Moby Dick

or
The White Whale

REGENT CLASSICS

THE world's best-loved and most famous stories, presented in an easily read type and in attractive format, giving an opportunity of building up a fine library of masterpieces at a moderate price.

Moby Dick
or
The White Whale

by

Herman Melville

REGENT
CLASSICS

THE THAMES PUBLISHING CO.
LONDON

MADE AND PRINTED IN GREAT BRITAIN BY PURNELL AND SONS, LTD
PAULTON (SOMERSET) AND LONDON

CONTENTS

CONTENTS

CONTENTS

CONTENTS

CHAPTER 1

LOOMINGS

CALL ME Ishmael. Some years ago—never mind how long precisely—having little or no money in my purse, and nothing particular to interest me on shore, I thought I would sail about a little and see the watery part of the world. It is a way I have of driving off the spleen, and regulating the circulation. Whenever I find myself growing grim about the mouth; whenever it is a damp, drizzly November in my soul; whenever I find myself involuntarily pausing before coffin warehouses, and bringing up the rear of every funeral I meet; and especially whenever my hypos get such an upper hand of me, that it requires a strong moral principle to prevent me from deliberately stepping into the street, and methodically knocking people's hats off—then, I account it high time to get to sea as soon as I can. This is my substitute for pistol and ball. With a philosophical flourish Cato throws himself upon his sword; I quietly take to the ship. There is nothing surprising in this. If they but knew it, almost all men in their degree, some time or other, cherish very nearly the same feelings towards the ocean with me.

No, when I go to sea, I go as a simple sailor, right before the mast, plumb down into the forecastle, aloft there to the royal mast-head. True, they rather order me about some, and make me jump from spar to spar, like a grasshopper in a May meadow. And at first, this sort of thing is unpleasant enough. It touches one's sense of honour, particularly if you come of an old established family in the land, the Van Rensselaers, or Randolphs, or Hardicanutes. And more than all, if just previous to putting your hand into the tar-pot, you have been lording it as a country schoolmaster, making the tallest boys stand in awe of you. The transition is a keen one, I assure you, from a schoolmaster to a sailor, and requires a strong decoction of Seneca and the Stoics to enable you to grin and bear it. But even this wears off in time.

Again, I always go to sea as a sailor, because they make a point of paying me for my trouble, whereas they never pay passengers a single penny that I ever heard of.

Finally, I always go to sea as a sailor, because of the wholesome exercise and pure air of the forecastle deck. For as in this world, head winds are far more prevalent than winds from astern (that is, if you never violate the Pythagorean maxim), so for the most part the Commodore on the quarter-deck gets his atmosphere at second hand from the sailors on the forecastle. He thinks he breathes it first; but not so. In much the same way do the commonalty lead their leaders in many other things, at the same time that the leaders little suspect it. But wherefore it was that after having repeatedly smelt the sea as a merchant sailor, I should now take it into my head to go on a whaling voyage; this the invisible police officer of the Fates, who has the constant surveillance of me, and secretly dogs me, and influences me in some unaccountable way—he can better answer than any one else.

CHAPTER 2

THE CARPET-BAG

I STUFFED a shirt or two into my old carpet-bag, tucked it under my arm, and started for Cape Horn and the Pacific. Quitting the good city of old Manhatto, I duly arrived in New Bedford. It was on a Saturday night in December. Much was I disappointed upon learning that the little packet for Nantucket had already sailed, and that no way of reaching that place would offer, till the following Monday.

Now having a night, a day, and still another night following before me in New Bedford, ere I could embark for my destined port, it became a matter of concernment where I was to eat and sleep meanwhile.

Moving on, I at last came to a dim sort of light not far from the docks, and heard a forlorn creaking in the air; and looking up, saw a swinging sign over the door with a white painting upon it, faintly representing a tall straight jet of misty spray, and these words underneath—'The Spouter-Inn:—Peter Coffin.'

It was a queer sort of place—a gable-ended old house, one side palsied as it were, and leaning over sadly. It stood on a sharp bleak corner, where that tempestuous wind Euroclydon kept up a worse howling than ever it did about poor Paul's tossed craft.

But no more of this blubbering now, we are going a-whaling, and there is plenty of that yet to come. Let us scrape the ice from our frosted feet, and see what sort of a place this "Spouter" may be.

CHAPTER 3

THE SPOUTER-INN

ENTERING that gable-ended Spouter-Inn, you found yourself in a wide, low, straggling entry with old-fashioned wainscots, reminding one of the bulwarks of some condemned old craft.

Upon entering the place I found a number of young seamen gathered about a table, examining by a dim light divers specimens of *skrimshander*. I sought the landlord, and telling him I desired to be accommodated with a room, received for answer that his house was full— not a bed unoccupied. "But avast," he added, tapping his forehead, "you haint no objections to sharing a harpooneer's blanket, have ye? I s'pose you are goin' a whalin', so you'd better get used to that sort of thing."

I told him that I never liked to sleep two in a bed; that if I should ever do so, it would depend upon who the harpooneer might be, and that if he (the landlord) really had no other place for me, and the harpooneer was not decidedly objectionable, why rather than wander further about a strange town on so bitter a night, I would put up with the half of any decent man's blanket.

"I thought so. All right; take a seat. Supper?—you want supper? Supper'll be ready directly."

At last some four or five of us were summoned to our meal in an adjoining room. It was cold as Iceland—no fire at all—the landlord said he couldn't afford it. Nothing but two dismal tallow candles, each in a winding sheet. We were fain to button up our monkey jackets, and hold to our lips cups of scalding tea with our half frozen fingers. But the fare was of the most substantial kind—not only meat and potatoes, but dumplings; good heavens! dumplings for supper! One young fellow in a green box coat, addressed himself to these dumplings in a most direful manner.

Supper over, the company went back to the bar-room, when, knowing not what else to do with myself, I resolved to spend the rest of the evening as a looker on.

Presently a rioting noise was heard without. Staring up, the landlord cried, "That's the *Grampus's* crew. I seed her reported in the offing this morning; a three years' voyage, and a full ship. Hurrah, boys; now we'll have the latest news from the Feegees."

A tramping of sea boots was heard in the entry; the door was flung open, and in rolled a wild set of mariners enough. Enveloped in their shaggy watch coats, and with their heads muffled in woollen comforters, all bedarned and ragged, and their beards stiff with icicles, they seemed an eruption of bears from Labrador. They had just landed from their boat, and this was the first house they entered. No wonder, then, that they made a straight wake for the whale's mouth—the bar —when the wrinkled little old Jonah, there officiating, soon poured them out brimmers all round.

The liquor soon mounted into their heads, as it generally does even with the arrantest topers newly landed from sea, and they began capering about most obstreperously.

I observed, however, that one of them held somewhat aloof, and though he seemed desirous not to spoil the hilarity of his shipmates by his own sober face, yet upon the whole he refrained from making as much noise as the rest. When the revelry of his companions had mounted to its height, this man slipped away unobserved, and I saw no more of him till he became my comrade on the sea. In a few minutes, however, he was missed by his shipmates, and being, it seems, for some reason a huge favourite with them, they raised a cry of "Bulkington! Bulkington! where's Bulkington?" and darted out of the house in pursuit of him.

It was now about nine o'clock, but though the other boarders kept coming in by ones, twos, and threes, and going to bed, yet no sign of my harpooneer.

"Landlord!" said I, "what sort of a chap is he—does he always keep such late hours?" It was now hard upon twelve o'clock.

The landlord chuckled again with his lean chuckle, and seemed to be mightily tickled at something beyond my comprehension. "No," he answered, "generally he's an early bird—airley to bed and airley to rise—yea, he's the bird what catches the worm.—But to-night he went out a peddling, you see, and I don't see what on airth keeps him so late, unless, may be, he can't sell his head."

"Can't sell his head?—What sort of a bamboozingly story is this you are telling me?" getting into a towering rage. "Do you pretend to say, landlord, that this harpooneer is actually engaged this blessed Saturday night, or rather Sunday morning, in peddling his head around this town?"

"Wall," said the landlord, fetching a long breath, "be easy, this here harpooneer I have been tellin' you of has just arrived from the south seas, where he bought up a lot of 'balmed New Zealand heads (great curios, you know), and he's sold all on 'em but one, and that one he's trying to sell to-night, cause to-morrow's Sunday, and it would not do to be sellin' human heads about the streets when folks is goin' to churches. He wanted to, last Sunday, but I stopped him just as he was goin' out of the door with four heads strung on a string, for all the airth like a string of inions."

This account cleared up the otherwise unaccountable mystery, and showed that the landlord, after all, had had no idea of fooling me— but at the same time what could I think of a harpooneer who stayed out of a Saturday night clean into the holy Sabbath, engaged in such a cannibal business as selling the heads of dead idolators?

"Depend upon it, landlord, that harpooneer is a dangerous man."

"He pays reg'lar," was the rejoinder. "But come, it's getting dreadful late, you had better be turning flukes—it's a nice bed, Sal and me slept in that ere bed the night we were spliced. There's plenty room for two to kick about in that bed; it's an almighty big bed that. Why, afore we give it up, Sal used to put our Sam and little Johnny in the foot of it. But I got a dreaming and sprawling about one night, and somehow, Sam got pitched on the floor, and came near breaking his arm. Arter that, Sal said it wouldn't do. Come along here, I'll give ye a glim in a jiffy;" and so saying he lighted a candle and held it towards me, offering to lead the way. But I stood irresolute; when looking at a clock in the corner, he exclaimed "I vum it's Sunday— you won't see that harpooneer to-night; he's come to anchor somewhere—come along then; *do* come; *won't* ye come?"

I considered the matter a moment, and then upstairs we went, and I was ushered into a small room, cold as a clam, and furnished, sure enough, with a prodigious bed, almost big enough indeed for any four harpooneers to sleep abreast.

"There," said the landlord, placing the candle on a crazy old sea chest that did double duty as a washstand and centre table; "there, make yourself comfortable now, and good night to ye." I turned round from eyeing the bed, but he had disappeared.

Folding back the counterpane, I stooped over the bed. Though none of the most elegant, it yet stood the scrutiny tolerably well. I then glanced round the room; and besides the bedstead and centre table, could see no other furniture belonging to the place, but a rude shelf, the four walls, and a papered fireboard representing a man striking a whale. Of things not properly belonging to the room, there was a hammock lashed up, and thrown upon the floor in one corner; also a large seaman's bag, containing the harpooneer's wardrobe, no doubt in lieu of a land trunk. Likewise, there was a parcel of outlandish bone fish hooks on the shelf over the fire-place, and a tall harpoon standing at the head of the bed.

But what is this on the chest? I took it up, and held it close to

the light, and felt it, and smelt it, and tried every way possible to
arrive at some satisfactory conclusion concerning it. I can compare it
to nothing but a large door mat, ornamented at the edges with little
tinkling tags something like the stained porcupine quills round an
Indian moccasin. There was a hole or slit in the middle of this mat,
as you see the same in South American ponchos. But could it be possible that any sober harpooneer would get into a door mat, and parade
the streets of any Christian town in that sort of guise? I put it on,
to try it, and it weighed me down like a hamper, being uncommonly
shaggy and thick, and I thought a little damp, as though this mysterious harpooneer had been wearing it of a rainy day. I went up in
it to a bit of glass stuck against the wall, and I never saw such a
sight in my life. I tore myself out of it in such a hurry that I gave
myself a kink in the neck.

I sat down on the side of the bed, and commenced thinking about
this head-peddling harpooneer, and his door mat. After thinking some
time on the bedside, I got up and took off my monkey jacket, and then
stood in the middle of the room thinking. I then took off my coat,
and thought a little more in my shirt-sleeves. But beginning to feel
very cold now, half undressed as I was, and remembering what the
landlord said about the harpooneer's not coming home at all that night,
it being so very late, I made no more ado, but jumped out of my
pantaloons and boots, and then blowing out the light tumbled into
bed, and commended myself to the care of heaven.

Whether that mattress was stuffed with corn-cobs or broken crockery,
there is no telling, but I rolled about a good deal, and could not sleep
for a long time. At last I slid off into a light doze, and had pretty
nearly made a good offing towards the land of Nod, when I heard
a heavy footfall in the passage, and saw a glimmer of light come into
the room from under the door.

Lord save me, thinks I, that must be the harpooneer, the infernal
head-peddler. But I lay perfectly still, and resolved not to say a word
till spoken to. Holding a light in one hand, and that identical New
Zealand head in the other, the stranger entered the room, and without
looking towards the bed, placed his candle a good way off from me
on the floor in one corner, and then began working away at the knotted
cords of the large bag I before spoke of as being in the room. I was all
eagerness to see his face, but he kept it averted for some time while
employed in unlacing the bag's mouth. This accomplished, however,
he turned round—when, good heavens! what a sight! Such a face!
It was of a dark, purplish, yellow colour, here and there stuck over
with large, blackish looking squares. Yes, it's just as I thought, he's

a terrible bed-fellow; he's been in a fight, got dreadfully cut, and here he is, just from the surgeon. But at that moment he chanced to turn his face so towards the light, that I plainly saw they could not be sticking-plasters at all, those black squares on his cheeks. They were stains of some sort or other. At first I knew not what to make of this; but soon an inkling of the truth occurred to me. I remembered a story of a white man—a whaleman too—who, falling among the cannibals, had been tattooed by them. I concluded that this harpooneer, in the course of his distant voyages, must have met with a similar adventure. And what is it, thought I, after all! It's only his outside; a man can be honest in any sort of skin. But then, what to make of his unearthly complexion, that part of it, I mean, lying round about, and completely independent of the squares of tattooing. To be sure, it might be nothing but a good coat of tropical tanning; but I never heard of a hot sun's tanning a white man into a purplish yellow one. However, I had never been in the South Seas; and perhaps the sun there produced these extraordinary effects upon the skin. Now, while all these ideas were passing through me like lightning, this harpooneer never noticed me at all. But, after some difficulty having opened his bag, he commenced fumbling in it, and presently pulled out a sort of tomahawk, and a seal-skin wallet with the hair on. Placing these on the old chest in the middle of the room, he then took the New Zealand head—a ghastly thing enough—and crammed it down into the bag. He now took off his hat—a new beaver hat—when I came nigh singing out with fresh surprise. There was no hair on his head —none to speak of at least—nothing but a small scalp-knot twisted up on his forehead. His bald purplish head now looked for all the world like a mildewed skull. Had not the stranger stood between me and the door, I would have bolted out of it quicker than ever I bolted a dinner.

Meanwhile, he continued the business of undressing, and at last showed his chest and arms. As I live, these covered parts of him were checkered with the same squares as his face; his back, too, was all over the same dark squares; he seemed to have been in a Thirty Years' War, and just escaped from it with a sticking-plaster shirt. Still more, his very legs were marked, as if a parcel of dark green frogs were running up the trunks of young palms. It was now quite plain that he must be some abominable savage or other shipped aboard of a whaleman in the South Seas, and so landed in this Christian country. I quaked to think of it. A peddler of heads too—perhaps the heads of his own brothers. He might take a fancy to mine—heavens! look at that tomahawk!

But there was no time for shuddering, for now the savage went about something that completely fascinated my attention, and convinced me that he must indeed be a heathen. Going to his heavy grego, or wrap-all, or dreadnought, which he had previously hung on a chair, he fumbled in the pockets, and produced at length a curious little deformed image with a hunch on its back, and exactly the colour of a three days' old Congo baby. Remembering the embalmed head, at first I almost thought that this black manikin was a real baby preserved in some similar manner. But seeing that it was not at all limber, and that it glistened a good deal like polished ebony, I concluded that it must be nothing but a wooden idol, which indeed it proved to be. For now the savage goes up to the empty fireplace, and removing the papered fire-board, sets up this little hunch-backed image, like a tenpin, between the andirons. The chimney jambs and all the bricks inside were very sooty, so that I thought this fire-place made a very appropriate little shrine or chapel for his Congo idol.

I now screwed my eyes hard towards the half hidden image, feeling but ill at ease meantime—to see what was next to follow. First he takes about a double handful of shavings out of his grego pocket, and places them carefully before the idol; then laying a bit of ship biscuit on top and applying the flame from the lamp, he kindled the shavings into a sacrificial blaze. Presently, after many hasty snatches into the fire, and still hastier withdrawals of his fingers (whereby he seemed to be scorching them badly), he at last succeeded in drawing out the biscuit; then blowing off the heat and ashes a little, he made a polite offer of it to the little negro. But the little devil did not seem to fancy such dry sort of fare at all; he never moved his lips. All these strange antics were accompanied by still stranger guttural noises from the devotee, who seemed to be praying in a sing-song or else singing some pagan psalmody or other, during which his face twitched about in the most unnatural manner. At last extinguishing the fire, he took the idol up very unceremoniously, and bagged it again in his grego pocket as carelessly as if he were a sportsman bagging a dead woodcock.

All these queer proceedings increased my uncomfortableness, and seeing him now exhibiting strong symptoms of concluding his business operations, and jumping into bed with me, I thought it was high time, now or never, before the light was put out, to break the spell in which I had so long been bound.

But the interval I spent in deliberating what to say, was a fatal one. Taking up his tomahawk from the table, he examined the head of it for an instant, and then holding it to the light, with his mouth at the handle, he puffed out great clouds of tobacco smoke. The next moment the light was extinguished, and this wild cannibal, tomahawk between his teeth, sprang into bed with me. I sang out, I could not help it now; and giving a sudden grunt of astonishment he began feeling me.

Stammering out something, I knew not what, I rolled away from him against the wall, and then conjured him, whoever or whatever he might be, to keep quiet, and let me get up and light the lamp again. But his guttural responses satisfied me at once that he but ill comprehended my meaning.

"Who-e debel you?"—he at last said—"you no speak-e, dam-me, I kill-e." And so saying the lighted tomahawk began flourishing about me in the dark.

"Landlord, for God's sake, Peter Coffin!" shouted I. "Landlord! Watch! Coffin! Angels! save me!"

"Speak-e! tell-ee me who-ee be, or dam-me, I kill-e!" again growled the cannibal, while his horrid flourishings of the tomahawk scattered the hot tobacco ashes about me till I thought my linen would get on fire. But thank heaven, at that moment the landlord came into the room light in hand, and leaping from the bed I ran up to him.

"Don't be afraid now," said he, grinning again. "Queequeg here wouldn't harm a hair of your head."

"Stop your grinning," shouted I, "and why didn't you tell me that that infernal harpooneer was a cannibal?"

"I thought ye know'd it;—didn't I tell ye, he was a peddlin' heads around town?—but turn flukes again and go to sleep. Queequeg, look here—you sabbee me, I sabbee you—this man sleepe you—you sabbee?"

"Me sabbee plenty"—grunted Queequeg, puffing away at his pipe and sitting up in bed.

"You gettee in," he added, motioning to me with his tomahawk, and throwing the clothes to one side. He really did this in not only a civil but a really kind and charitable way. I stood looking at him a moment. For all his tattooings he was on the whole a clean, comely looking cannibal. What's all this fuss I have been making about, thought I to myself—the man's a human being just as I am: he has just as much reason to fear me, as I have to be afraid of him. Better sleep with a sober cannibal than a drunken Christian.

"Landlord," said I, "tell him to stash his tomahawk there, or pipe, or whatever you call it; tell him to stop smoking, in short, and I will turn in with him. But I don't fancy having a man smoking in bed with me. It's dangerous. Besides, I ain't insured."

This being told to Queequeg, he at once complied, and again politely motioned me to get into bed—rolling over to one side as much as to say—I won't touch a leg of ye.

"Good night, landlord," said I, "you may go."

I turned in, and never slept better in my life.

CHAPTER 4

THE COUNTERPANE

UPON WAKING next morning about daylight, I found Queequeg's arm thrown over me in the most loving and affectionate manner. You had almost thought I had been his wife. The counterpane was of patchwork, full of odd little parti-coloured squares and triangles; and this arm of his tattooed all over with an interminable Cretan labyrinth of a figure, looked for all the world like a strip of that same patchwork quilt. Indeed, partly lying on it as the arm did when I first awoke, I could hardly tell it from the quilt, they so blended their hues together; and it was only by the sense of weight and pressure that I could tell that Queequeg was hugging me.

Though I tried to move his arm—unlock his bridegroom clasp—yet, sleeping as he was, he still hugged me tightly, as though naught but death should part us twain. I now strove to rouse him—"Queequeg!"—but his only answer was a snore. At length, by dint of much wriggling, and loud and incessant expostulations upon the unbecomingness of his hugging a fellow male in that matrimonial sort of style, I succeeded in extracting a grunt; and presently, he drew back his arm, shook himself all over like a Newfoundland dog just from the water, and sat up in bed, stiff as a pike-staff, looking at me, and rubbing his eyes as if he did not altogether remember how I came to be there, though a dim consciousness of knowing something about me seemed slowly dawning over him. Meanwhile, I lay quietly eyeing him, having no serious misgivings now, and bent upon narrowly observing so curious a creature. When, at last, his mind seemed made up touching the character of his bed-fellow, and he became, as it were, reconciled to the fact; he jumped out upon the floor, and by certain signs and sounds gave me to understand that, if it pleased me, he would dress first and then leave me to dress afterwards, leaving the whole apartment to myself.

He commenced dressing at top by donning his beaver hat, a very tall one, by the by, and then—still minus his trousers—he hunted up his boots. What under the heavens he did it for, I cannot tell, but his next movement was to crush himself—boots in hand, and hat on —under the bed; when, from sundry violent gaspings and strainings, I inferred he was hard at work booting himself; though by no law of propriety that I ever heard of, is any man required to be private when putting on his boots. But Queequeg, do you see, was a creature in the transition stage—neither caterpillar nor butterfly. He was just enough civilized to show off his outlandishness in the strangest possible manner. At last, he emerged with his hat very much dented and crushed down over his eyes, and began creaking and limping about the room, as if, not being much accustomed to boots, his pair of damp, wrinkled cowhide ones—probably not made to order either —rather pinched and tormented him at the first go off of a bitter cold morning.

Seeing, now, that there were no curtains to the window, and that the street being very narrow, the house opposite commanded a plain view into the room, and observing more and more the indecorous figure that Queequeg made, staving about with little else but his hat and boots on; I begged him as well as I could, to accelerate his toilet somewhat, and particularly to get into his pantaloons as soon as possible. He complied, and then proceeded to wash himself. At that time in the morning any Christian would have washed his face; but Queequeg, to my amazement, contented himself with restricting his ablutions to his chest, arms, and hands. He then donned his waistcoat, and taking up a piece of hard soap on the wash-stand centre-table, dipped it into water and commenced lathering his face. I was watching to see where he kept his razor, when lo and behold, he takes the harpoon from the bed corner, slips out the long wooden stock, unsheathes the head, whets it a little on his boot, and striding up to the bit of mirror against the wall, begins a vigorous scraping, or rather harpooning of his cheeks. Thinks I, Queequeg, this is using Rogers's best cutlery with a vengeance. Afterwards I wondered the less at this operation when I came to know of what fine steel the head of a harpoon is made, and how exceedingly sharp the long straight edges are always kept.

The rest of his toilet was soon achieved, and he proudly marched out of the room, wrapped up in his great pilot monkey jacket, and sporting his harpoon like a marshal's baton.

CHAPTER 5

BREAKFAST

I QUICKLY followed suit, and descending into the bar-room accosted the grinning landlord very pleasantly. I cherished no malice towards him, though he had been skylarking with me not a little in the matter of my bedfellow.

The bar-room was now full of the boarders who had been dropping in the night previous, and whom I had not as yet had a good look at. They were nearly all whalemen; chief mates, and second mates, and third mates, and sea carpenters, and sea-coopers, and sea black-smiths, and harpooners, and ship-keepers; a brown and brawny company, with bosky beards; an unshorn, shaggy set, all wearing monkey jackets for morning gowns.

"Grub, ho!" now cried the landlord, flinging open a door, and in we went to breakfast.

They say that men who have seen the world, thereby become quite at ease in manner, quite self-possessed in company. Not always, though: after we were all seated at the table, and I was preparing to hear some good stories about whaling; to my no small surprise nearly every man maintained a profound silence. And not only that, but they looked embarrassed. Yes, here were a set of sea-dogs, many of whom without the slightest bashfulness had boarded great whales on the high seas— entire strangers to them—and duelled them dead without winking; and yet, here they sat at a social breakfast table—all of the same call-ing, all of kindred tastes—looking round as sheepishly at each other as though they had never been out of sight of some sheepfold among the Green Mountains. A curious sight; these bashful bears, these timid warrior whalemen!

But as for Queequeg—why, Queequeg sat there among them—at the head of the table, too, it so chanced; as cool as an icicle. To be sure I cannot say much for his breeding. His greatest admirer could not have cordially justified his bringing his harpoon into breakfast with him, and using it there without ceremony; reaching over the table with it, to the imminent jeopardy of many heads, and grappling the beefsteaks towards him. But *that* was certainly very coolly done by him, and every one knows that in most people's estimation, to do anything coolly is to do it genteelly.

We will not speak of all Queequeg's peculiarities here; how he eschewed coffee and hot rolls, and applied his undivided attention to beefsteaks, done rare. Enough, that when breakfast was over he withdrew like the rest into the public room, lighted his tomahawk-pipe, and was sitting there quietly digesting and smoking with his inseparable hat on, when I sallied out for a stroll.

CHAPTER 6

THE STREET

IF I HAD been astonished at first catching a glimpse of so outlandish an individual as Queequeg circulating among the polite society of a civilized town, that astonishment soon departed upon taking my first daylight stroll through the streets of New Bedford.

In thoroughfares nigh the docks, any considerable seaport will frequently offer to view the queerest looking nondescripts from foreign parts. Even in Broadway and Chestnut streets, Mediterranean mariners will sometimes jostle the affrighted ladies. Regent Street is not unknown to Lascars and Malays; and at Bombay, in the Apollo Green, live Yankees have often scared the natives. But New Bedford beats all Water Street and Wapping. In these last-mentioned haunts you see only sailors; but in New Bedford, actual cannibals stand chatting at street corners; savages outright many of whom yet carry on their bones unholy flesh. It makes a stranger stare.

But think not that this famous town has only harpooneers, cannibals, and bumpkins to show her visitors. Not at all. Still New Bedford is a queer place. Had it not been for us whalemen, that tract of land would this day perhaps have been in as howling condition as the coast of Labrador. As it is, parts of her back country are enough to frighten one, they look so bony. The town itself is perhaps the dearest place to live in, in all New England. It is a land of oil, true enough: but not like Canaan; a land, also, of corn and wine. The streets do not run with milk; nor in the spring-time do they pave them with fresh eggs. Yet, in spite of this, nowhere in all America will you find more patrician-like houses; parks and gardens more opulent, than in New Bedford. Whence came they? how planted upon this once scraggy scoria of a country?

In summer time, the town is sweet to see; full of fine maples—long avenues of green and gold. And in August, high in air, the beautiful and bountiful horse-chestnuts, candelabra-wise, proffer the passer-by their tapering upright cones of congregated blossoms. So omnipotent is art; which in many a district of New Bedford has superinduced bright terraces of flowers upon the barren refuse rocks thrown aside at creation's final day.

And the women of New Bedford, they bloom like their own red roses. But roses only bloom in summer; whereas the fine carnation of their cheeks is perennial as sunlight in the seventh heavens. Elsewhere match that bloom of theirs, ye cannot, save in Salem, where they tell me the young girls breathe such musk, their sailor sweethearts smell them miles off shore, as though they were drawing nigh the odorous Moluccas instead of the Puritanic sands.

CHAPTER 7

THE CHAPEL

IN THE same New Bedford there stands a Whalemen's Chapel, and few are the moody fishermen, shortly bound for the Indian Ocean or Pacific, who fail to make a Sunday visit to the spot. I am sure that I did not.

Returning from my first morning stroll, I again sallied out upon this special errand. The sky had changed from clear, sunny cold, to driving sleet and mist. Wrapping myself in my shaggy jacket of the cloth called bearskin, I fought my way against the stubborn storm. Entering, I found a small scattered congregation of sailors, and sailors' wives and widows. A muffled silence reigned, only broken at times by the shrieks of the storm. Each silent worshipper seemed purposely sitting apart from the other, as if each silent grief were insular and incommunicable. The chaplain had not yet arrived; and there these silent islands of men and women sat steadfastly eyeing several marble tablets, with black borders, masoned into the wall on either side the pulpit.

Shaking off the sleet from my ice-glazed hat and jacket, I seated myself near the door, and turning sideways was surprised to see Queequeg near me. Affected by the solemnity of the scene, there was a wondering gaze of incredulous curiosity in his countenance. This savage was the only person present who seemed to notice my entrance; because he was the only one who could not read, and, therefore, was not reading those frigid inscriptions on the wall. Whether any of the relatives of the seamen whose names appeared there were now among the congregation, I knew not; but so many are the unrecorded accidents in the fishery, and so plainly did several women present wear the countenance if not the trappings of some unceasing grief, that I fee sure that here before me were assembled those, in whose unhealing hearts the sight of those bleak tablets sympathetically caused the old wounds to bleed afresh.

It needs scarcely to be told, with what feelings, on the eve of a Nantucket voyage, I regarded those marble tablets, and by the murky light of that darkened, doleful day read the fate of the whalemen who had gone before me. Yes, Ishmael, the same fate may be thine. But, somehow I grew merry again. Delightful inducements to embark, fine chance for promotion, it seems—aye, a stove boat will make me an immortal by brevet. Yes, there is death in this business of whaling—a speechlessly quick chaotic bundling of a man into Eternity. But what then? Methinks we have hugely mistaken this matter of Life and Death. Methinks that what they call my shadow here on earth is my true substance. Methinks that in looking at things spiritual, we are too much like oysters observing the sun through the water, and thinking that thick water the thinnest of air. Methinks my body is but the lees of my better being. In fact take my body who will, take it I say, it is not me. And therefore three cheers for Nantucket; and come a stove boat and stove body when they will, for stave my soul, Jove himself cannot.

CHAPTER 8

THE PULPIT

I HAD not been seated very long ere a man of a certain venerable robustness entered; immediately as the storm-pelted door flew back upon admitting him, a quick regardful eyeing of him by all the congregation, sufficiently attested that this fine old man was the chaplain. Yes, it was the famous Father Mapple, so called by the whalemen, among whom he was a very great favourite. He had been a sailor and a harpooneer in his youth, but for many years past had dedicated his life to the ministry. At the time I now write of, Father Mapple was in the hardy winter of a healthy old age; that sort of old age which seems merging into a second flowering youth, for among all the fissures of his wrinkles, there shone certain mild gleams of a newly developing bloom—the spring verdure peeping forth even beneath February's snow. No one having previously heard his history, could for the first time behold Father Mapple without the utmost interest, because there were certain engrafted clerical peculiarities about him, imputable to that adventurous maritime life he had led. When he entered I observed that he carried no umbrella, and certainly had not come in his carriage, for his tarpaulin hat ran down with melting sleet, and his great pilot cloth jacket seemed almost to drag } im to the floor with the weight of the water it had absorbed. However, hat and coat and overshoes were one by one removed, and hung up in a little space in an adjacent corner: when, arrayed in a decent suit, he quietly approached the pulpit.

Nor was the pulpit itself without a trace of sea-taste. Its panelled front was in the likeness of ship's bluff bows, and the Holy Bible rested on a projecting piece of scroll work, fashioned after a ship's fiddle-headed beak.

What could be more full of meaning?—for the pulpit is ever this earth's foremost part; all the rest comes in its rear; the pulpit leads the world. From thence it is the storm of God's quick wrath is first descried, and the bow must bear the earliest brunt. From thence it is the God of breezes fair or foul is first invoked for favourable winds. Yes, the world's a ship on its passage out, and not a voyage complete; and the pulpit is its prow.

CHAPTER 9

THE SERMON

FATHER MAPPLE rose, and in a mild voice of unassuming authority ordered the scattered people to condense. "Starboard gangway, there! side away to larboard—larboard gangway to starboard! Midships! midships!"

There was a low rumbling of heavy sea-boots among the benches, and a still slighter shuffling of women's shoes, and all was quiet again, and every eye on the preacher.

He paused a little; then kneeling in the pulpit's bows, folded his large brown hands across his chest, uplifted his closed eyes, and offered a prayer so deeply devout that he seemed kneeling and praying at the bottom of the sea.

This ended, in prolonged solemn tones, like the continual tolling of a bell in a ship that is foundering at sea in a fog—in such tones he commenced reading the following hymn; but changing his manner towards the concluding stanzas, burst forth with a pealing exultation and joy—

"The ribs and terrors in the whale,
Arched over me a dismal gloom,
While all God's sun-lit waves rolled by,
And lift me deepening down to doom.

"I saw the opening maw of hell,
With endless pains and sorrows there;
Which none but they that feel can tell—
Oh, I was plunging to despair.

"In black distress, I called my God,
When I could scarce believe him mine,
He bowed his ear to my complaints—
No more the whale did me confine.

"With speed he flew to my relief,
As on a radiant dolphin borne;
Awful, yet bright, as lightning shone
The face of my Deliverer God.

"My song for ever shall record
That terrible, that joyful hour;
I give the glory to my God,
His all the mercy and the power."

Nearly all joined in singing this hymn, which swelled high above the howling of the storm. A brief pause ensued; the preacher slowly turned over the leaves of the Bible, and at last, folding his hand down upon the proper page, said, "Beloved shipmates, clinch the last verse of the first chapter of Jonah—'And God had prepared a great fish to swallow up Jonah.'

"Shipmates, this book, containing only four chapters—four yarns—is one of the smallest strands in the mighty cable of the Scriptures. Yet what depths of the soul does Jonah's deep sealine sound! what a pregnant lesson to us is this prophet! What a noble thing is that canticle in the fish's belly! How billow-like and boisterously grand! We feel the floods surging over us, we sound with him to the kelpy bottom of the waters; sea-weed and all the slime of the sea is about us! But *what* is this lesson that the book of Jonah teaches? Shipmates, it is a two-stranded lesson; a lesson to us all as sinful men, and a lesson to me as a pilot of the living God. As sinful men, it is a lesson to us all, because it is a story of the sin, hard-heartedness, suddenly awakened fears, the swift punishment, repentance, prayers, and finally the deliverance and joy of Jonah. As with all sinners among men, the sin of this son of Amittai was in his wilful disobedience of the command of God—never mind now what that command was, or how conveyed—which he found a hard command. But all the things that God would have us do are hard for us to do—remember that—and hence, he oftener commands us than endeavours to persuade. And if we obey God, we must disobey ourselves; and it is in this disobeying ourselves, wherein the hardness of obeying God consists.

"With this sin of disobedience in him, Jonah still further flouts at God, by seeking to flee from Him. He thinks that a ship made by men, will carry him into countries where God does not reign, but only the Captains of this earth. He skulks about the wharves of Joppa, and seeks a ship that's bound for Tarshish. There lurks, perhaps, a hitherto unheeded meaning here. By all accounts Tarshish could have been no other city than the modern Cadiz. That's the opinion of learned men. Miserable man! At last, after much dodging search, he finds the Tarshish ship receiving the last items of her cargo; and as he steps on board to see its Captain in the cabin, all the sailors for the moment desist from hoisting in the goods, to mark the stranger's evil eye. Jonah sees this; but in vain he tries to look all ease and confidence; in vain essays his wretched smile. Strong intuitions of the man assure the mariners he can be no innocent. He descends into the cabin.

"'Who's there?' cries the Captain at his busy desk, hurriedly making out his papers for the Customs—'Who's there?' Oh! how that harmless question mangles Jonah! For the instant he almost turns to flee again. But he rallies. 'I seek a passage in this ship to Tarshish; how soon sail ye, sir?' Thus far the busy Captain had not looked up to Jonah, though the man now stands before him; but no sooner does he hear that hollow voice, than he darts a scrutinizing glance. 'We sail with the next coming tide,' at last he slowly answered, still intently eyeing him. 'No sooner, sir?'—'Soon enough for any honest man that goes a passenger.' Ha! Jonah, that's another stab. But he swiftly calls away the Captain from that scent. 'I'll sail with ye,'—he says,—'the passage money, how much is that?—I'll pay now.' For it is particularly written, shipmates, as if it were a thing not to be overlooked in this history, 'that he paid the fare thereof' ere the craft did sail. And taken with the context, this is full of meaning.

"And now the time of the tide has come; the ship casts off her cables; and from the deserted wharf the uncheered ship for Tarshish, all careening, glides to sea. That ship, my friends, was the first of recorded smugglers! the contraband was Jonah. But the sea rebels; he will not bear the wicked burden. A dreadful storm comes on, the ship is like to break. But now when the boatswain calls all hands to lighten her; when boxes, bales, and jars are clattering overboard; when the wind is shrieking, and the men are yelling, and every plank thunders with trampling feet right over Jonah's head.

"Terrors upon terrors run shouting through his soul. In all his cringing attitudes, the God-fugitive is now too plainly known. The sailors mark him; more and more certain grow their suspicions of him, and at last, fully to test the truth, by referring the whole matter to high Heaven, they fall to casting lots, so see for whose cause this great tempest was upon them. The lot is Jonah's; that discovered, then how furiously they mob him with their questions. 'What is thine occupation? Whence comest thou? Thy country? What people?' But mark now, my shipmates, the behaviour of poor Jonah. The eager mariners but ask him who he is, and where from; whereas, they not only receive an answer to those questions, but likewise another answer to a question not put by them, but the unsolicited answer is forced from Jonah by the hard hand of God that is upon him.

"'I am a Hebrew,' he cries—and then—'I fear the Lord the God of Heaven who hath made the sea and the dry land!' Fear him, O Jonah? Aye, well mightest thou fear the Lord God *then*! Straightway, he now goes on to make a full confession; whereupon the mariners became more and more appalled, but still are pitiful. For when Jonah, not yet supplicating God for mercy, since he but too well knew the darkness of his deserts,—when wretched Jonah cries out to them to take him and cast him forth into the sea, for he knew that for *his* sake this great tempest was upon them; they mercifully turn from him, and seek by other means to save the ship. But all in vain; the indignant gale howls louder; then, with one hand raised invokingly to God, with the other they not unreluctantly lay hold of Jonah.

"And now behold Jonah taken up as an anchor and dropped into the sea; when instantly an oily calmness floats out from the east, and the sea is still, as Jonah carries down the gale with him, leaving smooth water behind. He goes down in the whirling heart of such a masterless commotion that he scarce heeds the moment when he drops seething into the yawning jaws awaiting him; and the whale shoots-to all his ivory teeth, like so many white bolts, upon his prison. Then Jonah prayed unto the Lord out of the fish's belly. But observe his prayer, and learn a weighty lesson. For sinful as he is, Jonah does not weep and wail for direct deliverance. He feels that his dreadful punishment is just. He leaves all his deliverance to God, contenting himself with this, that in spite of all his pains and pangs, he will still look towards His holy temple. And here, shipmates, is true and faithful repentance; not clamorous for pardon, but grateful for punishment. And how pleasing to God was this conduct in Jonah, is shown in the eventual deliverance of him from the sea and the whale. Shipmates, I do not place Jonah before you to be copied for his sin but I do place him before you as a model for repentance. Sin not; but if you do, take heed to repent of it like Jonah."

While he was speaking these words, the howling of the shrieking, slanting storm without seemed to add new power to the preacher, who, when describing Jonah's sea-storm, seemed tossed by a storm himself. His deep chest heaved as with a groundswell; his tossed arms seemed the warring elements at work; and the thunders that rolled away from off his swarthy brow, and the light leaping from his eye, made all his simple hearers look on him with a quick fear that was strange to them.

There now came a lull in his look, as he silently turned over the leaves of the Book once more; and, at last, standing motionless, with closed eyes, for the moment, seemed communing with God and himself.

He said no more, but slowly waving a benediction, covered his face with his hands, and so remained kneeling, till all the people had departed, and he was left alone in the place.

CHAPTER 10

A BOSOM FRIEND

RETURNING to the Spouter-Inn from the Chapel, I found Queequeg there quite alone; he having left the Chapel before the benediction some time. He was waiting on a bench before the fire, with his feet on the stove hearth, and in one hand was holding close up to his face the little negro idol of his; peering hard into its face, and with a jack-knife gently whittling away at its nose, meanwhile humming to himself in his heathenish way.

But being now interrupted, he put up the image, and pretty soon, going to the table, took up a large book there, and placing it on his lap began counting the pages with deliberate regularity; at every fiftieth page—as I fancied—stopping for a moment, looking vacantly around him, and giving utterance to a long-drawn gurgling whistle of astonishment. He would then begin again at the next fifty; seeming to commence at number one each time, as though he could not count more than fifty, and it was only by such a large number of fifties being found together, that his astonishment at the multitude of pages was excited.

With much interest I sat watching him. Savage though he was, and hideously marred about the face—at least to my taste—his countenance yet had something in it which was by no means disagreeable. You cannot hide the soul. Through all his unearthly tattooings, I thought I saw the traces of a simple honest heart; and in his large, deep eyes,

fiery black and bold, there seemed tokens of a spirit that would dare
a thousand devils. And besides all this, there was a certain lofty bearing about the Pagan, which even his uncouthness could not altogether
maim. He looked like a man who had never cringed and never had
a creditor.

Whilst I was thus closely scanning him, half-pretending meanwhile
to be looking out at the storm from the casement, he never heeded my
presence, never troubled himself with so much as a single glance; but
appeared wholly occupied with counting the pages of the marvellous
book. I drew my bench near him, and made some friendly signs and
hints, doing my best to talk with him meanwhile. At first he little
noticed these advances; but presently, upon my referring to his last
night's hospitalities, he made out to ask me whether we were again
to be bedfellows. I told him yes; whereat I thought he looked pleased,
perhaps a little complimented.

We then turned over the book together and I endeavoured to explain
to him the purpose of the printing, and the meaning of the few pictures
that were in it. Thus I soon engaged his interest; and from that we
went to jabbering the best we could about the various outer sights to
be seen in this famous town. Soon I proposed a social smoke; and,
producing his pouch and tomahawk, he quietly offered me a puff. And
then we sat exchanging puffs from that wild pipe of his, and keeping
it regularly passing between us.

If there yet lurked any ice of indifference towards me in the Pagan's
breast, this pleasant, genial smoke we had soon thawed it out, and left
us cronies. He seemed to take to me quite as naturally and unbiddenly
as I to him; and when our smoke was over, he pressed his forehead
against mine, clasped me round the waist, and said that henceforth
we were married; meaning, in his country's phrase, that we were
bosom friends; he would gladly die for me, if need should be. In a
countryman, this sudden flame of friendship would have seemed far
too premature, a thing to be much distrusted; but in this simple savage
those old rules would not apply.

After supper, and another social chat and smoke, we went to our
room together. He made me a present of his embalmed head; took out
his enormous tobacco wallet, and groping under the tobacco, drew out
some thirty dollars in silver; then spreading them on the table, and
mechanically dividing them into two equal portions, pushed one of
them towards me, and said it was mine. I was going to remonstrate;
but he silenced me by pouring them into my trousers' pockets. I let
them stay. He then went about his evening prayers, took out his idol,
and removed the paper fireboard. By certain signs and symptoms, I

B

thought he seemed anxious for me to join him; but well knowing what was to follow, I deliberated a moment whether, in case he invited me, I would comply or otherwise.

I was a good Christian; born and bred in the bosom of the infallible Presbyterian Church. How then could I unite with this wild idolator in worshipping his piece of wood? But what is worship? thought I. Now, Queequeg is my fellow man. And what do I wish that this Queequeg would do to me? Why, unite with me in my particular Presbyterian form of worship. Consequently, I must then unite with him in his; ergo, I must turn idolator. So I kindled the shavings; helped prop up the innocent little idol; offered him burnt biscuit with Queequeg; salaamed before him twice or thrice; kissed his nose; and that done, we undressed and went to bed, at peace with our consciences and all the world. But we did not go to sleep without some little chat.

How it is I know not; but there is no place like a bed for confidential disclosures between friends. Man and wife, they say, there open the very bottom of their souls to each other; and some old couples often lie and chat over old times till nearly morning. Thus, then, in our hearts' honeymoon, lay I and Queequeg—a cosy, loving pair.

CHAPTER II

NIGHTGOWN

WE HAD lain thus in bed, chatting and napping at short intervals, and Queequeg now and then affectionally throwing his brown tattooed legs over mine, and then drawing them back; so entirely sociable and free and easy were we; when, at last, by reason of our confabulations, what little nappishness remained in us altogether departed, and we felt like getting up again, though daybreak was yet some way down the future.

Yes, we became very wakeful; so much so that our recumbent position began to grow wearisome, and by little and little we found ourselves sitting up; the clothes well tucked around us, leaning against the head-board with our four knees drawn up close together, and our two noses bending over them, as if our knee-pans were warming-pans. We felt very nice and snug, the more so since it was so chilly out of doors; indeed out of bedclothes too, seeing that there was no fire in the room.

We had been sitting in this crouching manner for some time, when all at once I thought I would open my eyes; for when between sheets, whether by day or by night, and whether asleep or awake, I have a way of always keeping my eyes shut, in order the more to concentrate the snugness of being in bed. Because no man can ever feel his own identity aright except his eyes be closed; as if darkness were indeed the proper element of our essences, though light be more congenial to our clayey part. Upon opening my eyes then, and coming out of my own pleasant and self-created darkness into the imposed and coarse outer gloom of the unilluminated twelve-o'clock-at-night, I experienced a disagreeable revulsion. Nor did I at all object to the hint from Queequeg that perhaps it were best to strike a light, seeing that we were so wide awake; and besides he felt a strong desire to have a few quiet puffs from his Tomahawk. Be it said, that though I had felt such a strong repugnance to his smoking in the bed the night before, yet see how elastic our stiff prejudices grow when once love comes to bend them. For now I liked nothing better than to have Queequeg smoking by me, even in bed, because he seemed to be full of such serene household joy then. I no more felt unduly concerned for the landlord's policy of insurance. I was only alive to the condensed and confidential comfortableness of sharing a pipe and a blanket with a real friend. With our shaggy jackets drawn about our shoulders we now passed the Tomahawk from one to the other, till slowly there grew over us a blue hanging tester of smoke, illuminated by the flame of the new-lit lamp.

Whether it was that his undulating tester rolled the savage away to far distant scenes, I know not, but he now spoke of his native island; and, eager to hear his history, I begged him to go on and tell it. He gladly complied. Though at the time I but ill comprehended not a few of his words, yet subsequent disclosures, when I had become more familiar with his broken phraseology, now enable me to present the whole story such as it may prove in the mere skeleton I give.

CHAPTER 12

BIOGRAPHICAL

QUEEQUEG was a native of Rokovoko, an island far away to the West and South. It is not down in any map; true places never are.

When a new-hatched savage running wild about his native woodlands in a grass clout, followed by the nibbling goats, as if he were a green sapling; even then, in Queequeg's ambitious soul, lurked a strong desire to see something more of Christendom than a specimen whaler or two. His father was a High Chief, a King; his uncle a High Priest; and on the maternal side he boasted aunts who were the wives of unconquerable warriors. There was excellent blood in his veins—royal stuff; though sadly vitiated, I fear, by the cannibal propensity he nourished in his untutored youth.

A Sag Harbour ship visited his father's bay, and Queequeg sought a passage to Christian lands. But the ship, having her full complement of seamen, spurned his suit; and not all the King his father's influence could prevail. But Queequeg vowed a vow. Alone in his canoe, he paddled off to a distant strait, which he knew the ship must pass through when she quitted the island. On one side was a coral reef; on the other a low tongue of land, covered with mangrove thickets that grew out into the water. Hiding his canoe, still afloat, among these thickets, with its prow seaward, he sat down in the stern, paddle low in hand; and when the ship was gliding by, like a flash he darted out; gained her side; with one backward dash of his foot capsized and sank his canoe; climbed up the chains; and throwing himself at full length upon the deck, grappled a ring-bolt there, and swore not to let it go, though hacked in pieces.

In vain the captain threatened to throw him overboard; suspended a cutlass over his naked wrists; Queequeg was the son of a King, and Queequeg budged not. Struck by his desperate dauntlessness, and his wild desire to visit Christendom, the captain at last relented, and told him he might make himself at home. But this fine young savage— this sea Prince of Wales, never saw the Captain's cabin. They put him down among the sailors, and made a whaleman of him. But like Czar Peter content to toil in the shipyards of foreign cities, Queequeg disdained no seeming ignominy, if thereby he might happily gain the power of enlightening his untutored countrymen. For at bottom—so he told me—he was actuated by a profound desire to learn among the Christians, the arts whereby to make his people still happier than they were; and more than that, still better than they were. But, alas! the practices of whalemen soon convinced him that even Christians could be both miserable and wicked; infinitely more so, than all his father's heathens. Arrived at last in old Sag Harbour; and seeing what the sailors did there; and then going on to Nantucket, and seeing how they spent their wages in *that* place also, poor Queequeg gave it up for lost. Thought he, it's a wicked world in all meridians; I'll die a pagan.

And thus an old idolator at heart he yet lived among these Christians, wore their clothes, and tried to talk their gibberish. Hence the queer ways about him, though now some time from home.

By hints I asked him whether he did not propose going back, and having a coronation; since he might now consider his father dead and gone, he being very old and feeble at the last accounts. He answered no, not yet; and added that he was fearful Christianity, or rather Christians, had unfitted him for ascending the pure and undefiled throne of thirty pagan Kings before him. But by and by, he said, he would return,—as soon as he felt himself baptised again. For the nonce, however, he proposed to sail about, and sow his wild oats in all four oceans. They had made a harpooneer of him, and that barbed iron was in lieu of a sceptre now.

I asked him what might be his immediate purpose, touching his future movements. He answered to go to sea again, in his old vocation. Upon this, I told him that whaling was my own design, and informed him of my intention to sail out of Nantucket, as being the most promising port for an adventurous whaleman to embark from. He at once resolved to accompany me to that island, ship aboard the same vessel, get into the same watch, the same boat, the same mess with me, in short to share my every hap; with both my hands in his, boldly dip into the Potluck of both worlds. To all this I joyously assented; for besides the affection I now felt for Queequeg, he was an experienced harpooneer, and as such, could not fail to be of great usefulness to one, who, like me, was wholly ignorant of the mysteries of whaling, though well acquainted with the sea, as known to merchant seamen.

His story being ended with his pipe's last dying puff, Queequeg embraced me, pressed his forehead against mine, and blowing out the light, we rolled over from each other, this way and that, and very soon were sleeping.

CHAPTER 13

WHEELBARROW

NEXT MORNING, Monday, after disposing of the embalmed head to a barber, for a block, I settled my own and comrade's bill; using, however, my comrade's money. The grinning landlord, as well as the boarders, seemed amazingly tickled at the sudden friendship which had sprung up between me and Queequeg—especially as Peter Coffin's cock-and-bull stories about him had previously so much alarmed me concerning the very person whom I now companied with.

We borrowed a wheelbarrow, and embarking our things, including my own poor carpet-bag, and Queequeg's canvas sack and hammock, away we went down to "the *Moss,*" the little Nantucket packet schooner moored at the wharf. As we were going along the people stared; not at Queequeg so much—for they were used to seeing cannibals like him in their streets,—but at seeing him and me upon such confidential terms. But we heeded them not, going along wheeling the barrow by turns, and Queequeg now and then stopping to adjust the sheath on his harpoon barbs. I asked him why he carried such a troublesome thing with him ashore, and whether all whaling ships did not find their own harpoons. To this, in substance, he replied, that though what I hinted was true enough, yet he had a particular affection for his own harpoon, because it was of assured stuff, well tried in many a mortal combat, and deeply intimate with the hearts of whales. In short, like many reapers and mowers, who go into the farmer's meadows armed with their own scythes—though in no wise obliged to furnish them—even so, Queequeg, for his own private reasons, preferred his own harpoon.

At last, passage paid, and luggage safe, we stood on board the schooner. Hoisting sail, it glided down the Acushnet river. On one side, New Bedford rose in terraces of streets, their ice-covered trees all glittering in the clear, cold air. Huge hills and mountains of casks were piled upon wharves, and side by side the world-wandering whale ships lay silent and safely moored at last; while from others came a sound of carpenters and coopers, with blended noises of fires and forges to melt the pitch, all betokening that new cruisers were on the start; that one most perilous and long voyage ended, only begins a second; and a second ended, only begins a third, and so on, for ever and for aye. Such is the endlessness, yea, the intolerableness of all earthly effort.

Gaining the more open water, the bracing breeze waxed fresh; the little *Moss* tossed the quick foam from her bows, as a young colt his snortings. How I snuffed that Tartar air!—how I spurned that turnpike earth!—that common highway all over dented with the marks of slavish heels and hoofs; and turned me to admire the magnanimity of the sea which will permit no records.

At the same foam-fountain, Queequeg seemed to drink and reel with me. His dusky nostrils swelled apart; he showed his filed and pointed teeth. On, on we flew, and our offing gained, the *Moss* did homage to the blast; ducked and dived her bows as a slave before the Sultan. Sideways leaning, we sideways darted; every ropeyarn tingling like a wire; the two tall masts buckling like Indian canes in land tornadoes. So full of this reeling scene were we, as we stood by the plunging bowsprit, that for some time we did not notice the jeering glances of the passengers, a lubber-like assembly, who marvelled that two fellow

beings should be so companionable; as though a white man were anything more dignified than a whitewashed negro. But there were some
boobies and bumpkins there, who, by their intense greenness, must have
come from the heart and centre of all verdure. Queequeg caught one
of these young saplings mimicking him behind his back. I thought
the bumpkin's hour of doom was come. Dropping his harpoon, the
brawny savage caught him in his arms, and by an almost miraculous
dexterity and strength, sent him high up bodily into the air; then
slightly tapping his stern in mid-somerset, the fellow landed with
bursting lungs upon his feet, while Queequeg, turning his back upon
him, lighted his tomahawk pipe and passed it to me for a puff.

"Capting! Capting!" yelled the bumpkin, running towards that
officer: "Capting, Capting, here's the devil."

"Hallo, *you* sir," cried the Captain, a gaunt rib of the sea, stalking
up to Queequeg, "what in thunder do you mean by that? Don't you
know you might have killed that chap?"

"What him say?" said Queequeg, as he mildly turned to me.

"He say," said I, "that you came near kill-e that man there," pointing to the still shivering greenhorn.

"Kill-e," cried Queequeg, twisting his tattooed face into an unearthly expression of disdain, "ah! him bevy small-e fish-e; Queequeg
no kill-e so small-e fish-e; Queequeg kill-e big whale!"

"Look you," roared the Captain, "I'll kill-e *you*, you cannibal, if you
try any more of your tricks aboard here; so mind your eye."

But it so happened just then, that it was high time for the Captain
to mind his own eye. The prodigious strain upon the mainsail had
parted the weather-sheet, and the tremendous boom was now flying
from side to side, completely sweeping the entire after part of the deck.
The poor fellow whom Queequeg had handled so roughly, was swept
overboard; all hands were in a panic; and to attempt snatching at the
boom to stay it seemed madness. It flew from right to left, and back
again, almost in one ticking of a watch, and every instant seemed on the
point of snapping into splinters. Nothing was done, and nothing seemed
capable of being done; those on deck rushed towards the bows, and
stood eyeing the boom as if it were the lower jaw of an exasperated
whale. In the midst of this consternation, Queequeg dropped to his
knees, and crawling under the path of the boom, whipped hold of
a rope, secured one end to the bulwarks, and then flinging the other
like a lasso, caught it round the boom as it swept over his head, and
at the next jerk, the spar was that way trapped, and all was safe. The
schooner was run into the wind, and while the hands were clearing
away the stern boat, Queequeg stripped to the waist, darted from the

side with a long living arc of a leap. For three minutes or more he was seen swimming like a dog, throwing his long arms straight out before him, and by turns revealing his brawny shoulders through the freezing foam. I looked at the grand and glorious fellow, but saw no one to be saved. The greenhorn had gone down. Shooting himself perpendicularly from the water, Queequeg now took an instant's glance around him, and seeming to see just how matters were, dived down and disappeared. A few minutes more, and he rose again, one arm still striking out, and with the other dragging a lifeless form. The boat soon picked them up. The poor bumpkin was restored. All hands voted Queequeg a noble trump; the Captain begged his pardon. From that hour I clove to Queequeg like a barnacle; yea, till poor Queequeg took his last long dive.

CHAPTER 14

NANTUCKET

NOTHING MORE happened on the passage worthy the mentioning; so, after a fine run, we safely arrived in Nantucket.

Nantucket! Take out your map and look at it. See what a real corner of the world it occupies; how it stands there, away off shore, more lonely than the Eddystone lighthouse. Look at it—a mere hillock, and elbow of sand; all beach, without a background. There is more sand there than you would use in twenty years as a substitute for blotting paper. Some gamesome wights will tell you that they have to plant weeds there, they don't grow naturally; that they import Canada thistles; that they have to send beyond seas for a spile to stop a leak in an oil cask; that pieces of wood in Nantucket are carried about like bits of the true cross in Rome; that people there plant toadstools before their houses, to get under the shade in summer time; that one blade of grass makes an oasis, three blades in a day's walk a prairie; that they wear quicksand shoes, something like Laplander snow-shoes; that they are so shut up, belted about, every way inclosed, surrounded, and made an utter island of by the ocean, that to their very chair and tables small clams will sometimes be found adhering, as to the backs of sea turtles. But these extravaganzas only show that Nantucket is no Illinois.

Look now at the wondrous traditional story of how this island was settled by the red-men. Thus goes the legend. In olden times an eagle swooped down upon the New England coast, and carried off an infant Indian in his talons. With loud lament the parents saw their child borne out of sight over the wide waters. They resolved to follow in the same direction. Setting out in their canoes, after a perilous passage they discovered the island, and there they found an empty ivory casket,—the poor little Indian's skeleton.

What wonder, then, that these Nantucketers, born on a beach, should take to the sea for a livelihood? They first caught crabs and quohogs in the sand; grown bolder, they waded out with nets for mackerel; more experienced, they pushed off in boats and captured cod; and at last, launching a navy of great ships on the sea, explored this watery world; put an incessant belt of circumnavigations round it; peeped in at Behring's Straits; and in all seasons and all oceans declared everlasting war with the mightiest animated mass that has survived the flood; most monstrous and most mountainous! That Himmalehan, salt-sea Mastodon, clothed with such portentousness of unconscious power, that his very panics are more to be dreaded than his most fearless and malicious assaults!

And thus have these naked Nantucketers, these sea hermits, issuing from their ant-hill in the sea, overrun and conquered the watery world like so many Alexanders; parcelling out among them the Atlantic, Pacific, and Indian oceans, as the three pirate powers did Poland. Let America add Mexico to Texas, and pile Cuba upon Canada; let the English overswarm all India, and hang out their blazing banner from the sun; two thirds of this terraqueous globe are the Nantucketer's. For the sea is his; he owns it, as Emperors own empires; other seamen having but a right of way through it. Merchant ships are but extension bridges; armed ones but floating forts; even pirates and privateers, though following the sea as highwaymen the road, they but plunder other ships, other fragments of the land like themselves, without seeking to draw their living from the bottomless deep itself. The Nantucketer, he alone resides and riots on the sea; he alone, in Bible language, goes down to it in ships; to and fro ploughing it as his own special plantation. *There* is his home; *there* lies his business, which a Noah's flood would not interrupt, though it overwhelmed all the millions in China. He lives on the sea, as prairie cocks in the prairie; he hides among the waves, he climbs them as chamois hunters climb the Alps. For years he knows not the land; so that when he comes to it at last, it smells like another world, more strangely than the moon would to an Earthsman. With the landless gull, that at sunset folds her wings and is rocked to sleep between billows; so at nightfall, the Nantucketer, out of sight of land, furls his sails, and lays him to his rest, while under his very pillow rush herds of walruses and whales.

CHAPTER 15

CHOWDER

I<small>T WAS</small> quite late in the evening when the little *Moss* came snugly to anchor, and Queequeg and I went ashore; so we could attend to no business that day, at least none but a supper and a bed. The landlord of the Spouter-Inn had recommended us to his cousin Hosea Hussey of the Try Pots, whom he asserted to be the proprietor of one of the best kept hotels in all Nantucket, and moreover he had assured us that Cousin Hosea, as he called him, was famous for his chowders. In short, he plainly hinted that we could not possibly do better than try pot-luck at the Try Pots. But the directions he had given us about keeping a yellow warehouse on our starboard hand till we opened a white church to the larboard, and then keeping that on the larboard hand till we made a corner three points to the starboard, and that done, then ask the first man we met where the place was: these crooked directions of his very much puzzled us at first, especially as, at the outset, Queequeg insisted that the yellow warehouse—our first point of departure—must be left on the larboard hand, whereas I had understood Peter Coffin to say it was on the starboard. However, by dint of beating about a little in the dark, and now and then knocking up a peaceful inhabitant to inquire the way, we at last came to something which there was no mistaking.

Two enormous wooden pots painted black, and suspended by asses' ears swung from the cross-trees of an old top-mast, planted in front of an old doorway. The horns of the cross-trees were sawed off on the other side, so that this old top-mast looked not a little like a gallows. Perhaps I was over sensitive to such impressions at the time, but I could not help staring at this gallows with a vague misgiving. A sort of crick was in my neck as I gazed up to the two remaining horns; yes, *two* of them, one for Queequeg, and one for me. It's ominous, thinks I. A Coffin my Innkeeper upon landing in my first whaling port; tombstones staring at me in the whalemen's chapel; and here a gallows! and a pair of prodigious black pots too! Are these last throwing out oblique hints touching Tophet?

I was called from these reflections by the sight of a freckled woman with yellow hair and a yellow gown, standing in the porch of the inn, under a dull red lamp swinging there, that looked much like an injured eye, and carrying on a brisk scolding with a man in a purple woollen shirt.

"Get along with ye," said she to the man, "or I'll be combing ye!"

"Come on, Queequeg," said I, "all right. There's Mrs. Hussey."

And so it turned out; Mr. Hosea Hussey being away from home, but leaving Mrs. Hussey entirely competent to attend to all his affairs. Upon making known our desires for a supper and a bed, Mrs. Hussey, postponing further scolding for the present, ushered us into a little room, and seating us at a table spread with the relics of a recently concluded repast, turned around to us and said—"Clam or Cod?"

"What's that about Cods, ma'am?" said I, with much politeness.

"Clam or Cod?" she repeated.

"A clam for supper? a cold clam; is *that* what you mean, Mrs. Hussey?" says I; "but that's a rather cold and clammy reception in the winter time, ain't it, Mrs. Hussey?"

But being in a great hurry to resume scolding the man in the purple shirt, who was waiting for her in the entry, and seeming to hear nothing but the word "clam," Mrs. Hussey hurried towards an open door leading to the kitchen, and bawling out "clam for two," disappeared.

"Queequeg," said I, "do you think that we can make out a supper for us both on one clam?"

However, a warm savoury steam from the kitchen served to belie the apparently cheerless prospect before us. But when that smoking chowder came in, the mystery was delightfully explained. Oh! sweet friends, hearken to me. It was made of small juicy clams, scarcely bigger than hazel nuts, mixed with pounded ship biscuits, and salted pork cut up into little flakes; the whole enriched with butter, and plentifully seasoned with pepper and salt. Our appetites being sharpened by the frosty voyage, and in particular, Queequeg seeing his favourite fishing food before him, and the chowder being surpassingly excellent, we despatched it with great expedition.

Supper concluded, we received a lamp, and directions from Mrs. Hussey concerning the nearest way to bed; but, as Queequeg was about to precede me up the stairs, the lady reached forth her arm, and demanded his harpoon; she allowed no harpoon in her chambers. "Why not?" said I; "every true whaleman sleeps with his harpoon—but why not?" "Because it's dangerous," says she. "Ever since young Stiggs coming from that unfort'nt v'y'ge of his, when he was gone four years and a half, with only three barrels of *ile,* was found dead in my first floor back, with his harpoon in his side; ever since then I allow no boarders to take sich dangerous weepons in their bedrooms at night.

So, Mr. Queequeg," (for she had learned his name) "I will just take
this here iron, and keep it for you till morning. But the chowder;
clam or cod to-morrow for breakfast, men?"

"Both," said I; "and let's have a couple of smoked herring by way
of variety."

CHAPTER 16

THE SHIP

IN BED we concocted our plans for the morrow. But to my surprise
and no small concern, Queequeg now gave me to understand, that
he had been diligently consulting Yojo—the name of his black little
god—and Yojo had told him two or three times over, and strongly
insisted upon it everyway, that instead of our going together among
the whaling-fleet in harbour, and in concert selecting our craft; instead
of this, I say, Yojo earnestly enjoined that the selection of the ship
should rest wholly with me, inasmuch as Yojo purposed befriend-
ing us; and, in order to do so, had already pitched upon a vessel,
which, if left to myself, I, Ishmael, should infallibly light upon, for
all the world as though it had turned out by chance; and in that
vessel I must immediately ship myself, for the present irrespective of
Queequeg.

I have forgotten to mention that, in many things, Queequeg placed
great confidence in the excellence of Yojo's judgment and surprising
forecast of things; and cherished Yojo with considerable esteem, as
a rather good sort of god, who perhaps meant well enough upon the
whole, but in all cases did not succeed in his benevolent designs.

Now, this plan of Queequeg's, or rather Yojo's, touching the selection
of our craft; I did not like that plan at all. I had not a little relied
upon Queequeg's sagacity to point out the whaler best fitted to carry
us and our fortunes securely. But as all my remonstrances produced
no effect upon Queequeg, I was obliged to acquiesce; and accordingly
prepared to set about this business with a determined rushing sort of
energy and vigour, that should quickly settle that trifling little affair.
Next morning early, leaving Queequeg shut up with Yojo in our little
bedroom—for it seemed that it was some sort of Lent or Ramadan, or
day of fasting, humiliation, and prayer with Queequeg and Yojo that
day; *how* it was I never could find out, for, though I applied myself
to it several times, I never could master his liturgies and XXXIX
Articles—leaving Queequeg, then, fasting on his tomahawk pipe, and
Yojo warming himself at his sacrificial fire of shavings, I sallied out

among the shipping. After much prolonged sauntering and many random inquiries, I learnt that there were three ships up for three-years' voyages—The *Devil-dam,* the *Tit-bit,* and the *Pequod. Devil-dam,* I do not know the origin of; *Tit-bit* is obvious; *Pequod,* you will no doubt remember, was the name of a celebrated tribe of Massachusetts Indians, now extinct as the ancient Medes. I peered and pryed about the *Devil-dam;* from her, hopped over to the *Tit-bit;* and, finally, going on board the *Pequod,* looked around her for a moment, and then decided that this was the very ship for us.

Now when I looked about the quarter-deck, for some one having authority, on order to propose myself as a candidate for the voyage, at first I saw nobody; but I could not well overlook a strange sort of tent, or rather wigwam, pitched a little behind the main-mast. It seemed only a temporary erection used in port. It was of a conical shape, some ten feet high; consisting of the long, huge slabs of limber black bone taken from the middle and highest part of the jaws of the right-whale. Planted with their broad ends on the deck, a circle of these slabs laced together, mutually sloped towards each other, and at the apex united in a tufted point, where the loose hairy fibres waved to and fro like the top-knot on some old Pottowottamie Sachem's head. A triangular opening faced towards the bows of the ship, so that the insider commanded a complete view forward.

And half concealed in this queer tenement, I at length found one who by his aspect seemed to have authority; and who, it being noon, and the ship's work suspended, was now enjoying respite from the burden of command. He was seated on an old-fashioned oaken chair, wriggling all over with curious carving; and the bottom of which was formed of a stout interlacing of the same elastic stuff of which the wigwam was constructed.

There was nothing so very particular, perhaps, about the appearance of the elderly man I saw; he was brown and brawny, like most old seamen, and heavily rolled up in blue pilot-cloth, cut in the Quaker style; only there was a fine and almost microscopic net-work of the minutest wrinkles interlacing round his eyes, which must have arisen from his continual sailings in many hard gales, and always looking to windward;—for this causes the muscles about the eyes to become pursed together. Such eye-wrinkles are very effectual in a scowl.

"Is this the Captain of the *Pequod?*" said I, advancing to the door of the tent.

"Supposing it be the Captain of the *Pequod,* what dost thou want of him?" he demanded.

"I was thinking of shipping."

"Thou wast, wast thou? I see thou art no Nantucketer—ever been in a stove boat?"

"No, sir, I never have."

"Dost know nothing at all about whaling, I dare say—eh?"

"Nothing, sir; but I have no doubt I shall soon learn. I've been several voyages in the merchant service, and I think that——"

"Merchant service be damned. Talk not that lingo to me. Dost see that leg?—I'll take that leg away from thy stern, if ever thou talkest of the marchant service to me again. Marchant service indeed! I suppose now ye feel considerable proud of having served in those marchant ships. But flukes! man, what makes thee want to go a-whaling, eh?—it looks a little suspicious, don't it, eh?—Hast not been a pirate, hast thou?—Didst not rob thy last Captain, didst thou?—Dost not think of murdering the officers when thou gettest to sea?"

I protested my innocence of these things. I saw that under the mask of these half humorous innuendoes, this old seaman, as an insulated Quakerish Nantucketer, was full of his insular prejudices, and rather distrustful of all aliens, unless they hailed from Cape Cod or the Vineyard.

"But what takes thee a-whaling? I want to know that before I think of shipping ye."

"Well, sir, I want to see what whaling is. I want to see the world."

"Want to see what whaling is, eh? Have ye clapped eye on Captain Ahab?"

"Who is Captain Ahab, sir?"

"Aye, aye, I thought so. Captain Ahab is the Captain of this ship."

"I am mistaken then. I thought I was speaking to the Captain himself."

"Thou art speaking to Captain Peleg—that's who ye are speaking to, young man. It belongs to me and Captain Bildad to see the *Pequod* fitted out for the voyage, and supplied with all her needs, including crew. We are part owners and agents. But as I was going to say, if thou wantest to know what whaling is, as thou tellest ye do, I can put ye in a way of finding it out before ye bind yourself to it, past backing out. Clap eye on Captain Ahab, young man, and thou wilt find that he has only one leg."

"What do you mean, sir? Was the other one lost by a whale?"

"Lost by a whale! Young man, come nearer to me: it was devoured, chewed up, crouched by the monstrousest parmacetty, that ever chipped a boat!—ah, ah!"

I was a little alarmed by his energy, perhaps also a little touched at the hearty grief in his concluding exclamation, but said as calmly as I could, "What you say is no doubt true enough, sir; but how could I know there was any peculiar ferocity in that particular whale, though indeed I might have inferred as much from the simple fact of the accident."

"Look ye, now, young man, thy lungs are a sort of soft, d'ye see; thou dost not talk shark a bit. *Sure,* ye've been to sea before now; sure of that?"

"Sir," said I, "I thought I told you that I had been four voyages in the merchant——"

"Hard down out of that! Mind what I said about the marchant service—don't aggravate me—I won't have it. But let us understand each other. I have given thee a hint about what whaling is; do ye still feel inclined for it?"

"I do, sir."

"Very good. Now, art thou the man to pitch a harpoon down a live whale's throat, and then jump after it? Answer, quick!"

"I am, sir, if it should be positively indispensable to do so; not to be got rid of, that is; which I don't take to be the fact."

"Good again. Now then, thou not only wantest to go a-whaling, to find out by experience what whaling is, but ye also want to go in order to see the world? Was not that what ye said! I thought so. Well then, just step forward there, and take a peep over the weather-bow, and then back to me and tell me what ye see there."

For a moment I stood a little puzzled by this curious request, not knowing exactly how to take it, whether humorously or in earnest. But concentrating all his crow's feet into one scowl, Captain Peleg started me on the errand.

Going forward and glancing over the weather bow, I perceived that the ship swinging to her anchor with the flood-tide was now obliquely pointing towards the open ocean. The prospect was unlimited, but exceedingly monotonous and forbidding; not the slightest variety that I could see.

"Well, what's the report?" said Peleg when I came back; "what did ye see?"

"Not much," I replied—"nothing but water; considerable horizon though, and there's a squall coming up, I think."

"Well, what dost thou think then of seeing the world? Do ye wish to go round Cape Horn to see any more of it, eh? Can't ye see the world where you stand?"

I was a little staggered, but go a-whaling I must, and I would; and the *Pequod* was as good a ship as any—I thought the best—and all this I now repeated to Peleg. Seeing me so determined, he expressed his willingness to ship me.

"And thou mayest as well sign the papers right off," he added— "come along with ye." And so saying, he led the way below deck into the cabin.

Seated on the transom was what seemed to me a most uncommon and surprising figure. It turned out to be Captain Bildad, who along with Captain Peleg was one of the largest owners of the vessel; the other shares, as is sometimes the case in these ports, being held by a crowd of old annuitants; widows, fatherless children, and chancery wards; each owning about the value of a timber head, or a foot of plank, or a nail or two in the ship. People in Nantucket invest their money in whaling vessels, the same way that you do yours in approved state stocks bringing in good interest.

Like Captain Peleg, Captain Bildad was a well-to-do, retired whaleman. But unlike Captain Peleg—who cared not a rush for what are called serious things, and indeed deemed those self-same serious things the veriest of all trifles—Captain Bildad had not only been originally educated according to the strictest sect of Nantucket Quakerism, but all his subsequent ocean life, and the sight of many unclad, lovely island creatures, round the Horn—all that had not moved this native born Quaker one single jot, had not so much as altered one angle of his vest. Still, for all this immutableness, was there some lack of common consistency about worthy Captain Peleg. Though refusing, from conscientious scruples, to bear arms against land invaders, yet himself had illimitably invaded the Atlantic and Pacific; and though a sworn foe to human bloodshed, yet had he in his straight-bodied coat spilled tuns upon tuns of leviathan gore.

Now Bildad, I am sorry to say, had the reputation of being an incorrigible old hunks, and in his sea-going days, a bitter, hard taskmaster. They told me in Nantucket, though it certainly seems a curious story, that when he sailed the old Categut whaleman, his crew, upon arriving home, were mostly all carried ashore to the hospital, sore exhausted and worn out. For a pious man, especially for a Quaker, he was certainly rather hard-hearted, to say the least. He never used to swear, though, at his men, they said; but somehow he got an inordinate quantity of cruel, unmitigated hard work out of them. When Bildad was a chief-mate, to have his drab-coloured eye intently looking at you made you feel completely nervous, till you could clutch something— a hammer or a marling-spike, and go to work like mad, at something or other, never mind what. Indolence and idleness perished from before him. His own person was the exact embodiment of his utilitarian character. On his long, gaunt body, he carried no spare flesh, no superfluous beard, his chin having a soft economical nap to it, like the worn nap of his broad-brimmed hat.

Such, then, was the person that I saw seated on the transom when I followed Captain Peleg down into the cabin. The space between the decks was small; and there, bolt upright, sat old Bildad, who always sat so, and never leaned, and this to save his coat-tails. His broad-brim was placed beside him; his legs were stiffly crossed; his drab vesture was buttoned up to his chin; and spectacles on nose, he seemed absorbed in reading from a ponderous volume.

"Bildad," cried Captain Peleg, "at it again, Bildad, eh? Ye have been studying those Scriptures, now, for the last thirty years, to my certain knowledge. How far ye got, Bildad?"

As if long habituated to such profane talk from his old shipmate, Bildad, without noticing his present irreverence, quietly looked up, and seeing me, glanced again inquiringly towards Peleg.

"He says he's our man, Bildad," said Peleg, "he wants to ship."

"Dost thee?" said Bildad, in a hollow tone, and turning round to me.

"I *dost*," said I unconsciously, he was so intense a Quaker.

"What do ye think of him, Bildad?" said Peleg.

"He'll do," said Bildad, eyeing me, and then went on spelling away at his book in a mumbling tone quite audible.

I thought him the queerest old Quaker I ever saw, especially as Peleg, his friend and old shipmate, seemed such a blusterer. But I said nothing, only looking round me sharply. Peleg now threw open a chest, and drawing forth the ship's articles, placed pen and ink before him, and seated himself at a little table. I began to think it was high time to settle with myself at what terms I would be willing to engage for the voyage. I was already aware that in the whaling business they paid no wages; but all hands, including the captain, received certain shares of the profits called *lays,* and that these lays were proportioned to the degree of importance pertaining to the respective duties of the ship's company. I was also aware that being a green hand at whaling, my own lay would not be very large; but considering that I was used to the sea, could steer a ship, splice a rope, and all that, I made no doubt that from all I had heard I should be offered at least the 275th lay—that is, the 275th part of the clear nett proceeds of the voyage, whatever that might eventually amount to. And though the 275th lay was what they call a rather *long lay,* yet it was better than nothing; and if we had a lucky voyage, might pretty nearly pay for the clothing I would wear out on it, not to speak of my three years' beef and board, for which I would not have to pay one stiver.

Now while Peleg was vainly trying to mend a pen with his jack-knife, old Bildad, to my no small surprise, considering that he was such an interested party in these proceedings; Bildad never heeded us, but went on mumbling to himself out of his book, "*Lay* not up for yourselves treasures upon earth, where moth——"

"Well, Captain Bildad," interrupted Peleg, "what d'ye say, what lay shall we give this young man?"

"Thou knowest best," was the sepulchral reply, "the seven hundred and seventy-seventh wouldn't be too much, would it?—'where moth and rust do corrupt, but *lay*——' "

"Why, blast your eyes, Bildad," cried Peleg, "thou dost not want to swindle this young man! he must have more than that."

"Seven hundred and seventy-seventh," again said Bildad, without lifting his eyes; and then went on mumbling—"for where your treasure is, there will your heart be also."

"I am going to put him down for the three hundredth," said Peleg, "do ye hear that, Bildad! The three hundredth lay, I say. Now then, my young man, Ishmael's thy name, didn't ye say? Well then, down ye go here, Ishmael, for the three hundredth lay."

"Captain Peleg," said I, "I have a friend with me who wants to ship too—shall I bring him down to-morrow?"

"To be sure," said Peleg. "Fetch him along, and we'll look at him."

"What lay does he want?" groaned Bildad, glancing up from the book in which he had again been burying himself.

"Oh! never thee mind about that, Bildad," said Peleg. "Has he ever whaled it any?" turning to me.

"Killed more whales than I can count, Captain Peleg."

"Well, bring him along then."

And, after signing the papers, off I went; nothing doubting that I had done a good morning's work, and that the *Pequod* was the identical ship that Yojo had provided to carry Queequeg and me round the Cape.

But I had not proceeded far, when I began to bethink me that the Captain with whom I was to sail yet remained unseen by me; though, indeed, in many cases, a whale-ship will be completely fitted out, and receive all her crew on board, ere the captain makes himself visible by arriving to take command: for sometimes these voyages are so prolonged, and the shore intervals at home so exceedingly brief, that if the captain have a family, or any absorbing concernment of that sort, he does not trouble himself much about his ship in port, but leaves her to the owners till all is ready for sea. However, it is always as well to have a look at him before irrevocably committing yourself into his hands. Turning back I accosted Captain Peleg, inquiring where Captain Ahab was to be found.

"And what doest thou want of Captain Ahab? It's all right enough; thou art shipped."

"Yes, but I should like to see him."

"But I don't think thou wilt be able to at present. I don't know exactly what's the matter with him; but he keeps close inside the house; a sort of sick, and yet he don't look so. In fact, he ain't sick; but no, he isn't well either. Any how, young man, he won't always see me, so I don't suppose he will thee. He's a queer man, Captain Ahab—so some think—but a good one. Oh, thou'lt like him well enough; no fear, no fear. He's a grand, ungodly, godlike man, Captain Ahab; doesn't speak much; but, when he does speak, then you may well listen. Mark ye, be forewarned; Ahab's above the common; Ahab's been in colleges, as well as 'mong the cannibals; been used to deeper wonders than the waves; fixed his fiery lance in mightier, stranger foes than whales. His lance! aye, the keenest and surest that out of all our isle! Oh! he ain't Captain Bildad; no, and he ain't Captain Peleg; *he's Ahab*, boy; and Ahab of old, thou knowest, was a-crowned king!

"And once for all, let me tell thee and assure thee, young man, it's better to sail with a moody good captain than a laughing bad one. So good-bye to thee—and wrong not Captain Ahab, because he happens to have a wicked name. Besides, my boy, he has a wife—not three voyages wedded—a sweet, resigned girl. Think of that; by that sweet girl that old man had a child: hold ye then there can be any utter, hopeless harm in Ahab? No, no, my lad; stricken, blasted, if he be, Ahab has his humanities!"

As I walked away, I was full of thoughtfulness; what had been incidentally revealed to me of Captain Ahab, filled me with a certain wild vagueness of painfulness concerning him. And somehow, at the time, I felt a sympathy and a sorrow for him, but for I don't know what, unless it was the cruel loss of his leg. And yet I also felt a strange awe of him; but that sort of awe, which I cannot at all describe, was not exactly awe; I do not know what it was. But I felt it; and it did not disincline me towards him; though I felt impatience at what seemed like mystery in him, so imperfectly as he was known to me then. However, my thoughts were at length carried in other directions, so that for the present dark Ahab slipped my mind.

CHAPTER 17

THE RAMADAN

As Queequeg's Ramadan, or Fasting and Humiliation, was to continue all day, I did not choose to disturb him till towards nightfall; for I cherish the greatest respect towards everybody's religious obligations, never mind how comical, and could not find it in my heart to undervalue even a congregation of ants worshipping a toadstool; or those other creatures in certain parts of our earth, who with a degree of footmanism quite unprecedented in other planets, bow down before the torso of a deceased landed proprietor merely on account of the inordinate possessions yet owned and rented in his name.

Towards evening, when I felt assured that all his performances and rituals were over, I went up to his room and knocked at the door; but no answer. I tried to open it, but it was fastened inside. "Queequeg," said I softly through the keyhole—all silent. "I say, Queequeg! why don't you speak? It's I—Ishmael." But all remained still as before. I began to grow alarmed. I had allowed him such abundant time; I thought he might have had an apoplectic fit. I looked through the key-hole; but the door opening into an odd corner of the room, the keyhole prospect was but a crooked and sinister one. I could only see part of the foot-board of the bed and a line of the wall, but nothing more. I was surprised to behold resting against the wall the wooden shaft of Queequeg's harpoon, which the landlady the evening previous had taken from him, before our mounting to the chamber. That's strange, thought I; but at any rate since the harpoon stands yonder, and he seldom or never goes abroad without it, therefore he must be inside here, and no possible mistake.

"Queequeg!—Queequeg!"—all still. Something must have happened. Apoplexy! I tried to bust open the door; but it stubbornly resisted. Running down stairs, I quickly stated my suspicions to the first person I met—the chambermaid. "La! la!" she cried, "I thought something must be the matter. I went to make the bed, after breakfast, and the door was locked; and not a mouse to be heard; and it's been just so silent ever since. But I thought, may be, you had both gone off and locked your baggage in for safe keeping. La! La! ma'am, —Mistress! murder! Mrs. Hussey! apoplexy!"—and with these cries she ran along towards the kitchen, I following.

Mrs. Hussey soon appeared with a mustard-pot in one hand and a vinegar-cruet in the other, having just broken away from the occupation of attending to the casters, and scolding her little black boy meantime.

"Wood-house!" cried I, "which way to it? Run for God's sake, and fetch something to pry open the door—the axe!—the axe!—he's had a stroke; depend upon it!"—and so saying I was unmethodically rushing up stairs again empty-handed, when Mrs. Hussey interposed the mustard-pot and vinegar-cruet, and the entire caster of her countenance.

"What's the matter with you, young man?"

"Get the axe! For God's sake, run for the doctor, some one, while I pry it open!"

"Look here," said the landlady, quickly putting down the vinegar-cruet, so as to have one hand free; "look here; are you talking about prying open any of my doors?"—and with that she seized my arm. "What's the matter with you? What's the matter with you, shipmate?"

In as calm, but rapid a manner as possible, I gave her to understand the whole case. Unconsciously clapping the vinegar-cruet to one side of her nose, she ruminated for an instant; then exclaimed—"No! I haven't seen it since I put it there." Running to a little closet under the landing of the stairs, she glanced in, and returning, told me that Queequeg's harpoon was missing. "He's killed himself," she cried. "It's unfort'nate Stiggs done over again—there goes another counterpane—God pity his poor mother!—it will be the ruin of my house. Has the poor lad a sister? Where's that girl?—there, Betty, go to Snarles the Painter, and tell him to paint me a sign, with—'no suicides permitted here and no smoking in the parlour'; might as well kill both birds at once. Kill? The Lord be merciful to his ghost! What's that noise there? You, young man, avast there!"

And running after me, she caught me as I was again trying to force open the door.

"I won't allow it; I won't have my premises spoiled. Go for the locksmith, there's one about a mile from here. But avast!" putting her hand in her side pocket, "here's a key that'll fit, I guess; let's see." And with that, she turned it in the lock; but, alas! Queequeg's supplemental bolt remained unwithdrawn within.

"Have to burst it open," said I, and was running down the entry a little, for a good start, when the landlady caught at me, again vowing I should not break down her premises; but I tore from her, and with a sudden bodily rush dashed myself full against the mark.

With a prodigious noise the door flew open, and the knob slamming

against the wall, sent the plaster to the ceiling; and there, goo
heavens! there sat Queequeg, altogether cool and self-collected; righ
in the middle of the room; squatting on his hams, and holding Yoj
on top of his head. He looked neither one way nor the other way, bu
sat like a carved image with scarce a sign of active life.

"Queequeg," said I, going up to him, "Queequeg, what's the matte
with you?"

"He hain't been a sittin' so all day, has he?" said the landlady.

But all we said, not a word could we drag out of him; I almos
felt like pushing him over so as to change his position, for it wa
almost intolerable, it seemed so painfully and unnaturally constrained
especially, as in all probability he had been sitting so for upwards c
eight or ten hours, going too without his regular meals.

"Mrs. Hussey," said I, "he's *alive* at all events; so leave us, if yo
please, and I will see to this strange affair myself."

Closing the door upon the landlady, I endeavoured to prevail upo
Queequeg to take a chair; but in vain. There he sat; and all he coul
do—for all my polite arts and blandishments—he would not move
peg, nor say a word, not even look at me nor notice my presence in ar
the slightest way.

I wonder, thought I, if this can possibly be a part of his Ramadar
do they fast on their hams that way in his native island. It must
so; yes, it's a part of his creed, I suppose; well, then, let him rest; he
get up sooner or later, no doubt. It can't last for ever, thank God, ar
his Ramadan only comes once a year; and I don't believe it's ve.
punctual then.

I went down to supper. After sitting a long time listening to t
long stories of some sailors who had just come from a plum-puddir
voyage, as they called it (that is, a short whaling-voyage in a schoon
or brig confined to the north of the line, in the Atlantic Ocean only
after listening to these plum-puddingers till nearly eleven o'clock,
went up stairs to go to bed, feeling quite sure by this time Queequ
must certainly have brought his Ramadan to a termination. But n
there he was just where I had left him; he had not stirred an inch.
began to grow vexed with him; it seemed so downright senseless ar
insane to be sitting there all day and half the night on his hams in
cold room, holding a piece of wood on his head.

"For heaven's sake, Queequeg, get up and shake yourself; get
and have some supper. You'll starve; you'll kill yourself, Queequeg
But not a word did he reply.

Despairing of him, therefore, I determined to go to bed and to slee
and no doubt, before a great while, he would follow me. But previo

to turning in, I took my heavy bearskin jacket and threw it over him, as it promised to be a very cold night; and he had nothing but his ordinary jacket on. For some time, do all I would, I could not get into the faintest doze. I had blown out the candle; and the mere thought of Queequeg—not four feet off—sitting there in that uneasy position, stark alone in the cold and dark; this made me really wretched. Think of it; sleeping all night in the same room with a wide awake pagan on his hams in this dreary, unaccountable Ramadan!

But somehow I dropped off at last, and knew nothing more till break of day; when, looking over the bedside, there squatted Queequeg, as if he had been screwed down to the floor. But as soon as the first glimpse of sun entered the window, up he got, with stiff and grating joints, but with a cheerful look; limped towards me where I lay; pressed his forehead again against mine; and said his Ramadan was over.

At last we rose and dressed; and Queequeg, taking a prodigious hearty breakfast of chowders of all sorts, so that the landlady should not make much profit by reason of his Ramadan, we sallied out to board the *Pequod,* sauntering along, and picking our teeth with halibut bones.

CHAPTER 18

HIS MARK

As we were walking down the end of the wharf towards the ship, Queequeg carrying his harpoon, Captain Peleg in his gruff voice loudly hailed us from his wigwam, saying he had not suspected my friend was a cannibal, and furthermore announcing that he let no cannibals on board that craft, unless they previously produced their papers.

"What do you mean by that, Captain Peleg?" said I, now jumping on the bulwarks, and leaving my comrade standing on the wharf.

"I mean," he replied, "he must show his papers."

"Yea," said Captain Bildad in his hollow voice, sticking his head from behind Peleg's out of the wigwam. "He must show that he's converted. Son of darkness," he added, turning to Queequeg, "art thou at present in communion with any Christian church?"

"Why," said I, "he's a member of the first Congregational Church." Here be it said, that many tattooed savages sailing in Nantucket ships at last come to be converted into the churches.

"Young man," said Bildad sternly, "thou art skylarking with me—explain thyself thou young Hittite. What church doest thee mean? answer me."

Finding myself thus hard pushed, I replied. "I mean, sir, the same ancient Catholic Church to which you and I, and Captain Peleg there, and Queequeg here, and all of us, and every mother's son and soul of us belong; the great and everlasting First Congregation of this whole worshipping world; we all belong to that; only some of us cherish some crotchets noways touching the grand belief; in *that* we all join hands."

"Splice, thou mean'st *splice* hands," cried Peleg, drawing nearer. "Young man, you'd better ship for a missionary, instead of a fore-mast hand; I never heard a better sermon. Deacon Deuteronomy—why Father Mapple himself couldn't beat it, and he's reckoned something. Come aboard, come aboard; never mind about the papers. I say, tell Quohog there—what's that you call him? tell Quohog to step along. By the great anchor, what a harpoon he's got there! looks like good stuff that; and he handles it about right. I say, Quohog, or whatever your name is, did you ever stand in the head of a whale-boat? did you ever strike a fish?"

Without saying a word, Queequeg, in his wild sort of way, jumped upon the bulwarks, from thence into the bows of one of the whale-boats hanging to the side; and then bracing his left knee, and poising his harpoon, cried out in some such way as this:

"Cap'ain, you see him small drop tar on water dere? You see him? well, spose him one whale eye, well, den!" and taking sharp aim at it, he darted the iron right over old Bildad's broad brim clean across the ship's decks, and struck the glistening tar spot out of sight.

"Now," said Queequeg, quietly hauling in the line, "spos-ee him whale-e eye; why, dad whale dead."

"Quick, Bildad," said Peleg, his partner, who, aghast at the close vicinity of the flying harpoon, had retreated towards the cabin gangway. "Quick, I say, you Bildad, and get the ship's papers. We must have Hedgehog there, I mean Quohog, in one of our boats. Look ye Quohog, we'll give ye the nintieth lay, and that's more than ever was given a harpooneer yet out of Nantucket."

So down we went into the cabin, and to my great joy Queequeg was soon enrolled among the same ship's company to which I myself belonged.

When all preliminaries were over and Peleg had got everything ready for signing, he turned to me and said, "I guess, Quohog there doesn'

know how to write, does he? I say, Quohog, blast ye! dost thou sign
thy name or make thy mark?"

But at this question, Queequeg, who had twice or thrice before taken
part in similar ceremonies, looked no ways abashed; but taking the
offered pen, copied upon the paper, in the proper place, an exact
counterpart of a queer round figure which was tattooed upon his arm;
so that through Captain Peleg's obstinate mistake touching his appella-
tive, it stood something like this:

Quohog.
his ✠ mark.

Meanwhile Captain Bildad sat earnestly and steadfastly eyeing Queequeg, and at last rising solemnly and fumbling in the huge pockets
of his broad-skirted drab coat, took out a bundle of tracts, and selecting
one entitled "The Latter Day Coming; or No Time to Lose," placed it
in Queequeg's hands, and then grasping them and the book with both
his, looked earnestly into his eyes, and said, "Son of darkness, I must
do my duty by thee; I am part owner of this ship, and feel concerned
for the souls of all its crew; if thou still clingest to thy Pagan ways,
which I sadly fear, I beseech thee, remain not for aye a Belial bonds-
man. Spurn the idol Bell, and the hideous dragon; turn from the wrath
to come; mind thine eye, I say; oh! goodness gracious! steer clear of
the fiery pit!"

Bildad said no more, but buttoning up his coat, stalked on deck,
where we followed him. There he stood, very quietly overlooking
some sail-makers who were mending a top-sail in the waist. Now and
then he stooped to pick up a patch, or save an end of the tarred twine,
which otherwise might have been wasted.

CHAPTER 19

THE PROPHET

'SHIPMATES, have ye shipped in that ship?"
Queequeg and I had just left the *Pequod,* and were sauntering
away from the water, for the moment each occupied with his own
thoughts, when the above words were put to us by a stranger, who,
pausing before us, levelled his massive forefinger at the vessel in question. He was but shabbily apparelled in faded jacket and patched

trousers; a rag of a black handkerchief investing his neck. A confluent small-pox had in all directions flowed over his face, and left it like the complicated ribbed bed of a torrent, when the rushing waters have been dried up.

"Have ye shipped in her?" he repeated.

"Yes," said I, "we have just signed the articles."

"Ye hav'n't seen Old Thunder yet, have ye?"

"Who's Old Thunder?" said I, again riveted with the insane earnestness of his manner.

"Captain Ahab."

"What! the captain of our ship, the *Pequod*?"

"Aye, among some of us old sailor chaps, he goes by that name. Ye hav'n't seen him yet, have ye?"

"No, we hav'n't. He's sick they say, but is getting better, and will be all right again before long."

"All right again before long!" laughed the stranger with a solemnly derisive sort of laugh. "Look ye; when Captain Ahab is all right, then this left arm of mine will be all right; not before."

"Look here, friend," said I, "if you have anything important to tell us, out with it; but if you are only trying to bamboozle us, you are mistaken in your game; that's all I have to say."

"And it's said very well, and like to hear a chap talk up that way; you are just the man for him—the likes of ye. Morning to ye, shipmates, morning! Oh! when ye get there, tell 'em I've concluded not to make one of 'em."

"Ah, my dear fellow, you can't fool us that way—you can't fool us. It is the easiest thing in the world for a man to look as if he had a great secret in him."

"Morning to ye, shipmates, morning."

"Morning it is," said I. "Come along, Queequeg, let's leave this crazy man. But stop, tell me your name, will you?"

"Elijah."

Elijah! thought I, and we walked away, both commenting after each other's fashion, upon this ragged old sailor; and agreed that he was nothing but a humbug, trying to be a bugbear. But we had not gone perhaps above a hundred yards, when chancing to turn a corner, and looking back as I did so, who should be seen but Elijah following us, though at a distance. Somehow, the sight of him struck me so, that I said nothing to Queequeg of his being behind, but passed on with my comrade, anxious to see whether the stranger would turn the same corner that we did. He did; and then it seemed to me that he was dogging us, but with what intent I could not for the life of me imagine.

I was resolved to satisfy myself whether this ragged Elijah was really dogging us or not, and with that intent crossed the way with Queequeg, and on that side of it retraced our steps. But Elijah passed on, without seeming to notice us. This relieved me; and once more, and finally as it seemed to me, I pronounced him in my heart, a humbug.

CHAPTER 20

ALL ASTIR

A DAY or two passed, and there was great activity aboard the *Pequod*. Not only were the old sails being mended, but new sails were coming on board, and bolts of canvas, and coils of rigging; in short everything betokened that the ship's preparations were hurrying to a close. Captain Peleg seldom or never went ashore, but sat in his wig-wam keeping a sharp look-out upon the hands. Bildad did all the purchasing and providing at the stores; and the men employed in the hold and on the rigging were working till long after nightfall.

On the day following Queequeg's signing articles, word was given at all the inns where the ship's company were stopping, that their chests must be on board before night, for there was no telling how soon the vessel might be sailing. So Queequeg and I got down our traps, resolving, however, to sleep ashore till the last. But it seems they always give very long notice in these cases, and the ship did not sail for several days. But no wonder; there was a good deal to be done, and there is no telling how many things to be thought of, before the *Pequod* was fully equipped.

At the period of our arrival at the Island, the heaviest storage of the *Pequod* had been almost completed; comprising her beef, bread, water, fuel, and iron hoops and staves. But, as before hinted, for some time was a continual fetching and carrying on board of divers odds and ends of things, both large and small.

Chief among those who did this fetching and carrying was Captain Bildad's sister, a lean old lady of a most determined and indefatigable spirit, but withal very kindhearted, who seemed resolved that, if *she* could help it, nothing should be found wanting in the *Pequod*, after once fairly getting to sea. At one time she would come on board with a jar of pickles for the steward's pantry; another time with a bunch of quills for the chief mate's desk, where he kept his log; a third time with a roll of flannel for the small of some one's rheumatic back.

Never did any woman better deserve her name, which was Charity—
Aunt Charity, as everybody called her.

During these days of preparation, Queequeg and I often visited the
craft, and as often I asked about Captain Ahab, and how he was, and
when he was going to come on board his ship. To these questions
they would answer, that he was getting better and better, and was
expected aboard every day; meantime, the two Captains, Peleg and
Bildad, could attend to everything necessary to fit the vessel for the
voyage. If I had been downright honest with myself, I would have
seen very plainly in my heart that I did but half fancy being committed
this way to so long a voyage, without once laying my eyes on the man
who was to be the absolute dictator of it, so soon as the ship sailed out
upon the open sea. But when a man suspects any wrong, it sometimes
happens that if he be already involved in the matter, he insensibly
strives to cover up his suspicions even from himself. And much this
way it was with me. I said nothing, and tried to think nothing.

At last it was given out that some time next day the ship would
certainly sail. So next morning Queequeg and I took a very early
start.

CHAPTER 21

GOING ABOARD

IT WAS nearly six o'clock, but only grey imperfect misty dawn,
when we drew nigh the wharf.

"There are some sailors running ahead there, if I see right," said I to
Queequeg, "it can't be shadow; she's off by sunrise, I guess; come on!"

"Avast!" cried a voice, whose owner at the same time coming close
behind us, laid a hand upon both our shoulders, and then insinuating
himself between us, stood stooping forward a little, in the uncertain
twilight, strangely peering from Queequeg to me. It was Elijah.

"Going aboard?"

"Hands off, will you," said I.

"Lookee here," said Queequeg, shaking himself, "go 'way!"

"Ain't going aboard, then?"

"Yes, we are," said I, "but what business is that of yours? Do you
know, Mr. Elijah, that I consider you a little impertinent?"

"No, no, no; I wasn't aware of that," said Elijah, slowly and won-
deringly looking from me to Queequeg, with the most unaccountable
glances.

"Elijah," said I, "you will oblige my friend and me by withdrawing.

We are going to the Indian and Pacific Oceans, and would prefer not to be detained."

"Ye be, be ye? Coming back afore breakfast?"

"He's cracked, Queequeg," said I, "come on."

"Holloa!" cried stationary Elijah, hailing us when we had removed a few paces.

"Never mind him," said I, "Queequeg, come on."

But he stole up to us again, and suddenly clapping his hand on my shoulder, said, "Did ye see anything looking like men going toward that ship a while ago?"

Struck by this plain matter-of-fact question, I answered, saying "Yes, I thought I did see four or five men; but it was too dim to be sure."

"Very dim, very dim," said Elijah. " 'Morning to ye."

Once more we quitted him; but once more he came softly after us; and touching my shoulder again, said, "See if you can find 'em now, will ye?"

"Find who?"

" 'Morning to ye! 'morning to ye!" he rejoined, again moving off. "Oh! I was going to warn ye against—but never mind, never mind—it's all one, all in the family too;—sharp frost this morning, ain't it? Good-bye to ye. Shan't see ye again very soon, I guess; unless it's before the Grand Jury." And with these cracked words he finally departed, leaving me, for the moment, in no small wonderment at his frantic impudence.

At last, stepping on board the *Pequod*, we found everything in profound quiet, not a soul moving. The cabin entrance was locked within; the hatches were all on, and lumbered with coils of rigging. Going forward to the forecastle, we found the slide of the scuttle open. Seeing a light, we went down, and found only an old rigger there, wrapped in a tattered pea-jacket. He was thrown at whole length upon two chests, his face downwards and inclosed in his folded arms. The profoundest slumber slept upon him.

"Those sailors we saw, Queequeg, where can they have gone to?" said I, looking dubiously at the sleeper. But it seemed that, when on the wharf, Queequeg had not at all noticed what I now alluded to; hence I would have thought myself to have been optically deceived in that matter, were it not for Elijah's otherwise inexplicable question.

Queequeg removed himself to just beyond the head of the sleeper, and lighted his tomahawk pipe. I sat at the feet. We kept the pipe passing over the sleeper, from one to the other.

He was going on with some wild reminiscences about his tomahawk-pipe, which, it seemed, had in its two uses both brained his foes and

soothed his soul, when we were directly attracted to the sleepin
rigger. The strong vapour now completely filling the contracted hol
it began to tell upon him. He breathed with a sort of mufflednes
then seemed troubled in the nose; then revolved over once or twice
then sat up and rubbed his eyes.

"Holloa!" he breathed at last, "who be ye smokers?"

"Shipped men," answered I, "when does she sail?"

"Aye aye, ye are going in her, be ye? She sails to-day. The Captai
came aboard last night."

"What Captain?—Ahab?"

"Who but him indeed?"

I was going to ask him some further questions concerning Aha
when we heard a noise on deck.

"Halloa! Starbuck's astir," said the rigger. "He's a lively chie
mate, that; good man, and a pious; but all alive now, I must turn to
And so saying he went on deck, and we followed.

It was now clear sunrise. Soon the crew came on board in twos ar
threes; the riggers bestirred themselves; the mates were actively e
gaged; and several of the shore people were busy in bringing vario
last things on board. Meanwhile Captain Ahab remained invisib
enshrined within his cabin.

CHAPTER 22

MERRY CHRISTMAS

At length, towards noon, upon the final dismissal of the shij
riggers, and after the *Pequod* had been hauled out from tl
wharf, and after the ever-thoughtful Charity had come off in a whal
boat, with her last gift—a night-cap for Stubb, the second mate, b
brother-in-law, and a spare Bible for the steward—after all this, tl
two Captains, Peleg and Bildad, issued from the cabin, and turnii
to the chief mate, Peleg said:

"Now, Mr. Starbuck, are you sure everything is right? Capta
Ahab is all ready—just spoke to him—nothing more to be got fro
shore, eh? Well, call all hands, then. Muster 'em aft here—bla
'em!"

"No need of profane words, however great the hurry, Peleg," sa
Bildad, "but away with thee, friend Starbuck, and do our bidding."

Now, in getting under weigh, the station generally occupied by t
pilot is the forward part of the ship. And here Bildad, who, wi

Peleg, be it known, in addition to his other offices, was one of the licensed pilots of the port—he being suspected to have got himself made a pilot in order to save the Nantucket pilot-fee to all the ships he was concerned in, for he never piloted any other craft—Bildad, I say, might now be seen actively engaged in looking over the bows for the approaching anchor, and at intervals singing what seemed a dismal stave of psalmody, to cheer the hands at the windlass, who roared forth some sort of a chorus about the girls in Booble Alley, with hearty good will. Nevertheless, not three days previous, Bildad had told them that no profane songs would be allowed on board the *Pequod*, particularly in getting under weigh; and Charity, his sister, had placed a small copy of Watts in each seaman's berth.

Meantime, overseeing the other part of the ship, Captain Peleg ripped and swore astern in the most frightful manner. I almost thought he would sink the ship before the anchor could be got up; involuntarily I paused on my handspike, and told Queequeg to do the same, thinking of the perils we both ran, in starting on the voyage with such a devil for a pilot. I was comforting myself, however, with the thought that in pious Bildad might be found some salvation, spite of his seven hundred and seventy-seventh lay, when I felt a sudden sharp poke in my rear, and turning round was horrified at the apparition of Captain Peleg in the act of withdrawing his leg from my immediate vicinity. That was my first kick.

"Is that the way they heave in the merchant service?" he roared. "Spring, thou sheep-head; spring, and break thy back-bone! Why don't ye spring, I say, all of ye—spring! Quohog! spring, thou chap with the red whiskers; spring there, Scotch-cap; spring, thou green pants. Spring, I say, all of ye, and spring your eyes out!" And so saying he moved along the windlass, here and there using his leg very freely, while imperturbable Bildad kept leading off with his psalmody. Thinks I, Captain Peleg must have been drinking something to-day.

At last the anchor was up, the sails were set, and off we glided. It was a short, cold Christmas; and as the short northern day merged into night, we found ourselves almost broad upon the wintry ocean, whose freezing spray cased us in ice as in polished armour. The long rows of teeth on the bulwarks glistened in the moonlight; and like the white ivory tusks of some huge elephant, vast curving icicles depended from the bows.

Lank Bildad, as pilot, headed the first watch, and ever and anon, as the old craft deep dived in to the green seas, and sent the shivering frost all over her, and the winds howled, and the cordage rang, his steady notes were heard—

"Sweet fields beyond the swelling flood,
Stand dressed in living green.
So to the Jews old Canaan stood,
While Jordan rolled between."

At last we gained such an offing, that the two pilots were needed no longer. The stout sail-boat that had accompanied us began ranging alongside.

"God bless ye, and have ye in His holy keeping, men," murmured old Bildad, almost incoherently. "I hope ye'll have fine weather now, so that Captain Ahab may soon be moving among ye—a pleasant sun is all he needs, and ye'll have plenty of them in the tropic voyage ye go. Be careful in the hunt, ye mates. Don't stave the boats needlessly, ye harpooneers; good white cedar plank is raised three per cent within the year. Don't forget your prayers, either. Mr. Starbuck, mind that cooper don't waste the spare staves. Oh! the sail-needles are in the green locker! Don't whale it too much a' Lord's days, men; but don't miss a fair chance either, that's rejecting Heaven's good gifts. Have an eye to the molasses tierce, Mr. Stubb; it was a little leaky, I thought. If ye touch at the islands, Mr. Flask, beware of fornication. Good-bye, good-bye! Don't keep that cheese too long down in the hold, Mr. Starbuck; it'll spoil. Be careful with the butter—twenty cents the pound it was, and mind ye, if——"

"Come, come, Captain Bildad; stop palavering,—away!" and with that, Peleg hurried him over the side, and both dropped into the boat.

Ship and boat diverged; the cold, damp night breeze blew between; a screaming gull flew overhead; the two hulls wildly rolled; we gave three heavy-hearted cheers, and blindly plunged like fate into the lone Atlantic.

CHAPTER 23

THE LEE SHORE

Some chapters back, one Bulkington was spoken of, a tall, new-landed mariner, encountered in New Bedford at the inn.

When on that shivering winter's night, the *Pequod* thrust her vindictive bows into the cold malicious waves, who should I see standing at her helm but Bulkington! I looked with sympathetic awe and fearfulness upon the man, who in mid-winter just landed from a four-years' dangerous voyage, could so unrestingly push off again for still another tempestuous term. The land seemed scorching to his feet. Wonderfullest things are ever the unmentionable; deep memories yield no epitaphs; this six-inch chapter is the stoneless grave of Bulkington. Let me only say that it fared with him as with the storm-tossed ship, that miserably drives along the leeward land. The port would fain give succour; the port is pitiful; in the port is safety, comfort, hearthstone, supper, warm blankets, friends, all that's kind to our mortalities. But in that gale, the port, the land, is that ship's direst jeopardy; she must fly all hospitality; one touch of land, though it but graze the keel, would make her shudder through and through. With all her might she crowds all sail off shore; in so doing, fights 'gainst the very winds that fain would blow her homeward; seeks all the lashed sea's landlessness again; for refuge's sake forlornly rushing into peril; her only friend her bitterest foe!

Know ye now, Bulkington? Glimpses do ye seem to see of that mortally intolerable truth; that all deep, earnest thinking is but the intrepid effort of the soul to keep the open independence of her sea; while the wildest winds of heaven and earth conspire to cast her on the treacherous, slavish shore?

But as in landlessness alone resides the highest truth, shoreless, indefinite as God—so, better is it to perish in that howling infinite, than be ingloriously dashed upon the lee, even if that were safety! For worm-like, then, oh! who would craven crawl to land! Terrors of the terrible! is all this agony so vain? Take heart, take heart, O Bulkington! Bear thee grimly, demigod! Up from the spray of thy ocean-perishing—straight up, leaps thy apotheosis!

CHAPTER 24

THE ADVOCATE

As Queequeg and I are now fairly embarked in this business of whaling; and as this business of whaling has somehow come to be regarded among landsmen as a rather unpoetical and disreputable pursuit; therefore, I am all anxiety to convince ye, ye landsmen, of the injustice hereby done to us hunters of whales.

Doubtless one leading reason why the world declines honouring us whalemen, is this: they think that, at best, our vocation amounts to a butchering sort of business; and that when actively engaged therein, we are surrounded by all manner of defilements. Butchers we are, that is true. But butchers, also, and butchers of the bloodiest badge

C

have been all Martial Commanders whom the world invariably delights
to honour. And as for the matter of the alleged uncleanliness of our
business, ye shall soon be initiated into certain facts hitherto pretty
generally unknown, and which, upon the whole, will triumphantly
plant the sperm whale-ship at least among the cleanliest things of this
tidy earth. But even granting the charge in question to be true; what
disordered slippery decks of a whale-ship are comparable to the unspeakable carrion of those battle-fields from which so many soldiers
return to drink in all ladies' plaudits? And if the idea of peril so much
enhances the popular conceit of the soldier's profession; let me assure
ye that many a veteran who has freely marched up to a battery, would
quickly recoil at the apparition of the sperm-whale's vast tail, fanning
into eddies the air over his head. For what are the comprehensible
terrors of man compared with the interlinked terrors and wonders of
God!

But, though the world scouts at us whale-hunters, yet does it unwittingly pay us the profoundest homage; yea, an all-abounding
adoration! for almost all the tapers, lamps, and candles that burn
round the globe, burn, as before so many shrines, to our glory!

Grant it, since you cite it; but, say what you will, there is no real
dignity in whaling.

No dignity in whaling? The dignity of our calling the very heavens
attest. Cetus is a constellation in the South! No more! Drive down
your hat in presence of the Czar, and take it off to Queequeg! No
more! I know a man that, in his lifetime, has taken three hundred
and fifty whales. I account that man more honourable than that
great captain of antiquity who boasted of taking as many walled
towns.

And, as for me, if, by any possibility, there be any as yet undiscovered prime thing in me; if I shall ever deserve any real repute in
that small but high hushed world which I might not be unreasonably
ambitious of; if hereafter I shall do anything that, upon the whole, a
man might rather have done than to have left undone; if at my death,
my executors, or more properly my creditors, find any precious MSS.
in my desk, then here I prospectively ascribe all the honour and the
glory go to whaling; for a whale-ship was my Yale College and my
Harvard.

CHAPTER 25

POSTSCRIPT

IN BEHALF of the dignity of whaling, I would fain advance naught but substantiated facts. But after embattling his facts, an advocate who should wholly suppress a not unreasonable surmise which might tell eloquently upon his cause—such an advocate, would he not be blameworthy?

It is well known that at the coronation of kings and queens, even modern ones, a certain curious process of seasoning them for their functions is gone through. There is a salt-cellar of state so called, and there may be a caster of state. How they use the salt, precisely—who knows? Certain I am, however, that a king's head is solemnly oiled at his coronation, even as a head of salad. Can it be, though, that they anoint it with a view of making its interior run well, as they anoint machinery? Much might be ruminated here, concerning the essential dignity of this regal process, because in common life we esteem but meanly and contemptibly a fellow who anoints his hair, and palpably smells of that anointing. In truth, a mature man who uses hair-oil, unless medicinally, that man has probably got a quoggy spot in him somewhere. As a general rule, he can't amount to much in his totality. But the only thing to be considered here, is this—what kind of oil is used at coronations? Certainly it cannot be olive oil, nor macassar oil, nor castor oil, nor bear's oil, nor train oil, nor cod-liver oil. What then can it possibly be, but the sperm oil in its unmanufactured, unpolluted state, the sweetest of all oils?

Think of that, ye loyal Britons! we whalemen supply your kings and queens with coronation stuff!

CHAPTER 26

KNIGHTS AND SQUIRES

THE CHIEF mate of the *Pequod* was Starbuck, a native of Nantucket, and a Quaker by descent. He was a long, earnest man, and though born on an icy coast, seemed well adapted to endure hot latitudes, his flesh being hard as twice-baked biscuit. Only some thirty arid summers had he seen; those summers had dried up all his physical superfluousness. But this, his thinness, so to speak, seemed no more the token of wasting anxieties and cares, than it seemed the indication of any bodily blight. It was merely the condensation of the man. He was by no means ill-looking; quite the contrary. Uncommonly conscientious for a seaman, and endued with a deep natural reverence, the wild watery loneliness of his life did therefore strongly incline him to superstition; but to that sort of superstition, which in some organizations seems rather to spring, somehow, from intelligence than from ignorance. Outward portents and inward presentiments were his. And if at times these things bent the welded iron of his soul much more did his far away domestic memories of his young Cape wife and child, tend to bend him still more from the original ruggedness of his nature, and open him still further to those latent influences which, in some honest hearted men, restrain the gush of dare-devil daring, so often evinced by others in the more perilous vicissitudes of the fishery.

Starbuck was no crusader after perils; in him courage was not a sentiment; but a thing simply useful to him, and always at hand upon all mortally practical occasions. Besides, he thought, perhaps, that in this business of whaling, courage was one of the great staple outfits of the ship, like her beef and her bread, and not to be foolishly wasted. Wherefore he had no fancy for lowering for whales after sun-down; nor for persisting in fighting a fish that too much persisted in fighting him. For, thought Starbuck, I am here in this critical ocean to kill whales for my living, and not to be killed by them for theirs; and that hundreds of men had been so killed Starbuck well knew. What doom was his own father's? Where, in the bottomless deeps, could he find the torn limbs of his brother?

With memories like these in him, and, moreover, given to a certain superstitiousness, as has been said; the courage of this Starbuck, which could, nevertheless, still flourish, must indeed have been extreme. But it was not in reasonable nature that a man so organized, and with such terrible experiences and remembrances as he had; it was not in nature that these things should fail in latently engendering an element in him which under suitable circumstances, would break out from its confinement, and burn all his courage up. And brave as he might be, it was that sort of bravery chiefly, visible in some intrepid men, which, while generally abiding firm in the conflict with seas, or winds, or whales, or any of the ordinary irrational horrors of the world, yet cannot withstand those more terrific, because more spiritual terrors, which sometimes menace you from the concentrating brow of an enraged and mighty man.

CHAPTER 27

KNIGHTS AND SQUIRES

STUBB was the second mate. He was a native of Cape Cod; and hence, according to local usage, was called a Cape-Cod-man. A happy-go-lucky; neither craven nor valiant; taking perils as they came with an indifferent air; and while engaged in the most imminent crisis of the chase, toiling away, calm and collected as a journeyman joiner engaged for the year. Good-humoured, easy, and careless, he presided over his whale-boat as if the most deadly encounter were but a dinner, and his crew all invited guests. He was as particular about the comfortable arrangements of his part of the boat, as an old stage-driver is about the snugness of his box. When close to the whale, in the very death-lock of the fight, he handled his unpitying lance coolly and off-handedly, as a whistling tinker his hammer. He would hum over his old rigadig tunes while flank and flank with the most exasperated monster.

What, perhaps, with other things, made Stubb such an easy-going, unfearing man, so cheerily trudging off with the burden of life in a world full of grave peddlers, all bowed to the ground with their packs; what helped to bring about that almost impious good-humour of his; that thing must have been his pipe. For, like his nose, his short, black little pipe was one of the regular features of his face. You would almost as soon have expected him to turn out of his bunk without his nose as without his pipe. He kept a whole row of pipes there ready loaded, stuck in a rack, within easy reach of his hand; and, whenever he turned in, he smoked them all out in succession, lighting one from the other to the end of the chapter; then loading them again to be in readiness anew. For, when Stubbs dressed, instead of first putting his legs into his trousers, he put his pipe into his mouth.

The third mate was Flask, a native of Tisbury, in Martha's Vineyard. A short, stout, ruddy young fellow, very pugnacious concerning whales, who somehow seemed to think that the great Leviathans had personally and hereditarily affronted him; and therefore it was a sort of point of honour with him, to destroy them whenever encountered. So utterly lost was he to all sense of reverence for the many marvels of their majestic bulk and mystic ways; and so dead to anything like an apprehension of any possible danger from encountering them; that in his poor opinion the wondrous whale was but a species of magnified mouse, or at least water-rat, requiring only a little circumvention and some small application of time and trouble in order to kill and boil.

This ignorant, unconscious fearlessness of his made him a little waggish in the matter of whales; he followed these fish for the fun of it; and a three-years' voyage round Cape Horn was only a jolly joke that lasted that length of time. As a carpenter's nails are divided into wrought nails and cut nails; so mankind may be similarly divided. Little Flask was one of the wrought ones; made to clinch tight and last long. They called him King-Post on board of the *Pequod*; because, in form, he could be well likened to the short, square limber known by that name in Arctic whalers; and which by the means of many radiating side timbers inserted into it, serves to brace the ship against the icy concussions of those battering seas.

Now these three mates—Starbuck, Stubb, and Flask, were momentous men. They it was who by universal prescription commanded three of the *Pequod's* boats as headsmen. In that grand order of battle in which Captain Ahab would probably marshal his forces to descend on the whales, these three headsmen were as captains of companies. Or, being armed with their long keen whaling spears, they were as a picked trio of lancers; even as the harpooneers were flingers of javelins.

And since in this famous fishery, each mate or headsman, like a Gothic Knight of old, is always accompanied by his boat-steerer or harpooneer, who in certain conjunctures provides him with a fresh lance, when the former one has been badly twisted, or elbowed in the assault; and moreover, as there generally subsists between the two, a close intimacy and friendliness; it is therefore but meet, that in this place we set down who the *Pequod's* harpooneers were, and to what headsman each of them belonged.

First of all was Queequeg, whom Starbuck, the chief mate, had selected for his squire. Queequeg is already known.

Next was Tashtego, an unmixed Indian from Gay Head, the most westerly promontory of Martha's Vineyard, where there still exists the last remnant of a village of red men, which has long supplied the neighbouring island of Nantucket with many of her most daring harpooneers. In the fishery, they usually go by the generic name of Gay-Headers. Tashtego's long, lean, sable hair, his high cheek bones, and black rounding eyes—for an Indian, Oriental in their largeness, but Antarctic in their glittering expression—all this sufficiently proclaimed him an inheritor of the unvitiated blood of those proud warrior hunters, who, in quest of the great New England moose, had scoured, bow in hand, the aboriginal forests of the main. But no longer snuffing in the trail of the wild beasts of the woodland, Tashtego now hunted in the wake of the great whales of the sea; the unerring harpoon of the son fitly replacing the infallible arrow of the sires.

To look at the tawny brawn of his lithe snaky limbs, you would almost have credited the superstitions of some of the earlier Puritans, and half-believed this wild Indian to be a son of the Prince of the Powers of the Air. Tashtego was Stubb the second mate's squire.

Third among the harpooneers was Daggoo, a gigantic, coal-black negro-savage, with a lion-like tread—an Ahasuerus to behold. Suspended from his ears were two golden hoops, so large that the sailors called them ring-bolts, and would talk of securing the top-sail halyards to them. In his youth Daggoo had voluntarily shipped on board of a whaler, lying in a lonely bay on his native coast. And never having been anywhere in the world but in Africa, Nantucket, and the pagan harbours most frequented by whale men; and having now led for many years the bold life of the fishery in the ships of owners uncommonly heedful of what manner of men they shipped; Daggoo retained all his barbaric virtues, and erect as a giraffe, moved about the decks in all the pomp of six feet five in his socks. There was a corporeal humility in looking up at him; and a white man standing before him seemed a white flag come to beg truce of a fortress. Curious to tell, this imperial negro, Ahasuerus Daggoo, was the Squire of little Flask, who looked like a chessman beside him. As for the residue of the *Pequod's* company, be it said, that at the present day not one in two of the many thousand men before the mast employed in the American whale fishery are Americans born, though pretty nearly all the officers are. An Anacharsis Clootz deputation from all the isles of the sea, and all the ends of the earth, accompanying Old Ahab in the *Pequod* to lay the world's grievances before that bar from which not very many of them ever come back. Black Little Pip—he never did—oh, no! he went before. Poor Alabama boy! On the grim *Pequod's* forecastle, ye shall ere long see him, beating his tambourine; prelusive of the eternal time, when sent for, to the great quarter-deck on high, he was bid strike in with angels, and beat his tambourine in glory; called a coward here, hailed a hero there!

CHAPTER 28

AHAB

FOR SEVERAL days after leaving Nantucket, nothing above hatches was seen of Captain Ahab. The mates regularly relieved each other at the watches, and for aught that could be seen to the contrary, they seemed to be the only commanders of the ship; only they sometimes

issued from the cabin with orders so sudden and peremptory, that
after all it was plain they but commanded vicariously. Yes, their
supreme lord and dictator was there, though hitherto unseen by any
eyes not permitted to penetrate into the now sacred retreat of the
cabin.

Now, it being Christmas when the ship shot from out her harbour,
for a space we had biting Polar weather, though all the time running
away from it to the southward; and by every degree and minute of
latitude which we sailed, gradually leaving that merciless winter, and
all its intolerable weather behind us. It was one of those less lowering,
but still grey and gloomy enough mornings of the transition, when
with a fair wind the ship was rushing through the water with a vindictive sort of leaping and melancholy rapidity, that as I mounted to
the deck at the call of the forenoon watch, so soon as I levelled my
glance towards the taffrail, foreboding shivers ran over me. Reality
outran apprehension; Captain Ahab stood upon his quarter-deck.

There seemed no sign of common bodily illness about him, nor of
the recovery from any. He looked like a man cut away from the stake,
when the fire has overrunningly wasted all the limbs without consum-
ing them, or taking away one particle from their compacted aged
robustness. His whole high, broad form seemed made of solid bronze,
and shaped in an unalterable mould, like Cellini's cast Perseus. Threading its way out from among his grey hairs, and continuing right down
one side of his tawny scorched face and neck, till it disappeared in his
clothing, you saw a slender rod-like mark, lividly whitish. It resembled
that perpendicular seam sometimes made in the straight, lofty trunk of
a great tree, when the upper lightning tearingly darts down it, and
without wrenching a single twig, peels and grooves out the bark from
top to bottom, ere running off into the soil, leaving the tree still greenly
alive, but branded. Whether that mark was born with him, or whether
it was the scar left by some desperate wound, no one could certainly
say. By some tacit consent, throughout the voyage little or no allusion
was made to it, especially by the mates.

So powerfully did the whole grim aspect of Ahab affect me, and the
livid brand which streaked it, that for the first few moments I hardly
noted that not a little of this overbearing grimness was owing to the
barbaric white leg upon which he partly stood. It had previously come
to me that this ivory leg had at sea been fashioned from the polished
bone of the sperm-whale's jaw.

I was struck with the singular posture he maintained. Upon each
side of the *Pequod's* quarter-deck, and pretty close to the mizzen
shrouds, there was an auger hole, bored about half an inch or so, into

the plank. His bone leg steadied in that hole; one arm elevated, and holding by a shroud; Captain Ahab stood erect, looking straight out beyond the ship's ever-pitching prow. There was an infinity of firmest fortitude, a determinate, unsurrenderable wilfulness, in the fixed and fearless, forward dedication of that glance. Not a word he spoke; nor did his officers say aught to him; though by all their minutest gestures and expressions, they plainly showed the uneasy, if not painful, consciousness of being under a troubled master-eye. And not only that, but moody stricken Ahab stood before them with a crucifixion in his face; in all the nameless regal overbearing dignity of some mighty woe.

Ere long, from his first visit in the air, he withdrew into his cabin. But after that morning, he was every day visible to the crew; either standing in his pivot-hole, or seated upon an ivory stool he had; or heavily walking the deck. As the sky grew less gloomy; indeed, began to grow a little genial, he became still less and less a recluse; as if, when the ship had sailed from home, nothing but the dead wintry bleakness of the sea had then kept him so secluded. And, by and by, it came to pass, that he was almost continually in the air; but, as yet, for all that he said, or perceptibly did, on the at last sunny deck, he seemed as unnecessary there as another mast. But the *Pequod* was only making a passage now; not regularly cruising; nearly all whaling preparatives needing supervision the mates were fully competent to, so that there was little or nothing, out of himself, to employ or excite Ahab, now; and thus chase away for that one interval, the clouds that layer upon layer were piled upon his brow, as ever all clouds choose the loftiest peaks to pile themselves upon.

Nevertheless, ere long, the warm, warbling persuasiveness of the pleasant, holiday weather we came to, seemed gradually to charm him from his mood. For, as when the red-cheeked, dancing girls, April and May, trip home to the wintry, misanthropic woods; even the barest, ruggedest, most thunder-cloven old oak will at least send forth some few green sprouts, to welcome such glad-hearted visitants; so Ahab did, in the end, a little respond to the playful allurings of that girlish air. More than once did he put forth the faint blossom of a look which, in any other man, would have soon flowered out in a smile.

CHAPTER 29

ENTER AHAB; TO HIM, STUBB

Some days elapsed, and ice and icebergs all astern, the *Pequod* now went rolling through the bright Quito spring, which, at sea, almost perpetually reigns on the threshold of the eternal August of the Tropic.

Old age is always wakeful; as if, the longer linked with life, the less man has to do with aught that looks like death. Among sea-commanders, the old greybeards will oftenest leave their berths to visit the night-cloaked deck. It was so with Ahab; only that now, of late, he seemed so much to live in the open air, that truly speaking, his visits were more to the cabin, than from the cabin to the planks. "It feels like going down into one's tomb,"—he would mutter to himself,—"for an old captain like me to be descending this narrow scuttle, to go to my grave-dug berth."

So, almost every twenty-four hours, when the watches of the night were set, and the band on deck sentinelled the slumbers of the band below; and when if a rope was to be hauled upon the forecastle, the sailors flung it not rudely down, as by day, but with some cautiousness dropped it to its place, for fear of disturbing their slumbering shipmates; when this sort of steady quietude would begin to prevail, habitually, the silent steersman would watch the cabin-scuttle; and ere long the old man would emerge, gripping at the iron banister, to help his crippled way. Some considerating touch of humanity was in him; for at times like these, he usually abstained from patrolling the quarter-deck; because to his wearied mates, seeking repose within six inches of his ivory heel, such would have been the reverberating crack and din of that bony step, that their dreams would have been of the crunching teeth of sharks. But once, the mood was on him too deep for common regardings; and as with heavy lumbering pace he was measuring the ship from taffrail to main-mast, Stubb, the old second mate, came up from below, with a certain unassured, deprecating humorousness, hinted that if Captain Ahab was pleased to walk the planks, then, no one could say nay; but there might be some way of muffling the noise; hinting something indistinctly and hesitatingly about a globe of tow, and the insertion into it, of the ivory heel. Ah! Stubb, thou didst not know Ahab then.

"Am I a cannon-ball, Stubb," said Ahab, "that thou wouldst wad me that fashion? But go thy ways; I had forgot. Below to thy nightly grave; where such as ye sleep between shrouds, to use ye to the filling one at last.—Down, dog, and kennel!"

Starting at the unforeseen concluding exclamation of the so suddenly scornful old man, Stubb was speechless a moment; then said excitedly, "I am not used to be spoken to that way, sir; I do but less than half like it, sir."

"Avast!" gritted Ahab between his set teeth, and violently moving away, as if to avoid some passionate temptation.

"No, sir; not yet," said Stubb, emboldened, "I will not tamely be called a dog, sir."

"Then be called ten times a donkey, and a mule, and an ass, and begone, or I'll clear the world of thee!"

As he said this, Ahab advanced upon him with such overbearing terrors in his aspect, that Stubb involuntarily retreated.

"I was never served so before without giving a hard blow for it," muttered Stubb, as he found himself descending the cabin-scuttle. "It's very queer. Stop, Stubb; somehow, now, I don't well know whether to go back and strike him, or—what's that?—down here on my knees and pray for him? Yes, that was the thought coming up in me; but it would be the first time I ever *did* pray. It's queer; very queer; and he's queer too; aye, take him fore and aft, he's about the queerest old man Stubb ever sailed with. How he flashed at me!—his eyes like powder-pans! is he mad? Anyway there's something on his mind, as sure as there must be something on a deck when it cracks. He ain't in his bed now, either, more than three hours out of the twenty-four; and he don't sleep then. Didn't that Dough-Boy, the steward, tell me that of a morning he always finds the old man's hammock clothes all rumpled and tumbled, and the sheets down at the foot, and the coverlid almost tied into knots, and the pillow a sort of frightful hot, as though a baked brick had been on it?"

CHAPTER 30

THE PIPE

WHEN STUBB had departed, Ahab stood for a while leaning over the bulwarks; and then, as had been usual with him of late, calling a sailor of the watch, he sent him below for his ivory stool, and also his pipe. Lighting the pipe at the binnacle lamp and planting the stool on the weather side of the deck, he sat and smoked.

Some moments passed, during which the thick vapour came from his mouth in quick and constant puffs, which blew back again into his face. "How now," he soliloquized at last, withdrawing the tube, "this smoking no longer soothes. Oh, my pipe! hard must it go with me if thy charm be gone! Here have I been unconsciously toiling, not pleasuring,—aye, and ignorantly smoking to windward all the while; to windward, and with such nervous whiffs, as if, like the dying whale, my final jets were the strongest and fullest of trouble. What business have I with this pipe? This thing that is meant for sereneness, to send up mild white vapours among mild white hairs, not among torn iron-grey locks like mine. I'll smoke no more——"

He tossed the still lighted pipe into the sea. The fire hissed in the waves; the same instant the ship shot by the bubble the sinking pipe made. With slouched hat, Ahab lurchingly paced the planks.

CHAPTER 31

QUEEN MAB

NEXT MORNING Stubb accosted Flask.

"Such a queer dream, King-Post, I never had. You know the old man's ivory leg, well I dreamed he kicked me with it; and when I tried to kick back, upon my soul, my little man, I kicked my leg right off! And then, presto! Ahab seemed a pyramid, and I, like a blazing fool, kept kicking at it. But what was still more curious, Flask—you know how curious all dreams are—through all this rage that I was in, I somehow seemed to be thinking to myself, that after all, it was not much of an insult, that kick from Ahab. 'Why,' thinks I, 'what's the row? It's not a real leg, only a false one.' And there's a mighty difference between a living thump and a dead thump. That's what makes a blow from the hand, Flask, fifty times more savage to bear than a blow from a cane. The living member—that makes the living insult, my little man. And thinks I to myself all the while, mind, while I was stubbing my silly toes against that cursed pyramid— so confoundedly contradictory was it all, all the while, I say, I was thinking to myself, 'what's his leg now, but a cane—a whalebone cane. Yes,' thinks I, 'it was only a playful cudgelling—in fact,' only a whale- boning that he gave me—not a base kick. Besides, thinks I, 'look at it once; why, the end of it—the foot part—what a small sort of end it is; whereas, if a broad-footed farmer kicked me, *there's* a devilish broad insult.' Now, what do you think of that dream, Flask?"

"I don't know; it seems a sort of foolish to me, tho'."

"May be; may be. But it's made a wise man of me, Flask. D'ye see Ahab standing there, sideways looking over the stern? Well, the best thing you can do, Flask, is to let that old man alone; never speak to him, whatever he says. Halloa! What's that he shouts? Hark!"

"Mast-head, there! Look sharp, all of ye! There are whales hereabouts! If ye see a white one, split your lungs for him!"

"What do you think of that now, Flask? ain't that there a small drop of something queer about that, eh? A white whale—did ye mark that, man? Look ye—there's something special in the wind. Stand by for it, Flask. Ahab has that that's bloody on his mind. But, mum; he comes this way."

CHAPTER 32

CETOLOGY

ALREADY WE are boldly launched upon the deep; but soon we shall be lost in its unshored, harbourless immensities. Ere that come to pass; ere the *Pequod's* weedy hull rolls side by side with the barnacled hulls of the leviathan; at the outset it is but well to attend to a matter almost indispensable to a thorough appreciative understanding of the more special leviathanic revelations and allusions of all sorts which are to follow.

It is some systematized exhibition of the whale in his broad genera, that I would now fain put before you. Yet is it no easy task. The classification of the constituents of a chaos, nothing less is here essayed. Listen to what the best and latest authorities have laid down.

"No branch of Zoology is so much involved as that which is entitled Cetology," says Captain Scoresby, A.D. 1820.

"It is not my intention, were it in my power, to enter into the inquiry as to the true method of dividing the cetacea into groups and families. * * * Utter confusion exists among the historians of this animal" (sperm whale), says Surgeon Beale, A.D. 1839.

"Unfitness to pursue our research in the unfathomable waters."—"Impenetrable veil covering our knowledge of the cetacea."—"A field strewn with thorns."—"All these incomplete indications but serve to torture us naturalists."

Thus spake of the whale, the great Cuvier, and John Hunter, and Lesson, those lights of zoology and anatomy. Nevertheless, though of real knowledge there be little, yet of books there are a plenty; and so in some small degree, with cetology, or the science of whales.

Of the whale authors, only one of them was a real professional harpooneer and whaleman. I mean Captain Scoresby. On the separate subject of the Greenland or right-whale, he is the best existing authority. But Scoresby knew nothing and says nothing of the great sperm-whale, compared with which the Greenland whale is almost unworthy mentioning.

There are only two books in being which at all pretend to put the living sperm-whale before you, and at the same time, in the remotest degree succeed in the attempt. Those books are Beale's and Bennett's; both in their time surgeons to the English South-Sea whale-ships, and both exact and reliable men. The original matter touching the sperm-whale to be found in their volumes is necessarily small; but so far as it goes, it is of excellent quality, though mostly confined to scientific description. As yet, however, the sperm-whale, scientific or poetic, lives not complete in any literature. Far above all other hunted whales, his is an unwritten life.

Now the various species of whales need some sort of popular comprehensive classification, if only an easy outline one for the present, hereafter to be filled in all its departments by subsequent labourers. As no better man advances to take this matter in hand, I hereupon offer my own poor endeavours. I promise nothing complete; because any human thing supposed to be complete, must for that very reason infallibly be faulty. I shall not pretend to a minute anatomical description of the various species, or—in this place at least —to much of any description. My object here is simply to project the draught of a systematization of cetology. I am the architect, not the builder.

But it is a ponderous task; and I will try. There are some preliminaries to settle.

First: The uncertain, unsettled condition of this science of Cetology is in the very vestibule attested by the fact, that in some quarters it still remains a moot point whether a whale be a fish. In his System of Nature, A.D. 1776, Linnæus declares, "I hereby separate the whales from the fish." But to my own knowledge, I know that down to the year 1850, sharks and shad, alewives and herring, against Linnæus's express edict, were still found dividing the possession of the same seas with the Leviathan.

The grounds upon which Linnæus would fain have banished the whales from the waters, he states as follows: "On account of their warm bilocular heart, their lungs, their moveable eyelids, their hollow ears, penem intrantem feminam mammis lactantem," and finally, "ex lege naturæ jure meritoque." I submitted all this to my friends Simeon

Macey and Charley Coffin, of Nantucket, both messmates of mine in a certain voyage, and they united in the opinion that the reasons set forth were altogether insufficient. Charley profanely hinted they were humbug.

Be it known that, waiving all argument, I take the good old-fashioned ground that the whale is a fish, and call upon holy Jonah to back me. This fundamental thing settled, the next point is, in what internal respect does the whale differ from other fish. Above, Linnæus has given you those items. But in brief, they are these: lungs and warm blood; whereas, all other fish are lungless and cold-blooded.

Next: how shall we define the whale, by his own obvious externals, so as conspicuously to label him for all time to come? To be short, then, a whale is *a spouting fish with a horizontal tail*. There you have him. However contracted, that definition is the result of expanded meditation. A walrus spouts much like a whale, but the walrus is not a fish, because he is amphibious. But the last term of definition is still more cogent, as coupled with the first. Almost any one must have noticed that all the fish familiar to landsmen have not a flat, but a vertical, or up and down tail. Whereas, among spouting fish the tail, though it may be similarly shaped, invariably assumes a hortizontal position.

By the above definition of what a whale is, I do by no means exclude from the leviathanic brotherhood any sea creature hitherto identified with the whale by the best informed Nantucketers; nor, on the other hand, link with it any fish hitherto authoritatively regarded as alien.[1] Hence, all the smaller, spouting, and horizontal tailed fish must be included in this ground-plan of Cetology. Now, then, come the grand divisions of the entire whale host.

First: According to magnitude I divide the whales into three primary BOOKS (subdivisible into CHAPTERS), and these shall comprehend them all, both small and large.

I. The FOLIO WHALE; II. the OCTAVO WHALE; III. the DUODECIMO WHALE.

As to the type of the FOLIO, I present the *Sperm Whale*; of the OCTAVO, the *Grampus*; of the DUODECIMO, the *Porpoise*.

FOLIOS. Among these I here include the following chapters: —
I. The *Sperm Whale*; II. the *Right Whale*; III. the *Fin Back Whale*;

[1] I am aware that down to the present time, the fish styled Lamatins and Dugongs (Pig-fish and Sow-fish of the Coffins of Nantucket) are included by many naturalists among the whales. But as these pig-fish are a noisy, contemptible set, mostly lurking in the mouths of rivers, and feeding on wet hay, and especially as they do not spout, I deny their credentials as whales and have presented them with their passports to quit the Kingdom of Cetology.

IV. the *Hump-backed Whale*; V. the *Razor Back Whale*; VI. the *Sulphur Bottom Whale*.

BOOK I. (*Folio*), CHAPTER I. (*Sperm Whale*)—This whale, among the English of old vaguely known as the Trumpa whale, and the Physeter whale, and the Anvil Headed whale, is the present Cachalot of the French, and the Pottsfich of the Germans, and the Macrocephalus of the Long Words. He is, without doubt, the largest inhabitant of the globe; the most formidable of all whales to encounter; the most majestic in aspect; and lastly, by far the most valuable in commerce; he being the only creature from which that valuable substance, spermaceti, is obtained. All his peculiarities will, in many other places, be enlarged upon.

BOOK I. (*Folio*), CHAPTER II. (*Right Whale*)—In one respect this is the most venerable of the leviathans, being the one first regularly hunted by man. It yields the article commonly known as whalebone or baleen; and the oil specially known as "whale oil," an inferior article in commerce. Among the fishermen, he is indiscriminately designated by all the following titles: The Whale; the Greenland Whale; the Black Whale; the Great Whale; the True Whale; the Right Whale. There is a deal of obscurity concerning the identity of the species thus multitudinously baptised. What then is the whale, which I include in the second species of my Folio? It is the Great Mysticetus of the English naturalists; the Greenland Whale of the English whalemen; the Baliene Ordinarie of the French whalemen; the Growlands Walfish of the Swedes. It is the whale which for more than two centuries past has been hunted by the Dutch and English in the arctic seas; it is the whale which the American fishermen have long pursued in the Indian Ocean, on the Brazil Banks, or the Nor' West Coast, and various other parts of the world, designated by them Right Whale Cruising Grounds.

BOOK I. (*Folio*), CHAPTER III. (*Fin-Back*)—Under this head I reckon a monster which, by the various names of Fin-Back, Tall-Spout, and Long-John, has been seen almost in every sea and is commonly the whale whose distant jet is often described by passengers crossing the Atlantic, in the New York packet-tracks. In the length he attains, and in his baleen, the Fin-Back resembles the right whale, but is of a less portly girth, and a lighter colour, approaching to olive. His great lips present a cable-like aspect, formed by the intertwisting, slanting folds of large wrinkles. His grand distinguishing feature, the fin, from which he derives his name, is often a conspicuous object. This fin is some three or four feet long, growing vertically from the hinder part of the back, of an angular shape, and with a very sharp pointed end. Even if not the slightest other part of the creature be visible, this isolated fin will, at times, be seen plainly projecting from the surface. When the sea is moderately calm, and slightly marked with spherical ripples, and this gnomon-like fin stands up and casts shadows upon the wrinkled surface, it may well be supposed that the watery circle surrounding it somewhat resembles a dial, with its style and wavy hour-lines graved on it. On that Ahaz-dial the shadow often goes back. The Fin-Back is not gregarious. He seems a whale-hater, as some men are man-haters. Very shy; always going solitary; unexpectedly rising to the surface in the remotest and most sullen waters; his straight and single lofty jet rising like a tall misanthropic spear upon a barren plain; gifted with such wondrous power and velocity in swimming, as to defy all present pursuit from man; this leviathan seems the banished and unconquerable Cain of his race, bearing for his mark that style upon his back. From having the baleen in his mouth, the Fin-Back is sometimes included with the right whale, among a theoretic species denominated *Whalebone whales,* that is, whales with baleen. Of these so-called Whalebone whales, there would seem to be several varieties, most of which, however, are little known. Broad-nosed whales and beaked whales; pike-headed whales; bunched whales; under-jawed whales and rostrated whales, are the fisherman's names for a few sorts.

BOOK I. (*Folio*), CHAPTER IV. (*Hump Back*)—This whale is often seen on the northern American coast. He has been frequently captured there, and towed into harbour. He has a great pack on him like a peddler; or you might call him the Elephant and Castle whale. At any rate, the popular name for him does not sufficiently distinguish him, since the sperm-whale also has a hump, though a smaller one. His oil is not very valuable. He has baleen. He is the most gamesome and light-hearted of all the whales, making more gay foam and white water generally than any other of them.

BOOK I. (*Folio*), CHAPTER V. (*Razor Back*)—Of this whale little is known but his name. I have seen him at a distance off Cape Horn. Of a retiring nature, he eludes both hunters and philosophers. Though no coward, he has never yet shown any part of him but his back, which rises in a long sharp ridge. Let him go. I know little more of him, nor does anybody else.

BOOK I. (*Folio*), CHAPTER VI. (*Sulphur Bottom*)—Another retiring gentleman, with a brimstone belly, doubtless got by scraping along the Tartarian tiles in some of his profounder divings. He is seldom seen; at least I have never seen him except in the remoter southern seas, and then always at too great a distance to study his countenance. He is

never chased; he would run away with ropewalks of line. Prodigies
are told of him. Adieu, Sulphur Bottom! I can say nothing more that
is true of ye, nor can the oldest Nantucketer.

Thus ends BOOK I. (*Folio*), and now begins BOOK II. (*Octavo*.)

OCTAVOS.[1] These embrace the whales of middling magnitude,
among which at present may be numbered:—I., the *Grampus*; II.,
the *Black Fish*; III., the *Narwhale*; IV., the *Thrasher*; V., the *Killer*.

BOOK II. (*Octavo*), CHAPTER I. (*Grampus*)—Though this fish,
whose loud sonorous breathing, or rather blowing, has furnished a
proverb to landsmen, he is so well known a denizen of the deep,
yet is he not popularly classed among whales. But possessing all the
grand distinctive features of the leviathan, most naturalists have recognized him for one. He is of moderate octavo size, varying from fifteen
to twenty-five feet in length, and of corresponding dimensions round
the waist. He swims in herds; he is never regularly hunted, though
his oil is considerable in quantity, and pretty good for light. By some
fishermen his approach is regarded as premonitory of the advance of
the great sperm-whale.

BOOK II. (*Octavo*), CHAPTER II (*Black Fish*)—I give the popular
fisherman's names for all these fish, for generally they are the best.
Where any name happens to be vague or inexpressive, I shall say so,
and suggest another. I do so now, touching the Black Fish so called,
because blackness is the rule among almost all whales. So, call him
the Hyena Whale, if you please. His voracity is well known, and from
the circumstance that the inner angles of his lips are curved upwards,
he carries an everlasting Mephistophelian grin on his face. This whale
averages some sixteen or eighteen feet in length. He is found in almost
all latitudes. He has a peculiar way of showing his dorsal hooked fin
in swimming, which looks something like a Roman nose. When not
more profitably employed, the sperm-whale hunters sometimes capture
the Hyena whale, to keep up the supply of cheap oil for domestic
employment—as some frugal housekeepers, in the absence of company,
and quite alone by themselves, burn unsavoury tallow instead of
odorous wax. Though their blubber is very thin, some of these whales
will yield you upwards of thirty gallons of oil.

BOOK II. (*Octavo*), CHAPTER III. (*Narwhale*), that is *Nostril whale*
—Another instance of a curiously named whale, so named I suppose
from his peculiar horn being originally mistaken for a peaked nose.

[1] Why this book of whales is not denominated the Quarto is very plain. Because,
while the whales of this order, though smaller than those of the former order, nevertheless retain a proportionate likeness to them in figure, yet the bookbinder's Quarto
volume in its diminished form does not preserve the shape of the Folio volume, but
the Octavo volume does.

The creature is some sixteen feet in length, while its horn averages five feet, though some exceed ten, and even attain to fifteen feet. Strictly speaking, this horn is but a lengthened tusk, growing out from the jaw in a line a little depressed from the horizontal. But it is only found on the sinister side, which has an ill effect, giving its owner something analogous to the aspect of a clumsy left-handed man. What precise purpose this ivory horn or lance answers, it would be hard to say. It does not seem to be used like the blade of the sword-fish and bill-fish; though some sailors tell me that the Narwhale employs it for a rake in turning over the bottom of the sea for food. Charley Coffin said it was used for an ice-piercer; for the Narwhale, rising to the surface of the Polar Sea, and finding it sheeted with ice, thrusts his horn up, and so breaks through. But you cannot prove either of these surmises to be correct. My own opinion is, that however this one-sided horn may really be used by the Narwhale—however that may be—it would certainly be very convenient to him for a folder in reading pamphlets. The Narwhale I have heard called the Tusked whale, the Horned whale, and the Unicorn whale. He is certainly a curious example of the Unicornism to be found in almost every kingdom of animated nature.

BOOK II. (*Octavo*), CHAPTER IV. (*Killer*)—Of this whale little is precisely known to the Nantucketer, and nothing at all to the professed naturalists. From what I have seen of him at a distance, I should say that he was about the bigness of a grampus. He is very savage—a sort of Feegee fish. He sometimes takes the great Folio whales by the lip, and hangs there like a leech, till the mighty brute is worried to death. The Killer is never hunted. I never heard what sort of oil he has. Exception might be taken to the name bestowed upon this whale, on the ground of its indistinctness. For we are all killers, on land and on sea; Bonapartes and Sharks included.

BOOK II. (*Octavo*), CHAPTER V. (*Thrasher*)—This gentleman is famous for his tail, which he uses for a ferule in thrashing his foes. He mounts the Folio whale's back, and as he swims, he works his passage by flogging him; as some schoolmasters get along in the world by a similar process. Still less is known of the Thrasher than of the Killer. Both are outlaws, even in the lawless seas.

Thus ends BOOK II. (*Octavo*), and begins BOOK III. (*Duodecimo*.) DUODECIMOS. These include the smaller whales. I. The Huzza Porpoise. II. The Algerine Porpoise. III. The Mealy-mouthed Porpoise.

To those who have not chanced specially to study the subject, it may possibly seem strange, that fishes not commonly exceeding four or five feet should be marshalled among WHALES—a word, which, in the popular sense, always conveys an idea of hugeness. But the creatures set down above as Duodecimos are infallibly whales, by the terms of my definition of what a whale is—i.e. a spouting fish, with a horizontal tail.

BOOK III. (*Duodecimo*), CHAPTER I. (*Huzza Porpoise*)—This is the common porpoise found almost all over the globe. The name is of my own bestowal; for there are more than one sort of porpoises, and something must be done to distinguish them. I call him thus, because he always swims in hilarious shoals, which upon the broad sea keep tossing themselves to heaven like caps in a Fourth-of-July crowd. Their appearance is generally hailed with delight by the mariner. Full of fine spirits, they invariably come from the breezy billows to windward. They are the lads that always live before the wind. They are accounted a lucky omen. If you yourself can withstand three cheers at beholding these vivacious fish, then heaven help ye; the spirit of godly gamesomeness is not in ye. A well-fed, plump Huzza Porpoise will yield you one good gallon of good oil. But the fine and delicate fluid extracted from his jaws is exceedingly valuable. It is in request among jewellers and watchmakers. Sailors put it on their hones. Porpoise meat is good eating, you know. It may never have occurred to you that a porpoise spouts. Indeed, his spout is so small that it is not very readily discernible. But the next time you have a chance, watch him; and you will then see the great sperm-whale himself in miniature.

BOOK III. (*Duodecimo*), CHAPTER II. (*Algerine Porpoise*)—A pirate. Very savage. He is only found, I think, in the Pacific. He is somewhat larger than the Huzza Porpoise, but much of the same general make. Provoke him, and he will buckle to a shark. I have lowered for him many times, but never yet saw him captured.

BOOK III. (*Duodecimo*), CHAPTER III. (*Mealy-mouthed Porpoise*)—The largest kind of Porpoise; and only found in the Pacific, so far as it is known. The only English name, by which he has hitherto been designated, is that of the fishers—Right-Whale Porpoise, from the circumstance that he is chiefly found in the vicinity of that Folio. In shape, he differs in some degree from the Huzza Porpoise, being of a less rotund and jolly girth; indeed, he is of quite a neat and gentleman-like figure. He has no fins on his back (most other porpoises have), he has a lovely tail, and sentimental Indian eyes of a hazel hue. But his mealy-mouth spoils him. Though his entire back down to his side fins is of a deep sable, yet a boundary line, distinct as the mark in a ship's hull, called the "bright-waist," that line streaks him from stem to stern, with two separate colours, black above and white below. The white comprises part of his head, and the whole of his mouth, which makes him look as if he had just escaped from a felonious visit to a meal-bag. A most mean and mealy aspect! His oil is much like that of the common porpoise.

.   .   .   .   .   .

Beyond the Duodecimo, this system does not proceed, inasmuch as the Porpoise is the smallest of the whales. Above you have all the Leviathans of note. But there are a rabble of uncertain, fugitive half-fabulous whales, which, as an American whaleman, I know by reputation, but not personally. I shall enumerate them by their fore-castle appellations; for possibly such a list may be valuable to future investigators, who may complete what I have here but begun. If any of the following whales, shall hereafter be caught and marked, then he can readily be incorporated into this System, according to his Folio, Octavo, or Duodecimo magnitude: The Bottle-Nose Whale; the Junk Whale; the Pudding-Headed Whale; the Cape Whale; the Leading Whale; the Cannon Whale; the Scragg Whale; the Coppered Whale; the Elephant Whale; the Iceberg Whale; the Quog Whale; the Blue Whale; etc. From Icelandic, Dutch, and old English authorities, there might be quoted other lists of uncertain whales, blessed with all manner of uncouth names. But I omit them as altogether obsolete; and can hardly help suspecting them for mere sounds, full of Leviathanism, but signifying nothing.

Finally: It was stated at the outset, that this system would not be here, and at once, perfected. You cannot but plainly see that I have kept my word. But I now leave my cetological System standing thus unfinished, even as the great Cathedral of Cologne was left, with the crane still standing upon the top of the uncompleted tower. For small erections may be finished by their first architects; grand ones, true ones, ever leave the copestone to posterity. God keep me for ever completing anything. This whole book is but a draught of a draught. Oh, Time, Strength, Cash, and Patience!

CHAPTER 33

THE SPECKSYNDER

CONCERNING THE officers of the whale-craft, this seems as good a place as any to set down a little domestic peculiarity on shipboard, arising from the existence of the harpooneer class of officers, a class unknown of course in any other marine than the whale-fleet.

The large importance attached to the harpooneer's vocation is evinced by the fact, that originally in the old Dutch Fishery, two centuries and more ago, the command of a whale-ship was not wholly lodged in the person now called the captain, but was divided between him and an officer called the Specksynder. Literally this word means Fat-Cutter; usage, however, in time made it equivalent to Chief Harpooneer. In those days, the captain's authority was restricted to the navigation and general management of the vessel: while over the whale-hunting department and all its concerns, the Specksynder or Chief Harpooneer reigned supreme. At present he ranks simply as senior Harpooneer; and as such, is but one of the captain's more inferior subalterns. Nevertheless, as upon the good conduct of the harpooneers the success of a whaling voyage largely depends, and since in the American Fishery he is not only an important officer in the boat, but under certain circumstances (night watches on a whaling ground) the command of the ship's deck is also his; therefore the grand political maxim of the sea demands, that he should nominally live apart from the men before the mast, and be in some way distinguished as their professional superior; though always, by them, familiarly regarded as their social equal.

Now, the grand distinction drawn between officer and man at sea, is this—the first lives aft, the last forward. Hence, in whale-ships and merchantmen alike, the mates have their quarters with the captain; and so, too, in most of the American whalers the harpooneers are lodged in the after part of the ship. That is to say, they take their meals in the captain's cabin, and sleep in a place directly communicating with it.

Though the long period of a Southern whaling voyage (by far the longest of all voyages now or ever made by man), the peculiar perils of it, and the community of interest prevailing among a company, all of whom, high or low, depend for their profits, not upon fixed wages, but upon their common luck, together with the common vigilance, intrepidity, and hard work; though all these things do in some cases tend to beget a less rigorous discipline than in merchantmen generally; yet, never mind how much like an old Mesopotamian family these whalemen may, in some primitive instances, live together; for all that, the punctilious externals, at least, of the quarter-deck are seldom materially relaxed, and in no instance done away. Indeed, many are the Nantucket ships in which you will see the skipper parading his quarter-deck with an elated grandeur not surpassed in any military navy; nay, extorting almost as much outward homage as if he wore the imperial purple, and not the shabbiest of pilot-cloth.

And though of all men the moody captain of the *Pequod* was the

least given to that sort of shallowest assumption; and though the only
homage he ever exacted was implicit, instantaneous obedience; though
he required no man to remove the shoes from his feet ere stepping upon
the quarter-deck; and though there were times when, owing to peculiar
circumstances connected with events hereafter to be detailed, he addressed them in unusual terms, whether of condescension or in
terrorem, or otherwise; yet even Captain Ahab was by no means un-
observant of the paramount forms and usages of the sea.

CHAPTER 34

THE CABIN-TABLE

IT IS noon; and Dough-Boy, the steward, thrusting his pale loaf-of-
bread face from the cabin-scuttle, announces dinner to his lord and
master; who, sitting in the lee quarter-boat, has just been taking an
observation of the sun; and is now mutely reckoning the latitude on
the smooth, medallion shaped tablet, reserved for that daily purpose
on the upper part of his ivory leg. From his complete inattention to
the tidings, you would think that moody Ahab had not heard his
menial. But presently catching hold of the mizzen-shrouds, he swings
himself to the deck, and in an even, unexhilarated voice, saying,
"Dinner, Mr. Starbuck," disappears into the cabin.

When the last echo of his sultan's step has died away, and Starbuck,
the first Emir, has every reason to suppose that he is seated, then
Starbuck rouses from his quietude, takes a few turns along the planks,
and, after a grave peep into the binnacle, says, with some touch of
pleasantness, "Dinner, Mr. Stubb," and descends the scuttle. The
second Emir lounges about the rigging awhile, and then slightly
shaking the main brace, to see whether it will be all right with that
important rope, he likewise takes up the old burden, and with a rapid
"Dinner, Mr. Flask," follows after his predecessors.

But the third Emir, now seeing himself all alone on the quarter-
deck, seems to feel relieved from some curious restraint; for, tipping
all sorts of knowing winks in all sorts of directions, and kicking off
his shoes, he strikes into a sharp but noiseless squall of a hornpipe right
over the Grand Turk's head; and then, by a dexterous sleight, pitching
his cap into the mizzen-top for a shelf, he goes down rollicking, so far
at least as he remains visible from the deck, reversing all other proces-
sions, by bringing up the rear with music. But ere stepping into the
cabin doorway below, he pauses, ships a new face altogether, and, then,

independent, hilarious little Flask enters King Ahab's presence, in the character of Abjectus, or the Slave.

Over his ivory-inlaid table, Ahab presided like a mute, maned sea-lion on the white coral-beach, surrounded by his warlike but still deferential cubs. In his own proper turn, each officer waited to be served. They were as little children before Ahab; and yet, in Ahab, there seemed not to lurk the smallest social arrogance. With one mind, their intent eyes all fastened upon the old man's knife, as he carved the chief dish before him. These cabin meals were somehow solemn meals, eaten in awful silence; and yet at the table old Ahab forbade not conversation; only he himself was dumb. What a relief it was to choking Stubb, when a rat made a sudden racket in the hold below.

Now, Ahab and his three mates formed what may be called the first table in the *Pequod's* cabin. After their departure, taking place in inverted order to their arrival, the canvas cloth was cleared, or rather was restored to some hurried order by the pallid steward. And then the three harpooneers were bidden to the feast, they being its residuary legatees. They made a sort of temporary servants' hall of the high and mighty cabin.

In strange contrast to the hardly tolerable constraint and nameless invisible domineerings of the captain's table, was the entire care-free licence and ease, the almost frantic democracy of those inferior fellows the harpooneers. While their masters, the mates, seemed afraid of the sound of the hinges of their own jaws, the harpooneers chewed their food with such a relish that there was a report to it. They dined like lords; they filled their bellies like Indian ships all day loading with spices. Such portentous appetites had Queequeg and Tashtego, that to fill out the vacancies made by the previous repast, often the pale Dough-Boy was fain to bring on a great baron of salt-junk, seemingly quarried out of the solid ox.

It was a sight to see Queequeg seated over against Tashtego opposing his filed teeth to the Indian's: crosswise to them, Daggoo seated on the floor, for a bench would have brought his hearse-plumed head to the low carlines; at every motion of his colossal limbs, making the low cabin framework to shake, as when an African elephant goes passenger in a ship.

But, though these barbarians dined in the cabin, and nominally lived there; still, being anything but sedentary in their habits, they were scarcely ever in it except at meal-times, and just before sleeping-time, when they passed through it to their own peculiar quarters.

CHAPTER 35

THE MAST-HEAD

IT was during the more pleasant weather, that in due rotation with the other seamen my first mast-head came round.

In most American whalemen the mast-heads are manned almost simultaneously with the vessel's leaving her port; even though she may have fifteen thousand miles, and more, to sail ere reaching her proper cruising ground. And if, after a three, four, or five years' voyage she is drawing nigh home with anything empty in her—say, an empty vial even—then, her mast-heads are kept manned to the last; and not till her skysail-poles sail in among the spires of the port, does she altogether relinquish the hope of capturing one whale more.

The three mast-heads are kept manned from sunrise to sunset; the seamen taking their regular turns (as at the helm), and relieving each other every two hours. In the serene weather of the tropics it is exceedingly pleasant, the mast-head; nay, to a dreamy meditative man it is delightful. There you stand, a hundred feet above the silent decks, striding along the deep, as if the masts were gigantic stilts, while beneath you and between your legs, as it were, swim the hugest monsters of the sea, even as ships once sailed between the boots of the famous Colossus at old Rhodes. There you stand, lost in the infinite series of the sea, with nothing ruffled but the waves. The tranced ship indolently rolls; the drowsy trade winds blow; everything resolves you into languor.

In one of those southern whalemen, on a long three or four years' voyage, as often happens, the sum of the various hours you spend at the mast-head would amount to several entire months. Your most usual point of perch is the head of the t' gallant-mast, where you stand upon two thin parallel sticks (almost peculiar to whalemen) called the t' gallant cross-trees. Here, tossed about by the sea, the beginner feels about as cosy as he would standing on a bull's horns.

Let me make a clean breast of it here, and frankly admit that I kept but sorry guard. With the problem of the universe revolving in me, how could I—being left completely to myself at such a thought-engendering altitude,—how could I but lightly hold my obligations to observe all whale-ships' standing orders, "Keep your weather eye open, and sing out every time."

And let me in this place movingly admonish you, ye ship-owners of Nantucket! Beware of enlisting in your vigilant fisheries any lad with lean brow and hollow eye; given to unseasonable meditativeness; and who offers to ship with the Phædon instead of Bowditch in his head. Beware of such an one, I say: your whales must be seen before they can be killed; and this sunken-eyed young Platonist will tow you ten wakes round the world, and never make you one pint of sperm the richer. Nor are these monitions at all unneeded. For nowadays, the whale-fishery furnishes an asylum for many romantic, melancholy, and absent-minded young men, disgusted with the carking care of earth, and seeking sentiment in tar and blubber.

"Why, thou monkey," said a harpooneer to one of these lads, "we've been cruising now hard upon three years, and thou hast not raised a whale yet. Whales are scarce as hen's teeth whenever thou art up here." Perhaps they were; or perhaps there might have been shoals of them in the far horizon; but lulled into such an opium-like listlessness of vacant, unconscious reverie is this absent-minded youth by the blending cadence of waves with thoughts, that at last he loses his identity; takes the mystic ocean at his feet for the visible image of that deep, blue, bottomless soul, pervading mankind and nature; and every strange, half-seen, gliding, beautiful thing that eludes him; every dimly-discovered, uprising fin of some undiscernible form, seems to him the embodiment of those elusive thoughts that only people the soul by continually flitting through it. In this enchanted mood, thy spirit ebbs away to whence it came; becomes diffused through time and space; like Cranmer's sprinkled Pantheistic ashes, forming at last a part of every shore the round globe over.

There is no life in thee, now, except that rocking life imparted by a gentle rolling ship; by her, borrowed from the sea; by the sea, from the inscrutable tides of God. But while this sleep, this dream is on ye, move your foot or hand an inch; slip your hold at all; and your identity comes back in horror. Over Descartian vortices you hover. And perhaps, at mid-day, in the fairest weather, with one half-throttled shriek you drop through that transparent air into the summer sea, no more to rise for ever. Heed it well, ye Pantheists!

CHAPTER 36

THE QUARTER-DECK
(Enter Ahab: Then, all)

IT WAS not a great while after the affair of the pipe, that one morning shortly after breakfast, Ahab, as was his wont, ascended the cabin-gangway to the deck. There most sea-captains usually walk at that hour, as country gentlemen, after the same meal, take a few turns in the garden.

"D'ye mark him, Flask?" whispered Stubb; "the chick that's in him pecks the shell. 'Twill soon be out."

The hours wore on;—Ahab now shut up within his cabin; anon, pacing the deck, with the same intense bigotry of purpose in his aspect.

It drew near the close of day. Suddenly he came to a halt by the bulwarks, and inserting his bone leg into the auger hole there, and with one hand grasping a shroud, he ordered Starbuck to send everybody aft.

"Sir!" said the mate, astonished at an order seldom or never given on ship-board except in some extraordinary case.

"Send everybody aft," repeated Ahab. "Mast-heads, there! come down!"

When the entire ship's company were assembled, and with curious and not wholly unapprehensive faces, were eyeing him, for he looked not unlike the weather horizon when a storm is coming up, Ahab, after rapidly glancing over the bulwarks, and then darting his eyes among the crew, started from his standpoint; and as though not a soul were nigh him resumed his heavy turns upon the deck. With bent head and half-slouched hat he continued to pace, unmindful of the wondering whispering among the men; till Stubb cautiously whispered to Flask, that Ahab must have summoned them there for the purpose of witnessing a pedestrian feat. But this did not last long. Vehemently pausing, he cried:

"What do ye do when ye see a whale, men?"

"Sing out for him!" was the impulsive rejoinder from a score of clubbed voices.

"Good!" cried Ahab, with a wild approval in his tones; observing the hearty animation into which his unexpected question had so magnetically thrown them.

"And what do ye next, men?"

"Lower away, and after him!"

"And what tune is it ye pull to, men?"

"A dead whale or a stove boat!"

More and more strangely and fiercely glad and approving, grew the countenance of the old man at every shout; while the mariners began to gaze curiously at each other, as if marvelling how it was that they themselves became so excited at such seemingly purposeless questions.

But, they were all eagerness again, as Ahab, now half-revolving in his pivot-hole, with one hand reaching high up a shroud, and tightly, almost convulsively grasping it, addressed them thus:

"All ye mast-headers have before now heard me give orders about a white whale. Look ye! d'ye see this Spanish ounce of gold?"— holding up a broad bright coin to the sun—"it is a sixteen-dollar piece, men. D'ye see it? Mr. Starbuck, hand me yon top-maul."

While the mate was getting the hammer, Ahab, without speaking, was slowly rubbing the gold piece against the skirts of his jacket, as if to heighten its lustre, and without using any words was meanwhile lowly humming to himself, producing a sound so strangely muffled and inarticulate that it seemed the mechanical humming of the wheels of his vitality in him.

Receiving the top-maul from Starbuck, he advanced towards the main-mast with the hammer uplifted in one hand, exhibiting the gold with the other, and with a high raised voice exclaiming: "Whosoever of ye raises me a white-headed whale with a wrinkled brow and a crooked jaw; whosoever of ye raises me that white-headed whale, with three holes punctured in his starboard fluke—look ye, whosoever of ye raises me that same white whale, he shall have this gold ounce, my boys!"

"Huzza! huzza!" cried the seamen, as with swinging tarpaulins they hailed the act of nailing the gold to the mast.

"It's a white whale, I say," resumed Ahab, as he threw down the top-maul; "a white whale. Skin your eyes for him, men; look sharp for white water; if ye see but a bubble, sing out."

All this while Tashtego, Daggoo, and Queequeg had looked on with even more intense interest and surprise than the rest, and at the mention of the wrinkled brow and crooked jaw they had started as if each was separately touched by some specific recollection.

"Captain Ahab," said Tashtego, "that white whale must be the same that some call Moby Dick."

"Moby Dick?" shouted Ahab. "Do ye know the white whale then, Tash?"

"Does he fan-tail a little curious, sir, before he goes down?" said the Gay-Header deliberately.

"And has he a curious spout, too," said Daggoo, "very bushy, even for a parmacetty, and mighty quick, Captain Ahab?"

"And he have one, two, tree—oh! good many iron in him hide, too, Captain," cried Queequeg disjointedly, "all twiske-tee be-twisk, like him—him—" faltering hard for a word, and screwing his hand round and round as though uncorking a bottle—"like him—him——"

"Corkscrew!" cried Ahab, "aye, Queequeg, the harpoons lie all twisted and wrenched in him; aye, Daggoo, his spout is a big one, like a whole shock of wheat, and white as a pile of our Nantucket wool after the great annual sheep-shearing; aye, Tashtego, and he fan-tails like a split jib in a squall. Death and devils! men, it is Moby Dick ye have seen—Moby Dick—Moby Dick!"

"Captain Ahab," said Starbuck, who, with Stubb and Flask, had thus far been eyeing his superior with increasing surprise, but at last seemed struck with a thought which somewhat explained all the wonder. "Captain Ahab, I have heard of Moby Dick—but it was not Moby Dick that took off thy leg?"

"Who told thee that?" cried Ahab; then pausing, "Aye, Starbuck; aye, my hearties all round; it was Moby Dick that dismasted me; Moby Dick that brought me to this dead stump I stand on now. Aye, aye," he shouted with a terrific, loud, animal sob, like that of a heart-stricken moose; "Aye, aye! it was that accursed white whale that razeed me; made a poor pegging lubber of me for ever and a day!" Then tossing both arms, with measureless imprecations he shouted out: "Aye, aye! and I'll chase him round Good Hope, and round the Horn, and round the Norway Maelstrom, and round perdition's flames before I give him up. And this is what ye have shipped for, men! to chase that white whale on both sides of land, and over all sides of earth, till he spouts black blood and rolls fin out. What say ye, men, will ye splice hands on it, now? I think ye do look brave."

"Aye, aye!" shouted the harpooneers and seamen, running closer to the excited old man: "A sharp eye for the white whale; a sharp lance for Moby Dick!"

"God bless ye," he seemed to half sob and half shout. "God bless ye, men. Steward! go draw the great measure of grog."

Receiving the brimming pewter, and turning to the harpooneers, he ordered them to produce their weapons. Then ranging them before him near the capstan, with their harpoons in their hands, while his three mates stood at his side with their lances, and the rest of the ship's company formed a circle round the group; he stood for an instant searchingly eyeing every man of his crew. But those wild eyes met his, as the bloodshot eyes of the prairie wolves meet the eye of their leader, ere he rushes on at their head in the trail of the bison; but, alas! only to fall into the hidden snare of the Indian.

"Drink and pass!" he cried, handing the heavy charged flagon to the nearest seaman. "The crew alone now drink. Round with it, round! Short draughts—long swallows, men; 'tis hot as Satan's hoof. So, so; it goes round excellently. It spiralizes in ye; forks out at the serpent-snapping eye. Well done; almost drained. That way it went, this way it comes. Hand it me—here's a hollow! Men, ye seem the years; so brimming life is gulped and gone. Steward, refill!

"Attend now, my braves. I have mustered ye all round this cap-stan; and ye mates, flank me with your lances; and ye harpooneers, stand there with your irons; and ye, stout mariners, ring me in, that I may in some sort revive a noble custom of my fishermen fathers before me. O men, you will yet see that—— Ha! boy, come back? bad pennies come not sooner. Hand it me. Why, now, this pewter had run brimming again, wer't not thou St. Vitus' imp—away, thou ague!

"Advance, ye mates! Cross your lances full before me. Well done! Let me touch the axis." So saying, with extended arm, he grasped the three level, radiating lances at their crossed centre; while so doing, suddenly and nervously twitched them; meanwhile, glancing intently from Starbruck to Stubb; from Stubb to Flask. It seemed as though, by some nameless, interior volition, he would fain have shocked into them the same fiery emotion accumulated within the Leyden jar of his own magnetic life. The three mates quailed before his strong, sustained, and mystic aspect. Stubb and Flask looked sideways from him; the honest eye of Starbuck fell downright.

"In vain!" cried Ahab; "but, maybe, 'tis well. For did ye three but once take the full-forced shock, then mine own electric thing, *that* had perhaps expired from out me. Perchance, too, it would have dropped ye dead. Perchance ye need it not. Down lances! And now, ye mates I do appoint ye three cupbearers to my three pagan kinsmen there— you three most honourable gentlemen and noblemen, my valiant har-pooneers. Disdain the task? What, when the great Pope washes the feet of beggars, using his tiara for ewer? Oh, my sweet cardinals! your own condescension, *that* shall bend ye to it. I do not order ye; ye will it. Cut your seizings and draw the poles, ye harpooneers!"

Silently obeying the order, the three harpooneers now stood with the detached iron part of their harpoons, some three feet long, held, barbs up, before him.

"Stab me not with that keen steel! Cant them; cant them over! know ye not the goblet end? Turn up the socket! So, so; now, ye cup-bearers, advance. The irons! take them; hold them while I fill!" Forthwith, slowly going from one officer to the other, he brimmed the harpoon sockets with the fiery waters from the pewter.

"Now, three to three, ye stand. Commend the murderous chalices! bestow them, ye who are now made parties to this indissoluble league. Ha! Starbuck! but the deed is done! Yon ratifying sun now waits to sit upon it. Drink, ye harpooneers! drink and swear, ye men that man the deathful whaleboat's bow—Death to Moby Dick! God hunt us all, if we do not hunt Moby Dick to his death!" The long, barbed steel goblets were lifted; and to cries and maledictions against the white whale, the spirits were simultaneously quaffed down with a hiss. Starbuck paled, and turned, and shivered. Once more, and finally, the replenished pewter went the rounds among the frantic crew; when, waving his free hand to them, they all dispersed; and Ahab retired within his cabin.

CHAPTER 37

MOBY DICK

WITH GREEDY ears I learned the history of that murderous monster against whom I and all the others had taken our oaths of violence and revenge.

For some time past, though at intervals only, the unaccompanied, secluded white whale had haunted those uncivilized seas mostly frequented by the sperm-whale fishermen. But not all of them knew of his existence; only a few of them, comparatively, had knowingly seen him; while the number who as yet had actually and knowingly given battle to him, was small indeed. For, owing to the large number of whale-cruisers; the disorderly way they were sprinkled over the entire watery circumference, many of them adventurously pushing their quest along solitary latitudes, so as seldom or never for a whole twelvemonth or more on a stretch, to encounter a single news-telling sail of any sort; the inordinate length of each separate voyage; the irregularity of the times of sailing from home; all these, with other circumstances, direct and indirect, long obstructed the spread through the whole world-wide whaling-fleet of the special individualizing tidings concerning Moby Dick. It was hardly to be doubted, that several vessels reported to have encountered, at such or such a time, or on such or such a meridian, a sperm-whale of uncommon magnitude and malignity, which whale, after doing great mischief to his assailants, had completely escaped them; to some minds it was not an unfair presumption, I say, that the whale in question must have been no other than Moby Dick.

There was enough in the earthly make and incontestable character of the monster to strike the imagination with unwonted power. For, it was not so much his uncommon bulk that so much distinguished him from other sperm-whales, but, as was elsewhere thrown out—a peculiar snow-white wrinkled forehead, and a high, pyramidical white hump. These were his prominent features; the tokens whereby, even in the limitless, uncharted seas, he revealed his identity, at a long distance, to those who knew him.

The rest of his body was so streaked, and spotted, and marbled with the same shrouded hue, that, in the end, he had gained his distinctive appellation of the white whale; a name, indeed, literally justified by his vivid aspect, when seen gliding at high noon through a dark blue sea, leaving a milky-way wake of creamy foam, all spangled with golden gleamings.

Nor was it his unwonted magnitude, nor his remarkable hue, nor yet his deformed lower jaw, that so much invested the whale with natural terror, as that unexampled, intelligent malignity which, according to specific accounts, he had over and over again evinced in his assaults. More than all, his treacherous retreats struck more of dismay than perhaps aught else. For, when swimming before his exulting pursuers, with every apparent symptom of alarm, he had several times been known to turn round suddenly, and, bearing down upon them, either stave their boats to splinters, or drive them back in consternation to their ship.

Already several fatalities had attended his chase. But though similar disasters, however little bruited ashore, were by no means unusual in the fishery; yet, in most instances, such seemed the white whale's infernal aforethought of ferocity, that every dismembering or death that he caused, was not wholly regarded as having been inflicted by an unintelligent agent.

Judge, then, to what pitches of inflamed, distracted fury the minds of his more desperate hunters were impelled, when amid the chips of chewed boats, and the sinking limbs of torn comrades, they swam out of the white curds of the whale's direful wrath into the serene, exasperating sunlight, that smiled on, as if at a birth or a bridal.

His three boats stove around him, and oars and men both whirling in the eddies; one captain, seizing the line-knife from his broken prow, had dashed at the whale, as an Arkansas duellist at his foe, blindly seeking with a six-inch blade to reach the fathom-deep life of the whale. That captain was Ahab. And then it was, that suddenly sweeping his sickle-shaped lower jaw beneath him, Moby Dick had reaped away Ahab's leg, as a mower a blade of grass in the field. No turbaned Turk, no hired Venetian or Malay, could have smote him with more seeming malice. Small reason was there to doubt, then, that ever since that almost fatal encounter, Ahab had cherished a wild vindictiveness against the whale, all the more fell for that in his frantic morbidness he at last came to identify with him, not only all his bodily woes, but all his intellectual and spiritual exasperations. The white whale swam before him as the monomaniac incarnation of all those malicious agencies which some deep men feel eating in them, till they are left living on with half a heart and half a lung. But be all this as it may, certain it is, that with the mad secret of his unabated rage bolted up and keyed in him, Ahab had purposely sailed upon the present voyage with the one only and all-engrossing object of hunting the white whale. Had any one of his old acquaintances on shore but half dreamed of what was lurking in him then, how soon would their aghast and righteous souls have wrenched the ship from such a fiendish man! They were bent on profitable cruises, the profit to be counted down in dollars from the mint. He was intent on an audacious, immitigable, and supernatural revenge.

Here, then, was this grey-headed, ungodly old man, chasing with curses a Job's whale round the world, at the head of a crew, too, chiefly made up of mongrel renegades, and castaways, and cannibals —morally enfeebled also, by the incompetence of mere unaided virtue or right-mindedness in Starbuck, the invulnerable jollity of indifference and recklessness in Stubb, and the pervading mediocrity in Flask. Such a crew, so officered, seemed specially picked and packed by some infernal fatality to help him to his monomaniac revenge. How it was that they so aboundingly responded to the old man's ire—by what evil magic their souls were possessed, that at times his hate seemed almost theirs; the white whale as much their insufferable foe as his; how all this came to be—what the white whale was to them, or how to their unconscious understandings, also, in some dim, unsuspected way, he might have seemed the gliding great demon on the seas of life, all this to explain, would be to dive deeper than Ishmael can go. The subterranean miner that works in us all, how can one tell whither leads his shaft by the ever shifting, muffled sound of his pick? Who does not feel the irresistible arm drag? What skiff in tow of a seventy-four can stand still? For one, I gave myself up to the abandonment of the time and the place; but while yet all a-rush to encounter the whale, could see naught in that brute but the deadliest ill.

CHAPTER 38

HARK!

"HIST! DID you hear that noise, Cabaco?"

It was the middle-watch: a fair moonlight; the seamen were standing in a cordon, extending from one of the fresh-water butts in the waist, to the scuttle-butt near the taffrail. In this manner, they passed the buckets to fill the scuttle-butt. Standing, for the most part,

D

on the hallowed precincts of the quarter-deck, they were careful not
to speak or rustle their feet. From hand to hand, the buckets went in
the deepest silence, only broken by the occasional flap of a sail, and the
steady hum of the unceasingly advancing keel.

It was in the midst of this repose, that Archy, one of the cordon,
whose post was near the after-hatches, whispered to his neighbour, a
Cholo, the words above.

"Hist! did you hear that noise, Cabaco?"

"Take the bucket, will ye, Archy? what noise d'ye mean?"

"There it is again—under the hatches—don't you hear it—a cough
—it sounded like a cough."

"Cough be damned! Pass along that return bucket."

"There again—there it is!—it sounds like two or three sleepers turning over, now!"

"Caramba! have done, shipmate, will ye? It's the three soaked
biscuits ye eat for supper turning over inside of ye—nothing else. Look
to the bucket!"

"Say what ye will, shipmate; I've sharp ears."

"Aye, you are the chap, ain't ye, that heard the hum of the old
Quakeress's knitting-needles fifty miles at sea from Nantucket; you're
the chap."

"Grin away; we'll see what turns up. Hark ye, Cabaco, there is
somebody down in the after-hold that has not yet been seen on deck;
and I suspect our old Mogul knows something of it too. I heard Stubb
tell Flask, one morning watch, that there was something of that sort
in the wind."

"Tish! the bucket!"

CHAPTER 39

THE CHART

HAD you followed Captain Ahab down into his cabin after the
squall that took place on the night succeeding that wild ratifica-
tion of his purpose with his crew, you would have seen him go to a
locker in the transom, and bringing out a large wrinkled roll of
yellowish sea charts, spread them before him on his screwed-down
table. Then seating himself before it, you would have seen him intently
study the various lines and shadings which there met his eye; and
with slow but steady pencil trace additional courses over spaces that
before were blank. At intervals, he would refer to piles of old-log-
books beside him, wherein were set down the seasons and places in

which, on various former voyages of various ships, sperm-whales had been captured or seen.

While thus employed, the heavy pewter lamp suspended in chains over his head, continually rocked with the motion of the ship, and for ever threw shifting gleams and shadows of lines upon his wrinkled brow, till it almost seemed that while he himself was marking out lines and courses on the wrinkled charts, some invisible pencil was also tracing lines and courses upon the deeply marked chart of his forehead.

But it was not this night in particular that, in the solitude of his cabin, Ahab thus pondered over his charts. Almost every night they were brought out; almost every night some pencil marks were effaced, and others were substituted. For with the charts of all four oceans before him, Ahab was threading a maze of currents and eddies, with a view to the more certain accomplishment of that monomaniac thought of his soul.

Now, to any one not fully acquainted with the ways of the leviathans, it might seem an absurdly hopeless task thus to seek out one solitary creature in the unhooped oceans of this planet. But not so did it seem to Ahab, who knew the sets of all tides and currents; and thereby calculating the driftings of the sperm-whale's food; and, also, calling to mind the regular, ascertained seasons for hunting him in particular latitudes; could arrive at reasonable surmises, almost approaching to certainties, concerning the timeliest day to be upon this or that ground in search of his prey.

There was a circumstance which at first sight seemed to entangle his delirious but still methodical scheme. But not so in the reality, perhaps. Though the gregarious sperm-whales have their regular seasons for particular grounds, yet in general you cannot conclude that the herds which haunted such and such a latitude or longitude this year, say, will turn out to be identically the same with those that were found there the preceding season; though there are peculiar and unquestionable instances where the contrary of this has proved true. In general, the same remark, only within a less wide limit, applies to the solitaries and hermits among the matured, aged sperm-whales. So that though Moby Dick had in a former year been seen, for example, on what is called the Seychelle ground in the Indian ocean, or Volcano Bay on the Japanese Coast; yet it did not follow, that were the *Pequod* to visit either of those spots at any subsequent corresponding season, she would infallibly encounter him there. So, too, with some other feeding grounds, where he had at times revealed himself. But all these seemed only his casual stopping-places and ocean-inns, so to speak, not his places of prolonged abode. And where Ahab's chances of accomplishing his object have hitherto been spoken of, allusion has only been made to whatever wayside, antecedent, extra prospects were his, ere a particular set time or place were attained, when all possibilities would become probabilities, and, as Ahab fondly thought, every possibility the next thing to a certainty. That particular set time and place were conjoined in the one technical phrase—the Season-on-the-Line. For there and then, for several consecutive years, Moby Dick had been periodically descried, lingering in those waters for awhile, as the sun, in its annual round, loiters for a predicted interval in any one sign of the Zodiac. There it was, too, that most of the deadly encounters with the white whale had taken place; there the waves were storied with his deeds; there also was that tragic spot where the monomaniac old man had found the awful motive to his vengeance. But in the cautious comprehensiveness and unloitering vigilance with which Ahab threw his brooding soul into this unfaltering hunt, he would not permit himself to rest all his hopes upon the one crowning fact above mentioned, however flattering it might be to those hopes; nor in the sleeplessness of his vow could he so tranquillize his unquiet heart as to postpone all intervening quest.

Now, the *Pequod* had sailed from Nantucket at the very beginning of the Season-on-the-Line. No possible endeavour then could enable her commander to make the great passage southwards, double Cape Horn, and then running down sixty degrees of latitude arrive in the equatorial Pacific in time to cruise there. Therefore, he must wait for the next ensuing season. Yet the premature hour of the *Pequod's* sailing had, perhaps, been correctly selected by Ahab, with a view to this very complexion of things. Because an interval of three hundred and sixty-five days and nights was before him; an interval which, instead of impatiently enduring ashore, he would spend in a miscellaneous hunt; if by a chance the white whale, spending his vacation in seas far remote from his periodical feeding-grounds, should turn up his wrinkled brow off the Persian Gulf, or in the Bengal Bay, or China Seas, or in any other waters haunted by his race. So that Monsoons, Pampas, Nor'-Westers, Harmattans, Trades; any wind but the Levanter and Simoom, might blow Moby Dick into the devious zig-zag world-circle of the *Pequod's* circum-navigating wake.

CHAPTER 40

THE AFFIDAVIT

So FAR as what there may be of a narrative in this book; and, indeed, as indirectly touching one or two very interesting and curious particulars in the habits of sperm-whales, the foregoing chapter, in its earlier part, is as important a one as will be found in this volume; but the leading matter of it requires to be still further and more familiarly enlarged upon, in order to be adequately understood, and moreover to take away any incredulity which a profound ignorance of the entire subject may induce in some minds, as to the natural verity of the main points of this affair.

I care not to perform this part of my task methodically; but shall be content to produce the desired impression by separate citations of items, practically or reliably known to me as a whale-man; and from these citations, I take it—the conclusion aimed at will naturally follow of itself.

First: I have personally known three instances where a whale, after receiving a harpoon, has effected a complete escape; and, after an interval (in one instance of three years), has been again struck by the same hand, and slain; when the two irons, both marked by the same private cypher, have been taken from the body. In the instance where three years intervened between the flinging of the two harpoons; and I think it may have been something more than that; the man who darted them happening, in the interval, to go in a trading ship on a voyage to Africa, went ashore there, joined a discovery party, and penetrated far into the interior, where he travelled for a period of nearly two years, often endangered by serpents, savages, tigers, poisonous miasmas, with all the other common perils incident to wandering in the heart of unknown regions. Meanwhile, the whale he had struck must also have been on its travels; no doubt it had thrice circumnavigated the globe, brushing with its flanks all the coasts of Africa; but to no purpose. This man and this whale again came together, and the one vanquished the other. I say I, myself, have known three instances similar to this; that is in two of them I saw the whales struck; and, upon the second attack, saw the two irons with the respective marks cut in them, afterwards taken from the dead fish. In the three-year instance, it so fell out that I was in the boat both times, first and last, and the last time distinctly recognized a peculiar sort of huge mole under the whale's eye, which I had observed there three

years previous. I say three years, but I am pretty sure it was more than
that. Here are three instances, then, which I personally know the
truth of; but I have heard of many other instances from persons whose
veracity in the matter there is no good ground to impeach.

Secondly: People ashore have indeed some indefinite idea that a
whale is an enormous creature of enormous power; but I have ever
found that when narrating to them some specific example of this two-
fold enormousness, they have significantly complimented me upon my
facetiousness; when, I declare upon my soul, I had no more idea of
being facetious than Moses, when he wrote the history of the plagues
of Egypt.

But fortunately the special point I here seek can be established upon
testimony entirely independent of my own. That point is this: The
sperm-whale is in some cases sufficiently powerful, knowing, and
judiciously malicious, as with direct aforethought to stave in, utterly
destroy, and sink a large ship; and what is more, the sperm-whale
has done it.

First: In the year 1820 the ship *Essex*, Captain Pollard, of Nantucket,
was cruising in the Pacific Ocean. One day she saw spouts, lowered
her boats, and gave chase to a shoal of sperm-whales. Ere long, several
of the whales were wounded; when, suddenly, a very large whale
escaping from the boats, issued from the shoal, and bore directly down
upon the ship. Dashing his forehead against her hull, he so stove her
in, that in less than "ten minutes" she settled down and fell over.
Not a surviving plank of her has been seen since. After the severest
exposure, part of the crew reached the land in their boats. Being
returned home at last, Captain Pollard once more sailed for the Pacific
in command of another ship, but the gods ship-wrecked him again upon
unknown rocks and breakers; for the second time his ship was utterly
lost, and forthwith forswearing the sea, he has never tempted it since.
At this day Captain Pollard is a resident of Nantucket. I have seen
Owen Chace, who was chief mate of the *Essex* at the time of the
tragedy; I have read his plain and faithful narrative; I have conversed
with his son; and all this within a few miles of the scene of the
catastrophe.

Secondly: The ship *Union,* also of Nantucket, was in the year 1807
totally lost off the Azores by a similar onset, but the authentic particulars of this catastrophe I have never chanced to encounter, though from
the whale hunters I have now and then heard casual allusions to it.

I might proceed with several more examples, one way or another
known to me, of the great power and malice at times of the sperm-
whale. In more than one instance, he has been known, not only to

chase the assailing boats back to their ships, but to pursue the ship itself, and long withstand all the lances hurled at him from its decks. The English ship *Pusie Hall* can tell a story on that head; and, as for his strength, let me say that there have been examples where the lines attached to a running sperm-whale have, in a calm, been transferred to the ship, and secured there; the whale towing her great hull through the water, as a horse walks off with a cart. Again, it is very often observed that, if the sperm-whale, once struck, is allowed time to rally, he then acts, not so often with blind rage, as with wilful, deliberate designs of destruction to his pursuers; nor is it without conveying some eloquent indication of his character, that upon being attacked he will frequently open his mouth, and retain it in that dread expansion for several consecutive minutes.

CHAPTER 41

THE MAT-MAKER

IT WAS a cloudy, sultry afternoon; the seamen were lazily lounging about the decks, or vacantly gazing over into the lead-coloured waters. Queequeg and I were mildly employed weaving what is called a sword-mat, for an additional lashing to our boat. So still and subdued and yet somehow preluding was all the scene, and such an incantation of revelry lurked in the air, that each silent sailor seemed resolved into his own invisible self.

I was the attendant or page of Queequeg, while busy at the mat. As I kept passing and repassing the filling or woof of marline between the long yarns of the warp, using my own hand for the shuttle, and as Queequeg, standing sideways, ever and anon slid his heavy oaken sword between the threads, and idly looking off upon the water, carelessly and unthinkingly drove home every yarn: I say so strange a dreaminess did there then reign all over the ship and all over the sea, only broken by the intermitting dull sound of the sword, that it seemed as if this were the Loom of Time, and I myself were a shuttle mechanically weaving and weaving away at the Fates. There lay the fixed threads of the warp subject to but one single, ever returning, unchanging vibration, and that vibration merely enough to admit of the crosswise interblending of other threads with its own. This warp seemed necessity; and here, thought I, with my own hand I ply my own shuttle and weave my own destiny into these unalterable threads. Meantime, Queequeg's impulsive, indifferent sword, sometimes hitting

the woof slantingly, or crookedly, or strongly, or weakly, as the ca
might be; and by this difference in the concluding blow producing
corresponding contrast in the final aspect of the completed fabric; th
savage's sword, thought I, which thus finally shapes and fashions bot
warp and woof; this easy, indifferent sword must be chance—ay
chance, free will, and necessity—no wise incompatible—all interwea
ingly working together. The straight warp of necessity, not to l
swerved from its ultimate course—its every alternating vibratio
indeed, only tending to that; free will still free to ply her shutt
between given threads; and chance, though restrained in its play withi
the right lines of necessity, and sideways in its motions directed l
free will, though thus prescribed to by both, chance by turns rul
either, and has the last featuring blow at events.

. . . . .

Thus we were weaving and weaving away when I started at a sou
so strange, long drawn, and musically wild and unearthly, that th
ball of free will dropped from my hand, and I stood gazing up
the clouds whence that voice dropped like a wing. High aloft in th
cross-trees was that mad Gay-Header, Tashtego. His body was reac
ing eagerly forward, his hand stretched out like a wand, and at bri
sudden intervals he continued his cries. To be sure the same sou
was that very moment perhaps being heard all over the seas, fro
hundreds of whalemen's look-outs perched as high in the air; but fro
few of those lungs could that accustomed old cry have derived su
a marvellous cadence as from Tashtego the Indian's.

As he stood hovering over you half suspended in air, so wild
and eagerly peering towards the horizon, you would have thoug
him some prophet or seer beholding the shadows of Fate, and by tho
wild cries announcing their coming.

"There she blows! there! there! there! she blows! she blows!"

"Where-away?"

"On the lee-beam, about two miles off! a school of them!"

Instantly all was commotion.

The sperm-whale blows as a clock ticks, with the same undeviati
and reliable uniformity. And thereby whalemen distinguish this fi
from other tribes of his genus.

"There go flukes!" was now the cry from Tashtego; and the wha
disappeared.

"Quick, steward!" cried Ahab. "Time! time!"

Dough-Boy hurried below, glanced at the watch, and reported t
exact minute to Ahab.

The ship was now kept away from the wind, and she went gently rolling before it. Tashtego reporting that the whales had gone down heading to leeward, we confidently looked to see them again directly in advance of our bows. For that singular craft at times evinced by the sperm-whale when, sounding with his head in one direction, he nevertheless, while concealed beneath the surface, mills round, and swiftly swims off in the opposite quarter—this deceitfulness of his could not now be in action; for there was no reason to suppose that the fish seen by Tashtego had been in any way alarmed, or indeed knew at all of our vicinity. One of the men selected for shipkeepers—that is, those not appointed to the boats, by this time relieved the Indian at the main-mast head. The sailors at the fore and mizzen had come down; the line tubs were fixed in their places; the cranes were thrust out; the mainyard was backed, and the three boats swung over the sea like three samphire baskets over high cliffs. Outside of the bulwarks their eager crews with one hand clung to the rail, while one foot was expectantly poised on the gunwale. So look the long line of man-of-war's men about to throw themselves on board an enemy's ship.

But at this critical instant a sudden exclamation was heard that took every eye from the whale. With a start all glared at dark Ahab, who was surrounded by five dusky phantoms that seemed fresh formed out of air.

CHAPTER 42

THE FIRST LOWERING

THE PHANTOMS, for so they then seemed, were flitting on the other side of the deck, and, with a noiseless celerity, were casting loose the tackles and bands of the boat which swung there. This boat had always been deemed one of the spare boats, though technically called the captain's, on account of its hanging from the starboard quarter. The figure that now stood by its bows was tall and swart, with one white tooth evilly protruding from its steel-like lips. A rumpled Chinese jacket of black cotton funereally invested him, with wide black trousers of the same dark stuff. But strangely crowning this ebonness was a glistening white plaited turban, the living hair braided and coiled round and round upon his head. Less swart in aspect, the companions of this figure were of that vivid, tiger-yellow complexion peculiar to some of the aboriginal natives of the Manillas;—a race notorious for a certain diabolism of subtlety, and by some honest white mariners supposed to be the paid spies and secret confidential agents on the water of the devil, their lord, whose counting-room they suppose to be elsewhere.

While yet the wondering ship's company were gazing upon these strangers, Ahab cried out to the white-turbaned old man at their head. "All ready there, Fedallah?"

"Ready," was the half-hissed reply.

"Lower away then; d'ye hear?" shouting across the deck. "Lower away there, I say."

Such was the thunder of his voice, that spite of their amazement the men sprang over the rail; the sheaves whirled round in the blocks; with a wallow, the three boats dropped into the sea; while, with a dexterous, off-handed daring, unknown in any other vocation, the sailors, goat-like, leaped down the rolling ship's side into the tossed boats below.

Hardly had they pulled out from under the ship's lee, when a fourth keel, coming from the windward side, pulled round under the stern, and showed the five strangers rowing Ahab, who, standing erect in the stern, loudly hailed Starbuck, Stubb, and Flask, to spread themselves widely, so as to cover a large expanse of water.

In obedience to a sign from Ahab, Starbuck was now pulling obliquely across Stubb's bow; and when for a minute or so the two boats were pretty near to each other, Stubb hailed the mate.

"Mr. Starbuck! larboard boat there, ahoy! a word with ye, sir, if ye please!"

"Halloa!" returned Starbuck, turning round not a single inch as he spoke; still earnestly but whisperingly urging his crew; his face set like a flint from Stubb's.

"What think ye of those yellow boys, sir!"

"Smuggled on board, somehow, before the ship sailed. (Strong, strong boys!)" in a whisper to his crew, then speaking out loud again: "A sad business, Mr. Stubb! (seethe her, seethe her, my lads!) but never mind, Mr. Stubb, all for the best. Let all your crew pull strong, come what will. (Spring, my men, spring!) There's hogsheads of sperm ahead, Mr. Stubb, and that's what ye came for. (Pull, my boys!) Sperm, sperm's the play! This at least is duty; duty and profit hand in hand."

"Aye, aye, I thought as much," soliloquized Stubb, when the boats diverged, "as soon as I clapped eye on 'em, I thought so. Aye, and that's what he went in to the after hold for, so often, as Dough-Boy long suspected. They were hidden down there. The white whale's at the bottom of it. Well, well, so be it! Can't be helped! All right! Give away, men! It ain't the white whale to-day! Give away!"

Now the advent of these outlandish strangers at such a critical instant as the lowering of the boats from the deck, this had not unreasonably awakened a sort of superstitious amazement in some of the ship's company; but Archy's fancied discovery having some time previous got abroad among them, though indeed not credited then, this had in some small measure prepared them for the event. It took off the extreme edge of their wonder; and so what with all this and Stubb's confident way of accounting for their appearance, they were for the time freed from superstitious surmisings; though the affair still left abundant room for all manner of wild conjectures as to dark Ahab's precise agency in the matter from the beginning. For me, I silently recalled the mysterious shadows I had seen creeping on board the *Pequod* during the dim Nantucket dawn, as well as the enigmatical hintings of the unaccountable Elijah.

Meantime, Ahab, out of hearing of his officers, having sided the farthest to windward, was still ranging ahead of the other boats; a circumstance bespeaking how potent a crew was pulling him. Those tiger-yellow creatures of his seemed all steel and whalebone; like five trip-hammers they rose and fell with regular strokes of strength, which periodically started the boat along the water like a horizontal burst boiler out of a Mississippi steamer. As for Fedallah, who was seen pulling the harpooneer oar, he had thrown aside his black jacket, and displayed his naked chest with the whole part of his body above the gunwale, clearly cut against the alternating depressions of the watery horizon; while at the other end of the boat Ahab, with one arm, like a fencer's, thrown half backward into the air, as if to counter-balance any tendency to trip; Ahab was seen steadily managing his steering oar as in a thousand boat lowerings ere the white whale had torn him. All at once the outstretched arm gave a peculiar motion and then remained fixed, while the boat's five oars were seen simul-taneously peaked. Boat and crew sat motionless on the sea. Instantly the three spread boats in the rear paused on their way. The whales had irregularly settled bodily down into the blue, thus giving no distantly discernible token of the movement, though from his closer vicinity Ahab had observed it.

"Every man look out along his oars!" cried Starbuck. "Thou Queequeg, stand up."

Nimbly springing up on the triangular raised box in the bow, the savage stood erect there, and with intensely eager eyes gazed off towards the spot where the chase had last been descried. Likewise upon the extreme stern of the boat where it was also triangularly plat-formed level with the gunwale, Starbuck himself was seen coolly and adroitly balancing himself to the jerking tossings of his chip of a craft, and silently eyeing the vast blue eye of the sea.

Not very far distant Flask's boat was also lying breathlessly still; its commander recklessly standing upon the top of the loggerhead, a stout sort of post rooted in the keel, and rising some two feet above the level of the stern platform. It is used for catching turns with the whale line. Its top is not more spacious than the palm of a man's hand, and standing upon such a base as that, Flask seemed perched at the mast-head of some ship which had sunk to all but her trucks. But little King-Post was small and short, and at the same time little King-Post was full of a large and tall ambition, so that this logger-head stand-point of his did by no means satisfy King-Post.

"I can't see three seas off; tip us up an oar there, and let me on to that."

Upon this, Daggoo, with either hand upon the gunwale to steady his way, swiftly slid aft, and then erecting himself volunteered his lofty shoulders for a pedestal.

"Good a mast-head as any, sir. Will you mount?"

"That I will, and thank ye very much, my fine fellow; only I wish you fifty feet taller."

Whereupon planting his feet firmly against two opposite planks of the boat, the gigantic negro, stooping a little, presented his flat palm to Flask's foot, and then putting Flask's hand on his hearse-plumed head and bidding him spring as he himself should toss, with one dex-terous fling landed the little man high and dry on his shoulders. And here was Flask now standing, Daggoo with one lifted arm furnishing him with a breastband to lean against and steady himself by.

At any time it is a strange sight to the tyro to see with what wondrous habitude of unconscious skill the whaleman will maintain an erect posture in his boat, even when pitched about by the most riotously perverse and cross-running seas. Still more strange to see him giddily perched upon the logger-head itself under such circumstances. But the sight of little Flask mounted upon gigantic Daggoo was yet more curious; for sustaining himself with a cool, indifferent, easy, un-thought of, barbaric majesty, the noble negro to every roll of the sea harmoniously rolled his fine form. On his broad back, flaxen-haired Flask seemed a snow-flake. The bearer looked nobler than the rider. Though truly vivacious, tumultuous, ostentatious little Flask would now and then stamp with impatience; but not one added heave did he thereby give to the negro's lordly chest. So have I seen Passion and Vanity stamping the living magnanimous earth, but the earth did not alter her tides and her seasons for that.

Meanwhile Stubb, the third mate, betrayed no such far-gazing solici-
tudes. The whales might have made one of their regular soundings,
not a temporary dive from mere fright; and if that were the case, Stubb,
as his wont in such cases, it seems, was resolved to solace the languish-
ing interval with his pipe. He withdrew it from his hatband, where
he always wore it aslant like a feather. He loaded it, and rammed
home the loading with his thumb-end; but hardly had he ignited his
match across the rough sandpaper of his hand, when Tashtego, his
harpooneer, whose eyes had been setting to windward like two fixed
stars, suddenly dropped like light from his erect attitude to his seat,
crying out in a quick phrensy of hurry, "Down, down all, and give
way!—there they are!"

To a landsman, no whale, nor any sign of a herring, would have been
visible at that moment; nothing but a troubled bit of greenish white
water, and thin scattered puffs of vapour hovering over it, and suffus-
ingly blowing off to leeward, like the confused scud from white rolling
billows. The air around suddenly vibrated and tingled, as it were, like
the air over intensely heated plates of iron. Beneath this atmospheric
waving and curling, and partially beneath a thin layer of water, also,
the whales were swimming. Seen in advance of all the other indications, the puffs of vapour they spouted, seemed their fore-running
couriers and detached flying outriders.

All four boats were now in keen pursuit of that one spot of troubled
water and air. But it bade fair to outstrip them; it flew on and on, as
a mass of interblending bubbles borne down a rapid stream from the
hills.

The dancing white water made by the chase was now becoming more
and more visible, owing to the increasing darkness of the dun cloud-
shadows flung upon the sea. The jets of vapour no longer blended,
but tilted everywhere to right and left; the whales seemed separating
their wakes. The boats were pulled more apart; Starbuck giving chase
to three whales running dead to leeward. Our sail was now set, and,
with the still rising wind, we rushed along; the boat going with such
madness through the water, that the lee oars could scarcely be worked
rapidly enough to escape being torn from the row-locks.

Soon we were running through a suffusing wide veil of mist; neither
ship nor boat to be seen.

"Give way, men," whispered Starbuck, drawing still further aft
the sheet of his sail; "there is time to kill a fish yet before the squall
comes. There's white water again!—close to! Spring!"

Soon after, two cries in quick succession on each side of us denoted
that the other boats had got fast; but hardly were they overheard,

when with a lightning-like hurtling whisper Starbuck said: "Stand up!" and Queequeg, harpoon in hand, sprang to his feet.

Though not one of the oarsmen was then facing the life and death peril so close to them ahead, yet with their eyes on the intense countenance of the mate in the stern of the boat, they knew that the imminent instant had come; they heard, too, an enormous wallowing sound as of fifty elephants stirring in their litter. Meanwhile the boat was still booming through the mist, the waves curling and hissing around us like the erected crests of enraged serpents.

"That's his hump. *There, there,* give it to him!" whispered Starbuck.

A short rushing sound leaped out of the boat; it was the darted iron of Queequeg. Then all in one welded commotion came an invisible push from astern, while forward the boat seemed striking on a ledge; the sail collapsed and exploded; a gush of scalding vapour shot up near by; something rolled and tumbled like an earthquake beneath us. The whole crew were half suffocated as they were tossed helter-skelter into the white curdling cream of the squall. Squall, whale, and harpoon had all blended together; and the whale, merely grazed by the iron, escaped.

Though completely swamped, the boat was nearly unharmed. Swimming round it we picked up the floating oars, and lashing them across the gunwale, tumbled back to our places. There we sat up to our knees in the sea, the water covering every rib and plank, so that to our downward gazing eyes the suspended craft seemed a coral boat grown up to us from the bottom of the ocean.

The wind increased to a howl; the waves dashed their bucklers together; the whole squall roared, forked, and crackled around us like a white fire upon the prairie, in which, unconsumed, we were burning; immortal in these jaws of death! In vain we hailed the other boats; as well roar to the live coals down the chimney of a flaming furnace as hail those boats in that storm. Meanwhile the driving scud, rack, and mist, grew darker with the shadows of night; no sign of the ship could be seen. The rising sea forbade all attempts to bale out the boat. The oars were useless as propellers, performing now the office of life-preservers. So, cutting the lashing of the waterproof match keg, after many failures Starbuck contrived to ignite the lamp in the lantern; then stretching it on a waif pole, handed it to Queequeg as the standard-bearer of this forlorn hope. There, then, he sat, holding up that imbecile candle in the heart of that almighty forlornness. There, then, he sat, the sign and symbol of a man without faith, hopelessly holding up hope in the midst of despair.

Wet, drenched through, and shivering cold, despairing of ship or boat, we lifted up our eyes as the dawn came on. The mist still spread over the sea, the empty lantern lay crushed in the bottom of the boat. Suddenly Queequeg started to his feet, hollowing his hand to his ear. We all heard a faint creaking, as of ropes and yards hitherto muffled by the storm. The sound came nearer and nearer; the thick mists were dimly parted by a huge, vague form. Affrighted, we all sprang into the sea as the ship at last loomed into view, bearing right down upon us within a distance of not much more than its length.

Floating on the waves we saw the abandoned boat, as for one instant it tossed and gaped beneath the ship's bows like a chip at the base of a cataract; and then the vast hull rolled over it, and it was seen no more till it came up weltering astern. Again we swam for it, were dashed against it by the seas, and were at last taken up and safely landed on board. Ere the squall came close to, the other boats had cut loose from their fish and returned to the ship in good time. The ship had given us up, but was still cruising, if haply it might light upon some token of our perishing,—an oar or a lance pole.

CHAPTER 43

THE "ALBATROSS"

SOUTH-EASTWARD from the Cape, off the distant Crozetts, a good cruising ground for Right Whalemen, a sail loomed ahead, the *Goney* ("Albatross") by name. As she slowly drew nigh, from my lofty perch at the fore-mast-head, I had a good view of that sight so remarkable to a tyro in the far ocean fisheries—a whaler at sea, and long absent from home.

As if the waves had been fullers, this craft was bleached like the skeleton of a stranded walrus. All down her sides, this spectral appearance was traced with long channels of reddened rust, while all her spars and her rigging were like the thick branches of trees furred over with hoar-frost. Only her lower sails were set. A wild sight it was to see her long-bearded lookouts at those three mast-heads. They seemed clad in the skins of beasts, so torn and bepatched the raiment that had survived nearly four years of cruising. Standing in iron hoops nailed to the mast, they swayed and swung over a fathomless sea; and though, when the ship slowly glided close under our stern, we six men in the air came so nigh to each other that we might almost have leaped from the mast-heads of one ship to those of the other; yet, those forlorn-looking fishermen, mildly eyeing us as they passed, said not one word to our own look-outs, while the quarter-deck hail was being heard from below.

"Ship ahoy! Have ye seen the white whale?"

But as the strange captain, leaning over the pallid bulwarks, was in the act of putting his trumpet to his mouth, it somehow fell from his hand into the sea; and the wind now rising amain, he in vain strove to make himself heard without it. Meantime his ship was still increasing the distance between. While in various silent ways the seamen of the *Pequod* were evincing their observance of this ominous incident at the first mere mention of the white whale's name to another ship, Ahab for a moment paused; it almost seemed as though he would have lowered a boat to board the stranger, had not the threatening wind forbade. But taking advantage of his windward position, he again seized his trumpet, and knowing by her aspect that the stranger vessel was a Nantucketer and shortly bound for home, he loudly hailed—"Ahoy there! This is the *Pequod,* bound round the world! Tell them to address all future letters to the Pacific ocean! and this time three years, if I am not at home, tell them to address them to——"

At that moment the two wakes were fairly crossed, and instantly, then, in accordance with their singular ways, shoals of small harmless fish, that for some days before had been placidly swimming by our side, darted away with what seemed shuddering fins, and ranged themselves fore and aft with the stranger's flanks. Though in the course of his continual voyagings Ahab must often before have noticed a similar sight, yet, to any monomaniac man, the veriest trifles capriciously carry meanings.

"Swim away from me, do ye?" murmured Ahab, gazing over into the water. There seemed but little in the words, but the tone conveyed more of deep helpless sadness than the insane old man had ever before evinced. But turning to the steersman, who thus far had been holding the ship in the wind to diminish her headway, he cried out in his old lion voice,—"Up helm! Keep her off round the world!"

Round the world! There is much in that sound to inspire proud feelings; but whereto does all that circumnavigation conduct? Only through numberless perils to the very point whence we started, where those that we left behind secure, were all the time before us.

Were this world an endless plain, and by sailing eastward we could for ever reach new distances, and discover sights more sweet and strange than any Cyclades or Islands of King Solomon, then there were promise in the voyage. But in pursuit of those mysteries we dream of, or in tormented chase of that demon phantom that, some time or other, swims before all human hearts; while chasing such over this round globe, they either lead us on in barren mazes or midway leave us whelmed.

CHAPTER 44

THE GAM

THE OSTENSIBLE reason why Ahab did not go on board of the whaler we had spoken was this: the wind and sea betokened storms. But even had this not been the case, he would not after all, perhaps, have boarded her—judging by his subsequent conduct on similar occasions —if so it had been that, by the process of hailing, he had obtained a negative answer to the question he put. For, as it eventually turned out, he cared not to consort, even for five minutes, with any stranger captain, except he could contribute some of that information he so absorbingly sought. But all this might remain inadequately estimated, were not something said here of the peculiar usages of whaling-vessels when meeting each other in foreign seas, and especially on a common cruising-ground.

If two strangers crossing the Pine Barrens in New York State, or the equally desolate Salisbury Plain in England; if casually encountering each other in such inhospitable wilds, these twain, for the life of them, cannot well avoid a mutual salutation; and stopping for a moment to interchange the news; and, perhaps, sitting down for a while and resting in concert: then, how much more natural that upon the illimitable Pine Barrens and Salisbury Plains of the sea, two whaling vessels descrying each other at the ends of the earth—off lone Fanning's Island, or the far away King's Mills; how much more natural, I say, that under such circumstances these ships should not only interchange hails, but come into still closer, more friendly and sociable contact. And especially would this seem to be a matter of course, in the case of vessels owned in one seaport, and whose captains, officers, and not a few of the men are personally known to each other; and consequently, have all sorts of dear domestic things to talk about.

For the long absent ship, the outward-bounder, perhaps, has letters on board; at any rate, she will be sure to let her have some papers of a date a year or two later than the last one on her blurred and thumbworn files. And in return for that courtesy, the outward-bound ship would receive the latest whaling intelligence from the cruising-ground to which she may be destined, a thing of the utmost importance to her.

And in degree, all this will hold true concerning whaling vessels crossing each other's track on the cruising-ground itself, even though they are equally long absent from home. For one of them may have received a transfer of letters from some third, and now far remote vessel; and some of those letters may be for the people of the ship she now meets. Besides, they would exchange the whaling news, and have an agreeable chat. For not only would they meet with all the sympathies of sailors, but likewise with all the peculiar congenialities arising from a common pursuit and mutually shared privations and perils.

Nor would difference of country make any very essential difference; that is, so long as both parties speak one language, as is the case with Americans and English. Though, to be sure, from the small number of English whalers, such meetings do not very often occur, and when they do occur there is too apt to be a sort of shyness between them; for your Englishman is rather reserved, and your Yankee, he does not fancy that sort of thing in anybody but himself. Besides, the English whalers sometimes affect a kind of metropolitan superiority over the American whalers; regarding the long, lean Nantucketer, with his nondescript provincialisms, as a sort of sea-peasant. But where this superiority in the English whaleman does really consist, it would be hard to say, seeing that the Yankees in one day, collectively, kill more whales than all the English, collectively, in ten years. But this is a harmless little foible in the English whale-hunters, which the Nantucketer does not take much to heart; probably, because he knows that he has a few foibles himself.

So, then, we see that of all ships separately sailing the sea, the whalers have most reason to be sociable—and they are so. Whereas, some merchant ships crossing each other's wake in the mid-Atlantic, will oftentimes pass on without so much as a single word of recognition, mutually cutting each other on the high seas, like a brace of dandies in Broadway; and all the time indulging, perhaps, in finical criticism upon each other's rig. As for men-of-war, when they chance to meet at sea, they first go through such a string of silly bowings and scrapings, such a ducking of ensigns, that there does not seem to be much right-down hearty good-will and brotherly love about it at all. As touching slave-ships meeting, why, they are in such a prodigious hurry, they run away from each other as soon as possible. And as for pirates, when they chance to cross each other's cross-bones, the first hail is—"How many skulls?"—the same way that whalers hail—"How many barrels?" And that question once answered, pirates straightway steer apart, for they are infernal villains on both sides, and don't like to see overmuch of each other's villainous likenesses.

But look at the godly, honest, unostentatious, hospitable, sociable, free-and-easy whaler! What does the whaler do when she meets another whaler in any sort of decent weather? She has a "*Gam*," a thing so utterly unknown to all other ships that they never heard of the name even; and if by chance they should hear of it, they only grin at it, and repeat gamesome stuff about "spouters" and "blubber-boilers," and such like pretty exclamations. Why it is all merchant-seamen, and also all pirates and man-of-war's men, and slave-ship sailors, cherish such a scornful feeling towards whale-ships; this is a question it would be hard to answer. Because, in the case of pirates, say, I should like to know whether that profession of theirs has any peculiar glory about it. It sometimes ends in uncommon elevation, indeed; but only at the gallows. And besides, when a man is elevated in that odd fashion, he has no proper foundation for his superior altitude. Hence, I conclude, that in boasting himself to be high lifted above a whaleman, in that assertion the pirate has no solid basis to stand on.

But what is a *Gam*? You might wear out your index-finger running up and down the columns of dictionaries, and never find the word. Dr. Johnson never attained to that erudition; Noah Webster's ark does not hold it. Nevertheless, this same expressive word has now for many years been in constant use among some fifteen thousand true born Yankees. Certainly, it needs a definition, and should be incorporated into the Lexicon. With that view, let me learnedly define it.

GAM. Noun—*A social meeting of two (or more) Whale-ships, generally on a cruising-ground; when, after exchanging hails, they exchange visits by boats' crews; the two captains remaining, for the time, on board of one ship, and the two chief mates on the other.*

There is another little item about Gamming which must not be forgotten here. All professions have their own little peculiarities of detail; so has the whale fishery. In a pirate, man-of-war, or slave-ship, when the captain is rowed anywhere in his boat, he always sits in the stern sheets on a comfortable, sometimes cushioned, seat there, and often steers himself with a pretty little milliners' tiller decorated with gay cords and ribbons. But the whale-boat has no seat astern, no sofa of that sort whatever, and no tiller at all. High times indeed, if whaling captains were wheeled about the water on castors like gouty old aldermen in patent chairs. And as for a tiller, the whale-boat never admits of any such effeminacy; and therefore as in gamming a complete boat's crew must leave the ship, and hence as the boat steerer or harpooneer is of the number, that subordinate is the steersman upon the occasion, and the captain, having no place to sit in, is pulled off to his visit standing like a pine tree. And often you will notice that being conscious of the eyes of the whole visible world resting on him from the sides of the two ships, this standing captain is all alive to the importance of sustaining his dignity by maintaining his legs. Nor is this any very easy matter; for in his rear is the immense projecting steering oar hitting him now and then in the small of his back, the after-oar reciprocating by rapping his knees in front. He is thus completely wedged before and behind, and can only expand himself sideways by settling down on his stretched legs; but a sudden violent pitch of the boat will often go far to topple him, because length of foundation is nothing without corresponding breadth. Merely make a spread angle of two poles, and you cannot stand them up. Then, again, it would never do in plain sight of the world's riveted eyes, it would never do, I say, for this straddling captain to be seen steadying himself the slightest particle by catching hold of anything with his hands; indeed, as token of his entire, buoyant self-command, he generally carries his hands in his trousers' pockets; but perhaps being generally very large, heavy hands, he carries them there for ballast. Nevertheless there have occurred instances, well authenticated ones too, where the captain has been known for an uncommonly critical moment or two, in a sudden squall say—to seize hold of the nearest oarsman's hair, and hold on there like grim death.

CHAPTER 45

THE "TOWN-HO'S" STORY
(*As told at the Golden Inn*)

THE CAPE of Good Hope, and all the watery region round about there, is much like some noted four corners of a great highway, where you meet more travellers than in any other part.

It was not very long after speaking the *Goney* that another home-ward-bound whaleman, the *Town-Ho*,[1] was encountered. She was manned almost wholly by Polynesians. In the short gam that ensued she gave us strong news of Moby Dick. To some the general interest in the white whale was now wildly heightened by a circumstance of the *Town-Ho's* story, which seemed obscurely to involve with the whale a certain wondrous, inverted visitation of one of those so called judgments of God which at times are said to overtake some men. This

---

[1] The ancient whale-cry upon first sighting a whale from the masthead, still used by whalemen in hunting the famous Gallipago terrapin.

latter circumstance with its own particular accompaniments, forming what may be called the secret part of the tragedy about to be narrated, never reached the ears of Captain Ahab or his mates. For that secret part of the story was unknown to the captain of the *Town-Ho* himself. It was the private property of three confederate white seamen of that ship, one of whom, it seems, communicated it to Tashtego with Romish injunctions of secrecy, but the following night Tashtego rambled in his sleep, and revealed so much of it in that way, that when he was wakened he could not well withhold the rest. Nevertheless, so potent an influence did this thing have on those seamen in the *Pequod* who came to the full knowledge of it, and by such a strange delicacy, to call it so, were they governed in this matter, that they kept the secret among themselves so that it never transpired abaft the *Pequod*'s main-mast. Interweaving in its proper place this darker thread with the story as publicly narrated on the ship, the whole of this strange affair I now proceed to put on lasting record.

For my humour's sake, I shall preserve the style in which I once narrated it at Lima, to a lounging circle of my Spanish friends, one saint's eve, smoking upon the thick-gilt tiled piazza of the Golden Inn. Of those fine cavaliers, the young Dons, Pedro and Sebastian, were on the closer terms with me; and hence the interluding questions they occasionally put, and which were duly answered at the time.

"Some two years prior to my first learning the events which I am about rehearsing to you, gentlemen, the *Town-Ho,* sperm-whaler of Nantucket, was cruising in your Pacific here, not very many days' sail eastward from the eaves of this Golden Inn. She was somewhere to the northward of the Line. One morning upon handling the pumps, according to daily usage, it was observed that she made more water in her hold than common. They supposed a sword-fish had stabbed her, gentlemen. But the captain, having some unusual reason for believing that rare good luck awaited him in those latitudes; and therefore being very averse to quit them, and the leak not being then considered at all dangerous, though, indeed, they could not find it after searching the hold as low down as was possible in rather heavy weather, the ship still continued her cruisings, the mariners working at the pumps at wide and easy intervals; but no good luck came; more days went by, and not only was the leak yet undiscovered, but it sensibly increased. So much so, that now taking some alarm, the captain, making all sail, stood away for the nearest harbour among the islands, there to have his hull hove out and repaired.

"Though no small passage was before her, yet, if the commonest chance favoured, he did not at all fear that his ship would founder by the way, because his pumps were of the best, and being periodically relieved at them, those six-and-thirty men of his could easily keep the ship free; never mind if the leak should double on her. In truth, well nigh the whole of this passage being attended by very prosperous breezes, the *Town-Ho* had all but certainly arrived in perfect safety at her port without the occurrence of the least fatality, had it not been for the brutal overbearing of Radney, the mate, a Vineyarder, and the bitterly provoked vengeance of Steelkilt, a Lakeman and desperado from Buffalo.

"It was not more than a day or two at the furthest after pointing her prow for her island haven, that the *Town-Ho's* leak seemed again increasing, but only so as to require an hour or more at the pumps every day. You must know that in a settled and civilized ocean like our Atlantic, for example, some skippers think little of pumping their whole way across it; though of a still sleepy night, should the officer of the deck happen to forget his duty in that respect, the probability would be that he and his shipmate would never again remember it, on account of all hands gently subsiding to the bottom. Nor in the solitary and savage seas far from you to the westward, gentlemen, is it altogether unusual for ships to keep clanging at their pump-handles in full chorus even for a voyage of considerable length; that is, if it lie along a tolerably accessible coast, or if any other reasonable retreat is afforded them. It is only when a leaky vessel is in some very out of the way part of those waters, some really landless latitude, that her captain begins to feel a little anxious.

"Much this way it had been with the *Town-Ho*; so when her leak was found gaining once more, there was in truth some small concern manifested by several of her company; especially by Radney the mate. He commanded the upper sails to be well hoisted, sheeted home anew, and every way expanded to the breeze. Now this Radney, I suppose, was as little of a coward, and as little inclined to any sort of nervous apprehensiveness touching his own person as any fearless, unthinking creature on land or on sea that you can conveniently imagine, gentlemen. Therefore when he betrayed the solicitude about the safety of the ship, some of the seamen declared that it was only on account of his being part owner in her. So when they were working that evening at the pumps, there was on this head no small gamesomeness slyly going on among them as they stood with their feet continually overflowed by the rippling clear water; clear as any mountain spring, gentlemen— that bubbling from the pumps ran across the deck, and poured itself out in steady spouts at the lee scupper-holes.

"Now, as you well know, it is not seldom the case in this conventional world of ours—watery or otherwise; that when a person placed in command over his fellow-men finds one of them to be very significantly his superior in general pride of manhood, straightway against that man he conceives an unconquerable dislike and bitterness; and if he have a chance he will pull down and pulverize that subaltern's tower, and make a little heap of dust of it. Be this conceit ot mine as it may, gentlemen, at all events Steelkilt was a tall and noble animal with a head like a Roman, and a flowing golden beard like the tasselled housings of your last viceroy's snorting charger; and a brain, and a heart, and a soul in him, gentlemen, which had made Steelkilt Charlemagne, had he been born son to Charlemagne's father. But Radney, the mate, was ugly as a mule; yet as hardy, as stubborn, as malicious. He did not love Steelkilt, and Steelkilt knew it.

"Espying the mate drawing near as he was toiling at the pump with the rest, the Lakeman affected not to notice him, but unawed, went on with his gay banterings.

"'Aye, aye, my merry lads, it's a lively leak this; hold a cannikin, one of ye, and let's have a taste. By the Lord, it's worth bottling! I tell ye what, men, old Rad's investment must go for it! he had best cut away his part of the hull and tow it home. The fact is, boys, that sword-fish only began the job; he's come back again with a gang of ship-carpenters, saw-fish, and file-fish, and what not; and the whole posse of 'em are now hard at work cutting and slashing at the bottom; making improvements, I suppose. If old Rad were here now, I'd tell him to jump overboard and scatter 'em. They're playing the devil with his estate, I can tell him. But he's a simple old soul,—Rad, and a beauty too. Boys, they say the rest of his property is invested in looking-glasses. I wonder if he'd give a poor devil like me the model of his nose.'

"'Damn your eyes! what's that pump stopping for?' roared Radney, pretending not to have heard the sailors' talk. 'Thunder away at it!'

"'Aye, aye, sir,' said Steelkilt, merry as a cricket. 'Lively, boys, lively now!' And with that the pump clanged like fifty fire-engines; the men tossed their hats off to it, and ere long that peculiar gasping of the lungs was heard which denotes the fullest tension of life's utmost energies.

"Quitting the pump at last, with the rest of his band, the Lakeman went forward all panting, and sat himself down on the windlass; his face fiery red, his eyes bloodshot, and wiping the profuse sweat from his brow. Now what cozening fiend it was, gentlemen, that possessed Radney to meddle with such a man in that corporeally exasperated state, I know not; but so it happened. Intolerably striding along the deck, the mate commanded him to get a broom and sweep down the planks, and also a shovel, and remove some offensive matters consequent upon allowing a pig to run at large.

"Now, gentlemen, sweeping a ship's deck at sea is a piece of household work which in all times but raging gales is regularly attended to every evening; it has been known to be done in the case of ships actually foundering at the time. Such, gentlemen, is the inflexibility of sea-usages and the instinctive love of neatness in seamen; some of whom would not willingly drown without first washing their faces. But in all vessels this broom business is the prescriptive province of the boys, if boys there be aboard. Besides, it was the stronger men in the *Town-Ho* that had been divided into gangs, taking turns at the pumps; and being the most athletic seaman of them all, Steelkilt had been regularly assigned captain of one of the gangs; consequently he should have been freed from any trivial business not connected with truly nautical duties, such being the case with his comrades. I mention all these particulars so that you may understand exactly how this affair stood between the two men.

"But there was more than this: the order about the shovel was almost as plainly meant to sting and insult Steelkilt, as though Radney had spat in his face. Any man who has gone sailor in a whale ship will understand this; and all this and doubtless much more, the Lakeman fully comprehended when the mate uttered his command. But as he sat still for a moment, and as he steadfastly looked into the mate's malignant eye and perceived the stacks of powder-casks heaped up in him and the slow-match silently burning along towards them; as he instinctively saw all this, that strange forbearance and unwillingness to stir up the deeper passionateness in any already ireful being—a repugnance most felt, when felt at all, by really valiant men even when aggrieved—this nameless phantom feeling, gentlemen, stole over Steelkilt.

"Therefore, in his ordinary tone, only a little broken by the bodily exhaustion he was temporarily in, he answered him saying that sweeping the deck was not his business, and he would not do it. And then, without at all alluding to the shovel, he pointed to three lads as the customary sweepers; who, not being billeted at the pumps, had done little or nothing all day. To this, Radney replied with an oath, in a most domineering and outrageous manner unconditionally reiterating his command; meanwhile advancing upon the still seated Lakeman with an uplifted cooper's club hammer which he had snatched from a cask near by.

"Heated and irritated as he was by his spasmodic toil at the pumps, for all his nameless feeling of forbearance the sweating Steelkilt could but ill brook this bearing in the mate; but somehow still smothering the conflagration within him, without speaking he remained doggedly rooted to his seat, till at last the incensed Radney shook the hammer within a few inches of his face, furiously commanding him to do his bidding.

"Steelkilt rose, and slowly retreated round the windlass, steadily followed by the mate with his menacing hammer, deliberately repeated his intention not to obey. Seeing, however, that his forbearance had not the slightest effect, by an awful and unspeakable intimation with his twisted hand he warned off the foolish and infatuated man; but it was to no purpose. And in this way the two went once slowly round the windlass; when, resolved at last no longer to retreat, bethinking him that he had now forborne as much as comported with his humour, the Lakeman paused on the hatches and thus spoke to the officer:

"'Mr. Radney, I will not obey you. Take that hammer away, or look to yourself.' But the predestinated mate coming still closer to him, where the Lakeman stood fixed, now shook the heavy hammer within an inch of his teeth; meanwhile repeating a string of insufferable maledictions. Retreating not the thousandth part of an inch; stabbing him in the eye with the unflinching poniard of his glance, Steelkilt, clenching his right hand behind him and creepingly drawing it back, told his persecutor that if the hammer but grazed his cheek he (Steelkilt) would murder him. But, gentlemen, the fool had been branded for the slaughter by the gods. Immediately the hammer touched the cheek; the next instant the lower jaw of the mate was stove in his head; he fell on the hatch spouting blood like a whale.

"Ere the cry could go aft Steelkilt was shaking one of the backstays leading far aloft to where two of his comrades were standing their mast-heads. They were both Canallers.

"Sliding down the ropes like baleful comets, the two Canallers rushed into the uproar, and sought to drag their man out of it towards the forecastle. Others of the sailors joined with them in this attempt, and a twisted turmoil ensued; while standing out of harm's way, the valiant captain danced up and down with a whale-pike, calling upon his officers to manhandle that atrocious scoundrel, and smoke him along to the quarter-deck. At intervals, he ran close up to the revolving border of the confusion, and prying into the heart of it with his pike, sought to prick out the object of his resentment. But Steelkilt and his desperadoes were too much for them all; they succeeded in gaining the

forecastle deck, where, hastily slewing about three or four large casks
in a line with the windlass, these sea-Parisians entrenched themselves
behind the barricade.

"'Come out of that, ye pirates!' roared the captain, now menacing
them with a pistol in each hand, just brought to him by the steward.
'Come on out of that, ye cut-throats!'

"Steelkilt leaped on the barricade, and striding up and down there,
defied the worst the pistols could do; but gave the captain to understand distinctly, that his (Steelkilt's) death would be the signal for a
murderous mutiny on the part of all hands. Fearing in his heart lest
this might prove but too true, the captain a little desisted, but still
commanded the insurgents instantly to return to their duty.

"'Will you promise not to touch us, if we do?' demanded their
ringleader.

"'Turn to! turn to!—I make no promise;—to your duty! Do you
want to sink the ship, by knocking off at a time like this? Turn to!'
and he once more raised a pistol.

"'Sink the ship?' cried Steelkilt. 'Aye, let her sink. Not a man of
us turns to, unless you swear not to raise a rope-yarn against us. What
say ye, men?' turning to his comrades. A fierce cheer was their
response.

"The Lakeman now patrolled the barricade, all the while keeping
his eye on the captain, and jerking out such sentences as these: 'It's
not our fault; we didn't want it; I told him to take his hammer away;
it was boys' business; he might have known me before this; I told him
not to prick the buffalo; I believe I have broken a finger here against
his cursed jaw; ain't those mincing knives down in the forecastle
there, men? look to those handspikes, my hearties. Captain, by God,
look to yourself; say the word; don't be a fool; forget it all; we are
ready to turn to; treat us decently, and we're your men; but we won't
be flogged.'

"'Turn to! I make no promises, turn to, I say!'

"'Look ye, now,' cried the Lakeman, flinging out his arm towards
him, 'there are a few of us here (and I am one of them) who have
shipped for the cruise, d'ye see; now as you well know, sir, we can
claim our discharge as soon as the anchor is down; so we don't want
a row; it's not our interest; we want to be peaceable; we are ready to
work, but we won't be flogged."

"'Turn to!' roared the captain.

"Steelkilt glanced round him for a moment, and then said, 'I tell
you what it is now, Captain, rather than kill ye, and be hung for such
a shabby rascal, we won't lift a hand against ye unless ye attack us;

but till you say the word about not flogging us, we don't do a hand's turn."

"'Down into the forecastle then, down with ye, I'll keep ye there till ye're sick of it. Down ye go.'

"'Shall we?' cried the ringleader to his men. Most of them were against it; but at length, in obedience to Steelkilt, they preceded him down into their dark den, growlingly disappearing, like bears into a cave.

"As the Lakeman's bare head was just level with the planks, the captain and his posse leaped the barricade, and rapidly drawing over the slide of the scuttle, planted their group of hands upon it, and loudly called for the steward to bring the heavy brass padlock belonging to the companionway. Then opening the slide a little, the captain whispered something down the crack, closed it, and turned the key upon them—ten in number—leaving on deck some twenty or more, who thus far had remained neutral.

"All night a wide-awake watch was kept by all the officers, forward and aft, especially about the forecastle scuttle and fore hatchway; at which last place it was feared the insurgents might emerge, after breaking through the bulkhead below. But the hours of darkness passed in peace; the men who still remained at their duty toiling hard at the pumps, whose clinking and clanking at intervals through the dreary night dismally resounded through the ship.

"At sunrise the captain went forward, and knocking on the deck, summoned the prisoners to work; but with a yell they refused. Water was then lowered down to them, and a couple of handfuls of biscuit were tossed after it; when again turning the key upon them and pocketing it, the captain returned to the quarter-deck. Twice every day for three days this was repeated; but on the fourth morning a confused wrangling, and then a scuffling was heard, as the customary summons was delivered; and suddenly four men burst up from the forecastle, saying they were ready to turn to. The fetid closeness of the air, and a famishing diet, united perhaps to some fears of ultimate retribution, had constrained them to surrender at discretion. Emboldened by this, the captain reiterated his demand to the rest, but Steelkilt shouted up to him a terrific hint to stop his babbling and betake himself where he belonged. On the fifth morning three others of the mutineers bolted up into the air from the desperate arms below that sought to restrain them. Only three were left.

"'Better turn to, now?' said the captain with a heartless jeer.

"'Shut us up again, will ye!' cried Steelkilt.

"'Oh! certainly,' said the captain, and the key clicked.

"It was at this point, gentlemen, that enraged by the defection of seven of his former associates, and stung by the mocking voice that had last hailed him, and maddened by his long entombment in a place as black as the bowels of despair; it was then that Steelkilt proposed to the two Canallers, thus far apparently of one mind with him, to burst out of their hole at the next summoning of the garrison; and armed with their keen mincing knives (long, crescentic, heavy implements with a handle at each end) run amuck from the bowsprit to the taffrail; and if by any develishness of desperation possible, seize the ship. For himself, he would do this, whether they joined him or not. That was the last night he should spend in that den. But the scheme met with no opposition on the part of the other two; they swore they were ready for that, or for any other mad thing, for anything in short but a surrender. And what was more, they each insisted upon being the first man on deck, when the time to make the rush should come. But to this their leader had fiercely objected, reserving that priority for himself; particularly as his two comrades would not yield, the one to the other, in the matter; and both of them could not be first, for the ladder would but admit one man at a time. And here, gentlemen, the foul play of these miscreants must come out.

"Upon hearing the frantic project of their leader, each in his own separate soul had suddenly lighted it would seem, upon the same piece of treachery, namely: to be foremost in breaking out, in order to be the first of the three, though the last of the ten, to surrender; and thereby secure whatever small chance of pardon such conduct might merit. But when Steelkilt made known his determination still to lead them to the last, they in some way, by some subtle chemistry of villainy, mixed their before secret treacheries together; and when their leader fell into a doze, verbally opened their souls to each other in three sentences; and bound the sleeper with cords, and gagged him with cords; and shrieked out for the captain at midnight.

"Thinking murder at hand, and smelling in the dark for the blood, he and all his armed mates and harpooneers rushed for the forecastle. In a few minutes the scuttle was opened, and, bound hand and foot, the still struggling ringleader was shoved up into the air by his perfidious allies, who at once claimed the honour of securing a man who had been fully ripe for murder. But all these were collared, and dragged along the deck like dead cattle; and, side by side, were seized up into the mizzen rigging, like three quarters of meat, and there they hung till morning. 'Damn ye,' cried the captain, pacing to and fro before them, 'the vultures would not touch ye, ye villains!'

"At sunrise he summoned all hands; and separating those who had rebelled from those who had taken no part in the mutiny, he told the former that he had a good mind to flog them all round—thought, upon the whole, he would do so—he ought to—justice demanded it; but for the present, considering their timely surrender, he would let them go with a reprimand, which he accordingly administered in the vernacular.

"'But as for you, ye carrion rogues,' turning to the three men in the rigging—'for you, I mean to mince ye up for the try-pots'; and, seizing a rope, he applied it with all his might to the back of the two traitors, till they yelled no more, but lifelessly hung their heads sideways, as the two crucified thieves are drawn.

"'My wrist is sprained with ye;' he cried, at last; 'but there is still rope enough left for you, my fine bantam, that wouldn't give up. Take that gag from his mouth, and let us hear what he can say for himself.'

"For a moment the exhausted mutineer made a tremulous motion of his cramped jaws, and then painfully twisting round his head, said in a sort of hiss, 'What I say is this—and mind it well—if you flog me, I murder you!'

"'Say ye so? then see how ye frighten me'—and the captain drew off with the rope to strike.

"'Best not,' hissed the Lakeman.

"'But I must,'—and the rope was once more drawn back for the stroke.

"Steelkilt here hissed out something, inaudible to all but the captain; who, to the amazement of all hands, started back, paced the deck rapidly two or three times, and then suddenly throwing down his rope, said, 'I won't do it—let him go—cut him down: d'ye hear?'

"But as the junior mates were hurrying to execute the order, a pale man, with a bandaged head, arrested them—Radney the chief mate. Ever since the blow, he had lain in his berth; but that morning, hearing the tumult on the deck, he had crept out, and thus far had watched the whole scene. Such was the state of his mouth, that he could hardly speak; but mumbling something about *his* being willing and able to do what the captain dared not attempt, he snatched the rope and advanced to his pinioned foe.

"'You are a coward!' hissed the Lakeman.

"'So I am, but take that.' The mate was in the very act of striking, when another hiss stayed his uplifted arm. He paused: and then pausing no more, made good his word, spite of Steelkilt's threat, whatever that might have been. The three men were then cut down, all hands were turned to, and, sullenly worked by the moody seamen, the iron pumps clanged as before.

"Just after dark that day, when one watch had retired below, a clamour was heard in the forecastle; and the two trembling traitors running up, besieged the cabin door, saying they durst not consort with the crew. Entreaties, cuffs, and kicks could not drive them back, so at their own instance they were put down in the ship's run for salvation. Still, no sign of mutiny reappeared among the rest. On the contrary, it seemed, that mainly at Steelkilt's instigation, they had resolved to maintain the strictest peacefulness, obey all orders to the last, and, when the ship reached port, desert her in a body. But in order to insure the speediest end to the voyage, they all agreed to another thing—namely, not to sing out for whales, in case any should be discovered. For, spite of her leak, and spite of all her other perils, the *Town-Ho* still maintained her mast-heads, and her captain was just as willing to lower for a fish that moment, as on the day his craft first struck the cruising ground; and Radney the mate was quite as ready to change his berth for a boat, and with his bandaged mouth seek to gag in death the vital jaw of the whale.

"But though the Lakeman had induced the seamen to adopt this sort of passiveness in their conduct, he kept his own counsel (at least till all was over) concerning his own proper and private revenge upon the man who had stung him in the ventricles of his heart. He was in Radney the chief mate's watch; and as if the infatuated man sought to run more than half-way to meet his doom, after the scene at the rigging, he insisted, against the express counsel of the captain, upon resuming the head of his watch at night. Upon this, and one or two other circumstances, Steelkilt systematically built the plan of his revenge.

"During the night, Radney had an unseamanlike way of sitting on the bulwarks of the quarter-deck, and leaning his arm upon the gunwale of the boat which was hoisted up there, a little above the ship's side. In this attitude, it was well known, he sometimes dozed. There was a considerable vacancy between the boat and the ship, and down between this was the sea. Steelkilt calculated his time, and found that his next trick at the helm would come round at two o'clock, in the morning of the third day from that in which he had been betrayed. At his leisure, he employed the interval in braiding something very carefully in his watches below.

"'What are you making there?' said a shipmate.

"'What do you think? what does it look like?'

"'Like a lanyard for your bag; but it's an odd one, seems to me.'

" 'Yes, rather oddish,' said the Lakeman, holding it at arm's length before him; 'but I think it will answer. Shipmate, I haven't enough twine,—have you any?'

"But there was none in the forecastle.

" 'Then I must get some from old Rad'; and he rose to go aft.

" 'You don't mean to go begging to *him*!' said a sailor.

" 'Why not? Do you think he won't do me a turn, when it's to help himself in the end, shipmate?' and going to the mate, he looked at him quietly, and asked him for some twine to mend his hammock. It was given him—neither twine nor lanyard were seen again; but the next night an iron ball, closely netted, partly rolled from the pocket of the Lakeman's monkey jacket, as he was tucking the coat into his hammock for a pillow. Twenty-four hours after, his trick at the silent helm—nigh to the man who was apt to doze over the grave always ready dug to the seaman's hand—that fatal hour was then to come; and in the fore-ordaining soul of Steelkilt, the mate was already stark and stretched as a corpse, with his forehead crushed in.

"But, gentlemen, a fool saved the would-be murderer from the bloody deed he had planned. Yet complete revenge he had, and without being the avenger. For by a mysterious fatality, Heaven itself seemed to step in to take out of his hands into its own the damning thing he would have done.

"It was just between daybreak and sunrise of the morning of the second day, when they were washing down the decks, that a stupid Teneriffe man, drawing water in the main-chains, all at once shouted out, 'There she rolls! there she rolls!' Jesu, what a whale! It was Moby Dick.

"Now, gentlemen, so suddenly perceiving the snowy whale within fifty yards of the ship—forgetful of the compact among the crew—in the excitement of the moment, the Teneriffe man had instinctively and involuntarily lifted his voice for the monster, though for some little time past it had been plainly beheld from the three sullen mast-heads. All was now a frenzy. 'The white whale—the white whale!' was the cry from captain, mates, and harpooneers, who, undeterred by fearful rumours, were all anxious to capture so famous and precious a fish; while the dogged crew eyed askance, and with curses, the appalling beauty of the vast milky mass, that lit up by a horizontal spangling sun, shifted and glistened like a living opal in the blue morning sea. Gentlemen, a strange fatality pervades the whole career of these events, as if verily mapped out before the world was charted. The mutineer was the bowsman of the mate, and when fast to a fish, it was his duty to sit next him, while Radney stood up with his lance in the prow, and haul in or slacken the line, at the word of command. Moreover, when the four boats were lowered, the mate's got the start; and none howled more fiercely with delight than did Steelkilt, as he strained at his oar. After a stiff pull, their harpooneer got fast, and, spear in hand, Radney sprang to the bow. He was always a furious man, it seems, in a boat. And now his bandaged cry was, to beach him on the whale's topmost back. Nothing loath, his bowsman hauled him up and up, through a blinding foam that blent two whitenesses together; till of a sudden the boat struck as against a sunken ledge, and keeling over, spilled out the standing mate. That instant, as he fell on the whale's slippery back, the boat righted, and was dashed aside by the swell, while Radney was tossed over into the sea, on the other flank of the whale. He struck out through the spray, and, for an instant, was dimly seen through that veil, wildly seeking to remove himself from the eye of Moby Dick. But the whale rushed round in a sudden maelstrom; seized the swimmer between his jaws; and rearing high up with him, plunged headlong again, and went down.

"Meantime, at the first tap of the ship's bottom, the Lakeman had slackened the line, so as to drop astern from the whirlpool; calmly looking on, he thought his own thoughts. But a sudden, terrific downward jerking of the boat, quickly brought his knife to the line. He cut it; and the whale was free. But, at some distance, Moby Dick rose again, with some tatters of Radney's red woollen shirt, caught in the teeth that had destroyed him. All four boats gave chase again; but the whale eluded them, and finally wholly disappeared.

"In good time, the *Town-Ho* reached her port—a savage, solitary place—where no civilized creature resided. There, headed by the Lakeman, all but five or six of the foremast-men deliberately deserted among the palms; eventually, as it turned out, seizing a large double war-canoe of the savages, and setting sail for some other harbour.

"The ship's company being reduced to but a handful, the captain called upon the Islanders to assist him in the laborious business of heaving down the ship to stop the leak. But to such unresting vigilance over their dangerous allies was this small band of whites necessitated both by night and by day, and so extreme was the hard work they underwent, that upon the vessel being ready again for sea, they were in such a weakened condition that the captain durst not put off with them in so heavy a vessel. After taking counsel with his officers, he anchored the ship as far off shore as possible; loaded and ran out his two cannon from the bows; stacked his muskets on the poop; and warning the Islanders not to approach the ship at their peril, took one man

with him, and setting the sail of his best whale-boat, steered straight
before the wind for Tahiti, five hundred miles distant, to procure a
reinforcement to his crew.

"On the fourth day of the sail, a large canoe was descried, which
seemed to have touched at a low isle of corals. He steered away from it;
but the savage craft bore down on him; and soon the voice of Steelkilt
hailed him to heave to, or he would run him under water. The captain
presented a pistol. With one foot on each prow of the yoked war-
canoes, the Lakeman laughed him to scorn; assuring him that if the
pistol so much as clicked in the lock, he would bury him in bubbles
and foam.

"'What do you want of me?' cried the captain.

"'Where are you bound? and for what are you bound?' demanded
Steelkilt; 'no lies.'

"'I am bound to Tahiti for more men.'

"'Very good. Let me board you a moment—I come in peace.' With
that he leaped from the canoe, swam to the boat; and climbing the
gunwale, stood face to face with the captain.

"'Cross your arms, sir; throw back your head. Now, repeat after
me. As soon as Steelkilt leaves me, I swear to beach this boat on yonder
island, and remain there six days. If I do not, may lightnings strike
me!'

"'A pretty scholar,' laughed the Lakeman. 'Adios, Señor!' and
leaping into the sea, he swam back to his comrades.

"Watching the boat till it was fairly beached, and drawn up to the
roots of the coco-nut trees, Steelkilt made sail again, and in due time
arrived at Tahiti, his own place of destination. There, luck befriended
him; two ships were about to sail for France, and were providentially
in want of precisely that number of men which the sailor headed.
They embarked, and so for ever got the start of their former captain,
had he been at all minded to work them legal retribution.

"Some ten days after the French ships sailed, the whale-boat arrived,
and the captain was forced to enlist some of the more civilized Tahi-
tians, who had been somewhat used to the sea. Chartering a small
native schooner, he returned with them to his vessel; and finding all
right there, again resumed his cruisings.

"Where Steelkilt now is, gentlemen, none know; but upon the
island of Nantucket, the widow of Radney still turns to the sea which
refuses to give up its dead; still in dreams sees the awful white whale
that destroyed him. * * * *

"'Are you through?' said Don Sebastian, quietly.

"'I am, Don.'

F

" 'Then I entreat you, tell me if to the best of your own convictions, this your story is in substance really true? It is so passing wonderful! Did you get it from an unquestionable source? Bear with me if I seem to press.'

" 'Also bear with all of us, sir sailor; for we all join in Don Sebastian's suit,' cried the company, with exceeding interest.

" 'Is there a copy of the Holy Evangelists in the Golden Inn, gentlemen?'

" 'Nay,' said Don Sebastian; 'but I know a worthy priest near by, who will quickly procure one for me. I go for it; but are you well advised? this may grow too serious.'

" 'Will you be so good as to bring the priest also, Don?'

" 'Though there are no Auto-da-Fés in Lima now,' said one of the company to another; 'I fear our sailor friend runs risk of the archiepiscopacy. Let us withdraw more out of the moonlight. I see no need of this.'

" 'Excuse me for running after you, Don Sebastian; but may I also beg that you will be particular in procuring the largest sized Evangelists you can.'

.   .   .   .   .

" 'This is the priest, he brings you the Evangelists,' said Don Sebastian, gravely, returning with a tall and solemn figure.

" 'Let me remove my hat. Now, venerable priest, further into the light, and hold the Holy Book before me that I may touch it.

" 'So help me Heaven, and on my honour the story I have told ye, gentlemen, is in substance and its great items, true. I know it to be true; it happened on this ball; I trod the ship; I knew the crew; I have seen and talked with Steelkilt since the death of Radney.' "

CHAPTER 46

BRIT

STEERING north-eastward from the Crozetts, we fell in with vast meadows of brit, the minute, yellow substance, upon which the Right whale largely feeds. For leagues and leagues it undulated round us, so that we seemed to be sailing through boundless fields of ripe and golden wheat.

On the second day, numbers of Right whales were seen, who, secure from the attack of a sperm-whaler like the *Pequod*, with open jaws sluggishly swam through the brit, which, adhering to the fringing fibres of that wondrous Venetian blind in their mouths, was in that manner separated from the water that escaped at the lip.

As morning mowers, who side by side slowly and seethingly advance their scythes through the long wet grass of marshy meads; even so these monsters swam, making a strange, grassy, cutting sound; and leaving behind them endless swaths of blue upon the yellow sea.[1]

But it was only the sound they made as they parted the brit which at all reminded one of mowers. Seen from the mast-heads, especially when they paused and were stationary for a while, their vast black forms looked more like lifeless masses of rock than anything else. And as in the great hunting countries of India, the stranger at a distance will sometimes pass on the plains recumbent elephants without knowing them to be such, taking them for bare, blackened elevations of the soil, even so, often, with him, who for the first time beholds this species of the leviathans of the sea. And even when recognized at last, their immense magnitude renders it very hard really to believe that such bulky masses of overgrowth can possibly be instinct, in all parts, with the same sort of life that lives in a dog or a horse.

Indeed, in other respects, you can hardly regard any creatures of the deep with the same feelings that you do those of the shore. For though some old naturalists have maintained that all creatures of the land are of their kind in the sea; and though taking a broad general view of the thing, this may very well be; yet coming to specialities, where, for example, does the ocean furnish any fish that in disposition answers to the sagacious kindness of the dog? The accursed shark alone can in any generic respect be said to bear comparative analogy to him.

CHAPTER 47

SQUID

SLOWLY WADING through the meadows of brit, the *Pequod* still held on her way north-eastward towards the island of Java; a gentle air impelling her keel, so that in the surrounding serenity her three tall tapering masts mildly waved to that languid breeze, as three mild palms on a plain. And still, at wide intervals in the silvery night, the lonely, alluring jet would be seen.

[1] That part of the sea known among whalemen as the "Brazil Banks" does not bear that name as the Banks of Newfoundland do, because of there being shallows and soundings there, but because of this remarkable meadowlike appearance, caused by the vast drifts of brit continually floating in those latitudes, where the Right whale is often chased.

But one transparent blue morning, when stillness almost preternatural spread over the sea, however unattended with any stagnant calm; when the long burnished sun-glade on the waters seemed a golden finger laid across them, enjoying some secrecy; when the slippered waves whispered together as they softly ran on; in this profound hush of the visible sphere a strange spectre was seen by Daggoo from the main-mast-head.

In the distance, a great white mass lazily rose, and rising higher and higher, and disentangling itself from the azure, at last gleamed before our prow like a snow-slide, new slid from the hills. Thus glistening for a moment, as slowly it subsided, and sank. Then once more arose, and silently gleamed. It seemed not a whale; and yet is this Moby Dick? thought Daggoo. Again the phantom went down, but on reappearing once more, with a stiletto-like cry that startled every man from his nod, the negro yelled out—"There! there again! there she breaches! right ahead! The white whale, the white whale!"

Upon this, the seamen rushed to the yard-arms, as in swarming-time the bees rush to the boughs. Bare-headed in the sultry sun, Ahab stood on the bowsprit, and with one hand pushed far behind in readiness to wave his orders to the helmsman, cast his eager glance in the direction indicated aloft by the outstretched motionless arm of Daggoo.

Whether the flitting attendance of the one still and solitary jet had gradually worked upon Ahab, so that he was now prepared to connect the ideas of mildness and repose with the first sight of the particular whale he pursued; however this was, or whether his eagerness betrayed him; whichever way it might have been, no sooner did he distinctly perceive the white mass, than with a quick intensity he instantly gave orders for lowering.

The four boats were soon on the water; Ahab's in advance, and all swiftly pulling towards their prey. Soon it went down, and while, with oars suspended, we were awaiting its reappearance, lo! in the same spot where it sank, once more it slowly rose. Almost forgetting for the moment all thoughts of Moby Dick, we now gazed at the most wondrous phenomenon which the secret seas have hitherto revealed to mankind. A vast pulpy mass, furlongs in length and breadth, of a glancing cream-colour, lay floating on the water, innumerable long arms radiating from its centre, and curling and twisting like a nest of anacondas, as if blindly to catch at any hapless object within reach. No perceptible face or front did it have; no conceivable token of either sensation or instinct; but undulated there on the billows, an unearthly, formless, chance-like apparition of life.

As with a low sucking sound it slowly disappeared again, Starbuck still gazing at the agitated waters where it had sunk, with a wild voice exclaimed—"Almost rather had I seen Moby Dick and fought him, than to have seen thee, thou white ghost!"

"What was it, sir?" said Flask.

"The great live squid, which, they say, few whale-ships ever beheld, and returned to their ports to tell of it."

But Ahab said nothing; turning his boat, he sailed back to the vessel; the rest as silently following.

Whatever superstitions the sperm-whalemen in general have connected with the sight of this object, certain it is, that a glimpse of it being so very unusual, that circumstance has gone far to invest it with portentousness. So rarely is it beheld, that though one and all of them declare it to be the largest animated thing in the ocean, yet very few of them have any but the most vague ideas concerning its true nature and form; nothwithstanding, they believe it to furnish to the sperm-whale his only food. For though other species of whales find their food above water, and may be seen by man in the act of feeding, the spermaceti whale obtains his whole food in unknown zones below the surface; and only by inference is it that any one can tell of what, precisely, that food consists. At times, when closely pursued, he will disgorge what are supposed to be the detached arms of the squid; some of them thus exhibited exceeding twenty and thirty feet in length. They fancy that the monster to which these arms belonged ordinarily clings by them to the bed of the ocean; and that the sperm-whale, unlike other species, is supplied with teeth in order to attack and tear it.

There seems some ground to imagine that the great Kraken of Bishop Pontoppodan may ultimately resolve itself into Squid. The manner in which the Bishop describes it, as alternatively rising and sinking, with some other particulars he narrates, in all this the two correspond. But much abatement is necessary with respect to the incredible bulk he assigns it.

By some naturalists who have vaguely heard rumours of the mysterious creature, here spoken of, it is included among the class of cuttlefish, to which, indeed, in certain external respects it would seem to belong, but only as the Anak of the tribe.

CHAPTER 48

THE LINE

WITH REFERENCE to the whaling scene shortly to be described, as well as for the better understanding of all similar scenes elsewhere presented, I have here to speak of the magical, sometimes horrible whale-line.

The line originally used in the fishery was of the best hemp, slightly vapoured with tar, not impregnated with it, as in the case of ordinary ropes; for while tar, as ordinarily used, makes the hemp more pliable to the rope-maker, and also renders the rope itself more convenient to the sailor for common ship use; yet, not only would the ordinary quantity too much stiffen the whale-line for the close coiling to which it must be subjected; but as most seamen are beginning to learn, tar in general by no means adds to the rope's durability or strength, however much it may give it compactness and gloss.

Of late years the Manilla rope has in the American fishery almost entirely superseded hemp as a material for whale-lines; for, though not so durable as hemp, it is stronger, and far more soft and elastic; and I will add (since there is an æsthetics in all things), is much more handsome and becoming to the boat, than hemp. Hemp is a dusky dark fellow, a sort of Indian; but Manilla is as a golden-haired Circassian to behold.

The whale-line is only two thirds of an inch in thickness. At first sight, you would not think it so strong as it really is. By experiment its one and fifty yarns will each suspend a weight of one hundred and twenty pounds; so that the whole rope will bear a strain nearly equal to three tons. In length, the common sperm-whale-line measures something over two hundred fathoms. Towards the stern of the boat it is spirally coiled away in the tub, not like the worm-pipe of a still though, but so as to form one round, cheese-shaped mass of densely bedded "sheaves", or layers of concentric spiralizations, without any hollow but the "heart", or minute vertical tube formed at the axis of the cheese. As the least tangle or kink in the coiling would, in running out, infallibly take somebody's arm, leg, or entire body off, the utmost precaution is used in stowing the line in its tub. Some harpooneers will consume almost an entire morning in this business, carrying the line high aloft and then reeving it downwards through a block towards the tub, so as in the act of coiling to free it from all possible wrinkles and twists.

In the English boats two tubs are used instead of one; the same line being continuously coiled in both tubs. There is some advantage in this; because these twin-tubs being so small they fit more readily into the boat, and do not strain it so much; whereas, the American tub, nearly three feet in diameter and of proportionate depth, makes a rather bulky freight for a craft whose planks are but one half-inch in thickness; for the bottom of the whale-boat is like critical ice, which will bear up a considerable distributed weight, but not very much of a concentrated one. When the painted canvas cover is clapped on the American tub-line, the boat looks as if it were pulling off with a prodigious great wedding-cake to present to the whales.

Both ends of the line are exposed; the lower end terminating in an eye-splice or loop coming up from the bottom against the side of the tub, and hanging over its edge completely disengaged from everything. This arrangement of the lower end is necessary on two accounts. First: In order to facilitate the fastening to it of an additional line from a neighbouring boat, in case the stricken whale should sound so deep as to threaten to carry off the entire line originally attached to the harpoon. In these instances, the whale of course is shifted like a mug of ale, as it were, from the one boat to the other; though the first boat always hovers at hand to assist its consort. Second: This arrangement is indispensable for common safety's sake; for were the lower end of the line in any way attached to the boat, and were the whale then to run the line out to the end almost in a single, smoking minute as he sometimes does, he would not stop there, for the doomed boat would infallibly be dragged down after him into the profundity of the sea; and in that case no town-crier would ever find her again.

Before lowering the boat for the chase, the upper end of the line is taken aft from the tub, and passing round the loggerhead there, is again carried forward the entire length of the boat, resting crosswise upon the loom or handle of every man's oar, so that it jogs against his wrist in rowing; and also passing between the men, as they alternately sit at the opposite gunwales, to the leaded chocks or grooves in the extreme pointed prow of the boat, where a wooden pin or skewer the size of a common quill, prevents it from slipping out. From the chocks it hangs in a slight festoon over the bows, and is then passed inside the boat again; and some ten or twenty fathoms (called box-line) being coiled upon the box in the bows, it continues its way to the gunwale till a little further aft, and is then attached to the short-warp—the rope which is immediately connected with the harpoon; but previous to that connexion, the short-warp goes through sundry mystifications too tedious to detail.

Thus the whale-line folds the whole boat in its complicated coils, twisting and writhing around it in almost every direction. All the oarsmen are involved in its perilous contortions; so that to the timid eye of the landsman, they seem as Indian jugglers, with the deadliest snakes sportively festooning their limbs. Nor can any son of mortal man, for the first time, seat himself amid those hempen intricacies, and while straining his utmost at the oar, bethink him that at any unknown instant the harpoon may be darted, and all these horrible contortions be put in play like ringed lightnings; he cannot be thus circumstanced without a shudder that makes the very marrow in his bones to quiver in him like a shaken jelly. Yet habit—strange thing! what cannot habit accomplish?—Gayer sallies, more merry mirth, better jokes, and brighter repartees, you never heard over your mahogany than you will hear over the half-inch white cedar of the whale-boat when thus hung in hangman's nooses; and, like the six burghers of Calais before King Edward, the six men composing the crew pull into the jaws of death, with a halter around every neck, as you may say.

Perhaps a very little thought will now enable you to account for those repeated whaling disasters—some few of which are casually chronicled—of this man or that man being taken out of the boat by the line, and lost. For, when the line is darting out, to be seated then in the boat, is like being seated in the midst of the manifold whizzing of a steam engine in full play, when every flying beam, and shaft, and wheel, is grazing you. It is worse; for you cannot sit motionless in the heart of these perils, because the boat is rocking like a cradle, and you are pitched one way and the other, without the slightest warning; and only by a certain self-adjusting buoyancy and simultaneousness of volition and action, can you escape being made a Mazeppa of, and run away with where the all seeing sun himself could never pierce you out.

Again: as the profound calm which only apparently precedes and prophesies of the storm, is perhaps more awful than the storm itself; for, indeed, the calm is but the wrapper and envelope of the storm; and contains it in itself, as the seemingly harmless rifle holds the fatal powder, and the ball, and the explosion; so the graceful repose of the line, as it silently serpentines about the oarsmen before being brought into actual play—this is a thing which carries more of true terror than any other aspect of this dangerous affair. But why say more? All men live enveloped in whale-lines. All are born with halters round their necks; but it is only when caught in the swift, sudden turn of death, that mortals realize the silent, subtle, ever-present perils of life. And if you be a philosopher, though seated in the whale-boat, you would not at heart feel one whit more of terror, than though seated before your evening fire with a poker, and not a harpoon, by your side.

CHAPTER 49

STUBB KILLS A WHALE

IF TO Starbuck the apparition of the Squid was a thing of portents, to Queequeg it was quite a different object.

"When you see him 'quid," said the savage, honing his harpoon in the bow of his hoisted boat, "then you quick see him 'parm whale."

The next day was exceedingly still and sultry, and with nothing special to engage them, the *Pequod*'s crew could hardly resist the spell of sleep induced by such a vacant sea. For this part of the Indian Ocean through which we then were voyaging is not what whalemen call a lively ground; that is, it affords fewer glimpses of porpoises, dolphins, flying-fish, and other vivacious denizens of more stirring waters, than those off the Rio de la Plata, or the in-shore ground off Peru.

It was my turn to stand at the fore-mast-head; and with my shoulders leaning against the slackened royal shrouds, to and fro I idly swayed in what seemed an enchanted air. No resolution could withstand it; in that dreamy mood losing all consciousness, at last my soul went out of my body; though my body still continued to sway, as a pendulum will, long after the power which first moved it is withdrawn.

Ere forgetfulness altogether came over me, I had noticed that the seamen at the main and mizzen-mastheads were already drowsy. So that at last all three of us lifelessly swung from the spars, and for every swing that we made there was a nod from below from the slumbering helmsman. The waves, too, nodded their indolent crests; and across the wide trance of the sea, east nodded to west, and the sun over all.

Suddenly bubbles seemed bursting beneath my closed eyes; like vices my hands grasped the shrouds; some invisible, gracious agency preserved me; with a shock I came back to life. And lo! close under our lee, not forty fathoms off, a gigantic sperm-whale lay rolling in the water like the capsized hull of a frigate, his broad, glossy back, of an Ethiopian hue, glistened in the sun's rays like a mirror. But lazily undulating in the trough of the sea, and ever and anon tranquilly spouting his vapoury jet, the whale looked like a portly burgher smoking his pipe of a warm afternoon. But that pipe, poor whale, was thy last. As if struck by some enchanter's wand, the sleepy ship and every sleeper in it all at once started into wakefulness; and more than a score of voices from all parts of the vessel, simultaneously with the three notes from aloft, shouted forth the accustomed cry, as the great fish slowly and regularly spouted the sparkling brine into the air.

"Clear away the boats! Luff!" cried Ahab. And obeying his own order, he dashed the helm down before the helmsman could handle the spokes.

The sudden exclamations of the crew must have alarmed the whale; and ere the boats were down, majestically turning, he swam away to the leeward, but with such a steady tranquillity, and making so few ripples as he swam, that thinking after all he might not as yet be alarmed, Ahab gave orders that not an oar should be used, and no man must speak but in whispers. So seated like Ontario Indians on the gunwales of the boats, we swiftly but silently paddled along; the calm not admitting of the noiseless sails being set. Presently, as we thus glided in chase, the monster perpendicularly flitted his tail forty feet into the air, and then sank out of sight like a tower swallowed up.

"There go flukes!" was the cry, an announcement immediately followed by Stubb's producing his match and igniting his pipe, for now a respite was granted. After the full interval of his sounding had elapsed, the whale rose again, and being now in advance of the smoker's boat, and much nearer to it than to any of the others, Stubb counted upon the honour of the capture. It was obvious, now, that the whale had at length become aware of his pursuers. All silence of cautiousness was therefore no longer of use. Paddles were dropped, and oars came loudly into play. And still puffing at his pipe, Stubb cheered on his crew to the assault.

Yes, a mighty change had come over the fish. All alive to his jeopardy, he was going "head out"; that part obliquely projecting from the mad yeast which he brewed.[1]

"Start her, start her, my men! Don't hurry yourselves; take plenty of time—but start her; start her like thunder-claps, that's all," cried Stubb, spluttering out the smoke as he spoke. "Start her, now; give 'ein the long and strong stroke, Tashtego. Start her, Tash, my boy— start her, all; but keep cool, keep cool—cucumbers is the word—easy, easy—only start her like grim death and grinning devils, and raise the

[1] It will be seen in some other place of what a very light substance the entire interior of the sperm-whale's enormous head consists. Though apparently the most massive, it is by far the most buoyant part about him. So that with ease he elevates it in the air, and invariably does so when going at his utmost speed. Besides, such is the breadth of the upper part of the front of his head, and such the tapering cut-water formation of the lower part, that by obliquely elevating his head, he thereby may be said to transform himself from a bluff-bowed sluggish galliot into a sharp-pointed New York pilot-boat.

buried dead perpendicular out of their graves, boys—that's all. Start her!"

"Woo-hoo! Wa-hee!" screamed the Gay-Header in reply, raising some old war-whoop to the skies; as every oarsman in the strained boat involuntarily bounced forward with the one tremendous leading stroke which the eager Indian gave.

But his wild screams were answered by others quite as wild. "Khee-hee! Khee-hee!" yelled Daggoo, straining forwards and backwards on his seat, like a pacing tiger in his cage.

"Ka-la! Koo-loo!" howled Queequeg, as if smacking his lips over a mouthful of Grenadier's steak. And thus with oars and yells the keels cut the sea. Meanwhile Stubb, retaining his place in the van, still encouraged his men to the onset, all the while puffing the smoke from his mouth. Like desperadoes they tugged and they strained, till the welcome cry was heard—"Stand up, Tashtego!—give it to him!" The harpoon was hurled. "Stern all!" The oarsmen backed water; the same moment something went hot and hissing along every one of their wrists. It was the magical line. An instant before, Stubb had swiftly caught two additional turns with it round the loggerhead, whence, by reason of its increased rapid circlings, a hempen blue smoke now jetted up and mingled with the steady fumes from his pipe. As the line passed round and round the loggerhead; so also, just before reaching that point, it blisteringly passed through and through both of Stubb's hands, from which the hand-cloths, or squares of quilted canvas sometimes worn at these times, had accidentally dropped. It was like holding an enemy's sharp two-edged sword by the blade, and that enemy all the time striving to wrest it out of your clutch.

"Wet the line! wet the line!" cried Stubb to the tub oarsman (him seated by the tub) who, snatching off his hat, dashed the sea-water into it.[1] More turns were taken, so that the line began holding its place. The boat now flew through the boiling water like a shark all fins. Stubb and Tashtego here changed places—stem for stern—a staggering business truly in that rocking commotion.

From the vibrating line extending the entire length of the upper part of the boat, and from its now being more tight than a harpstring, you would have thought the craft had two keels—one cleaving the water, the other the air—as the boat churned on through both opposing elements at once. A continual cascade played at the bows; a ceaseless

[1] Partly to show the indispensableness of this act, it may here be stated, that, in the old Dutch fishery, a mop was used to dash the running line with water; in many other ships, a wooden piggin, or bailer, is set apart for that purpose. Your hat, however, is the most convenient.

whirling eddy in her wake; and, at the slightest motion from within, even but of a little finger, the vibrating, cracking craft canted over her spasmodic gunwale into the sea. Thus they rushed; each man with might and main clinging to his seat, to prevent being tossed to the foam; and the tall form of Tashtego at the steering oar crouching almost double, in order to bring down his centre of gravity. Whole Atlantics and Pacifics seemed passed as they shot on their way, till at length the whale somewhat slackened his flight.

"Haul in—haul in!" cried Stubb to the bowsman! and, facing round towards the whale, all hands began pulling the boat up to him, while yet the boat was being towed on. Soon ranging up by his flank, Stubb, firmly planting his knee in the clumsy cleat, darted dart after dart into the flying fish; at the word of command, the boat alternately sterning out of the way of the whale's horrible wallow, and then ranging up for another fling.

The red tide now poured from all sides of the monster like brooks down a hill. His tormented body rolled not in brine but in blood, which bubbled and seethed for furlongs behind in their wake. The slanting sun playing upon this crimson pond in the sea, sent back its reflection into every face, so that they all glowed to each other like red men. And all the while, jet after jet of white smoke was agonizingly shot from the spiracle of the whale, and vehement puff after puff from the mouth of the excited headsman; as at every dart, hauling in upon his crooked lance (by the line attached to it), Stubb straightened it again and again, by a few rapid blows against the gunwale, then again and again sent it into the whale.

"Pull up—pull up!" he now cried to the bowsman, as the waning whale relaxed in his wrath. "Pull up!—close to!" and the boat ranged along the fish's flank. When reaching far over the bow, Stubb slowly churned his long sharp lance into the fish, and kept it there, carefully churning and churning, as if cautiously seeking to feel after some gold watch that the whale might have swallowed, and which he was fearful of breaking ere he could hook it out. But that gold watch he sought was the innermost life of the fish. And now it is struck; for, starting from his trance into that unspeakable thing called his "flurry," the monster horribly wallowed in his blood, overwrapped himself in impenetrable, mad, boiling spray, so that the imperilled craft, instantly dropping astern, had much ado blindly to struggle out from that phrensied twilight into the clear air of the day.

And now abating in his flurry, the whale once more rolled out into view; surging from side to side; spasmodically dilating and contracting his spout-hole, with sharp, cracking, agonized respirations. At last, gush after gush of clotted red gore, as if it had been the purple lees of red wine, shot into the frighted air; and falling back again, ran dripping down his motionless flanks into the sea. His heart had burst!

"He's dead, Mr. Stubb," said Daggoo.

"Yes; both pipes smoked out!" and withdrawing his own from his mouth, Stubb scattered the dead ashes over the water; and, for a moment, stood thoughtfully eyeing the vast corpse he had made.

CHAPTER 50

THE DART

A WORD concerning an incident in the last chapter.

According to the invariable usage of the fishery, the whale-boat pushes off from the ship, with the headsman or whale-killer as temporary steersman, and the harpooneer or whale-fastener pulling the foremost oar, the one known as the harpooneer-oar. Now it needs a strong, nervous arm to strike the first iron into the fish; for often, in what is called a long dart, the heavy implement has to be flung to the distance of twenty or thirty feet. But however prolonged and exhausting the chase, the harpooneer is expected to pull his oar meanwhile to the uttermost; indeed, he is expected to set an example of superhuman activity to the rest, not only by incredible rowing, but by repeated loud and intrepid exclamations; and what it is to keep shouting at the top of one's compass, while all the other muscles are strained and half started—what that is none know but those who have tried it. For one, I cannot bawl very heartily and work very recklessly at one and the same time. In this straining, bawling state, then, with his back to the fish, all at once the exhausted harpooneer hears the exciting cry—"Stand up, and give it to him!" He now has to drop and secure his oar, turn round on his centre half way, seize his harpoon from the crotch, and with what little strength may remain, he assays to pitch it somehow into the whale. No wonder, taking the whole fleet of whalemen in a body, that out of fifty fair chances for a dart, not five are successful; no wonder that so many hapless harpooneers are madly cursed and disrated; no wonder that some of them actually burst their blood-vessels in the boat; no wonder that some sperm-whalemen are absent four years with four barrels; no wonder that to many ship owners, whaling is but a losing concern; for it is the harpooneer that makes the voyage, and if you take the breath out of his body how can you expect to find it there when most wanted!

Again, if the dart be successful, then at the second critical instant, that is, when the whale starts to run, the boat-header and harpooneer likewise start to running fore and aft, to the imminent jeopardy of themselves and everyone else. It is then they change places; and the headsman, the chief officer of the little craft, takes his proper station in the bows of the boat.

Now, I care not who maintains the contrary, but all this is both foolish and unnecessary. The headsman should stay in the bows from first to last; he should both dart the harpoon and the lance, and no rowing whatever should be expected of him, except under circumstances obvious to any fisherman. I know that this would sometimes involve a slight loss of speed in the chase; but long experience in various whalemen of more than one nation has convinced me that in the vast majority of failures in the fishery, it has not by any means been so much the speed of the whale as the before described exhaustion of the harpooneer that has caused them.

To insure the greatest efficiency in the dart, the harpooneers of this world must start to their feet from out of idleness, and not from out of toil.

CHAPTER 51

THE CROTCH

OUT OF the trunk, the branches grow; out of them, the twigs. So, in productive subjects, grow the chapters.

The crotch alluded to on a previous page deserves independent mention. It is a notched stick of a peculiar form, some two feet in length, which is perpendicularly inserted into the starboard gunwale near the bow, for the purpose of furnishing a rest for the wooden extremity of the harpoon, whose other naked, barbed end slopingly projects from the prow. Thereby the weapon is instantly at hand to its hurler, who snatches it up as readily from its rest as a backwoodsman swings his rifle from the wall. It is customary to have two harpoons reposing in the crotch, respectively called the first and second irons.

But these two harpoons, each by its own cord, are both connected with the line; the object being this: to dart them both, if possible, one instantly after the other into the same whale; so that if, in the coming drag, one should draw out, the other may still retain a hold. It is a doubling of the chances. But it very often happens that owing to the instantaneous, violent, convulsive running of the whale upon receiving the first iron, it becomes impossible for the harpooneer, however lightning-like in his movements, to pitch the second iron into him. Nevertheless, as the second iron is already connected with the line, and the line is running, hence that weapon must, at all events, be anticipatingly tossed out of the boat, somehow and somewhere; else the most terrible jeopardy would involve all hands. Tumbled into the water, it accordingly is in such cases; the spare coils of box line (mentioned in a preceding chapter) making this feat, in most instances, prudently practicable. But this critical act is not always unattended with the saddest and most fatal casualties.

Furthermore: you must know that when the second iron is thrown overboard, it thenceforth becomes a dangling, sharp-edged terror, skittishly curvetting about both boat and whale, entangling the lines, or cutting them, and making a prodigious sensation in all directions. Nor, in general, is it possible to secure it again until the whale it fairly captured and a corpse.

Consider, now, how it must be in the case of four boats all engaging one unusually strong, active, and knowing whale; when owing to these qualities in him, as well as to the thousand concurring accidents of such an audacious enterprise, eight or ten loose second irons may be simultaneously dangling about him. For, of course, each boat is supplied with several harpoons to bend on to the line should the first one be ineffectually darted without recovery. All these particulars are faithfully narrated here, as they will not fail to elucidate several most important, however intricate, passages in scenes hereafter to be painted.

CHAPTER 52

STUBB'S SUPPER

STUBB'S WHALE had been killed some distance from the ship. It was a calm; so, forming a tandem of three boats, we commenced the slow business of towing the trophy to the *Pequod*. And now, as we eighteen men with our thirty-six arms, and one hundred and eighty thumbs and fingers, slowly toiled hour after hour upon that inert, sluggish corpse in the sea; and it seemed hardly to budge at all, except at long intervals; good evidence was hereby furnished of the enormousness of the mass we moved. For, upon the great canal of Hang-Ho, or whatever they call it, in China, four or five labourers on the footpath will draw a bulky freighted junk at the rate of a mile an hour; but this grand argosy we towed heavily forged along, as if laden with pig-lead in bulk.

Darkness came on; but three lights up and down in the *Pequod's* main-rigging dimly guided our way; till drawing nearer we saw Ahab dropping one of several more lanterns over the bulwarks. Vacantly eyeing the heaving whale for a moment, he issued the usual orders for securing it for the night, and then handing his lantern to a seaman, went his way into the cabin, and did not come forward again until morning.

Though, in overseeing the pursuit of this whale, Captain Ahab had evinced his customary activity, to call it so; yet now that the creature was dead, some vague dissatisfaction, or impatience, or despair, seemed working in him; as if the sight of that dead body reminded him that Moby Dick was yet to be slain; and though a thousand other whales were brought to his ship, all that would not one jot advance his grand, monomaniac object. Very soon you would have thought from the sound on the *Pequod's* decks, that all hands were preparing to cast anchor in the deep; for heavy chains are being dragged along the deck, and thrust rattling out of the port-holes. But by those clanking links, the vast corpse itself, not the ship, is to be moored. Tied by the head to the stern, and by the tail to the bows, the whale now lies with its black hull close to the vessel's, and seen through the darkness of the night, which obscured the spars and rigging aloft, the two—ship and whale, seemed yoked together like colossal bullocks, whereof one reclines while the other remains standing.[1]

If moody Ahab was now all quiescence, at least so far as he could be known on deck, Stubb, his second mate, flushed with conquest, betrayed an unusual but still good-natured excitement. Such an unwonted bustle was he in that the staid Starbuck, his official superior, quietly resigned to him for the time the sole management of affairs. One small, helping cause of all this liveliness in Stubb, was soon made strangely manifest. Stubb was a high liver; he was somewhat intemperately fond of the whale as a flavourish thing to his palate.

"A steak, a steak, ere I sleep! You Daggoo! overboard you go, and cut me one from his small!"

[1] A little item may as well be related here. The strongest and most reliable hold which the ship has upon the whale when moored alongside, is by the flukes or tail; and as from its greater density that part is relatively heavier than any other (excepting the side-fins), its flexibility even in death, causes it to sink low beneath the surface; so that with the hand you cannot get at it from the boat, in order to put the chain round it. But this difficulty is ingeniously overcome: a small, strong line is prepared with a wooden float at its outer end, and a weight at its middle, while the other end is secured to the ship. By adroit management the wooden float is made to rise on the other side of the mass, so that now having girdled the whale, the chain is readily made to follow suit; and being slipped along the body, is at last locked fast round the smallest part of the tail, at the point of junction with its broad flukes or lobes.

Here be it known, that though these wild fishermen do not, as a general thing, and according to the great military maxim, make the enemy defray the current expenses of the war (at least before realizing the proceeds of the voyage), yet now and then you find some of these Nantucketers who have a genuine relish for that particular part of the sperm-whale designated by Stubb; comprising the tapering extremity of the body.

About midnight that steak was cut and cooked; and lighted by two lanterns of sperm oil, Stubb stoutly stood up to his spermaceti supper at the capstan-board, as if that capstan-head were a side-board. Nor was Stubb the only banqueter on whale's flesh that night. Mingling their mumblings with his own mastications, thousands on thousands of sharks, swarming round the dead leviathan, smackingly feasted on its fatness. The few sleepers below in their bunks were often startled by the sharp slapping of their tails against the hull, within a few inches of the sleepers' hearts. Peering over the side you could just see them (as before you heard them) wallowing in the sullen, black waters, and turning over on their backs as they scooped out huge globular pieces of the whale of the bigness of a human head. This particular feat of the shark seems all but miraculous. How, at such an apparently unassailable surface, they contrive to gouge out such symmetrical mouthfuls, remains a part of the universal problem of all things. The mark they thus leave on the whale, may best be likened to the hollow made by a carpenter in counter-sinking for a screw.

Though amid all the smoking horror and diabolism of a sea-fight, sharks will be seen longingly gazing up to the ship's decks, like hungry dogs round a table where red meat is being carved, ready to bolt down every killed man that is tossed to them; and though, while the valiant butchers over the deck-table are thus cannibally carving each other's live meat with carving-knives all gilded and tasselled, the sharks, also, with their jewel-hilted mouths, are quarrelsomely carving away under the table at the dead meat; and though, were you to turn the whole affair upside down, it would still be pretty much the same thing, that is to say, a shocking sharkish business enough for all parties; and though sharks also are the invariable outriders of slave-ships crossing the Atlantic, systematically trotting alongside, to be handy in case a parcel is to be carried anywhere, or a dead slave to be decently buried; and though one or two other like instances might be set down, touching the set terms, places, and occasions, when sharks do most socially congregate, and most hilariously feast; yet is there no conceivable time or occasion when you will find them in such countless numbers, and in gayer or more jovial spirits, than around a dead sperm-whale, moored by night to a whale-ship at sea. If you have never seen that sight, then suspend your decision about the propriety of devil-worship, and the expediency of conciliating the devil.

But, as yet, Stubb heeded not the mumblings of the banquet that was going on so nigh him, no more than the sharks heeded the smacking of his own epicurean lips.

CHAPTER 53

THE SHARK MASSACRE

WHEN IN the Southern Fishery, a captured sperm-whale, after long and weary toil, is brought alongside late at night, it is not, as a general thing at least, customary to proceed at once to the business of cutting him in. For that business is an exceedingly laborious one; is not very soon completed; and requires all hands to set about it. Therefore, the common usage is to take in all sail; lash the helm a'lee; and then send everyone below to his hammock till daylight, with the reservation that, until that time, anchor-watches shall be kept; that is, two and two for an hour, each couple, the crew in rotation shall mount the deck to see that all goes well.

But sometimes, especially upon the Line in the Pacific, this plan will not answer at all; because such incalculable hosts of sharks gather round the moored carcase, that were he left so for six hours, say, on a stretch, little more than the skeleton would be visible by morning. In most other parts of the ocean, however, where these fish do not so largely abound, their wondrous voracity can be at times considerably diminished, by vigorously stirring them up with sharp whaling-spades, a procedure notwithstanding, which, in some instances, only seems to tickle them into still greater activity. But it was not thus in the present case with the *Pequod*'s sharks; though, to be sure, any man unaccustomed to such sights, to have looked over her side that night, would have almost thought the whole round sea was one huge cheese, and those sharks the maggots in it.

Nevertheless, upon Stubb setting the anchor-watch after his supper was concluded; and when, accordingly, Queequeg and a forecastle seaman came on deck, no small excitement was created among the sharks; for immediately suspending the cutting stages over the side, and lowering three lanterns, so that they cast long gleams of light over the turbid sea, these two mariners, darting their long whaling-spades, kept up an incessant murdering of the sharks,[1] by striking the keen steel deep into their skulls, seemingly their only vital part. But in the foamy confusion of their mixed and struggling hosts, the marksmen could not always hit their mark; and this brought about new revelations of the incredible ferocity of the foe. They viciously snapped, not only at each other's disembowelments, but like flexible bows, bent round, and bit their own; till those entrails seemed swallowed over and over again by the same mouth, to be oppositely voided by the gaping wound. Nor was this all. It was unsafe to meddle with the corpses and ghosts of these creatures. A sort of generic or Pantheistic vitality seemed to lurk in their very joints and bones, after what might be called the individual life had departed. Killed and hoisted on deck for the sake of his skin, one of these sharks almost took poor Queequeg's hand off, when he tried to shut down the dead lid of his murderous jaw.

"Queequeg no care what god made him shark," said the savage, agonizingly lifting his hand up and down; "wedder Fejee god or Nantucket god; but de god wat made shark must be one dam Ingin."

CHAPTER 54

CUTTING IN

IT was a Saturday night, and such a Sabbath as followed! *Ex officio* professors of Sabbath breaking are all whalemen. The ivory *Pequod* was turned into what seemed a shamble; every sailor a butcher. You would have thought we were offering up ten thousand red oxen to the sea gods.

In the first place, the enormous cutting tackles, among other ponderous things comprising a cluster of blocks generally painted green, and which no single man can possibly lift—this vast bunch of grapes was swayed up to the main-top and firmly lashed to the lower mast-head, the strongest point anywhere above a ship's deck. The end of the hawser-like rope winding through these intricacies, was then conducted to the windlass, and the huge lower block of the tackles was swung over the whale; to this block the great blubber hook, weighing some one hundred pounds, was attached. And now suspended in stages over

[1] The whaling-spade used for cutting-in is made of the very best steel; is about the bigness of a man's spread hand; and in general shape, corresponds to the garden implement after which it is named; only its sides are perfectly flat, and its upper end considerably narrower than the lower. This weapon is always kept as sharp as possible; and when being used is occasionally honed, just like a razor. In its socket, a stiff pole, from twenty to thirty feet long, is inserted for a handle.

the side, Starbuck and Stubb, the mates, armed with their long spades, began cutting a hole in the body for the insertion of the hook just above the nearest of the two side-fins. This done, a broad, semi-circular line is cut round the hole, the hook is inserted, and the main body of the crew striking up a wild chorus, now commence heaving in one dense crowd at the windlass. When instantly, the entire ship careens over on her side; every bolt in her starts like the nail-heads of an old house in frosty weather; she trembles, quivers, and nods her frighted mast-heads to the sky. More and more she leans over to the whale, while every gasping heave of the windlass is answered by a helping heave from the billows; till at last, a swift, startling snap is heard; with a great swash the ship rolls upwards and backwards from the whale, and the triumphant tackle rises into sight dragging after it the disengaged semicircular end of the first strip of blubber. Now as the blubber envelopes the whale precisely as the rind does an orange, so is it stripped off from the body precisely as an orange is sometimes stripped by spiralizing it. For the strain constantly kept up by the windlass continually keeps the whale rolling over and over in the water, and as the blubber in one strip uniformly peels off along the line called the "scarf," simultaneously cut by the spades of Starbuck and Stubb, the mates; and just as fast as it is thus peeled off, and indeed by that very act itself, it is all the time being hoisted higher and higher aloft till its upper end grazes the main-top; the men at the windlass then cease heaving, and for a moment or two the prodigious blood-dripping mass sways to and fro as if let down from the sky, and everyone present must take good heed to dodge it when it swings, else it may box his ears and pitch him headlong overboard.

One of the attending harpooneers now advances with a long, keen weapon called a boarding-sword, and watching his chance he dexterously slices out a considerable hole in the lower part of the swaying mass. Into this hole, the end of the second alternating great tackle is then hooked so as to retain a hold upon the blubber, in order to prepare for what follows. Whereupon, this accomplished swordsman, warning all hands to stand off, once more makes a scientific dash at the mass, and with a few sidelong, desperate, lunging slicings, severs it completely in twain; so that while the short lower part is still fast, the long upper strip, called a blanket-piece, swings clear, and is all ready for lowering. The heavers forward now resume their song, and while the one tackle is peeling and hoisting a second strip from the whale, the other is slowly slackened away, and down goes the first strip through the main hatchway right beneath, into an unfurnished parlour called the blubber-room. Into this twilight apartment sundry nimble hands keep coiling away the long blanket-piece as if it were a great live mass of plaited serpents. And thus the work proceeds; the two tackles hoisting and lowering simultaneously; both whale and windlass heaving, the heavers singing, the blubber-room gentlemen coiling, the mates scarfing, the ship straining, and all hands swearing occasionally, by way of assuaging the general friction.

CHAPTER 55

THE BLANKET

I HAVE given no small attention to that not unvexed subject, the skin of the whale. I have had controversies about it with experienced whalemen afloat, and learned naturalists ashore. My original opinion remains unchanged; but it is only an opinion.

The question is, what and where is the skin of the whale? Already you know what his blubber is. That blubber is something of the consistence of firm, close-grained beef, but tougher, more elastic and compact, and ranges from eight or ten to twelve and fifteen inches in thickness.

Now, however preposterous it may at first seem to talk of any creature's skin as being of that sort of consistence and thickness, yet in point of fact these are no arguments against such a presumption; because you cannot raise any other dense enveloping layer from the whale's body but that same blubber; and the outermost enveloping layer of any animal, if reasonably dense, what can that be but the skin? True, from the unmarred dead body of the whale, you may scrape off with your hand an infinitely thin, transparent substance, somewhat resembling the thinnest shreds of isinglass, only it is almost as flexible and soft as satin; that is, previous to being dried, when it not only contracts and thickens, but becomes rather hard and brittle. I have several such dried bits, which I use for marks in my whale-books. It is transparent, as I said before; and being laid upon the printed page, I have sometimes pleased myself with fancying it exerted a magnifying influence. At any rate, it is pleasant to read about whales through their own spectacles, as you may say. But what I am driving at here is this. That same infinitely thin, isinglass substance, which, I admit, invests the entire body of the whale, is not so much to be regarded as the skin of the creature, as the skin of the skin so to speak; for it were simply ridiculous to say, that the proper skin of the tremendous whale is thinner and more tender than the skin of a new-born child. But no more of this.

Assuming the blubber to be the skin of the whale; then, when this skin, as in the case of a very large sperm-whale, will yield the bulk of one hundred barrels of oil; and, when it is considered that, in quantity, or rather weight, that oil, in its expressed state, is only three-fourths, and not the entire substance of the coat; some idea may hence be had of the enormousness of that animated mass, a mere part of whose mere integument yields such a lake of liquid as that. Reckoning ten barrels to the ton, you have ten tons for the net weight of only three-quarters of the stuff of the whale's skin.

In life, the visible surface of the sperm-whale it not the least among the many marvels he presents. Almost invariably it is all over obliquely crossed and re-crossed with numberless straight marks in thick array, something like those in the finest Italian line engravings. But these marks do not seem to be impressed upon the isinglass substance above mentioned, but seem to be seen through it, as if they were engraved upon the body itself. Nor is this all. In some instances, to the quick, observant eye, those linear marks, as in a veritable engraving, but afford the ground for far other delineations. These are hieroglyphical; that is, if you call those mysterious cyphers on the walls of pyramids hieroglyphics, then that is the proper word to use in the present connexion. By my retentive memory of the hieroglyphics upon one sperm-whale in particular, I was much struck with a plate representing the old Indian characters chiselled on the famous hieroglyphic palisades on the banks of the Upper Mississippi. Like those mystic rocks, too, the mystic-marked whale remains undecipherable. This allusion to the Indian rocks reminds me of another thing. Besides all the other phenomena which the exterior of the sperm-whale presents, he not seldom displays the back, and more especially his flanks, effaced in great part of the regular linear appearance, by reason of numerous rude scratches, altogether of an irregular, random aspect. I should say that those new England rocks on the sea-coast, which Agassiz imagines to bear the marks of violent scraping contact with vast floating icebergs —I should say, that those rocks must not a little resemble the sperm-whale in this particular. It also seems to me that such scratches in the whale are probably made by hostile contact with other whales; for I have most remarked them in the large, full-grown bulls of the species.

A word or two more concerning this matter of the skin or blubber of the whale. It has already been said, that it is stripped from him in long pieces, called blanket-pieces. Like most sea-terms, this one is very happy and significant. For the whale is indeed wrapped up in his blubber as in a real blanket or counterpane; or, still better, an Indian poncho slipped over his head, and skirting his extremity. It is by reason of this cosy blanketing of his body, that the whale is enabled to keep himself comfortable in all weathers, in all seas, times, and tides.

CHAPTER 56

THE FUNERAL

"Haul in the chains! Let the carcase go astern!"

The vast tackles have now done their duty. The peeled white body of the beheaded whale flashes like a marble sepulchre; though changed in hue, it has not perceptibly lost anything in bulk. It is still colossal. Slowly it floats more and more away, the water round it torn and splashed by the insatiate sharks, and the air above vexed with rapacious flights of screaming fowls, whose beaks are like so many insulting poniards in the whale. The vast white headless phantom floats farther and farther from the ship, and every rod that it so floats, what seem square roods of sharks and cubic roods of fowls, augment the murderous din. For hours and hours from the almost stationary ship that hideous sight is seen. Beneath the unclouded and mild azure sky, upon the fair face of the pleasant sea, wafted by the joyous breezes, that great mass of death floats on and on, till lost in infinite perspectives.

There's a most doleful and most mocking funeral! The sea-vultures all in pious mourning, the air-sharks all punctiliously in black or speckled. In life but few of them would have helped the whale, I ween, if peradventure he had needed it; but upon the banquet of his funeral they most piously do pounce. Oh, horrible vulturism of earth! from which not the mightiest whale is free.

Nor is this the end. Desecrated as the body is, a vengeful ghost survives and hovers over it to scare. Espied by some timid man-of-war or blundering discovery-vessel from afar, when the distance obscuring the swarming fowls nevertheless still shows the white mass floating in the sun, and the white spray heaving high against it; straightway the whale's unharming corpse, with trembling fingers is set down in the log—*shoals, rocks, and breakers hereabouts: beware!* And for years afterwards, perhaps, ships shun the place; leaping over it as silly sheep leap over a vacuum, because their leader originally leaped there when a stick was held. There's your law of precedents; there's your utility of traditions; there's the story of your obstinate survival of old beliefs never bottomed on the earth, and now not even hovering in the air! There's orthodoxy!

Thus, while in life the great whale's body may have been a real terror to his foes, in his death his ghost becomes a powerless panic to a world.

Are you a believer in ghosts, my friend? There are other ghosts than the Cock-Lane one, and far deeper men than Doctor Johnson who believe in them.

CHAPTER 57

THE SPHYNX

IT SHOULD not have been omitted that previous to completely stripping the body of the leviathan, he was beheaded. Now, the beheading of the sperm-whale is a scientific anatomical feat, upon which experienced whale surgeons very much pride themselves: and not without reason.

Consider that the whale has nothing that can properly be called a neck; on the contrary, where his head and body seem to join, there, in that very place, is the thickest part of him. Remember, also, that the surgeon must operate from above, some eight or ten feet intervening between him and his subject, and that subject almost hidden in a discoloured, rolling, and often times tumultuous and bursting sea. Bear in mind, too, that under these untoward circumstances he has to cut many feet deep in the flesh; and in that subterraneous manner, without so much as getting one single peep into the ever-contracting gash thus made, he must skilfully steer clear of all adjacent, interdicted parts, and exactly divide the spine at a critical point hard by its insertion into the skull. Do you not marvel, then, at Stubb's boast, that he demanded but ten minutes to behead a sperm-whale?

When first severed, the head is dropped astern and held there by a cable till the body is stripped. That done, if it belong to a small whale it is hoisted on deck to be deliberately disposed of. But, with a full grown leviathan this is impossible; for the sperm-whale's head embraces nearly one-third of his entire bulk, and completely to suspend such a burden as that, even by the immense tackles of a whaler, this were as vain a thing as to attempt weighing a Dutch barn in jewellers' scales.

The *Pequod*'s whale being decapitated and the body stripped, the head was hoisted against the ship's side—about half-way out of the sea, so that it might yet in great part be buoyed up by its native element. And there with the strained craft steeply leaning over it, by reason of the enormous downward drag from the lower mast-head, and every yard-arm on that side projecting like a crane over the waves, there, that blood-dripping head hung to the *Pequod*'s waist like the giant Holofernes's from the girdle of Judith.

When this last task was accomplished it was noon, and the seamen went below to their dinner. Silence reigned over the before tumultuous but now deserted deck. An intense copper calm, like a universal yellow lotus, was more and more unfolding its noiseless measureless leaves upon the sea.

CHAPTER 58

THE MONKEY-ROPE

IN THE tumultuous business of cutting-in and attending to a whale, there is much running backwards and forwards among the crew. Now hands are wanted here, and then again hands are wanted there. There is no staying in any one place; for at one and the same time everything has to be done everywhere. It is much the same with him who endeavours the description of the scene. We must now retrace our way a little. It was mentioned that upon first breaking ground in the whale's back, the blubber-hook was inserted into the original hole there cut by the spades of the mates. But how did so clumsy and weighty a mass as that same hook get fixed in that hole? It was inserted there by my particular friend Queequeg, whose duty it was, as harpooneer, to descend upon the monster's back for the special purpose referred to. But in very many cases, circumstances require that the harpooneer shall remain on the whale till the whole flensing or stripping operation is concluded. The whale, be it observed, lies almost entirely submerged, excepting the immediate parts operated upon. So down there, some ten feet below the level of the deck, the poor harpooneer flounders about, half on the whale and half in the water, as the vast mass revolves like a tread-mill beneath him. On the occasion in question, Queequeg figured in the Highland costume—a shirt and socks —in which to my eyes at least, he appeared to uncommon advantage; and no one had a better chance to observe him, as will presently be seen.

Being the savage's bowsman, that is, the person who pulled the bow-oar in his boat (the second one from forward), it was my cheerful duty to attend upon him while taking that hard-scrabble scramble upon the dead whale's back. You have seen Italian organ-boys holding a dancing-ape by a long cord. Just so, from the ship's steep side, did I hold Queequeg down there in the sea, by what is technically called in the fishery a monkey-rope, attached to a strong strip of canvas belted round his waist.

It was a humorously perilous business for both of us. For, before we proceed further, it must be said that the monkey-rope was fast at both ends; fast to Queequeg's broad canvas belt, and fast to my narrow leather one. So that for better or for worse, we two, for the time, were wedded; and should poor Queequeg sink to rise no more, then both usage and honour demanded, that instead of cutting the cord, it should drag me down in his wake. So, then, an elongated Siamese ligature united us. Queequeg was my own inseparable twin brother; nor could I any way get rid of the dangerous liabilities which the hempen bond entailed.

So strongly and metaphysically did I conceive of my situation then, that while earnestly watching his motions, I seemed distinctly to perceive that my own individuality was now merged in a joint-stock company of two: that my free will had received a mortal wound; and that another's mistake or misfortune might plunge innocent me into unmerited disaster and death. Therefore, I saw that here was a sort of interregnum in Providence; for its even-handed equity never could have sanctioned so gross an injustice. And yet still further pondering —while I jerked him now and then from between the whale and the ship, which would threaten to jam him—still further pondering, I say, I saw that this situation of mine was the precise situation of every mortal that breathes; only, in most cases, he, one way or other, has this Siamese connexion with a plurality of other mortals. If your banker breaks, you snap; if your apothecary by mistake sends you poison in your pills, you die. True, you may say that, by exceeding caution, you may possibly escape these and the multitudinous other evil chances of life. But handle Queequeg's monkey-rope heedfully as I would, sometimes he jerked it so, that I came very near sliding overboard. Nor could I possibly forget that, do what I would, I only had the management of one end of it.[1]

I have hinted that I would often jerk poor Queequeg from between the whale and the ship—where he would occasionally fall, from the incessant rolling and swaying of both. But this was not the only jamming jeopardy he was exposed to. Unappalled by the massacre made upon them during the night, the sharks now freshly and more keenly allured by the before pent blood which began to flow from the carcase—the rabid creatures swarmed round it like bees in a beehive. And right in among those sharks was Queequeg; who often pushed

---

[1] The monkey-rope is found in all whalers; but it was only in the *Pequod* that the monkey and his holder were ever tied together. This improvement upon the original usage was introduced by no less a man than Stubb, in order to afford to the imperilled harpooneer the strongest possible guarantee for the faithfulness and vigilance of his monkey-rope holder.

them aside with his floundering feet. A thing altogether incredible were it not that, attracted by such prey as a dead whale, the otherwise miscellaneously carnivorous shark will seldom touch a man.

Nevertheless, it may well be believed that since they have such a ravenous finger in the pie, it is deemed but wise to look sharp to them. Accordingly, besides the monkey-rope, with which I now and then jerked the poor fellow from too close a vicinity to the maw of what seemed a peculiarly ferocious shark—he was provided with still another protection. Suspended over the side in one of the stages, Tashtego and Daggoo continually flourished over his head a couple of keen whale-spades, wherewith they slaughtered as many sharks as they could reach. This procedure of theirs, to be sure, was very disinterested and benev-olent of them. They meant Queequeg's best happiness, I admit; but in their hasty zeal to befriend him, and from the circumstance that both he and the sharks were at times half hidden by the blood-mudded water, those indiscreet spades of theirs would come nearer amputating a leg than a tail. But poor Queequeg, I suppose, straining and gasping there with that great iron hook—poor Queequeg, I suppose, only prayed to his Yojo, and gave up his life into the hands of his gods.

Well, well, my dear comrade and twin-brother, thought I, as I drew in and then slacked off the rope to every swell of the sea—what matters it, after all? Are you not the precious image of each and all of us men in this whaling world? That unsounded ocean you gasp in, is Life; those sharks, your foes; those spades, your friends; and what between sharks and spades you are in a sad pickle and peril, poor lad.

But courage! there is good cheer in store for you, Queequeg. For now, as with blue lips and blood-shot eyes the exhausted savage at last climbs up the chains and stands all dripping and involuntarily trem-bling over the side; the steward advances, and with a benevolent, consolatory glance hands him some hot Cognac.

CHAPTER 59

STUBB AND FLASK KILL A RIGHT WHALE; AND THEN HAVE A TALK OVER HIM

IT MUST be borne in mind that all this time we have a sperm-whale's prodigious head hanging to the *Pequod*'s side. But we must let it continue hanging there a while till we can get a chance to attend to it. For the present other matters press, and the best we can do now for the head, is to pray heaven the tackles may hold.

Now, during the past night and forenoon, the *Pequod* had gradually drifted into a sea, which, by its occasional patches of yellow brit, gave unusual tokens of the vicinity of Right whales, a species of the Leviathan that but few supposed to be at this particular time lurking anywhere near. And though all hands commonly disdained the capture of those inferior creatures; and though the *Pequod* was not commissioned to cruise for them at all, and though she had passed numbers of them near the Crozetts without lowering a boat; yet now that a sperm-whale had been brought alongside and beheaded, to the surprise of all, the announcement was made that a Right whale should be captured that day, if opportunity offered.

Nor was this long wanting. Tall spouts were seen to leeward; and two boats, Stubb's and Flask's, were detached in pursuit. Pulling farther and farther away, they at last became almost invisible to the men at the mast-head. But suddenly in the distance, they saw a great heap of tumultuous white water, and soon after news came from aloft that one or both the boats must be fast. An interval passed and the boats were in plain sight, in the act of being dragged right towards the ship by the towing whale. So close did the monster come to the hull, that at first it seemed as if he meant it malice; but suddenly going down in a maelstrom, within three rods of the planks, he wholly disappeared from view, as if diving under the keel. "Cut, cut!" was the cry from the ship to the boats, which, for one instant, seemed on the point of being brought with a deadly dash against the vessel's side. But having plenty of line yet in the tubs, and the whale not sounding very rapidly, they paid out abundance of rope, and at the same time pulled with all their might so as to get ahead of the ship. For a few minutes the struggle was intensely critical; for while they still slacked out the tightened line in one direction, and still plied their oars in another, the contending strain threatened to take them under. But it was only a few feet advance they sought to gain. And they stuck to it till they did gain it; when instantly, a swift tremor was felt running like lightning along the keel, as the strained line, scraping beneath the ship, suddenly rose to view under her bows, snapping and quivering; and so flinging off its drippings, that the drops fell like bits of broken glass on the water, while the whale beyond also rose to sight, and once more the boats were free to fly. But the fagged whale abated his speed, and blindly altering his course, went round the stern of the ship towing the two boats after him, so that they performed a complete circuit.

Meantime, they hauled more and more upon their lines, till close flanking him on both sides, Stubb answered Flask with lance for lance; and thus round and round the *Pequod* the battle went, while the multitudes of sharks that had before swum round the sperm-whale's body, rushed to the fresh blood that was spilled, thirstily drinking at every new gash, as the eager Israelites did at the new bursting fountains that poured from the smitten rock.

At last his spout grew thick, and with a frightful roll and vomit, he turned upon his back a corpse.

While the two headsmen were engaged in making fast cords to his flukes, and in other ways getting the mass in readiness for towing, some conversation ensued between them.

"I wonder what the old man wants with this lump of foul lard," said Stubb, not without some disgust at the thought of having to do with so ignoble a leviathan.

"Wants with it?" said Flask, coiling some spare line in the boat's bow, "did you never hear that the ship which but once has a sperm-whale's head hoisted on her starboard side, and at the same time a Right whale's on the larboard; did you never hear, Stubb, that that ship can never afterwards capsize?"

"Well, then, pull ahead, and let's get the whale alongside."

The boats were hailed, to tow the whale on the larboard side, where fluke chains and other necessaries were already prepared for securing him.

"Didn't I tell you so?" said Flask; "yes, you'll soon see this Right whale's head hoisted up opposite that parmaceti's."

In good time, Flask's saying proved true. As before, the *Pequod* steeply leaned over towards the sperm-whale's head, now, by the counterpoise of both heads, she regained her even keel; though sorely strained, you may well believe. So, when on one side you hoist in Locke's head, you go over that way; but now, on the other side, hoist in Kant's and you come back again; but in very poor plight. Thus, some minds for ever keep trimming boat. Oh, ye foolish! throw all these thunder-heads overboard, and then you will float light and right.

In disposing of the body of a Right whale, when brought alongside the ship, the same preliminary proceedings commonly take place as in the case of the sperm-whale; only, in the latter instance, the head is cut off whole, but in the former the lips and tongue are separately removed and hoisted on deck, with all the well-known black bone attached to what is called the crown-piece. But nothing like this, in the present case, had been done. The carcase of both whales had dropped astern; and the head-laden ship not a little resembled a mule carrying a pair of over-burdening panniers.

Meantime, Fedallah was calmly eyeing the Right whale's head, and ever and anon glancing from the deep wrinkles there to the lines in his own hand. And Ahab chanced so to stand, that the Parsee occupied his shadow; while, if the Parsee's shadow was there at all it seemed only to blend with, and lengthen Ahab's. As the crew toiled on, Laplandish speculations were bandied among them, concerning all these passing things.

CHAPTER 60

THE SPERM-WHALE'S HEAD—CONTRASTED VIEW

HERE, NOW, are two great whales, laying their heads together; let us join them, and lay together our own.

Of the grand order of folio leviathans, the sperm-whale and the Right whale are by far the most noteworthy. They are the only whales regularly hunted by man. To the Nantucketer, they present the two extremes of all the known varieties of the whale. As the external difference between them is mainly observable in their heads; and as a head of each is this moment hanging from the *Pequod's* side; and as we may freely go from one to the other, by merely stepping across the deck:—where, I should like to know, will you obtain a better chance to study practical cetology than here?

In the first place, you are struck by the general contrast between these heads. Both are massive enough in all conscience; but there is a certain mathematical symmetry in the sperm-whale's which the Right whale's sadly lacks. There is more character in the sperm-whale's head. As you behold it, you involuntarily yield the immense superiority to him, in point of pervading dignity. In the present instance, too, this dignity is heightened by the pepper and salt colour of his head at the summit, giving token of advanced age and large experience. In short, he is what the fisherman technically call a "grey-headed whale."

Let us now note what is least dissimilar in these heads—namely, the two most important organs, the eye and the ear. Far back on the side of the head, and low down, near the angle of either whale's jaw, if you narrowly search, you will at last see a lashless eye, which you would fancy to be a young colt's eye; so out of all proportion is it to the magnitude of the head.

Now, from this peculiar sideway position of the whale's eyes, it is plain that he can never see an object which is exactly ahead, no more than he can one exactly astern. In a word, the position of the whale's eyes corresponds to that of a man's ears; and you may fancy, for yourself, how it would fare with you, did you sideways survey objects through your ears. You would find that you could only command some thirty degrees of vision in advance of the straight-side-line of sight; and about thirty more behind it. If your bitterest foe were walking straight towards you, with dagger uplifted in broad day, you would not be able to see him, any more than if he were stealing upon you from behind. In a word, you would have two backs, so to speak; but, at the same time, also, two fronts (side fronts): for what is it that makes the front, of a man—what, indeed, but his eyes?

Moreover, while in most other animals that I can now think of, the eyes are so planted as imperceptibly to blend their visual power, so as to produce one picture and not two to the brain; the peculiar position of the whale's eyes, effectually divided as they are by many cubic feet of solid head, which towers between them like a great mountain separating two lakes in valleys; this, of course, must wholly separate the impressions which each independent organ imparts. The whale, therefore, must see one distinct picture on this side, and another distinct picture on that side; while all between must be profound darkness and nothingness to him. Man may, in effect, be said to look out on the world from a sentry-box with two joined sashes for his window. But with the whale, these two sashes are separately inserted, making two distinct windows, but sadly impairing the view. This peculiarity of the whale's eyes is a thing always to be borne in mind in the fishery; and to be remembered by the reader in some subsequent scenes.

But the ear of the whale is full as curious as the eye. If you are an entire stranger to their race, you might hunt over these two heads for hours, and never discover that organ. The ear has no external leaf whatever; and into the hole itself you can hardly insert a quill, so wondrously minute is it. It is lodged a little behind the eye. With respect to their ears, this important difference is to be observed between the sperm-whale and the Right. While the ear of the former has an external opening, that of the latter is entirely and evenly covered over with a membrane, so as to be quite imperceptible from without.

Let us now with whatever levers and steam-engines we have at hand, cant over the sperm-whale's head, so that it may be bottom up; then, ascending by a ladder to the summit have a peep down the mouth; and were it not that the body is now completely separated from it, with a lantern we might descend into the great Kentucky Mammoth Cave of his stomach. But let us hold on here by this tooth, and look about us where we are. What a really beautiful and chaste-looking mouth! from floor to ceiling, lined, or rather papered with a glistening white membrane, glossy as bridal satins.

But come out now, and look at this portentous lower jaw, which seems like the long narrow lid of an immense snuff-box, with the hinge at one end, instead of one side. If you pry it up, so as to get it overhead, and expose its rows of teeth, it seems a terrific portcullis; and such, alas! it proves to many a poor wight in the fishery, upon whom these spikes fall with impaling force. But far more terrible is it to behold, when fathoms down in the sea, you see some sulky whale, floating there suspended, with his prodigious jaw, some fifteen feet long, hanging straight down at right-angles with his body, for all the world like a ship's jib-boom. This whale is not dead; he is only dispirited; out of sorts, perhaps; hypochondriac; and so supine, that the hinges of his jaw have relaxed, leaving him there in that ungainly sort of plight, a reproach to all his tribe, who must, no doubt, imprecate lock-jaws upon him.

In most cases this lower jaw—being easily unhinged by a practised artist—is disengaged and hoisted on deck for the purpose of extracting the ivory teeth, and furnishing a supply of the hard white whalebone with which the fishermen fashion all sorts of curious articles, including canes, umbrella-sticks, and handles to riding-whips.

With a long, weary hoist the jaw is dragged on board, as if it were an anchor; and when the proper time comes—some few days after the other work—Queequeg, Daggoo, and Tashtego, being all accomplished dentists, are set to drawing teeth. With a keen cutting-spade, Queequeg lances the gums; then the jaw is lashed down to ringbolts, and a tackle being rigged from aloft, they drag out these teeth, as Michigan oxen drag stumps of old oak out of wild wood-lands. There are generally forty-two teeth in all; in old whales, much worn down, but undecayed; nor filled after our artificial fashion. The jaw is afterwards sawn into slabs, and piled away like joists for building houses.

CHAPTER 61

THE RIGHT WHALE'S HEAD—CONTRASTED VIEW

CROSSING the deck, let us now have a good long look at the Right whale's head.

As in general shape the noble sperm-whale's head may be compared to a Roman war-chariot (especially in front, where it is so broadly rounded); so, at a broad view, the Right whale's head bears a rather inelegant resemblance to a gigantic galliot-toed shoe. Two hundred years ago an old Dutch voyager likened its shape to that of a shoe maker's last. And in this same last or shoe, that old woman of the nursery tale with the swarming brood, might very comfortably be lodged, she and all her progeny.

But as you come nearer to this great head it begins to assume different aspects, according to your point of view. If you stand on its summit and look at these two f-shaped spout-holes, you would take the whole head for an enormous bass-viol, and these spiracles, the apertures in its sounding-board. Then, again, if you fix your eye upon this strange, crested, comb-like incrustation on the top of the mass— this green, barnacled thing, which the Greenlanders call the "crown," and the Southern fishers the "bonnet," of the Right whale; fixing your eyes solely on this, you would take the head for the trunk of some huge oak, with a bird's nest in its crotch. At any rate, when you watch those live crabs that nestle here on this bonnet, such an idea will be almost sure to occur to you; unless, indeed, your fancy has been fixed by the technical term "crown" also bestowed upon it; in which case you will take great interest in thinking how this mighty monster is actually a diademed king of the sea, whose green crown has been put together for him in this marvellous manner. But if this whale be a king, he is a very sulky looking fellow to grace a diadem. Look at that hanging lower lip! what a huge sulk and pout is there! a sulk and pout, by carpenter's measurement, about twenty feet long and five feet deep; a sulk and pout that will yield you some 500 gallons of oil and more.

A great pity, now, that this unfortunate whale should be hare-lipped. The fissure is about a foot across. Probably the mother during an important interval was sailing down the Peruvian coast, when earthquakes caused the beach to gape. Over this lip, as over a slippery threshold, we now slide into the mouth. Upon my word were I at Mackinaw, I should take this to be the inside of an Indian wigwam. Good Lord! is this the road that Jonah went? The roof is about twelve feet high, and runs to a pretty sharp angle, as if there were a regular ridge-pole there; while these ribbed, arched, hairy sides, present us with those wondrous, half-vertical, scimitar-shaped slats of whalebone, say three hundred on a side, which, depending from the upper part of the head or crown bone, form those Venetian blinds which have elsewhere been cursorily mentioned. The edges of these bones are fringed with hairy fibres, through which the Right whale strains the water, and in whose intricacies he retains the small fish, when open-mouthed he goes through the seas of brit in feeding time. In the central blinds of bone, as they stand in their natural order, there are certain curious marks, curves, hollows, and ridges, whereby some whalemen calculate the creature's age, as the age of an oak by its circular rings. Though the

certainty of this criterion is far from demonstrable, yet it has the savour
of analogical probability. At any rate, if we yield to it, we must grant
a far greater age to the Right whale than at first glance will seem
reasonable.

In old times, there seem to have prevailed the most curious fancies
concerning these blinds. One voyager in Purchas calls them the
wondrous "whiskers" inside of the whale's mouth;[1] another, "hogs'
bristles"; a third old gentleman in Hakluyt uses the following elegant
language: "There are about two hundred and fifty fins growing on
each side of his upper *chop,* which arch his tongue on each side of his
mouth."

As everyone knows, these same "hogs' bristles," "fins," "whiskers,"
"blinds," or whatever you please, furnish to the ladies their busks and
other stiffening contrivances. But in this particular, the demand has
long been on the decline. It was in Queen Anne's time that the bone
was in its glory, the farthingale being then all the fashion. And as
those ancient dames moved about gaily, though in the jaws of the
whale, as you may say; even so, in a shower, with the like thoughtless-
ness do we nowadays fly under the same jaws for protection; the umbrella being a tent spread over the same bone.

But now forget all about blinds and whiskers for a moment, and,
standing in the Right whale's mouth, look around you afresh. Seeing
all these colonnades of bone so methodically ranged about, would you
not think you were inside of the great Haarlem organ, and gazing
upon its thousand pipes? For a carpet to the organ we have a rug of
the softest Turkey—the tongue, which is glued, as it were, to the floor
of the mouth. It is very fat and tender, and apt to tear in pieces in
hoisting it on deck. This particular tongue now before us; at a passing
glance I should say it was a six-barreller; that is, it will yield you
about that amount of oil.

Ere this, you must have plainly seen the truth of what I started with
—that the sperm-whale and the Right whale have almost entirely
different heads. To sum up, then: in the Right whale's there is no
great well of sperm; no ivory teeth at all; no long, slender mandible
of a lower jaw, like the sperm-whale's. Nor in the sperm-whale are
there any of those blinds of bone; no huge lower lip; and scarcely
anything of a tongue. Again, the Right whale has two external spout
holes, the sperm-whale only one.

---

[1] This reminds us that the Right whale really has a sort of whisker, or rather a moustache, consisting of a few scattered white hairs on the upper part of the outer end of
the lower jaw. Sometimes these tufts impart a rather brigandish expression to his
otherwise solemn countenance.

Look your last, now, on these venerable hooded heads, while they yet lie together; for one will soon sink, unrecorded, in the sea; the other will not be very long in following.

Can you catch the expression of the sperm-whale's there? It is the same he died with, only some of the longer wrinkles in the forehead seem now faded away. I think his broad brow to be full of a prairie-like placidity, born of a speculative indifference as to death. But mark the other head's expression. See that amazing lower lip, pressed by accident against the vessel's side, so as firmly to embrace the jaw. Does not this whole head seem to speak of an enormous practical resolution in facing death? This Right whale I take to have been a Stoic; the sperm-whale, a Platonian, who might have taken up Spinoza in his latter years.

CHAPTER 62

THE BATTERING-RAM

ERE QUITTING, for the nonce, the sperm-whale's head, I would have you, as a sensible physiologist, simply—particularly remark its front aspect, in all its compacted collectedness. I would have you investigate it now with the sole view of forming to yourself some unexaggerated, intelligent estimate of whatever battering-ram power may be lodged there. Here is a vital point; for you must either satisfactorily settle this matter with yourself, or for ever remain an infidel as to one of the most appalling, but not the less true, events perhaps anywhere to be found in all recorded history.

You observe that in the ordinary swimming position of the sperm-whale, the front of his head presents an almost wholly vertical plane to the water; you observe that the lower part of that front slopes considerably backwards, so as to furnish more of a retreat for the long socket which receives the boom-like lower jaw; you observe that the mouth is entirely under the head, much in the same way, indeed, as though your own mouth were entirely under your chin. Moreover you observe that the whale has no external nose; and that what nose he has—his spout hole—is on the top of his head; you observe that his eyes and ears are at the sides of his head; nearly one-third of his entire length from the front. Wherefore, you must now have perceived that the front of the sperm-whale's head is a dead, blind wall, without a single organ or tender prominence of any sort whatsoever. Furthermore, you are now to consider that only in the extreme, lower, backward sloping part of the front of the head, is there the slightest vestige of bone; and not till you get near twenty feet from the forehead do you come to the full cranial development. So that this whole enormous boneless mass is as one wad. Finally, though, as will soon be revealed, its contents partly comprise the most delicate oil; yet, you are now to be apprised of the nature of the substance which so impregnably invests all that apparent effeminacy. In some previous place I have described to you how the blubber wraps the body of the whale, as the rind wraps an orange. Just so with the head; but with this difference: about the head this envelope, though not so thick, is of a boneless toughness, inestimable by any man who has not handled it. The severest pointed harpoon, the sharpest lance darted by the strongest human arm, impotently rebounds from it. It is as though the forehead of the sperm-whale were paved with horses' hoofs. I do not think that any sensation lurks in it.

Bethink yourself also of another thing. When two large, loaded Indiamen chance to crowd and crush towards each other in the docks, what do the sailors do? They do not suspend between them, at the point of coming contact, any merely hard substance, like iron or wood. No, they hold there a large, round wad of tow and cork, enveloped in the thickest and toughest of ox-hide. That bravely and uninjured takes the jam which would have snapped all their oaken handspikes and iron crowbars. By itself this sufficiently illustrates the obvious fact I drive at. But supplementary to this, it has hypothetically occurred to me that, as ordinary fish possess what is called a swimming bladder in them, capable, at will, of distension or contraction; and as the sperm-whale, as far as I know, has no such provision in him; considering, too, the otherwise inexplicable manner in which he now depresses his head altogether beneath the surface, and anon swims with it high elevated out of the water; considering the unobstructed elasticity of its envelope; considering the unique interior of his head; it has hypothetically occurred to me, I say, that those mystical lung-celled honeycombs there may possibly have some hitherto unknown and unsuspected connexion with the outer air, so as to be susceptible to atmospheric distension and contraction. If this be so, fancy the irresistibleness of that might, to which the most impalpable and destructive of all elements contributes.

Now, mark. Unerringly impelling this dead, impregnable, uninjurable wall, and this most buoyant thing within; there swims behind it all a mass of tremendous life, only to be adequately estimated as piled wood is—by the cord; and all obedient to one volition, as the smallest insect. So that when I shall hereafter detail to you all the specialities and concentrations of potency everywhere lurking in this expansive monster; when I shall show you some of his more inconsiderable braining feats; I trust you will have renounced all ignorant incredulity, and be ready to abide by this; that though the sperm-whale stove a passage through the Isthmus of Darien, and mixed the Atlantic with the Pacific, you would not elevate one hair of your eye-brow. For unless you own the whale, you are but a provincial and sentimentalist in Truth. But clear Truth is a thing for salamander giants only to encounter; how small the chances for the provincials then? What befel the weakling youth lifting the dread goddess's veil at Laïs?

CHAPTER 63

THE GREAT HEIDELBURGH TUN

Now comes the Baling of the Case. But to comprehend it aright, you must know something of the curious internal structure of the thing operated upon.

Regarding the sperm-whale's head as a solid oblong, you may, on an inclined plane, sideways divide it into two quoins,[1] whereof the lower is the bony structure, forming the cranium and jaws, and the upper an unctuous mass wholly free from bones; its broad forward end forming the expanded vertical apparent forehead of the whale. At the middle of the forehead horizontally subdivide this upper quoin, and then you have two almost equal parts, which before were naturally divided by an internal wall of a thick tendinous substance.

The lower subdivided part, called the junk, is one immense honey-comb of oil, formed by the crossing and recrossing, into ten thousand infiltrated cells, of tough elastic white fibres throughout its whole extent. The upper part, known as the Case, may be regarded as the great Heidelburgh Tun of the sperm-whale. And as that famous great tierce is mystically carved in front, so the whale's vast plaited forehead forms innumerable strange devices for emblematical adornment of his wondrous tun. Moreover, as that of Heidelburgh was always re-plenished with the most excellent of the wines of the Rhenish valleys, so the tun of the whale contains by far the most precious of all his oily vintages; namely, the highly-prized spermaceti, in its absolutely pure, limpid, and odoriferous state. Nor is this precious substance found unalloyed in any other part of the creature. Though in life it

---

[1] Quoin is not a Euclidean term. It belongs to the pure nautical mathematics. I know not that it has been defined before. A quoin is a solid which differs from a wedge in having its sharp end formed by the steep inclination of one side, instead of the mutual tapering of both sides.

remains perfectly fluid, yet, upon exposure to the air, after death, it soon begins to concrete; sending forth beautiful crystalline shoots, as when the first thin delicate ice is just forming in water. A large whale's case generally yields about five hundred gallons of sperm, though from unavoidable circumstances, considerable of it is spilled, leaks, and dribbles away, or is otherwise irrevocably lost in the ticklish business of securing what you can.

I know not with what fine and costly material the Heidelburgh Tun was coated within, but in superlative richness that coating could not possibly have compared with the silken pearl-coloured membrane, like the lining of a fine pelisse, forming the inner surface of the sperm-whale's case.

It will have been seen that the Heidelburgh Tun of the sperm-whale embraces the entire length of the entire top of the head; and since—as has been elsewhere set forth—the head embraces one third of the whole length of the creature, then setting that length down at eighty feet for a good sized whale, you have more than twenty-six feet for the depth of the tun, when it is lengthwise hoisted up and down against a ship's side.

As in decapitating the whale, the operator's instrument is brought close to the spot where an entrance is subsequently forced into the spermaceti magazine; he has, therefore, to be uncommonly heedful, lest a careless, untimely stroke should invade the sanctuary and wastingly let out its invaluable contents. It is this decapitated end of the head, also, which is at last elevated out of the water, and retained in that position by the enormous cutting tackles, whose hempen combinations, on one side, make quite a wilderness of ropes in that quarter.

Thus much being said, attend now, I pray you, to that marvellous and—in this particular instance—almost fatal operation whereby the sperm-whale's great Heidelburgh Tun is tapped.

CHAPTER 64

CISTERN AND BUCKETS

NIMBLE AS a cat, Tashtego mounts aloft; and without altering his erect posture, runs straight out upon the overhanging mainyard-arm, to the part where it exactly projects over the hoisted Tun. He has carried with him a light tackle called a whip, consisting of only two parts, travelling through a single-sheaved block. Securing this block, so that it hangs down from the yard-arm, he swings one end of the rope, till it is caught and firmly held by a hand on the deck. Then, hand-over-hand, down the other part, the Indian drops through the air, till dexterously he lands on the summit of the head. There—still high elevated above the rest of the company, to whom he vivaciously cries— he seems some Turkish Muezzin calling the good people to prayers from the top of a tower. A short-handled sharp spade being sent up to him, he diligently searches for the proper place to begin breaking into the Tun. In this business he proceeds very heedfully, like a treasure-hunter in some old house, sounding the walls to find where the gold is masoned in. By the time this cautious search is over, a stout iron-bound bucket, precisely like a well-bucket, has been attached to one ond of the whip; while the other end, being stretched across the deck, is there held by two or three alert hands. These last now hoist the bucket within grasp of the Indian, to whom another person has reached up a very long pole. Inserting this pole into the bucket, Tash- tego downward guides the bucket into the Tun, till it entirely dis- appears; then giving the word to the seamen at the whip, up comes the bucket again, all bubbling like a dairymaid's pail of new milk. Carefully lowered from its height, the full-freighted vessel is caught by an appointed hand, and quickly emptied into a large tub. Then re-mounting aloft, it again goes through the same round until the deep cistern will yield no more. Towards the end, Tashtego has to ram his long pole harder and harder, and deeper and deeper into the Tun, until some twenty feet of the pole have gone down.

Now, the people of the *Pequod* had been baling some time in this way; several tubs had been filled with the fragrant sperm; when all at once a queer accident happened. Whether it was that Tashtego, that wild Indian, was so heedless and reckless as to let go for a moment his one-handed hold on the great cabled tackles suspending the head; or whether the place where he stood was so treacherous and oozy; or whether the Evil One himself would have it to fall out so, without stating his particular reasons; how it was exactly, there is no telling now, but, on a sudden, as the eightieth or ninetieth bucket came suckingly up—my God! poor Tashtego—like the twin reciprocating bucket in a veritable well, dropped head-foremost down into this great Tun of Heidelburgh and with a horrible oily gurgling, went clean out of sight!

"Man overboard!" cried Daggoo, who amid the general consterna- tion first came to his senses. "Swing the bucket this way!" and putting one foot into it, so as the better to secure his slippery hand- hold on the whip itself, the hoisters ran him high up to the top of the head, almost before Tashtego could have reached its interior bottom. Meanwhile, there was a terrible tumult. Looking over the side, they saw the before lifeless head throbbing and heaving just below the surface of the sea, as if that moment seized with some momentous idea; whereas it was only the poor Indian unconsciously revealing by those struggles the perilous depth to which he had sunk.

At this instant, while Daggoo, on the summit of the head, was clearing the whip—which had somehow got foul of the great cutting tackles —a sharp cracking noise was heard; and to the unspeakable horror of all, one of the two enormous hooks suspending the head tore out, and with a vast vibration the enormous mass sideways swung, till the drunk ship reeled and shook as if smitten by an iceberg. The one remaining hook, upon which the entire strain now depended, seemed every instant to be on the point of giving way; an event still more likely from the violent motions of the head.

"Come down, come down!" yelled the seamen to Daggoo, but with one hand holding on to the heavy tackles, so that if the head should drop, he would still remain suspended; the negro having cleared the foul line, rammed down the bucket into the now collapsed well, meaning that the buried harpooneer should grasp it, and so be hoisted out.

"In heaven's name, man," cried Stubb, "are you ramming home a cartridge there?—Avast! How will that help him; jamming that ironbound bucket on top of his head! Avast, will ye!"

"Stand clear of the tackle!" cried a voice like the bursting of a rocket.

Almost in the same instant, with a thunderboom, the enormous mass dropped into the sea, like Niagara's Table-Rock into the whirlpool; the suddenly relieved hull rolled away from it, to far down her glittering copper; and all caught their breath, as half swinging—now over the sailors' heads, and now over the water—Daggoo, through a thick mist of spray, was dimly beheld clinging to the pendulous tackles, while poor, buried-alive Tashtego was sinking utterly down to the bottom of the sea! But hardly had the blinding vapour cleared away, when a naked figure with a boarding-sword in his hand, was for one swift moment seen hovering over the bulwarks. The next, a loud splash announced that my brave Queequeg had dived to the rescue. One packed rush was made to the side, and every eye counted every ripple, as moment followed moment, and no sign of either the sinker or the diver could be seen. Some hands now jumped into a boat alongside, and pushed a little off from the ship.

"Ha! ha!" cried Daggoo, all at once, from his now quiet, swinging perch overhead; and looking further off from the side, we saw an arm thrust upright from the blue waves; a sight strange to see, as an arm thrust forth from the grass over a grave.

"Both! both!—it is both!" cried Daggoo again with a joyful shout; and soon after, Queequeg was seen boldly striking out with one hand, and with the other clutching the long hair of the Indian. Drawn into the waiting boat, they were quickly brought to the deck; but Tashtego was long in coming to, and Queequeg did not look very brisk.

Now, how had this noble rescue been accomplished? Why, diving after the slowly descending head, Queequeg with his keen sword had made side lunges near its bottom, so as to scuttle a large hole there; then dropping his sword, had thrust his long arm far inwards and upwards, and so hauled out our poor Tash by the head. He averred, that upon first thrusting in for him, a leg was presented; but well knowing that that was not as it ought to be, and might occasion great trouble;—he had thrust back the leg, and by a dexterous heave and toss, had wrought a somerset upon the Indian; so that with the next trial, he came forth in the good old way—head foremost. As for the great head itself, that was doing as well as could be expected.

And thus, through the courage and great skill in obstetrics of Queequeg, the deliverance, or rather, delivery of Tashtego, was successfully accomplished, in the teeth, too, of the most untoward and apparently hopeless impediments; which is a lesson by no means to be forgotten. Midwifery should be taught in the same course with fencing and boxing, riding and rowing.

CHAPTER 65

THE NUT

IF THE sperm-whale be physiognomically a Sphinx, to the phrenologist his brain seems that geometrical circle which it is impossible to square.

In the full-grown creature the skull will measure at least twenty feet in length. Unhinge the lower jaw, and the side view of this skull is as the side view of a moderately inclined plane resting throughout on a level base. But in life—as we have elsewhere seen—this inclined plane is angularly filled up, and almost squared by the enormous superincumbent mass of the junk and sperm. At the high end the skull forms a crater to bed that part of the mass; while under the long floor of this crater—in another cavity seldom exceeding ten inches in length and as many in depth—reposes the mere handful of this monster's brain. The brain is at least twenty feet from his apparent forehead in life; it is hidden away behind its vast outworks, like the innermost citadel within the amplified fortifications of Quebec. So like a choice casket is it secreted in him, that I have known some whalemen who peremptorily deny that the sperm-whale has any other brain than that palpable semblance of one formed by the cubic-yards of his sperm magazine. Lying in strange folds, courses, and convolutions, to their apprehensions, it seems more in keeping with the idea of his general might to regard that mystic part of him as the seat of his intelligence.

It is plain, then, that phrenologically the head of this Leviathan, in the creature's living intact state, is an entire delusion. As for his true brain, you can then see no indications of it, nor feel any. The whale, like all things that are mighty, wears a false bow to the common world.

CHAPTER 66

PITCHPOLING

To MAKE them run easily and swiftly, the axles of carriages are anointed; and for much the same purpose, some whalers perform an analogous operation upon their boat; they grease the bottom. Nor is it to be doubted that as such a procedure can do no harm, it may possibly be of no contemptible advantage; considering that oil and water are hostile; that oil is a sliding thing, and that the object in view is to make the boat slide bravely. Queequeg believed strongly in anointing his boat, and one morning took more than customary pains in that occupation; crawling under its bottom, where it hung over the side, and rubbing in the unctuousness as though diligently seeking to insure a crop of hair from the craft's bald keel. He seemed to be working in obedience to some particular presentiment. Nor did it remain unwarranted by the event.

Towards noon whales were raised; but so soon as the ship sailed down to them, they turned and fled with swift precipitancy; a disordered flight, as of Cleopatra's barges from Actium.

Nevertheless, the boats pursued, and Stubb's was foremost. By great exertion, Tashtego at last succeeded in planting one iron; but the stricken whale, without at all sounding, still continued his horizontal flight, with added fleetness. Such unintermitted strainings upon the planted iron must sooner or later inevitably extract it. It became imperative to lance the flying whale, or be content to lose him. But to haul the boat up to his flank was impossible, he swam so fast and furious. What then remained?

Of all the wondrous devices and dexterities, the sleights of hand and countless subtleties, to which the veteran whaleman is so often forced, none exceed that fine manœuvre with the lance called pitchpoling. Small sword, or broad sword, in all its exercises boasts nothing like it. It is only indispensable with an inveterate running whale; its grand fact and feature is the wonderful distance to which the long lance is accurately darted from a violently rocking, jerking boat, under extreme headway. Steel and wood included, the entire spear is some ten or twelve feet in length; the staff is much slighter than that of the harpoon, and also of a lighter material—pine. It is furnished with a small rope called a warp, of considerable length, by which it can be hauled back to the hand after darting.

But before going further, it is important to mention here, that though the harpoon may be pitchpoled in the same way with the lance, yet it is seldom done; and when done, is still less frequently successful, on account of the greater weight and inferior length of the harpoon as compared with the lance, which in effect become serious drawbacks. As a general thing, therefore, you must first get fast to a whale, before any pitchpoling comes into play.

Look now at Stubb; a man who from his humorous, deliberate coolness and equanimity in the direst emergencies, was specially qualified to excel in pitchpoling. Look at him; he stands upright in the tossed bow of the flying boat; wrapped in fleecy foam, the towing whale is forty feet ahead. Handling the long lance lightly, glancing twice or thrice along its length to see if it be exactly straight, Stubb whistlingly gathers up the coil of the warp in one hand, so as to secure its free end in his grasp, leaving the rest unobstructed. Then holding the lance full before his waistband's middle, he levels it at the whale; when, covering him with it, he steadily depresses the butt-end in his hand, thereby elevating the point till the weapon stands fairly balanced upon his palm, fifteen feet in the air. He minds you somewhat of a juggler, balancing a long staff on his chin. Next moment with a rapid, nameless impulse, in a superb lofty arch the bright steel spans the foaming distance, and quivers in the life spot of the whale. Instead of sparkling water, he now spouts red blood.

"That drove the spigot out of him!" cries Stubb. 'Tis July's immortal Fourth; all fountains must run wine to-day! Would now, it were old Orleans whiskey, or old Ohio, or unspeakable old Monongahela! Then, Tashtego, lad, I'd have ye hold a canakin to the jet, and we'd drink round it! Yea, verily, hearts alive, we'd brew choice punch in the spread of his spout-hole there, and from that live punch-bowl quaff the living stuff."

Again and again to such gamesome talk, the dexterous dart is repeated, the spear returning to its master like a greyhound held in skilful leash. The agonized whale goes into his flurry; the towline is slackened, and the pitchpoler dropping astern, folds his hands, and mutely watches the monster die.

CHAPTER 67

THE FOUNTAIN

THAT FOR SIX thousand years—and no one knows how many millions of ages before—the great whales should have been spouting all over the sea, and sprinkling and mystifying the gardens of the deep, as with so many sprinkling or mystifying pots; and that for some centuries back, thousand of hunters should have been close by the fountain of the whale, watching these sprinklings and spoutings—that all this should be, and yet, that down to this blessed minute (fifteen and a quarter minutes past one o'clock p.m. of this sixteenth day of December, A.D. 1851), it should still remain a problem, whether these spoutings are, after all, really water, or nothing but vapour—this is surely a noteworthy thing.

Let us, then, look at this matter, along with some interesting items contingent. Everyone knows that by the peculiar cunning of their gills, the finny tribes in general breathe the air which at all times is combined with the element in which they swim; hence, a herring or a cod might live a century, and never once raise its head above the surface. But owing to his marked internal structure which gives him regular lungs, like a human being's, the whale can only live by inhaling the disengaged air in the open atmosphere. Wherefore the necessity for his periodical visits to the upper world. But he cannot in any degree breathe through his mouth, for, in his ordinary attitude, the sperm whale's mouth is buried at least eight feet beneath the surface; and what is still more, his windpipe has no connexion with his mouth. No, he breathes through his spiracle alone; and this is on the top of his head.

If I say, that in any creature breathing is only a function indispensable to vitality, inasmuch as it withdraws from the air a certain element which being subsequently brought into contact with the blood imparts to the blood its vivifying principle, I do not think I shall err; though I may possibly use some superfluous scientific words. Assume it, and it follows that if all the blood in a man could be aerated with one breath, he might then seal up his nostrils and not fetch another for a considerable time. That is to say, he would then live without breathing. Anomalous as it may seem, this is precisely the case with the whale, who systematically lives, by intervals, his full hour and more (when at the bottom) without drawing a single breath, or so much as in any way inhaling a particle of air; for, remember, he has no gills. How is this? Between his ribs and on each side of his spine he is supplied with a remarkable involved Cretan labyrinth of vermicelli-like vessels, which vessels, when he quits the surface, are completely distended with oxygenated blood. So that for an hour or more, a thousand fathoms in the sea, he carries a surplus stock of vitality in him, just as the camel crossing the waterless desert carries a surplus supply of drink for future use in its four supplementary stomachs. The anatomical fact of this labyrinth is indisputable; and that the supposition founded upon it is reasonable and true, seems the more cogent to me, when I consider the otherwise inexplicable obstinacy of that leviathan in *having his spoutings out,* as the fishermen phrase it. This is what I mean. If unmolested, upon rising to the surface, the sperm-whale will continue there for a period of time exactly uniform with all his other unmolested risings. Say he stays eleven minutes, and jets seventy times, that is, respires seventy breaths; then whenever he rises again, he will be sure to have his seventy breaths over again, to a minute. Now, if after he fetches a few breaths you alarm him, so that he sounds, he will be always dodging up again to make good his regular allowance of air. And not till those seventy breaths are told, will he finally go down to stay out his full term below. Remark, however, that in different individuals these rates are different; but in anyone they are alike. Now, why should the whale thus insist upon having his spoutings out, unless it be to replenish his reservoir of air, ere descending for good? How obvious is it, too, that this necessity for the whale's rising exposes him to all the fatal hazards of the chase. For not by hook or by net could this vast leviathan be caught, when sailing a thousand fathoms beneath the sunlight. Not so much thy skill, then, O hunter, as the great necessities that strike the victory to thee!

In man, breathing is incessantly going on—one breath only serving for two or three pulsations; so that whatever other business he has to attend to, waking or sleeping, breathe he must, or die he will. But the sperm-whale only breathes about one-seventh or Sunday of his time.

It has been said that the whale only breathes through his spout-hole; if it could truthfully be added that his spouts are mixed with water, then I opine we should be furnished with the reason why his sense of smell seems obliterated in him; for the only thing about him that at all

answers to his nose is that identical spout-hole; and being so clogged
with two elements, it could not be expected to have the power of
smelling. But owing to the mystery of the spout—whether it be water
or whether it be vapour—no absolute certainty can as yet be arrived at
on this head. Sure it is, nevertheless, that the sperm-whale has no
proper olfactories. But what does he want of them? No roses, no
violets, no Cologne-water in the sea.

Furthermore, as his windpipe solely opens into the tube of his spouting canal, and as that long canal—like grand Erie Canal—is furnished
with a sort of locks (that open and shut) for the downward retention
of air or the upward exclusion of water, therefore the whale has no
voice; unless you insult him by saying, that when he so strangely
rumbles, he talks through his nose. But then again, what has the
whale to say? Seldom have I known any profound being that had
anything to say to this world, unless forced to stammer out something
by way of getting a living. Oh! happy that the world is such an
excellent listener!

Now, the spouting canal of the sperm-whale, chiefly intended as it
is for the conveyance of air, and for several feet laid along, horizontally, just beneath the upper surface of his head, and a little to one
side; this curious canal is very much like a gaspipe laid down in a
city on one side of a street. But the question returns whether this gaspipe is also a water-pipe; in other words, whether the spout of the
sperm-whale is the mere vapour of the exhaled breath, or whether
that exhaled breath is mixed with water taken in at the mouth, and
discharged through the spiracle. It is certain that the mouth indirectly
communicates with the spouting canal; but it cannot be proved that
this is for the purpose of discharging water through the spiracle. Because
the greatest necessity for so doing would seem to be, when in feeding
he accidentally takes in water. But the sperm-whale's food is far
beneath the surface, and there he cannot spout even if he would.
Besides, if you regard him very closely, and time him with your watch,
you will find that when unmolested, there is an undeviating rhythm
between the periods of his jets and the ordinary periods of respiration.

But why pester one with all this reasoning on the subject? Speak
out! You have seen him spout; then declare what the spout is; can
you not tell water from air? My dear sir, in this world it is not so
easy to settle these plain things. I have ever found your plain things
the knottiest of all. And as for this whale spout, you might almost
stand in it, and yet be undecided as to what it is precisely.

The central body of it is hidden in the snowy sparkling mist enveloping it; and how can you certainly tell whether any water falls from

it, when, always, you are close enough to a whale to get a close view of his spout, he is in a prodigious commotion, the water cascading all around him. And if at such times you should think that you really perceived drops of moisture in the spout, how do you know that they are not merely condensed from its vapour; or how do you know that they are not those identical drops superficially lodged in the spout-hole fissure, which is countersunk into the summit of the whale's head? For even when tranquilly swimming through the mid-day sea in a calm, with his elevated hump sun-dried as a dromedary's in the desert; even then, the whale always carries a small basin of water on his head, as under a blazing sun you will sometimes see a cavity in a rock filled up with rain.

Nor is it at all prudent for the hunter to be over curious touching the precise nature of the whale spout. It will not do for him to be peering into it, and putting his face in it. You cannot go with your pitcher to this fountain and fill it, and bring it away. For even when coming into slight contact with the outer, vapoury shreds of the jet, which will often happen, your skin will feverishly smart, from the acridness of the thing so touching it. And I know one, who coming into still closer contact with the spout, whether with some scientific object in view, or otherwise, I cannot say, the skin peeled off from his cheek and arm. Wherefore, among whalemen, the spout is deemed poisonous; they try to evade it. Another thing; I have heard it said, and I do not much doubt it, that if the jet is fairly spouted into your eyes, it will blind you. The wisest thing the investigator can do then, it seems to me, is to let this deadly spout alone.

CHAPTER 68

THE TAIL

OTHER POETS have warbled the praises of the soft eye of the antelope, and the lovely plumage of the bird that never alights; less celestial, I celebrate, a tail.

Reckoning the largest sized sperm-whale's tail to begin at that point of the trunk where it tapers to about the girth of a man, it comprises upon its upper surface alone, an area of at least fifty square feet. The compact round body of its root expands into two broad, firm, flat palms or flukes, gradually shoaling away to less than an inch in thickness. At the crotch or junction, these flukes slightly overlap, then sideways recede from each other like wings, leaving a wide vacancy between. In no living thing are the lines of beauty more exquisitely defined than in the crescentic borders of these flukes. At its utmost expansion in the full grown whale, the tail will considerably exceed twenty feet across.

The entire member seems a dense webbed bed of welded sinews; but cut into it, and you find that three distinct strata compose it:— upper, middle, and lower. The fibres in the upper and lower layers are long and horizontal; those of the middle one, very short, and running crosswise between the outside layers. This triune structure, as much as anything else, imparts power to the tail. To the student of old Roman walls, the middle layer will furnish a curious parallel to the thin course of tiles always alternating with the stone in those wonderful relics of the antique, and which undoubtedly contribute so much to the great strength of the masonry.

But as if this vast local power in the tendinous tail were not enough, the whole bulk of the leviathan is knit over with a warp and woof of muscular fibres and filaments, which passing on either side the loins and running down into the flukes, insensibly blend with them, and largely contribute to their might; so that in the tail the confluent measureless force of the whole whale seems concentrated to a point. Could annihilation occur to matter, this were the thing to do it.

Five great motions are peculiar to it. First, when used as a fin for progression; Second, when used as a mace in battle; Third, in sweeping; Fourth, in lobtailing; Fifth, in peaking flukes.

First: Being horizontal in its position, the leviathan's tail acts in a different manner from the tails of all other sea creatures. It never wriggles. In man or fish, wriggling is a sign of inferiority. To the whale, his tail is the sole means of propulsion. Scroll-wise coiled forwards beneath the body, and then rapidly sprung backwards, it is this which gives that singular darting, leaping, motion to the monster when furiously swimming. His side-fins only serve to steer by.

Second: It is a little significant, that while one sperm-whale only fights another sperm-whale with his head and jaw, nevertheless, in his conflicts with man, he chiefly and contemptuously uses his tail. In striking at a boat, he swiftly curves away his flukes from it, and the blow is only inflicted by the recoil. If it be made in the unobstructed air, especially if it descend to its mark, the stroke is then simply irresistible. No ribs of man or boat can withstand it. Your only salvation lies in eluding it; but if it comes sideways through the opposing water, then partly owing to the light buoyancy of the whale-boat, and the elasticity of its materials, a cracked rib or a dashed plank or two, a sort of stitch in the side, is generally the most serious result. These submerged side blows are so often received in the fishery, that they are accounted mere child's play. Someone strips off a frock, and the hole is stopped.

Third: I cannot demonstrate it, but it seems to me, that in the whale the sense of touch is concentrated in the tail; for in this respect there is a delicacy in it only equalled by the daintiness of the elephant's trunk. This delicacy is chiefly evinced in the action of sweeping, when in maidenly gentleness the whale with a certain soft slowness moves his immense flukes from side to side upon the surface of the sea; and if he feel but a sailor's whisker, woe to that sailor, whiskers and all. What tenderness there is in that preliminary touch! Had this tail any prehensile power, I should straightway bethink me of Darmonodes' elephant that so frequented the flower-market, and with low salutations presented nosegays to damsels, and then caressed their zones. On more accounts than one, a pity it is that the whale does not possess this prehensile virtue in his tail; for I have heard of yet another elephant, that when wounded in the fight, curved round his trunk and extracted the dart.

Fourth: Stealing unawares upon the whale in the fancied security of the middle of solitary seas, you find him unbent from the vast corpulence of his dignity, and kitten-like, he plays on the ocean as if it were a hearth. But still you see his power in his play. The broad palms of his tail are flirted high into the air; then smiting the surface, the thunderous concussion resounds for miles. You would almost think a great gun had been discharged; and if you noticed the light wreath of vapour from the spiracle at his other extremity, you would think that that was the smoke from the touch-hole.

Fifth: As in the ordinary floating posture of the Leviathan the flukes lie considerably below the level of his back, they are then completely out of sight beneath the surface; but when he is about to plunge into the deeps, his entire flukes with at least thirty feet of his body are tossed erect in the air, and so remain vibrating a moment, till they downwards shoot out of view. Excepting the sublime *breach*—somewhere else to be described—this peaking of the whale's flukes is perhaps the grandest sight to be seen in all animated nature.

The chance comparison in this chapter, between the whale and the elephant, so far as some aspects of the tail of the one and the trunk of the other are concerned, should not tend to place those two opposite organs on an equality, much less the creatures to which they respectively belong. For as the mightiest elephant is but a terrier to Leviathan, so, compared with Leviathan's tail, his trunk is but the stalk of a lily.

The most direful blow from the elephant's trunk were as the playful tap of a fan, compared with the measureless crush and crash of the sperm-whale's ponderous flukes, which in repeated instances have one after the other hurled entire boats with all their oars and crews into the air, very much as an Indian juggler tosses his balls.[1]

The more I consider this mighty tail, the more do I deplore my inability to express it. At times there are gestures in it, which, though they would well grace the hand of man, remain wholly inexplicable. In an extensive herd, so remarkable, occasionally, are these mystic gestures, that I have heard hunters who have declared them akin to Free-Mason signs and symbols; that the whale, indeed, by these methods intelligently conversed with the world. Nor are there wanting other motions of the whale in his general body, full of strangeness, and unaccountable to his most experienced assailant. Dissect him how I may, then, I but go skin deep; I know him not, and never will. But if I know not even the tail of this whale, how understand his head? Much more, how comprehend his face, when face he has none? Thou shalt see my back parts, my tail, he seems to say, but my face shall not be seen. But I cannot completely make out his back parts; and hint what he will about his face, I say again he has no face.

CHAPTER 69

THE GRAND ARMADA

THE LONG and narrow peninsula of Malacca, extending south-eastward from the territories of Burmah, forms the most southerly point of all Asia. In a continuous line from that peninsula stretch the long islands of Sumatra, Java, Bally, and Timor; which, with many others, form a vast mole, or rampart, lengthwise connecting Asia with Australia, and dividing the long unbroken Indian ocean from the thickly studded oriental archipelagos. This rampart is pierced by several sally-ports for the convenience of ships and whales; conspicuous among which are the straits of Sunda and Malacca. By the straits of Sunda, chiefly, vessels bound to China from the west, emerge into the China seas.

[1] Though all comparison in the way of general bulk between the whale and the elephant is preposterous, inasmuch as in that particular the elephant stands in much the same respect to the whale that a dog does to the elephant; nevertheless, there are not wanting some points of curious similitude; among these is the spout. It is well known that the elephant will often draw up water or dust in his trunk, and then elevating it, jet it forth in a stream.

Those narrow straits of Sunda divide Sumatra from Java; and standing midway in that vast rampart of islands, buttressed by that bold green promontory, known to seamen as Java Head; they not a little correspond to the central gateway opening into some vast walled empire: and considering the inexhaustible wealth of spices, and silks, and jewels, and gold, and ivory, with which the thousand islands of that oriental sea are enriched, it seems a significant provision of nature, that such treasures, by the very formation of the land, should at least bear the appearance, however ineffectual, of being guarded from the all-grasping western world. The shores of the Straits of Sunda are unsupplied with those domineering fortresses which guard the entrances to the Mediterranean, the Baltic, and the Propontis. Unlike the Danes, these Orientals do not demand the obsequious homage of lowered topsails from the endless procession of ships before the wind, which for centuries past, by night and by day, have passed between the islands of Sumatra and Java, freighted with the costliest cargoes of the east. But while they freely waive a ceremonial like this, they do by no means renounce their claim to more solid tribute.

Time out of mind the piratical proas of the Malays, lurking among the low shaded coves and islets of Sumatra, have sallied out upon the vessels sailing through the straits, fiercely demanding tribute at the point of their spears. Though by the repeated bloody chastisements they have received at the hands of European cruisers, the audacity of these corsairs has of late been somewhat repressed; yet even at the present day, we occasionally hear of English and American vessels, which, in those waters, have been remorselessly boarded and pillaged.

With a fair, fresh wind, the *Pequod* was now drawing nigh to these straits; Ahab purposing to pass through them into the Javan sea, and thence, cruising northwards, over waters known to be frequented here and there by the sperm-whale, sweep inshore by the Philippine Islands, and gain the far coast of Japan, in time for the great whaling season there. By these means, the circumnavigating *Pequod* would sweep almost all the known sperm-whale cruising grounds of the world, previous to descending upon the Line in the Pacific; where Ahab, though everywhere else foiled in his pursuit, firmly counted upon giving battle to Moby Dick, in the sea he was most known to frequent; and at a season when he might most reasonably be presumed to be haunting it.

But how now? in this zoned quest, does Ahab touch no land? does his crew drink air? Surely, he will stop for water. Nay. For a long time, now, the circus-running sun has raced within his fiery ring, and needs no sustenance but what's in himself. So Ahab. Mark this, too, in the whaler. While other hulls are loaded down with alien stuff, to be transferred to foreign wharves; the world-wandering whale-ship carries no cargo but herself and crew, their weapons and their wants. She has a whole lake's contents bottled in her ample hold. She is ballasted with utilities; not altogether with unusable pig-lead and kent-ledge. She carries years' water in her. Clear old prime Nantucket water; which, when three years afloat, the Nantucketer, in the Pacific, prefers to drink before the brackish fluid, but yesterday rafted off in casks, from the Peruvian or Indian streams. Hence it is, that, while other ships may have gone to China from New York, and back again, touching at a score of ports, the whale-ship, in all that interval, may not have sighted one grain of soil; her crew having seen no man but floating seamen like themselves. So that did you carry them the news that another flood had come; they would only answer—"Well, boys, here's the ark!"

Now, as many sperm-whales had been captured off the western coast of Java, in the near vicinity of the Straits of Sunda; indeed, as most of the ground, roundabout, was generally recognized by the fishermen as an excellent spot for cruising; therefore, as the *Pequod* gained more and more upon Java Head, the look-outs were repeatedly hailed, and admonished to keep wide awake. But though the green palmy cliffs of the land soon loomed on the starboard bow, and with delighted nostrils the fresh cinnamon was snuffed in the air, yet not a single jet was descried. Almost renouncing all thought of falling in with any game hereabouts, the ship had well nigh entered the straits, when the customary cheering cry was heard from aloft, and ere long a spectacle of singular magnificence saluted us.

But here be it premised, that owing to the unwearied activity with which of late they have been hunted over all four oceans, the sperm-whales, instead of almost invariably sailing in small detached companies, as in former times, are now frequently met with in extensive herds, sometimes embracing so great a multitude, that it would almost seem as if numerous nations of them had sworn solemn league and covenant for mutual assistance and protection. To this aggregation of the sperm-whale into such immense caravans, may be imputed the circumstance that even in the best cruising grounds, you may now sometimes sail for weeks and months together, without being greeted by a single spout; and then be suddenly saluted by what sometimes seems thousands on thousands.

Broad on both bows, at the distance of some two or three miles, and forming a great semicircle, embracing one half of the level horizon, a continuous chain of whale-jets were up-playing and sparkling in the noonday air. Unlike the straight perpendicular twin-jets of the Right whale, which, dividing at top, fall over in two branches, like the cleft drooping boughs of a willow, the single forward-slanting spout of the sperm-whale presents a thick curled bush of white mist, continually rising and falling away to leeward.

Crowding all sail the *Pequod* pressed after them; the harpooneers handling their weapons, and loudly cheering from the heads of their yet suspended boats. If the wind only held, little doubt had they, that chased through these Straits of Sunda, the vast host would only deploy into the Oriental seas to witness the capture of not a few of their number. And who could tell whether, in that congregated caravan, Moby Dick himself might not temporarily be swimming, like the worshipped white-elephant in the coronation procession of the Siamese! So with stun-sail piled on stun-sail, we sailed along, driving these leviathans before us; when, of a sudden, the voice of Tashtego was heard, loudly directing attention to something in our wake.

Corresponding to the crescent in our van, we beheld another in our rear. It seemed formed of detached white vapours, rising and falling something like the spouts of the whales; only they did not so completely come and go; for they constantly hovered, without finally disappearing. Levelling his glass at this sight, Ahab quickly revolved in his pivot-hole, crying, "Aloft there, and rig whips and buckets to wet the sails;—Malays, sir, and after us!"

As if long lurking behind the headlands, till the *Pequod* should fairly have entered the straits, these rascally Asiatics were now in hot pursuit, to make up for their over-cautious delay. But when the swift *Pequod*, with a fresh leading wind, was herself in hot chase; how very kind of these tawny philanthropists to assist in speeding her on to her own chosen pursuit,—mere riding-whips and rowels to her, that they were. As with glass under arm, Ahab to-and-fro paced the deck; in his forward turn beholding the monsters he chased, and in the after one the bloodthirsty pirates chasing *him;* some such fancy as the above seemed his. And when he glanced upon the green walls of the watery defile in which the ship was then sailing, and bethought him that through that gate lay the route to his vengeance, and beheld, how that through that same gate he was now both chasing and being chased to his deadly end; and not only that, but a herd of remorseless wild pirates and inhuman atheistical devils were infernally cheering him on with their curses;—when all these conceits had passed through his brain, Ahab's brow was left gaunt and ribbed, like the black sand beach after some stormy tide has been gnawing it, without being able to drag the firm thing from its place.

But thoughts like these troubled very few of the reckless crew; and when, after steadily dropping and dropping the pirates astern, the *Pequod* at last shot by the vivid green Cockatoo Point on the Sumatra side, emerging at last upon the broad waters beyond; then, the harpooneers seemed more to grieve that the swift whales had been gaining upon the ship, than to rejoice that the ship had so victoriously gained upon the Malays. But still driving on in the wake of the whales, at length they seemed abating their speed; gradually the ship neared them; and the wind now dying away, word was passed to spring to the boats. But no sooner did the herd, by some presumed wonderful instinct of the sperm-whale, become notified of the three keels that were after them,—though as yet a mile in their rear,—than they rallied again, and forming in close ranks and battalions, so that their spouts all looked like flashing lines of stacked bayonets, moved on with redoubled velocity.

Stripped to our shirts and drawers, we sprang to the white-ash, and after several hours' pulling were almost disposed to renounce the chase, when a general pausing commotion among the whales gave animating tokens that they were now at last under the influence of that strange perplexity of inert irresolution, which, when the fishermen perceive it in the whale, they say he is gallied. The compact martial columns in which they had been hitherto rapidly and steadily swimming, were now broken up in one measureless rout; and like King Porus' elephants in the Indian battle with Alexander, they seemed going mad with consternation. In all directions expanding in vast irregular circles, and aimlessly swimming hither and thither, by their short thick spoutings, they plainly betrayed their distraction of panic. This was still more strangely evinced by those of their number, who, completely paralysed as it were, helplessly floated like waterlogged dismantled ships on the sea. Had these Leviathans been but a flock of simple sheep, pursued over the pasture by three fierce wolves, they could not possibly have evinced such excessive dismay. But this occasional timidity is characteristic of almost all herding creatures. Though banding together in tens of thousands, the lion-maned buffaloes of the West have fled before a solitary horseman. Witness, too, all human beings, how when herded together in the sheepfold of a theatre's pit, they will, at the slightest alarm of fire, rush helter-skelter for the outlets, crowding, trampling, jamming, and remorselessly dashing each other to death. Best, therefore, withhold any amazement at the strangely gallied whales before us, for there is no folly of the beast of the earth which is not infinitely outdone by the madness of men.

Though many of the whales, as has been said, were in violent motion, yet it is to be observed that as a whole the herd neither advanced nor retreated, but collectively remained in one place. As is customary in those cases, the boats at once separated, each making for some one lone whale on the outskirts of the shoal. In about three minutes' time, Queequeg's harpoon was flung; the stricken fish darted blinding spray in our faces, and then running away with us like light, steered straight for the heart of the herd. Though such a movement on the part of the whale struck under such circumstances, is in no wise unprecedented; and indeed is almost always more or less anticipated; yet does it present one of the more perilous vicissitudes of the fishery. For as the swift monster drags you deeper and deeper into the frantic shoal, you bid adieu to circumspect life and only exist in a delirious throb.

As, blind and deaf, the whale plunged forward, as if by sheer power of speed to rid himself of the iron leach that had fastened to him; as we thus tore a white gash in the sea, on all sides menaced as we flew, by the crazed creatures to and fro rushing about us; our beset boat was like a ship mobbed by ice-isles in a tempest, and striving to steer through their complicated channels and straits, knowing not at what moment it may be locked in and crushed.

But not a bit daunted, Queequeg steered us manfully; now sheering off from this monster directly across our route in advance; now edging away from that, whose colossal flukes were suspended overhead, while all the time, Starbuck stood up in the bows, lance in hand, pricking out of our way whatever whales he could reach by short darts, for there was no time to make long ones. Nor were the oarsmen quite idle, though their wonted duty was now altogether dispensed with. They chiefly attended to the shouting part of the business. "Out of the way, Commodore!" cried one, to a great dromedary that of a sudden rose bodily to the surface, and for an instant threatened to swamp us. "Hard down with your tail there!" cried a second to another, which, close to our gunwale, seemed calmly cooling himself with his own fan-like extremity.

All whale-boats carry certain curious contrivances, originally invented by the Nantucket Indians, called druggs. Two thick squares of wood of equal size are stoutly clenched together, so that they cross each other's grain at right-angles; a line of considerable length is then attached to the middle of this block, and the other end of the line being looped, it can in a moment be fastened to a harpoon. It is chiefly among gallied whales that this drugg is used. For then, more whales are close round you than you can possibly chase at one time. But sperm-whales are not every day encountered; while you may, then, you must kill all you can. And if you cannot kill them all at once, you must wing them, so that they can be afterwards killed at your leisure. Hence it is, that at times like these the drugg comes into requisition. Our boat was furnished with three of them. The first and second were successfully darted, and we saw the whales staggeringly running off, fettered by the enormous sidelong resistance of the towing drugg. They were cramped like malefactors with the chain and ball. But upon flinging the third, in the act of tossing overboard the clumsy wooden block, it caught under one of the seats of the boat, and in an instant tore it out and carried it away, dropping the oarsman in the boat's bottom as the seat slid from under him. On both sides the sea came in at the wounded planks, but we stuffed two or three drawers and shirts in, and so stopped the leaks for the time.

It had been next to impossible to dart these drugged-harpoons, were it not that as we advanced into the herd, our whale's way greatly diminished; moreover, that as we went still farther and farther from the circumference of commotion, the direful disorders seemed waning. So that when at last the jerking harpoon drew out, and the towing whale sideways vanished; then, with the tapering force of his parting momentum, we glided between two whales into the innermost heart of the shoal, as if from some mountain torrent we had slid into a serene valley lake. Here the storms in the roaring glens between the outermost whales, were heard but not felt. In this central expanse the sea presented that smooth satin-like surface, called a sleek, produced by the subtle moisture thrown off by the whale in his more quiet moods. Yes, we were now in that enchanted calm which they say lurks at the heart of every commotion. And still in the distracted distance we beheld the tumults of the outer concentric circles, and saw successive pods of whales, eight or ten in each, swiftly going round and round, like multiplied spans of horses in a ring; and so closely shoulder to shoulder, that a Titanic circus-rider might easily have over-arched the middle ones, and so have gone round on their backs. Owing to the density of the crowd of reposing whales, more immediately surrounding the embayed axis of the herd, no possible chance of escape was at present afforded us. We must watch for a breach in the living wall that hemmed us in; the wall that had only admitted us in order to shut us up. Keeping at the centre of the lake, we were occasionally visited by small tame cows and calves; the women and children of this routed host.

Now, inclusive of the occasional wide intervals between the revolving outer circles, and inclusive of the spaces between the various pods in any one of those circles, the entire area at this juncture, embraced by the whole multitude, must have contained at least two or three square miles. At any rate—though indeed such a test at such a time might be deceptive—spoutings might be discovered from our low boat that seemed playing up almost from the rim of the horizon. I mention this circumstance, because, as if the cows and calves had been purposely locked up in this innermost fold; and as if the wide extent of the herd had hitherto prevented them from learning the precise cause of its stopping; or, possibly, being so young, unsophisticated, and every way innocent and inexperienced; however it may have been, these smaller whales—now and then visiting our becalmed boat from the margin of the lake—evinced a wondrous fearlessness and confidence, or else a still becharmed panic which it was impossible not to marvel at. Like household dogs they came snuffing round us, right up to our gun-wales, and touching them; till it almost seemed that some spell had suddenly domesticated them. Queequeg patted their foreheads; Starbuck scratched their backs with his lance; but fearful of the consequences, for the time refrained from darting it.

But far beneath this wondrous world upon the surface, another and still stranger world met our eyes as we gazed over the side. For, suspended in those watery vaults, floated the forms of the nursing mothers of the whales, and those that by their enormous girth seemed shortly to become mothers. The lake, as I have hinted, was to a considerable depth exceedingly transparent; and as human infants while suckling will calmly and fixedly gaze away from the breast, as if leading two different lives at the time; and while yet drawing mortal nourishment, be still spiritually feasting upon some unearthly reminiscence;—even so did the young of these whales seem looking up towards us, but not at us, as if we were but a bit of Gulf-weed in their new-born sight. Floating on their sides, the mothers also seemed quietly eyeing us. One of these little infants, that from certain queer tokens seemed hardly a day old, might have measured some fourteen feet in length, and some six feet in girth. He was a little frisky; though as yet his body seemed scarce yet recovered from that irksome position it had so lately occupied in the maternal reticule; where, tail to head, and all ready for the final spring, the unborn whale lies bent like a Tartar's bow. The delicate side-fins, and the palms of his flukes, still freshly retained the plaited crumpled appearance of a baby's ears newly arrived from foreign parts.

"Line! Line!" cried Queequeg, looking over the gunwale; "him fast! him fast!—Who line him! Who struck?—Two whale; one big, one little!"

"What ails ye, man?" cried Starbuck.

"Look-e here," said Queequeg pointing down.

As when the stricken whale, that from the tub has reeled out hundreds of fathoms of rope; as, after deep sounding, he floats up again and shows the slackened curling line buoyantly rising and spiralling towards the air; so now, Starbuck saw long coils of the umbilical cord of Madame Leviathan, by which the young cub seemed still tethered to its dam. Not seldom in the rapid vicissitudes of the chase, this natural line, with the maternal end loose, becomes entangled with the hempen one, so that the cub is thereby trapped. Some of the subtles secrets of the seas seemed divulged to us in this enchanted pond. We saw young Leviathan amours in the deep.[1]

And thus, though surrounded by circle upon circle of consternation and affrights, did these inscrutable creatures at the centre freely and fearlessly indulge in all peaceful concernments; yea, serenely revelled in dalliance and delight. But even so, amid the tornadoed Atlantic of my being, do I myself still for ever centrally disport in mute calm; and while ponderous planets of unwaning woe revolve round me, deep down and deep inland there I still bathe me in eternal mildness of joy.

Meanwhile, as we thus lay entranced, the occasional sudden frantic spectacles in the distance evinced the activity of the other boats, still engaged in drugging the whales on the frontier of the host; or possibly carrying on the war within the first circle, where abundance of room and some convenient retreats were afforded them. But the sight of the enraged drugged whales now and then blindly darting to and fro across the circles, was nothing to what at last met our eyes. It is sometimes the custom when fast to a whale more than commonly powerful and alert, to seek to hamstring him, as it were, by sundering or maiming his gigantic tail-tendon. It is done by darting a short-handled cutting-spade, to which is attached a rope for hauling it back again. A whale wounded (as we afterwards learned) in this part, but not effectually, as it seemed, had broken away from the boat, carrying along with him half of the harpoon line; and in the extraordinary agony of the wound, he was now dashing among the revolving circles like the lone mounted desperado Arnold, at the battle of Saratoga, carrying dismay wherever he went.

[1] The sperm-whale, as with all other species of the Leviathan, but unlike most other fish, breeds indifferently at all seasons; after a gestation which may probably be set down at nine months, producing but one at a time; though in some few known instances giving birth to an Esau and Jacob:—a contingency provided for in suckling by two teats curiously situated, one on each side of the anus; but the breasts themselves extend upwards from that. When by chance these precious parts in a nursing whale are cut by the hunter's lance, the mother's pouring milk and blood rivallingly discolour the sea for rods. The milk is very sweet and rich; it has been tasted by man; it might do well with strawberries. When overflowing with mutual esteem, the whales salute *more hominum*.

But agonizing as was the wound of this whale, and an appalling spectacle enough, any way; yet the peculiar horror with which he seemed to inspire the rest of the herd, was owing to a cause which at first the intervening distance obscured from us. But at length we perceived that by one of the unimaginable accidents of the fishery, this whale had become entangled in the harpoon-line that he towed; he had also run away with the cutting-spade in him; and while the free end of the rope attached to that weapon, had permanently caught in the coils of the harpoon-line round his tail, the cutting-spade itself had worked loose from his flesh. So that tormented to madness, he was now churning through the water, violently flailing with his flexible tail, and tossing the keen spade about him, wounding and murdering his own comrades.

This terrific object seemed to recall the whole herd from their stationary fright. First, the whales forming the margin of our lake began to crowd a little, and tumble against each other, as if lifted by half-spent billows from afar; then the lake itself began faintly to heave and swell; the submarine bridal-chambers and nurseries vanished; in more and more contracting orbits the whales in the more central circles began to swim in thickening clusters. Yes, the long calm was departing. A low advancing hum was soon heard; and then like to the tumultuous masses of block-ice when the great river Hudson breaks up in spring, the entire host of whales came tumbling upon their inner centre, as if to pile themselves up in one common mountain. Instantly Starbuck and Queequeg changed places; Starbuck taking the stern.

"Oars! Oars!" he intensely whispered, seizing the helm—"gripe your oars, and clutch your souls, now! My God, men, stand by! Shove him off, you Queequeg—the whale there!—prick him!—hit him! stand up—stand up, and stay so! Spring, men—pull, men; never mind their backs—scrape them!—scrape away!"

The boat was now all but jammed between two vast black bulks, leaving a narrow Dardanelles between their long lengths. But by desperate endeavour we at last shot into a temporary opening; then giving way rapidly, and at the same time earnestly watching for another outlet. After many similar hair-breadth escapes, we at last swiftly glided into what had just been one of the outer circles, but now crossed by random whales, all violently making for one centre. This lucky salvation was cheaply purchased by the loss of Queequeg's hat, who, while standing in the bows to prick the fugitive whales, had his hat taken clean from his head by the air-eddy made by the sudden passing of a pair of broad flukes close by.

Riotous and disordered as the universal commotion now was, it soo
resolved itself into what seemed a systematic movement; for havin
clumped together at last in one dense body, they then renewed thei
onward flight with augmented fleetness. Further pursuit was useless
but the boats still lingered in their wake to pick up what drugge
whales might be dropped astern, and likewise to secure one whic'
Flask had killed and waifed. The waif is a pennoned pole, two c
three of which are carried by every boat; and which, when addition;
game is at hand, are inserted upright into the floating body of a dea
whale, both to mark its place on the sea, and also as token of pric
possession, should the boats of any other ship draw near.

The result of this lowering was somewhat illustrative of that sag;
cious saying in the Fishery,—the more whales the less fish. Of ;
the drugged whales only one was captured. The rest contrived t
escape for the time, but only to be taken, as will hereafter be seer
by some other craft than the *Pequod*.

CHAPTER 70

SCHOOLS AND SCHOOLMASTERS

THE PREVIOUS chapter gave account of an immense body or herd c
sperm-whales, and there was also then given the probable caus
inducing those vast aggregations.

Now, though such great bodies are at times encountered, yet, a
must have been seen, even at the present day, small detached band
are occasionally observed, embracing from twenty to fifty individual
each. Such bands are known as schools. They generally are of tw
sorts; those composed almost entirely of females, and those muster
ing none but young vigorous males, or bulls as they are familiarl
designated.

In cavalier attendance upon the school of females, you invariably se
a male of full grown magnitude, but not old; who, upon any alarm
evinces his gallantry by falling in the rear and covering the flight c
his ladies. In truth, this gentleman is a luxurious Ottoman, swimmin
about over the watery world, surroundingly accompanied by all th
solaces and endearments of the harem. The contrast between thi
Ottoman and his concubines is striking; because, while he is alway
of the largest leviathanic proportions, the ladies, even at full growth
are not more than one-third of the bulk of an average-sized male. The
are comparatively delicate, indeed; I dare say, not to exceed half

dozen yards round the waist. Nevertheless, it cannot be denied, that upon the whole they are hereditarily entitled to *en bon point*.

It is very curious to watch this harem and its lord in their indolent ramblings. Like fashionables, they are for ever on the move in leisurely search of variety. You meet them on the Line in time for the full flower of the Equatorial feeding season, having just returned, perhaps, from spending the summer in the Northern seas, and so cheating summer of all unpleasant weariness and warmth. By the time they have lounged up and down the promenade of the Equator awhile, they start for the Oriental waters in anticipation of the cool season there, and so evade the other excessive temperature of the year.

Now, as the harem of whales is called by the fishermen a school, so is the lord and master of that school technically known as the schoolmaster. It is therefore not in strict character, however admirably satirical, that after going to school himself, he should then go abroad inculcating not what he learned there, but the folly of it.

The same secludedness and isolation to which the schoolmaster whale betakes himself in his advancing years, is true of all aged sperm-whales. Almost universally, a lone whale—as a solitary Leviathan is called—proves an ancient one.

The schools composing none but young and vigorous males, previously mentioned, offer a strong contrast to the harem schools. For while those female whales are characteristically timid, the young males, or Forty-barrel-bulls, as they call them, are by far the most pugnacious of all Leviathans, and proverbially the most dangerous to encounter; excepting those wondrous grey-headed, grizzled whales, sometimes met, and these will fight you like grim fiends exasperated by a penal gout.

The Forty-barrel-bull schools are larger than the harem schools. Like a mob of young collegians, they are full of fight, fun, and wickedness, tumbling round the world at such a reckless, rollicking rate, that no prudent underwriter would insure them any more than he would a riotous lad at Yale or Harvard. They soon relinquish this turbulence though, and when about three-fourths grown, break up, and separately go about in quest of settlements, that is, harems.

Another point of difference between the male and female schools is still more characteristic of the sexes. Say you strike a forty-barrel-bull —poor devil! all his comrades quit him. But strike a member of the harem school, and her companions swim around her with every token of concern, sometimes lingering so near her and so long, as themselves to fall a prey.

CHAPTER 71

FAST-FISH AND LOOSE-FISH

The allusion to the waifs and waif-poles in the last chapter but one necessitates some account of the laws and regulations of the whale fishery, of which the waif may be deemed the grand symbol and badge.

It frequently happens that when several ships are cruising in company, a whale may be struck by one vessel, then escape, and be finally killed and captured by another vessel; and herein are indirectly comprised many minor contingencies, all partaking of this one grand feature. For example,—after a weary and perilous chase and capture of a whale, the body may get loose from the ship by reason of a violent storm; and drifting far away to leeward, be retaken by a second whaler, who, in a calm, snugly tows it alongside, without risk of life or line. Thus the most vexatious and violent disputes would often arise between the fishermen, were there not some written or unwritten, universal, undisputed law applicable to all cases.

Perhaps the only formal whaling code authorized by legislative enactment, was that of Holland. It was decreed by the States-General in A.D. 1695. But though no other nation has ever had any written whaling law, yet the American fishermen have been their own legislators and lawyers in this matter. They have provided a system which for terse comprehensiveness surpasses Justinian's Pandects and the Bye-laws of the Chinese Society for the Suppression of Meddling with other People's Business. Yes; these laws might be engraven on a Queen Anne's farthing, or the barb of a harpoon, and worn round the neck, so small are they.

I. A Fast-Fish belongs to the party fast to it.

II. A Loose-Fish is fair game for anybody who can soonest catch it.

But what plays the mischief with this masterly code is the admirable brevity of it, which necessitates a vast volume of commentaries to expound it.

First: What is a Fast-Fish? Alive or dead a fish is technically fast, when it is connected with an occupied ship or boat, by any medium at all controllable by the occupant or occupants,—a mast, an oar, a nine-inch cable, a telegraph wire, or a strand of cobweb, it is all the same. Likewise a fish is technically fast when it bears a waif, or any other recognized symbol of possession; so long as the party waifing it plainly evince their ability at any time to take it alongside, as well as their intention so to do.

These are scientific commentaries; but the commentaries of the whalemen themselves sometimes consist in hard words and harder knocks—the Coke-upon-Littleton of the fist. True, among the more upright and honourable whalemen allowances are always made for peculiar cases, where it would be an outrageous moral injustice for one party to claim possession of a whale previously chased or killed by another party. But others are by no means so scrupulous.

CHAPTER 72

THE "PEQUOD" MEETS THE "ROSE-BUD"

In vain it was to rake for Ambergriese in the paunch of this Leviathan, insufferable fetor denying not inquiry.

Sir T. Browne, V.E.

IT WAS a week or two after the last whaling scene recounted, and when we were slowly sailing over a sleepy, vapoury, midday sea, that the many noses on the *Pequod's* deck proved more vigilant discoverers than the three pairs of eyes aloft. A peculiar and not very pleasant smell was smelt in the sea.

"I will bet something now," said Stubb, "that somewhere hereabouts are some of those drugged whales we tickled the other day. I thought they would keel up before long."

Presently, the vapours in advance slid aside; and there in the distance lay a ship, whose furled sails betokened that some sort of whale must be alongside. As we glided nearer, the stranger showed French colours from his peak; and by the eddying cloud of vulture sea-fowl that circled, and hovered, and swooped around him, it was plain that the whale alongside must be what the fishermen call a blasted whale, that is, a whale that has died unmolested on the sea, and so floated an unappropriated corpse. It may well be conceived, what an unsavoury odour such a mass must exhale; worse than an Assyrian city in the plague, when the living are incompetent to bury the departed. So intolerable indeed is it regarded by some, that no cupidity could persuade them to moor alongside of it. Yet are there those who will still do it; notwithstanding the fact that the oil obtained from such subjects is of a very inferior quality, and by no means of the nature of attar-of-rose.

Coming still nearer with the expiring breeze, we saw that the Frenchman had a second whale alongside; and this second whale seemed even more of a nosegay than the first. In truth, it turned out to be one of those problematical whales that seem to dry up and die with a sort of prodigious dyspepsia, or indigestion; leaving their defunct bodies almost entirely bankrupt of anything like oil. Nevertheless, in the proper place we shall see that no knowing fisherman will ever turn up his nose at such a whale as this, however much he may shun blasted whales in general.

The *Pequod* had now swept so nigh to the stranger, that Stubb vowed he recognized his cutting-spade pole entangled in the lines that were knotted round the tail of one of these whales.

By this time the faint air had become a complete calm; so that whether or no, the *Pequod* was now fairly entrapped in the smell, with no hope of escaping except by its breezing up again. Issuing from the cabin, Stubb now called his boat's crew, and pulled off for the stranger. Drawing across her bow, he perceived that in accordance with the fanciful French taste, the upper part of her stempiece was carved in the likeness of a huge drooping stalk, was painted green, and for thorns had copper spikes projecting from it here and there; the whole terminating in a symmetrical folded bulb of a bright red colour. Upon her head boards, in large gilt letters, he read "*Bouton de Rose*,"— *Rose-button,* or *Rose-bud*; and this was the romantic name of this aromatic ship.

Though Stubb did not understand the *Bouton* part of the inscription, yet the word *rose,* and the bulbous figure-head put together, sufficiently explained the whole to him.

"A wooden rose-bud, eh?" he cried with his hand to his nose, "that will do very well; but how like all creation it smells!"

Now in order to hold direct communication with the people on deck, he had to pull round the bows to the starboard side, and thus come close to the blasted whale; and so talk over it.

Arrived then at this spot, with one hand still to his nose, he bawled— "*Bouton-de-Rose,* ahoy! are there any of you *Bouton-de-Roses* that speak English?"

"Yes," rejoined a Guernsey-man from the bulwarks, who turned out to be the chief-mate.

"Well, then, my *Bouton-de-Rose-bud,* have you seen the white whale?"

"*What* whale?"

"The *white* whale—a sperm-whale—Moby Dick, have ye seen him?"

"Never heard of such a whale. Cachalot Blanche! White whale— no."

"Very good, then; good-bye now, and I'll call again in a minute."

Then rapidly pulling back towards the *Pequod* and seeing Ahab leaning over the quarter-deck rail awaiting his report, he moulded his two hands into a trumpet and shouted— "No, Sir! No!" Upon which Ahab retired, and Stubb returned to the Frenchman.

He now perceived that the Guernsey-man, who had just got into the chains, and was using a cutting-spade, had slung his nose in a sort of bag.

"What's the matter with your nose, there?" said Stubb. "Broke it?"

"I wish it was broken, or that I didn't have any nose at all!" answered the Guernsey-man, who did not seem to relish the job he was at very much. "But what are you holding *yours* for?"

"Oh, nothing! It's a wax nose; I have to hold it on. Fine day, ain't it? Air rather gardenny, I should say; throw us a bunch of posies, will ye, *Bouton-de-Rose*?"

"What in the devil's name do you want here?" roared the Guernsey-man, flying into a sudden passion.

"Oh! keep cool—cool? yes, that's the word; why don't you pack those whales in ice while you're working at 'em? But joking aside, though; do you know, Rose-bud, that it's all nonsense trying to get any oil out of such whales? As for that dried-up one, there, he hasn't a gill in his whole carcase."

"I know that well enough; but, d'ye see, the captain here won't believe it; this is the first voyage; he was a Cologne manufacturer before. But come aboard, and mayhap he'll believe you, if he won't me; and so I'll get out of this dirty scrape."

"Anything to oblige ye, my sweet and pleasant fellow," rejoined Stubb, and with that he soon mounted to the deck. There a queer scene presented itself. The sailors, in tasselled caps of red worsted, were getting the heavy tackles in readiness for the whales. But they worked rather slow and talked very fast, and seemed in anything but a good humour. All their noses upwardly projected from their faces like so many jib-booms. Now and then pairs of them would drop their work, and run up to the mast-head to get some fresh air. Some thinking they would catch the plague, dipped oakum in coal-tar, and at intervals held it to their nostrils. Others having broken the stems of their pipes almost short off at the bowl, were vigorously puffing tobacco-smoke, so that it constantly filled their olfactories.

Stubb was struck by a shower of outcries and anathemas proceeding from the captain's round-house abaft; and looking in that direction saw a fiery face thrust from behind the door, which was held ajar from within. This was the tormented surgeon, who, after in vain remonstrating against the proceedings of the day, had betaken himself to

G

the captain's round-house (*cabinet*, he called it) to avoid the pest; but still, could not help yelling out his entreaties and indignations at times.

Marking all this, Stubb argued well for his scheme, and turning to the Guernsey-man had a little chat with him, during which the stranger mate expressed his detestation of his captain as a conceited ignoramus, who had brought them all into so unsavoury and unprofitable a pickle. Sounding him carefully, Stubb further perceived that the Guernsey-man had not the slightest suspicion concerning the ambergris. He therefore held his peace on that head, but otherwise was quite frank and confidential with him, so that the two quickly concocted a little plan for both circumventing and satirizing the captain, without his at all dreaming of distrusting their sincerity. According to this little plan of theirs, the Guernsey-man, under cover of an interpreter's office, was to tell the captain what he pleased, but as coming from Stubb; and as for Stubb, he was to utter any nonsense that should come uppermost in him during the interview.

By this time their destined victim appeared from his cabin. He was a small and dark, but rather delicate looking man for a sea-captain, with large whiskers and moustache, however; and wore a red cotton velvet vest with watch-seals at his side. To this gentleman, Stubb was now politely introduced by the Guernsey-man, who at once ostentatiously put on the aspect of interpreting between them.

"What shall I say to him first?" said he.

"Why," said Stubb, eyeing the velvet vest and the watch and seals, "you may as well begin by telling him that he looks a sort of babyish to me, though I don't pretend to be a judge."

"He says, Monsieur," said the Guernsey-man, in French, turning to his captain, "that only yesterday his ship spoke a vessel, whose captain and chief-mate, with six sailors, had all died of a fever caught from a blasted whale they had brought alongside."

Upon this the captain started, and eagerly desired to know more.

"What now?" said the Guernsey-man to Stubb.

"Why, since he takes it so easy, tell him that now I have eyed him carefully, I'm quite certain that he's no more fit to command a whale-ship than a St. Jago monkey. In fact, tell him from me he's a baboon."

"He vows and declares, Monsieur, that the other whale, the dried one, is far more deadly than the blasted one; in fine, Monsieur, he conjures us, as we value our lives, to cut loose from these fish."

Instantly the captain ran forward, and in a loud voice commanded his crew to desist from hoisting the cutting-tackles, and at once cast loose the cables and chains confining the whales to the ship.

"What now?" said the Guernsey-man, when the captain had returned to them.

"Why, let me see; yes, you may as well tell him now that—that—in fact, tell him I've diddled him, and (aside to himself) perhaps somebody else."

"He says, Monsieur, that he's very happy to have been of any service to us."

Hearing this, the captain vowed that they were the grateful parties (meaning himself and mate) and concluded by inviting Stubb down into his cabin to drink a bottle of Bordeaux.

"He wants you to take a glass of wine with him," said the interpreter.

"Thank him heartily; but tell him it's against my principles to drink with the man I've diddled. In fact, tell him I must go."

"He says, Monsieur, that his principles won't admit of his drinking; but that if Monsieur wants to live another day to drink, then Monsieur had best drop all four boats, and pull the ship away from these whales, for it's so calm they won't drift."

By this time Stubb was over the side, and getting into his boat, hailed the Guernsey-man to this effect,—that having a long tow-line in his boat, he would do what he could to help them, by pulling out the lighter whale of the two from the ship's side. While the Frenchman's boats, then, were engaged in towing the ship one way, Stubb benevolently towed away at his whale the other way, ostentatiously slacking out a most unusually long tow-line.

Presently a breeze sprang up; Stubb feigned to cast off from the whale; hoisting his boats, the Frenchman soon increased his distance, while the *Pequod* slid in between him and Stubb's whale. Whereupon Stubb quickly pulled to the floating body, and hailing the *Pequod* to give notice of his intentions, at once proceeded to reap the fruit of his unrighteous cunning. Seizing his sharp boat-spade, he commenced an excavation in the body, a little behind the side fin. You would almost have thought he was digging a cellar there in the sea; and when at length his spade struck against the gaunt ribs, it was like turning up old Roman tiles and pottery buried in fat English loam. His boat's crew were all in high excitement, eagerly helping their chief, and looking as anxious as gold-hunters.

And all the time numberless fowls were diving, and ducking, and screaming, and yelling, and fighting around them. Stubb was beginning to look disappointed, especially as the horrible nosegay increased, when suddenly from out the very heart of this plague, there stole a faint stream of perfume, which flowed through the tide of bad smells without being absorbed by it, as one river will flow into and then along with another, without at all blending with it for a time.

"I have it, I have it," cried Stubb, with delight, striking something in the subterranean regions, "a purse! a purse!"

Dropping his spade, he thrust both hands in, and drew out handfuls of something that looked like ripe Windsor soap, or rich mottled old cheese; very unctuous and savoury withal. You might easily dent it with your thumb; it is of a hue between yellow and ash colour. And this, good friends, is ambergris, worth a gold guinea an ounce to any druggist. Some six handfuls were obtained, but more was unavoidably lost in the sea, and still more, perhaps, might have been secured were it not for impatient Ahab's loud command to Stubb to desist, and come on board, else the ship would bid them good-bye.

CHAPTER 73

AMBERGRIS

Now this ambergris is a very curious substance, and so important as an article of commerce, that in 1791 a certain Nantucket-born Captain Coffin was examined at the bar of the English House of Commons on that subject. For at that time, and indeed until a comparatively late day, the precise origin of ambergris remained, like amber itself, a problem to the learned. Though the word ambergris is but the French compound for grey amber, yet the two substances are quite distinct. For amber, though at times found on the sea-coast, is also dug up in some far inland soils, whereas ambergris is never found except upon the sea. Besides, amber is a hard, transparent, brittle, odourless substance, used for mouth-pieces to pipes, for beads and ornaments; but ambergris is soft, waxy, and so highly fragrant and spicy, that it is largely used in perfumery, in pastilles, precious candles, hair-powders, and pomatum. The Turks use it in cooking, and also carry it to Mecca, for the same purpose that frankincense is carried to St. Peter's in Rome. Some wine merchants drop a few grains into claret, to flavour it.

Who would think, then, that such fine ladies and gentlemen should regale themselves with an essence found in the inglorious bowels of a sick whale! Yet so it is. By some, ambergris is supposed to be the cause, and by others the effect, of the dyspepsia in the whale. How to cure such dyspepsia it were hard to say, unless by administering

hree or four boat loads of Brandreth's pills, and then running out of
arm's way, as labourers do in blasting rocks.

I have forgotten to say that there were found in this ambergris,
ertain hard, round, bony plates, which at first Stubb thought might
e sailors' trousers buttons; but it afterwards turned out that they
ere nothing more than pieces of small squid bones embalmed in that
manner.

CHAPTER 74

THE CASTAWAY

T WAS but some few days after encountering the Frenchman, that a
most significant event befell the most insignificant of the *Pequod*'s
rew; an event most lamentable; and which ended in providing the
ometimes madly merry and predestinated craft with a living and ever
ccompanying prophecy of whatever shattered sequel might prove her
wn.

Now, in the whale-ship, it is not everyone that goes in the boats.
ome few hands are reserved called ship-keepers, whose province it
to work the vessel while the boats are pursuing the whale. As a
eneral thing, these ship-keepers are as hardy fellows as the men com-
rising the boats' crews. But if there happen to be an unduly slender,
umsy, or timorous wight in the ship, that wight is certain to be made
ship-keeper. It was so in the *Pequod* with the little negro Pippin by
ickname, Pip by abbreviation.

It came to pass, that in the ambergris affair Stubb's after-oarsman
anced so to sprain his hand, as for a time to become quite maimed;
id, temporarily, Pip was put into his place.

The first time Stubb lowered with him, Pip evinced much nervous-
ess; but happily, for that time, escaped close contact with the whale;
id therefore came off not altogether discreditably; though Stubb
bserving him, took care, afterwards, to exhort him to cherish his
ourageousness to the utmost, for he might often find it needful.

Now upon the second lowering, the boat paddled upon the whale;
id as the fish received the darted iron, it gave its customary rap,
hich happened, in this instance, to be right under poor Pip's seat.
he involuntary consternation of the moment caused him to leap,
addle in hand, out of the boat; and in such a way, that part of the
ack whale-line coming against his chest, he breasted it overboard
ith him, so as to become entangled in it, when at last plumping into
e water. That instant the stricken whale started on a fierce run, the

line swiftly straightened; and presto! poor Pip came all foaming up to
the chocks of the boat, remorselessly dragged there by the line, which
had taken several turns around his chest and neck.

Tashtego stood in the bows. He was full of the fire of the hunt. He
hated Pip for a poltroon. Snatching the boat-knife from its sheath, he
suspended its sharp edge over the line, and turning towards Stubb, exclaimed interrogatively, "Cut?" Meantime Pip's blue, choked face
plainly looked, Do, for God's sake! All passed in a flash. In less than
half a minute, this entire thing happened.

"Damn him, cut!" roared Stubb; and so the whale was lost and Pip
was saved.

So soon as he recovered himself the poor little negro was assailed
by yells and execrations from the crew. Tranquilly permitting these
irregular cursings to evaporate, Stubb then in a plain, business-like
but still half humorous manner, cursed Pip officially; and that done
unofficially gave him much wholesome advice. The substance was,
Never jump from a boat, Pip, except—but all the rest was indefinite,
as the soundest advice ever is. Now, in general, *Stick to the boat* is your
true motto in whaling; but cases will sometimes happen when *Leap
from the boat* is still better. Moreover, as if perceiving at last that if
he should give undiluted conscientious advice to Pip, he would be
leaving him too wide a margin to jump in for the future; Stubb suddenly dropped all advice, and concluded with a peremptory command,
"Stick to the boat, Pip, or by the Lord, I won't pick you up if you
jump; mind that. We can't afford to lose whales by the likes of you;
a whale would sell for thirty times what you would, Pip, in Alabama.
Bear that in mind, and don't jump any more." Hereby perhaps Stubb
indirectly hinted, that though man loved his fellow, yet man is a
money-making animal, which propensity too often interferes with his
benevolence.

But we are all in the hands of the Gods; and Pip jumped again. It
was under very similar circumstances to the first performance; but this
time he did not breast out the line; and hence, when the whale started
to run, Pip was left behind on the sea, like a hurried traveller's trunk.
Alas! Stubb was but too true to his word. It was a beautiful, boun-
teous, blue day; the spangled sea calm and cool, and flatly stretching
away, all round, to the horizon, like gold-beater's skin hammered out
to the extremest. Bobbing up and down in that sea, Pip's ebon head
showed like a head of cloves. No boat-knife was lifted when he fell
so rapidly astern. Stubb's inexorable back was turned upon him; and
the whale was winged. In three minutes, a whole mile of shoreless
ocean was between Pip and Stubb. Out from the centre of the sea,

poor Pip turned his crisp, curling, black head to the sun, another lonely castaway, though the loftiest and the brightest.

Now, in calm weather, to swim in the open ocean is as easy to the practised swimmer as to ride in a spring-carriage ashore. But the awful lonesomeness is intolerable. The intense concentration of self in the middle of such a heartless immensity, my God! who can tell it? Mark, now when sailors in a dead calm bathe in the open sea—mark how closely they hug their ship and only coast along her sides.

But had Stubb really abandoned the poor little negro to his fate? No; he did not mean to, at least. Because there were two boats in his wake, and he supposed, no doubt, that they would of course come up to Pip very quickly, and pick him up; though, indeed, such considerations towards oarsmen jeopardized through their own timidity, is not always manifested by the hunters in all similar instances; and such instances not infrequently occur; almost invariably in the fishery, a coward, so called, is marked with the same ruthless detestation peculiar to military navies and armies.

But it so happened, that those boats, without seeing Pip, suddenly spying whales close to them on one side, turned, and gave chase; and Stubb's boat was now so far away, and he and all his crew so intent upon his fish, that Pip's ringed horizon began to expand around him miserably. By the merest chance the ship itself at last rescued him; but from that hour the little negro went about the deck an idiot; such, at least they said he was. The sea had jeeringly kept his finite body up, but drowned the infinite of his soul. Not drowned entirely, though. Rather carried down alive to wondrous depths, where strange shapes of the unwarped primal world glided to and fro before his passive eyes; and the miser-merman, Wisdom, revealed his hoarded heaps; and among the joyous, heartless, ever-juvenile eternities, Pip saw the multitudinous, God-omnipresent, coral insects, that out of the firmament of waters heaved the colossal orbs. He saw God's foot upon the treadle of the loom, and spoke it; and therefore his shipmates called him mad. So man's insanity is heaven's sense; and wandering from all mortal reason, man comes at last to that celestial thought, which, to reason, is absurd and frantic; and weal or woe, feels then uncompromised, indifferent as his God.

For the rest, blame not Stubb too hardly. The thing is common in that fishery; and in the sequel of the narrative, it will then be seen what like abandonment befell myself.

CHAPTER 75

A SQUEEZE OF THE HAND

THAT WHALE of Stubb's, so dearly purchased, was duly brought to the *Pequod*'s side, where all those cutting and hoisting operation previously detailed, were regularly gone through, even to the baling of the Heidelburgh Tun, or Case.

While some were occupied with this latter duty, others were employed in dragging away the larger tubs, so soon as filled with the sperm; and when the proper time arrived, this same sperm was carefully manipulated ere going to the try-works, of which anon.

It had cooled and crystallized to such a degree, that when, with several others, I sat down before a large Constantine's bath of it, found it strangely concreted into lumps, here and there rolling about in the liquid part. It was our business to squeeze these lumps back into fluid. A sweet and unctuous duty! No wonder that in old time sperm was such a favourite cosmetic. Such a clearer! such a sweetener such a softener! such a delicious mollifier! After having my hands in it for only a few minutes, my fingers felt like eels, and began, as it were, to serpentine and spiralize.

As I sat there at my ease, cross-legged on the deck; after the bitter exertion at the windlass; under a blue tranquil sky; the ship under indolent sail, and gliding so serenely along; as I bathed my hand among those soft, gentle globules of infiltrated tissues, wove almost within the hour; as they richly broke to my fingers, and discharged all their opulence, like fully ripe grapes their wine; as I snuffed up the uncontaminated aroma,—literally and truly, like the smell of spring violets; I declare to you, that for the time I lived as in a musk meadow; I forgot all about our horrible oath; in that inexpressible sperm, I washed my hands and my heart of it; I almost began to credit the old Paracelsian superstition that sperm is of rare virtue in allaying the heat of anger; while bathing in that bath, I felt divinely free from all ill-will, or petulance, or malice, of any sort whatsoever.

Squeeze! squeeze! squeeze! all the morning long; I squeezed that sperm till I myself almost melted into it; I squeezed that sperm till a strange sort of insanity came over me; and I found myself unwittingly squeezing my co-labourers' hands in it, mistaking their hands for the gentle globules. Such an abounding, affectionate, friendly, loving feeling did this avocation beget; that at last I was continually squeezing their hands, and looking up into their eyes sentimentally; as much as to say,—Oh! my dear fellow beings, why should we longer cherish any social acerbities, or know the slightest ill-humour or envy! Come; let us squeeze hands all round; nay, let us all squeeze ourselves into each other; let us squeeze ourselves universally into the very milk and sperm of kindness.

Would that I could keep squeezing that sperm for ever! For now, since by many prolonged, repeated experiences, I have perceived that in all cases man must eventually lower, or at least shift, his conceit of attainable felicity; not placing it anywhere in the intellect or the fancy; but in the wife, the heart, the bed, the table, the saddle, the fire-side, the country; now that I have perceived all this, I am ready to squeeze case eternally. In thoughts of the visions of the night, I saw long rows of angels in paradise, each with his hands in a jar of spermaceti.

. . . . * .

Now, while discoursing of sperm, it behoves to speak of other things akin to it, in the business of preparing the sperm-whale for the try-works.

First come white-horse, so called, which is obtained from the tapering part of the fish, and also from the thicker portions of his flukes. It is tough with congealed tendons—a wad of muscle—but still contains some oil. After being severed from the whale, the white-horse is first cut into portable oblongs ere going to the mincer. They look much like blocks of Berkshire marble.

Plum-pudding is the term bestowed upon certain fragmentary parts of the whale's flesh, here and there adhering to the blanket of blubber, and often participating to a considerable degree in its unctuousness. It is a most refreshing, convivial, beautiful object to behold. As its name imparts it is of an exceedingly rich, mottled tint, with a bestreaked snowy and golden ground, dotted with spots of the deepest crimson and purple. It is plums of rubies, in pictures of citron. Spite of reason, it is hard to keep yourself from eating it. I confess, that once I stole behind the foremast to try it. It tasted something as I should conceive a royal cutlet from the thigh of Louis le Gros might have tasted, supposing him to have been killed the first day after the venison season, and that particular venison season contemporary with an unusually fine vintage of the vineyards of Champagne.

There is another substance, and a very singular one, which turns up in the course of this business, but which I feel it to be very puzzling adequately to describe. It is called slobgollion; an appellation original with the whalemen, and even so is the nature of the substance. It is an ineffably oozy, stringy affair, most frequently found in the tubs of sperm, after a prolonged squeezing, and subsequent decanting. I hold it to be the wondrously thin, ruptured membranes of the case, coalescing.

Gurry, so called, is a term properly belonging to right whalemen, but sometimes incidentally used by the sperm fishermen. It designates the dark, glutinous substance which is scraped off the back of the Greenland or Right whale, and much of which covers the decks of those inferior souls who hunt that ignoble Leviathan.

Nippers. Strictly this word is not indigenous to the whale's vocabulary. But as applied by whalemen, it becomes so. A whaleman's nipper is a short firm strip of tendinous stuff cut from the tapering part of Leviathan's tail: it averages an inch in thickness, and for the rest, is about the size of the iron part of a hoe. Edgewise moved along the oily deck, it operates like a leathern squilgee; and by nameless blandishments, as of magic, allures along with it all impurities.

But to learn all about these recondite matters, your best way is at once to descend into the blubber-room, and have a long talk with its inmates. This place has previously been mentioned as the receptacle for the blanket-pieces, when stripped and hoisted from the whale. When the proper time arrives for cutting up its contents, this apartment is a scene of terror to all tyros, especially by night. On one side, lit by a dull lantern, a space has been left clear for the workmen. They generally go in pairs,—a pike-and-gaff-man and a spade-man. The whaling-pike is similar to a frigate's boarding-weapon of the same name. The gaff is something like a boat-hook. With his gaff the gaff-man hooks on to a sheet of blubber, and strives to hold it from slipping, as the ship pitches and lurches about. Meanwhile, the spade-man stands on the sheet itself, perpendicularly chopping it into portable horse-pieces. This spade is sharp as hone can make it; the spademan's feet are shoeless; the thing he stands on will sometimes irresistibly slide away from him like a sledge. If he cuts off one of his own toes, or one of his assistants', would you be very much astonished? Toes are scarce among veteran blubber-room men.

CHAPTER 76

THE CASSOCK

HAD YOU stepped on board the *Pequod* at a certain juncture of this post-mortemizing of the whale; and had you strolled forward nigh the windlass, pretty sure am I that you would have scanned with no small curiosity a very strange, enigmatical object, which you would have seen there, lying along lengthwise in the lee scuppers. Not the wondrous cistern in the whale's huge head; not the prodigy of his unhinged lower jaw; not the miracle of his symmetrical tail; none of these would so surprise you, as half a glimpse of that unaccountable cone,—longer than a Kentuckian is tall, nigh a foot in diameter at the base, and jet-black as Yojo, the ebony idol of Queequeg. And an idol, indeed, it is; or, rather, in old times, its likeness was. Such an idol as that found in the secret groves of Queen Maachah in Judea; and for worshipping which, King Asa, her son, did depose her, and destroyed the idol, and burnt it for an abomination at the brook Kedron as darkly set forth in the 15th chapter of the first book of Kings.

Look at the sailor, called the mincer, who now comes along, and assisted by two allies, heavily backs the grandissimus, as the mariners call it, and with bowed shoulders, staggers off with it as if he were a grenadier carrying a dead comrade from the field. Extending it upon the forecastle deck, he now proceeds cylindrically to remove its dark pelt, as an African hunter the pelt of a boa. This done he turns the pelt inside out, like a pantaloon leg; gives it a good stretching, so as almost to double its diameter; and at last hangs it, well spread, in the rigging, to dry. Ere long, it is taken down; when removing some three feet of it, towards the pointed extremity, and then cutting two slits for arm-holes at the other end, he lengthwise slips himself bodily into it. The mincer now stands before you invested in the full canonicals of his calling. Immemorial to all his order, this investiture alone will adequately protect him, while employed in the peculiar functions of his office.

That office consists in mincing the horse-pieces of blubber for the pots; an operation which is conducted at a curious wooden horse, planted endwise against the bulwarks, and with a capacious tub beneath it, into which the minced pieces drop, fast as the sheets from a rapt orator's desk. Arrayed in decent black; occupying a conspicuous pulpit; intent on bible leaves; what a candidate for an archbishopric, what a lad for a Pope were this mincer![1]

---

[1] Bible leaves! Bible leaves! This is the invariable cry from the mates to the mincer. It enjoins him to be careful, and cut his work into as thin slices as possible, inasmuch as by so doing the business of boiling out the oil is much accelerated, and its quantity considerably increased, besides perhaps improving it in quality.

CHAPTER 77

THE TRY-WORKS

BESIDES HER hoisted boats, an American whaler is outwardly distinguished by her try-works. She presents the curious anomaly of the most solid masonry joining with oak and hemp in constituting the completed ship. It is as if from the open field a brick-kiln were transported to her planks.

The try-works are planted between the foremast and the mainmast, the most roomy part of the deck. The timbers beneath are of a peculiar strength, fitted to sustain the weight of an almost solid mass of brick and mortar, some ten feet by eight square, and five in height. The foundation does not penetrate the deck, but the masonry is firmly secured to the surface by ponderous knees of iron bracing it on all sides, and screwing it down to the timbers. On the flanks it is cased with wood, and at top completely covered by a large, sloping, battened hatchway. Removing this hatch we expose the great try-pots, two in number, and each of several barrels' capacity. When not in use, they are kept remarkably clean. Sometimes they are polished with soapstone and sand, till they shine within like silver punch-bowls. During the night-watches some cynical old sailors will crawl into them and coil themselves away there for a nap. While employed in polishing them—one man in each pot, side by side—many confidential communications are carried on, over the iron lips. It is a place also for profound mathematical meditation. It was in the left-hand try-pot of the *Pequod*, with the soapstone diligently circling round me, that I was first indirectly struck by the remarkable fact, that in geometry all bodies gliding along the cycloid, my soapstone for example, will descend from any point in precisely the same time.

Removing the fire-board from the front of the try-works, the bare masonry of that side is exposed, penetrated by the two iron mouths of the furnaces, directly underneath the pots. These mouths are fitted with heavy doors of iron. The intense heat of the fire is prevented from communicating itself to the deck, by means of a shallow reservoir extending under the entire enclosed surface of the works. By a tunnel inserted at the rear, this reservoir is kept replenished with water as fast as it evaporates. There are no external chimneys; they open direct from the rear wall. And here let us go back for a moment.

It was about nine o'clock at night that the *Pequod's* try-works were first started on this present voyage. It belonged to Stubb to oversee the business.

"All ready there? Off hatch, then, and start her. You cook, fire the works." This was an easy thing, for the carpenter had been thrusting his shavings into the furnace throughout the passage. Here be it said that in a whaling voyage the first fire in the try-works has to be fed for a time with wood. After that no wood is used, except as a means of quick ignition to the staple fuel. In a word, after being tried out, the crisp, shrivelled blubber, now called scraps or fritters, still contains considerable of its unctuous properties. These fritters feed the flames. Like a plethoric burning martyr, or a self-consuming misanthrope, once ignited, the whale supplies his own fuel and burns by his own body. Would that he consumed his own smoke! for his smoke is horrible to inhale, and inhale it you must, and not only that, but you must live in it for the time. It has an unspeakable, wild, Hindoo odour about it, such as may lurk in the vicinity of funeral pyres. It smells like the left wing of the day of judgment; it is an argument for the pit.

By midnight the works were in full operation. We were clear from the carcase; sail had been made; the wind was freshening; the wild ocean darkness was intense. But that darkness was licked up by the fierce flames, which at intervals forked forth from the sooty flues, and illuminated every lofty rope in the rigging, as with the famed Greek fire. The burning ship drove on, as if remorselessly commissioned to some vengeful deed.

The hatch, removed from the top of the works, now afforded a wide hearth in front of them. Standing on this were the Tartarean shapes of the pagan harpooneers, always the whale-ship's stokers. With huge pronged poles they pitched hissing masses of blubber into the scalding pots, or stirred up the fires beneath, till the snaky flames darted, curling out of the doors to catch them by the feet. The smoke rolled away in sullen heaps. To every pitch of the ship there was a pitch of the boiling oil, which seemed all eagerness to leap into their faces. Opposite the mouth of the works, on the farther side of the wide wooden hearth, was the windlass. This served for a sea-sofa. Here lounged the watch, when not otherwise employed, looking into the red heat of the fire, till their eyes felt scorched in their heads. Their tawny features, now all begrimed with smoke and sweat, their matted beards, and the contrasting barbaric brilliancy of their teeth, all these were strangely revealed in the capricious emblazonings of the works. As they narrated to each other their unholy adventures, their tales of terror told in words of mirth; as their uncivilized laughter forked upwards out of them like the flame from the furnace; as to and fro, in their front, the harpooneers wildly gesticulated with their huge pronged forks and dippers; as the wind howled on, and the sea leaped, and the ship groaned and dived, and yet steadfastly shot her red hell farther and farther into the blackness of the sea and the night, and scornfully champed the white bone in her mouth, and viciously spat round her on all sides; then the rushing *Pequod,* freighted with savages, and laden with fire, and burning a corpse, and plunging into that blackness of darkness, seemed the material counterpart of her monomaniac commander's soul.

CHAPTER 78

STOWING DOWN AND CLEARING UP

ALREADY HAS it been related how the great leviathan is afar off described from the mast-head; how he is chased over the watery moors, and slaughtered in the valleys of the deep; how he is then towed alongside and beheaded; and how (on the principle which entitled the headsman of old to the garments in which the beheaded was killed) his great paddled surtout becomes the property of his executioner; how, in due time, he is condemned to the pots, and like Shadrach, Meshach, and Abednego, his spermaceti, oil, and bone pass unscathed through the fire;—but now it remains to conclude the last chapter of this part of the description by rehearsing—singing, if I may—the romantic proceeding of decanting off his oil into the casks and striking them down into the hold, where once again leviathan returns to his native profundities, sliding along beneath the surface as before; but, alas! never more to rise and blow.

While still warm, the oil, like hot punch, is received into the six-barrel casks; and while, perhaps, the ship is pitching and rolling this way and that in the midnight sea, the enormous casks are slewed round and headed over, end for end, and sometimes perilously scoot across the slippery deck, like so many land slides, till at last man-handled and stayed in their course; and all round the hoops, rap, rap, go as many hammers as can play upon them, for now, *ex officio,* every sailor is a cooper.

At length, when the last pint is casked, and all is cool, then the great hatchways are unsealed, the bowels of the ship are thrown open, and down go the casks to their final rest in the sea. This done, the hatches are replaced, and hermetically closed, like a closet walled up.

In the sperm fishery, this is perhaps one of the most remarkable incidents in all the business of whaling. One day the planks stream with freshets of blood and oil; on the sacred quarter-deck enormous masses of the whale's head are profanely piled; great rusty casks lie about, as in a brewery yard; the smoke from the try-works has besooted all the bulwarks; the mariners go about suffused with unctuousness; the entire ship seems great leviathan himself; while on all hands the din is deafening.

But a day or two after, you look about you, and prick your ears in this self-same ship; and were it not for the tell-tale boats and try-works, you would all but swear you trod some silent merchant vessel, with a most scrupulously neat commander. The unmanufactured sperm oil possesses a singularly cleansing virtue. This is the reason why the decks never look so white as just after what they call an affair of oil. Besides, from the ashes of the burned scraps of the whale, a potent ley is readily made; and whenever any adhesiveness from the back of the whale remains clinging to the side, that ley quickly exterminates it. Hands go diligently along the bulwarks and with buckets of water and rags restore them to their full tidiness. The soot is brushed from the lower rigging. All the numerous implements which have been in use are likewise faithfully cleansed and put away. The great hatch is scrubbed and placed upon the try-works, completely hiding the pots; every cask is out of sight; all tackles are coiled in unseen nooks; and when by the combined and simultaneous industry of almost the entire ship's company, the whole of this conscientious duty is at last concluded, then the crew themselves proceed to their own ablutions; shift themselves from top of toe; and finally issue to the immaculate deck, fresh and all aglow, as bridegrooms new-leaped from out the daintiest Holland.

Now, with elated step, they pace the planks in twos and threes, and humorously discourse of parlours, sofas, carpets, and fine cambrics; propose to mat the deck; think of having hangings to the top; object not to taking tea by moonlight on the piazza of the forecastle. To hint to such musked mariners of oil, and bone, and blubber, were little short of audacity. They know not the thing you distantly allude to. Away, and bring us napkins!

But mark: aloft there, at the three mast-heads, stand three men intent on spying out more whales, which, if caught, infallibly will again soil the old oaken furniture, and drop at least one small grease-spot somewhere. Yes; and many is the time, when, after the severest uninterrupted labours, which know no night; continuing straight through for ninety-six hours; when from the boat, where they have swelled

their wrists with all day rowing on the Line,—they only step to the
deck to carry vast chains, and heave the heavy windlass, and cut and
slash, yea, and in their very sweatings to be smoked and burned anew
by the combined fires of the equatorial sun and the equatorial try-
works; when, on the heel of all this, they have finally bestirred themselves to cleanse the ship, and make a spotless dairy room of it; many
is the time the poor fellows, just buttoning the necks of their clean
frocks, are startled by the cry of "There she blows!" and away they
fly to fight another whale, and go through the whole weary thing
again. Oh! my friends, but this is man-killing! Yet this is life. For
hardly have we mortals by long toilings extracted from this world's
vast bulk its small but valuable sperm; and then, with weary patience,
cleansed ourselves from its defilements, and learned to live here in clean
tabernacles of the soul; hardly is this done, when—*There she blows!*—
the ghost is spouted up, and away we sail to fight some other world,
and go through young life's old routine again.

Oh! the metempsychosis! Oh! Pythagoras, that in bright Greece,
two thousand years ago, did die, so good, so wise, so mild; I sailed with
thee along the Peruvian coast last voyage—and, foolish as I am, taught
thee, a green simple boy, how to splice a rope!

CHAPTER 79

A BOWER IN THE ARSACIDES

HITHERTO, in descriptively treating of the sperm-whale, I have
chiefly dwelt upon the marvels of his outer aspect; or separately
and in detail upon some few interior structural features. But to a large
and thorough sweeping comprehension of him, it behoves me now to
unbutton him still further, and untagging the points of his hose, un-
buckling his garters, and casting loose the hooks and the eyes of the
joints of his innermost bones, set him before you in his ultimatum; that
is to say, in his unconditional skeleton.

But how now, Ishmael? How is it, that you, a mere oarsman in the
fishery, pretend to know aught about the subterranean parts of the
whale? Did erudite Stubb, mounted upon your capstan, deliver lectures
on the anatomy of the Cetacea; and by help of the windlass, hold up a
specimen rib for exhibition? Explain thyself, Ishmael. Can you land
a full-grown whale on your deck for examination, as a cook dishes a
roast-pig? Surely not. A veritable witness have you hitherto been,
Ishmael; but have a care how you seize the privilege of Jonah alone;

the privilege of discoursing upon the joists and beams; the rafters, ridge-pole, sleepers, and under-pinnings, making up the framework of leviathan; and belike of the tallow-vats, dairy-rooms, butteries, and cheeseries in his bowels.

I confess, that since Jonah, few whalemen have penetrated very far beneath the skin of the adult whale; nevertheless, I have been blessed with an opportunity to dissect him in miniature. In a ship I belonged to, a small cub sperm-whale was once bodily hoisted to the deck for his poke or bag, to make sheaths for the barbs of the harpoons, and for the heads of the lances. Think you I let that chance go, without using my boat-hatchet and jack-knife, and breaking the seal and reading all the contents of that young cub?

And as for my exact knowledge of the bones of the leviathan in their gigantic, full grown development, for that rare knowledge I am indebted to my late royal friend Tranquo, king of Tranque, one of the Arsacides. For being at Tranque, years ago, when attached to the trading-ship *Dey of Algiers,* I was invited to spend part of the Arsacidean holidays with the lord of Tranque, at his retired palm villa at Pupella; a sea-side glen not very far distant from what our sailors called Bamboo-Town, his capital.

Among many other fine qualities, my royal friend Tranquo, being gifted with a devout love for all matters of barbaric vertù, had brought together in Pupella whatever rare things the more ingenious of his people could invent; chiefly carved woods of wonderful devices, chiselled shells, inlaid spears, costly paddles, aromatic canoes; and all these distributed among whatever natural wonders, the wonder-freighted, tribute-rendering waves had cast upon his shores.

Chief among these latter was a great sperm-whale, which, after an unusually long raging gale, had been found dead and stranded, with his head against a coco-nut tree, whose plumage-like, tufted droopings seemed his verdant jet. When the vast body had at last been stripped of its fathom-deep enfoldings, and the bones become dust dry in the sun, then the skeleton was carefully transported up the Pupella glen, where a grand temple of lordly palms now sheltered it.

CHAPTER 80

MEASUREMENT OF THE WHALE'S SKELETON

IN THE first place, I wish to lay before you a particular, plain statement, touching the living bulk of this leviathan, whose skeleton we
are briefly to exhibit. Such a statement may prove useful here.

According to a careful calculation I have made, and which I partly
base upon Captain Scoresby's estimate, of seventy tons for the largest
sized Greenland whale of sixty feet in length; according to my careful
calculation, I say, a sperm-whale of the largest magnitude, between
eighty-five and ninety feet in length, and something less than forty
feet in its fullest circumference, such a whale will weigh at least ninety
tons; so that, reckoning thirteen men to a ton, he would considerably
outweigh the combined population of a whole village of one thousand
one hundred inhabitants.

Think you then that brains, like yoked cattle, should be put to this
leviathan, to make him at all budge to any landsman's imagination?

Having already in various ways put before you his skull, spout-hole,
jaw, teeth, tail, forehead, fins, and divers other parts, I shall now
simply point out what is most interesting in the general bulk of his
unobstructed bones. But as the colossal skull embraces so very large a
proportion of the entire extent of the skeleton; as it is by far the most
complicated part; and as nothing is to be repeated concerning it in this
chapter, you must not fail to carry it in your mind, or under your arm,
as we proceed, otherwise you will not gain a complete notion of the
general structure we are about to view.

In length, the sperm-whale's skeleton at Tranque measured seventy-
two feet; so that when fully invested and extended in life, he must have
been ninety feet long; for in the whale, the skeleton loses about one fifth
in length compared with the living body. Of this seventy-two feet, his
skull and jaw comprised some twenty feet, leaving some fifty feet of
plain back-bone. Attached to this back-bone, for something less than
a third of its length, was the mighty circular basket of ribs which once
enclosed his vitals.

To me this vast ivory-ribbed chest, with the long, unrelieved spine,
extending far away from it in a straight line, not a little resembled
the hull of a great ship new-laid upon the stocks, when only some
twenty of her naked bow-ribs are inserted, and the keel is otherwise,
for the time, but a long, disconnected timber.

The ribs were ten on a side. The first, to begin from the neck, was nearly six feet long; the second, third, and fourth were each successively longer, till you came to the climax of the fifth, or one of the middle ribs, which measured eight feet and some inches. From that part, the remaining ribs diminished, till the tenth and last only spanned five feet and some inches. In general thickness, they all bore a seemly correspondence to their length. The middle ribs were the most arched. In some of the Arsacides they are used for beams whereon to lay footpath bridges over small streams.

In considering these ribs, I could not but be struck anew with the circumstance, so variously repeated in this book, that the skeleton of the whale is by no means the mould of his invested form. The largest of the Tranque ribs, one of the middle ones, occupied that part of the fish which, in life, is greatest in depth. Now, the greatest depth of the invested body of this particular whale must have been at least sixteen feet; whereas, the corresponding rib measured but little more than eight feet. So that this rib only conveyed half of the true notion of the living magnitude of that part. Besides, for some way, where I now saw but a naked spine, all that had been once wrapped round with tons of added bulk in flesh, muscle, blood, and bowels. Still more for the ample fins, I here saw but a few disordered joints; and in place of the weighty and majestic, but boneless flukes, an utter blank!

How vain and foolish, then, thought I, for timid untravelled man to try to comprehend aright this wondrous whale, by merely poring over his dead attenuated skeleton, stretched in this peaceful wood. No. Only in the heart of quickest perils; only when within the eddyings of his angry flukes; only on the profound unbounded sea, can the fully invested whale be truly and livingly found out.

But the spine. For that, the best way we can consider it is, with a crane, to pile its bones high up on end. No speedy enterprise. But now it's done, it looks much like Pompey's Pillar.

There are forty and odd vertebræ in all, which in the skeleton are not locked together. They mostly lie like the great knobbed blocks on a Gothic spire, forming solid courses of heavy masonry. The largest, a middle one, is in width something less than three feet, and in depth more than four. The smallest, where the spine tapers away into the tail, is only two inches in width, and looks something like a white billiard-ball. I was told that there were still smaller ones, but they had been lost by some little cannibal urchins, the priest's children, who had stolen them to play marbles with. Thus we see how the spine of even the hugest of living things tapers off at last into simple child's play.

CHAPTER 81

THE PACIFIC

WHEN GLIDING by the Bashee isles we emerged at last upon the great South Sea; were it not for other things, I could have greeted my dear Pacific with uncounted thanks, for now the long supplication of my youth was answered; that serene ocean rolled eastwards from me a thousand leagues of blue.

There is, one knows not what, sweet mystery about this sea, whose gently awful stirrings seem to speak of some hidden soul beneath; like those fabled undulations of the Ephesian sod over the buried Evangelist St. John. And meet it is, that over these sea-pastures, wide-rolling watery prairies and Potters' Fields of all four continents, the waves should rise and fall, and ebb and flow unceasingly; for here, millions of mixed shades and shadows, drowned dreams, somnambulisms, reveries; all that we call lives and souls, lie dreaming, dreaming, still; tossing like slumberers in their beds; the ever-rolling waves but made so by their restlessness.

To any meditative Magian rover, this serene Pacific, once beheld, must ever after be the sea of his adoption. It rolls the mid-most waters of the world, the Indian ocean and Atlantic being but its arms. The same waves wash the moles of the new-built Californian towns, but yesterday planted by the recentest race of men, and lave the faded but still gorgeous skirts of Asiatic lands, older than Abraham; while all between float milky-ways of coral isles, and low-lying, endless, unknown Archipelagoes, and impenetrable Japans. Thus this mysterious, divine Pacific zones the world's whole bulk about; makes all coasts one bay to it; seems the tide-beating heart of earth. Lifted by those eternal swells, you needs must own the seductive god, bowing your head to Pan.

But few thoughts of Pan stirred Ahab's brain, as standing like an iron statue at his accustomed place beside the mizzen rigging, with one nostril he unthinkingly snuffed the sugary musk from the Bashee isles (in whose sweet woods mild lovers must be walking), and with the other consciously inhaled the salt breath of the new found sea; that sea in which the hated white whale must even then be swimming. Launched at length upon these almost final waters, and gliding towards the Japanese cruising-ground, the old man's purpose intensified itself. His firm lips met like the lips of a vice; the Delta of his forehead's veins swelled like overladen brooks; in his very sleep, his ringing cry ran through the vaulted hull, "Stern all! the white whale spouts thick blood!"

CHAPTER 82

THE "PEQUOD" MEETS THE "BACHELOR"

JOLLY ENOUGH were the sights and the sounds that came bearing down before the wind.

It was a Nantucket ship, the *Bachelor*, which had just wedged in her last cask of oil, and bolted down her bursting hatches; and now, in glad holiday apparel, was joyously, though somewhat vain-gloriously, sailing round among the wide-separated ships on the ground, previous to pointing her prow for home.

The three men at her mast-head wore long streamers of narrow red bunting at their hats; from the stern, a whale-boat was suspended, bottom down; and hanging captive from the bowsprit was seen the long lower jaw of the last whale they had slain. Signals, ensigns, and jacks of all colours were flying from her rigging, on every side. Sideways lashed in each of her three basketed tops were two barrels of sperm; above which, in her top-mast cross-trees, you saw slender breakers of the same precious fluid; and nailed to her main truck was a brazen lamp.

As was afterwards learned, the *Bachelor* had met with the most surprising success; all the more wonderful, for that while cruising in the same seas numerous other vessels had gone entire months without securing a single fish. Not only had barrels of beef and bread been given away to make room for the far more valuable sperm, but additional supplemental casks had been bartered for, from the ships she had met; and these were stowed along the deck, and in the captain's and officers' state-rooms. Even the cabin table itself had been knocked into kindling-wood; and the cabin mess dined off the broad head of an oil-butt, lashed down to the floor for a centrepiece. In the forecastle, the sailors had actually caulked and pitched their chests, and filled them; it was humorously added, that the cook had clapped a head on his largest boiler, and filled it; that the steward had plugged his spare coffeepot and filled it; that the harpooneers had headed the sockets of their irons and filled them; that indeed everything was filled with sperm, except the pockets of the captain's pantaloons, and those he reserved to thrust his hands into, in self-complacent testimony of his entire satisfaction.

As this glad ship of good luck bore down upon the moody *Pequod*, the barbarian sound of enormous drums came from her forecastle; and drawing still nearer, a crowd of her men were seen standing round her huge try-pots, which, covered with the parchment-like *poke* or stomach skin of the black fish, gave forth a loud roar to every stroke of the clenched hands of the crew. On the quarter-deck, the mates and harpooneers were dancing with the olive-hued girls who had eloped with them from the Polynesian Isles; while suspended in an ornamented boat, firmly secured aloft between the fore-mast and mainmast, three Long Island negroes, with glittering fiddlebows of whale ivory, were presiding over the hilarious jig.

Lord and master over all this scene, the captain stood erect on the ship's elevated quarter-deck, so that the whole rejoicing drama was full before him, and seemed merely contrived for his own individual diversion.

And Ahab, he too was standing on his quarter-deck, shaggy and black, with a stubborn gloom; and as the two ships crossed each other's wakes—one all jubilations for things passed, the other all forebodings as to things to come—their two captains in themselves impersonated the whole striking contrast of the scene.

"Come aboard, come aboard!" cried the gay *Bachelor's* commander, lifting a glass and a bottle in the air.

"Hast seen the white whale?" gritted Ahab in reply.

"No; only heard of him; but don't believe in him at all," said the other good-humouredly. "Come aboard!"

"Thou art too damned jolly. Sail on. Hast lost any men?"

"Not enough to speak of—two islanders, that's all;—but come aboard, old hearty, come along. I'll soon take that black from your brow. Come along, will ye (merry's the play); a full ship, and homeward-bound."

"How wondrous familiar is a fool?" muttered Ahab; then aloud, "Thou art a full ship and homeward-bound, thou sayst; well, then, call me an empty ship, and outward-bound. So go thy ways, and I will mine. Forward there! Set all sail, and keep her to the wind!"

And thus, while the one ship went cheerily before the breeze, the other stubbornly fought against it; and so the two vessels parted; the crew of the *Pequod* looking with grave, lingering glances towards the receding *Bachelor*; but the *Bachelor's* men never heeding their gaze for the lively revelry they were in. And as Ahab, leaning over the taffrail, eyed the homeward-bound craft, he took from his pocket a small vial of sand, and then looking from the ship to the vial, seemed thereby bringing two remote associations together, for that vial was filled with Nantucket soundings.

CHAPTER 83

THE DYING WHALE

NOT SELDOM in this life, when, on the right side, fortune's favourites sail close by us, we, though all adroop before, catch somewhat of the rushing breeze, and joyfully feel our bagging sails fill out. So seemed it with the *Pequod*. For next day after encountering the gay *Bachelor*, whales were seen and four were slain; and one of them by Ahab.

It was far down the afternoon; and when all the spearings of the crimson fight were done: and floating in the lovely sunset sea and sky, sun and whale both stilly died together; then, such a sweetness and such plaintiveness, such inwreathing orisons curled up in that rosy air, that it almost seemed as if far over from the deep green convent valleys of the Manilla isles, the Spanish land-breeze, wantonly turned sailor, had gone to sea, freighted with these vesper hymns.

Soothed again, but only soothed to deeper gloom, Ahab, who had sterned off from the whale, sat intently watching his final wanings from the now tranquil boat. For that strange spectacle observable in all sperm-whales dying—the turning sunwards of the head, and so expiring—that strange spectacle, beheld of such a placid evening, somehow to Ahab conveyed a wondrousness unknown before.

CHAPTER 84

THE CANDLES

WARMEST climes but nurse the cruellest fangs: the tiger of Bengal crouches in spiced groves of ceaseless verdure. Skies the most effulgent but basket the deadliest thunders: gorgeous Cuba knows tornadoes that never swept tame northern lands. So, too, it is, that in these resplendent Japanese seas the mariner encounters the direst of all storms, the Typhoon. It will sometimes burst from out that cloudless sky, like an exploding bomb upon a dazed and sleepy town.

Towards evening of that day, the *Pequod* was torn of her canvas, and bare-poled was left to fight a Typhoon which had struck her directly ahead. When darkness came on, sky and sea roared and split with the thunder, and blazed with the lightning, that showed the

disabled masts fluttering here and there with the rags which the first
fury of the tempest had left for its after sport.

Holding by a shroud, Starbuck was standing on the quarterdeck;
at every flash of the lightning glancing aloft, to see what additional
disaster might have befallen the intricate hamper there; while Stubb
and Flask were directing the men in the higher hoisting and firmer
lashing of the boats. But all their pains seemed naught. Though lifted
to the very top of the cranes, the windward quarter boat (Ahab's) did
not escape. A great rolling sea, dashing high up against the reeling
ship's high teetering side, stove in the boat's bottom at the stern, and
left it again, all dripping through like a sieve.

CHAPTER 85

THE MUSKET

DURING the most violent shocks of the Typhoon, the man at the
Pequod's jaw-bone tiller had several times been reelingly hurled
to the deck by its spasmodic motions, even though preventer tackles
had been attached to it—for they were slack—because some play to the
tiller was indispensable.

In the midst of the storm poor Queequeg fell ill. So sick was he
that he begged the carpenter to make him a coffin. And that coffin
was made to his order. But ere long Queequeg recovered, and he
thereafter used his coffin as a sea-chest.

In a severe gale like this, while the ship is but a tossed shuttle-cock
to the blast, it is by no means uncommon to see the needles in the
compasses, at intervals, go round and round. It was thus with the
Pequod's; at almost every shock the helmsman had not failed to notice the
whirling velocity with which they revolved upon the cards; it is a sight
that hardly anyone can behold without some sort of unwonted emotion.

Some hours after midnight, the Typhoon abated so much, that
through the strenuous exertions of Starbuck and Stubb—one engaged
forward and the other aft—the shivered remnants of the jib and fore-
and main-top-sails were cut adrift from the spars, and went eddying
away to leeward, like the feathers of an albatross, which sometimes
are cast to the winds when that storm-tossed bird is on the wing.

The three corresponding new sails were now bent and reefed, and
a storm-trysail was set further aft; so that the ship soon went through
the water with some precision again; and the course—for the present,
East-south-east—which he was to steer, if practicable, was once more

given to the helmsman. For during the violence of the gale, he had only steered according to its vicissitudes. But as he was now bringing the ship as near her course as possible, watching the compass meanwhile! lo! a good sign! the wind seemed coming round astern; aye, the foul breeze became fair!

Instantly the yards were squared, to the lively song of "*Ho the fair wind! oh-ye-ho, cheerly, men!*" the crew singing for joy, that so promising an event should so soon have falsified the evil portents preceding it.

CHAPTER 86

THE NEEDLE

NEXT morning the not-yet-subsided sea rolled in long slow billows of mighty bulk, and striving in the *Pequod's* gurgling track, pushed her on like giants' palms outspread. The strong, unstaggering breeze abounded so, that sky and air seemed vast outbellying sails; the whole world boomed before the wind. Muffled in the full morning light, the invisible sun was only known by the spread intensity of his place; where his bayonet rays moved on in stacks. Emblazonings, as of crowned Babylonian kings and queens, reigned over everything. The sea was as a crucible of molten gold, that bubblingly leaps with light and heat.

Long maintaining an enchanted silence, Ahab stood apart; and every time the teetering ship loweringly pitched down her bowsprit, he turned to eye the bright sun's rays produced ahead; and when she profoundly settled by the stern, he turned behind, and saw the sun's rearward place, and how the same yellow rays were blending with his undeviating wake.

"Ha, ha, my ship! thou mightest well be taken now for the seachariot of the sun. Ho, ho! all ye nations before my prow, I bring the sun to ye! Yoke on the further billows; hallo! a tandem, I drive the sea!"

But suddenly reined back by some counter thought, he hurried towards the helm, huskily demanding how the ship was heading.

"East-sou-east, sir," said the frightened steersman.

"Thou liest!" smiting him with his clenched fist. "Heading East at this hour in the morning, and the sun astern?"

Upon this every soul was confounded; for the phenomenon just then observed by Ahab had unaccountably escaped everyone else; but its very blinding palpableness must have been the cause.

Thrusting his head half-way into the binnacle, Ahab caught one glimpse of the compasses; his uplifted arm slowly fell; for a moment he almost seemed to stagger. Standing behind him Starbuck looked, and lo! the two compasses pointed East, and the *Pequod* was as infallibly going West.

But ere the first wild alarm could get out abroad among the crew, the old man with a rigid laugh exclaimed, "I have it! It has happened before. Mr. Starbuck, last night's thunder turned our compasses—that's all. Thou hast before now heard of such a thing, I take it."

"Aye; but never before has it happened to me, sir," said the pale mate, gloomily.

Here it must needs be said, that accidents like this have in more than one case occurred to ships in violent storms. The magnetic energy, as developed in the mariner's needle, is, as all know, essentially one with the electricity beheld in heaven; hence it is not to be much marvelled at, that such things should be. In instances where the lightning has actually struck the vessel, so as to smite down some of the spars and rigging, the effect upon the needle has at times been still more fatal; all its loadstone virtue being annihilated, so that the before magnetic steel was of no more use than an old wife's knitting needle. But in either case, the needle never again, of itself, recovers the original virtue thus marred or lost; and if the binnacle compasses be affected, the same fate reaches all the others that may be in the ship; even were the lowermost one inserted into the kelson.

Deliberately standing before the binnacle, and eyeing the transpointed compasses, the old man, with the sharp of his extended hand, now took the precise bearing of the sun, and satisfied that the needles were exactly inverted, shouted out his orders for the ship's course to be changed accordingly. The yards were hard up; and once more the *Pequod* thrust her undaunted bows into the opposing wind, for the supposed fair one had only been juggling her.

Meanwhile, whatever were his own secret thoughts, Starbuck said nothing, but quietly he issued all requisite orders; while Stubb and Flask—who in some small degree seemed then to be sharing his feelings—likewise unmurmuringly acquiesced. As for the men, though some of them lowly rumbled, their fear of Ahab was greater than their fear of fate. But as ever before, the pagan harpooneers remained almost wholly unimpressed; or if impressed, it was only with a certain magnetism shot into their congenial hearts from inflexible Ahab's.

CHAPTER 87

THE LIFE-BUOY

STEERING now south-eastward, the *Pequod* held on her path towards the Equator. Making so long a passage through such unfrequented waters, descrying no ships, and ere long, sideways impelled by unvarying trade winds, over waves monotonously mild; all these seemed the strange calm things preluding some riotous and desperate scene.

At last, when the ship drew near to the outskirts, as it were, of the Equatorial fishing-ground, and in the deep darkness that goes before the dawn, was sailing by a cluster of rocky islets; the watch—then headed by Flask—was startled by a cry so plaintively wild and unearthly—like half-articulated wailings of the ghosts of all Herod's murdered Innocents—that one and all, they started from their reveries, and for the space of some moments stood, or sat, or leaned all transfixedly listening, like the carved Roman slave, while that wild cry remained within hearing. The Christian or civilized part of the crew said it was mermaids and shuddered; but the pagan harpooneers remained unappalled. Yet the grey Manxman—the oldest mariner of all—declared that the wild thrilling sounds that were heard, were the voices of newly drowned men in the sea.

Below in his hammock, Ahab did not hear of this till grey dawn, when he came to the deck; it was then recounted to him by Flask, not unaccompanied with hinted dark meanings. He hollowly laughed, and thus explained the wonder.

Those rocky islands the ship had passed were the resort of great numbers of seals, and some young seals that had lost their dams, or some dams that had lost their cubs, must have risen nigh the ship and kept company with her, crying and sobbing with their human sort of wail. But this only the more affected some of them, because most mariners cherish a very superstitious feeling about seals, arising not only from their peculiar tones when in distress, but also from the human look of their round heads and semi-intelligent faces, seen peeringly uprising from the water alongside. In the sea, under certain circumstances, seals have more than once been mistaken for men.

But the bodings of the crew were destined to receive a most plausible confirmation in the fate of one of their number that morning. At sunrise this man went from his hammock to his mast-head at the fore; and whether it was that he was not yet half waked from his sleep (for sailors sometimes go aloft in a transition state), whether it was thus with the man, there is now no telling; but, be that as it may, he had not been long at his perch, when a cry was heard—a cry and a rushing —and looking up, they saw a falling phantom in the air; and looking down, a little tossed heap of white bubbles in the blue of the sea.

The life-buoy—a long slender cask—was dropped from the stern, where it always hung obedient to a cunning spring; but no hand rose to seize it, and the sun having long beat upon this cask it had shrunken, so that it slowly filled, and the parched wood also filled at its every pore; and the studded iron-bound cask followed the sailor to the bottom, as if to yield to him his pillow, though in sooth but a hard one.

And thus the first man of the *Pequod* that mounted the mast to look out for the white whale, on the white whale's own peculiar ground; that man was swallowed up in the deep. But few, perhaps, thought of that at the time. Indeed, in some sort, they were not grieved at this event, at least as a portent; for they regarded it, not as a foreshadowing of evil in the future, but as the fulfilment of an evil already presaged. They declared that now they knew the reason of those wild shrieks they had heard the night before. But again the old Manxman said nay.

The lost life-buoy was now to be replaced; Starbuck was directed to see to it; but as no cask of sufficient lightness could be found, and as in the feverish eagerness of what seemed the approaching crisis of the voyage, all hands were impatient of any toil but what was directly connected with its final end, whatever that might prove to be; therefore, they were going to leave the ship's stern unprovided with a buoy, when by certain strange signs and innuendoes Queequeg hinted a hint concerning his coffin.

"A life-buoy of a coffin!" cried Starbuck, starting.

"Rather queer, that, I should say," said Stubb.

"It will make a good enough one," said Flask, "the carpenter here can arrange it easily."

"Bring it up; there's nothing else for it," said Starbuck, after a melancholy pause. "Rig it, carpenter, do not look at me so—the coffin, I mean. Dost thou hear me? Rig it."

"And shall I nail down the lid, sir?" moving his hand as with a hammer.

"Aye."

"And shall I caulk the seams, sir?" moving his hand as with a caulking-iron.

"Aye."

"And shall I then pay over the same with pitch, sir?" moving his hand as with a pitch-pot.

"Away! what possesses thee to this? Make a life-buoy of the coffin, and no more.—Mr. Stubb, Mr. Flask, come forward with me."

"He goes off in a huff. The whole he can endure; at the parts he baulks. Now I don't like this. I make a leg for Captain Ahab, and he wears it like a gentleman; but I make a bandbox for Queequeg, and he won't put his head into it. Are all my pains to go for nothing with that coffin? And now I'm ordered to make a life-buoy of it. It's like turning an old coat; going to bring the flesh on the other side now. I don't like this cobbling sort of business—I don't like it at all; it's undignified; it's not my place. Let tinkers' brats do tinkerings; we are their betters. I like to take in hand none but clean, virgin, fair-and-square mathematical jobs, something that regularly begins at the beginning, and is at the middle when midway, and comes to an end at the conclusion; not a cobbler's job, that's at an end in the middle, and at the beginning at the end. It's the old woman's tricks to be giving cobbling jobs. Lord! what an affection all old women have for tinkers. I know an old woman of sixty-five who ran away with a bald-headed young tinker once. And that's the reason I never would work for lonely widow old women ashore, when I kept my job-shop in the Vineyard; they might have taken it into their lonely old heads to run off with me. But heigh-ho! there are no caps at sea but snow-caps. Let me see. Nail down the lid; caulk the seams; pay over the same with pitch; batten them down tight, and hang it with the snap-spring over the ship's stern. Were ever such things done before with a coffin? Some superstitious old carpenters, now, would be tied up in the rigging, ere they would do the job. But I'm made of knotty Aroostook hemlock; I don't budge. Cruppered with a coffin! Sailing about with a grave-yard tray! But never mind. We workers in woods make bridal-bed-steads and card-tables, as well as coffins and hearses. We work by the month, or by the job, or by the profit; not for us to ask the why and wherefore of our work, unless it be too confounded cobbling, and then we stash it if we can. Hem! I'll do the job, now, tenderly. I'll have me—let's see—how many in the ship's company, all told? But I've forgotten. Any way, I'll have me thirty separate. Turk's-headed life-lines, each three feet long hanging all round to the coffin. Then, if the hull go down, there'll be thirty lively fellows all fighting for one coffin, a sight not seen very often beneath the sun! Come hammer, caulking-iron, pitch-pot, and marling-spike! Let's to it."

CHAPTER 88

THE "PEQUOD" MEETS THE "RACHEL"

NEXT DAY, a large ship, the *Rachel*, was descried, bearing directly down upon the *Pequod*, all her spars thickly clustering with men. At the time the *Pequod* was making good speed through the water; but as the broad-winged windward stranger shot nigh to her, the boastful sails all fell together as blank bladders that are burst, and all life fled from the smitten hull.

"Bad news; she brings bad news," muttered the old Manxman. But ere her commander, who with trumpet to mouth, stood up in his boat; ere he could hopefully hail, Ahab's voice was heard.

"Hast seen the white whale?"

"Aye, yesterday. Have ye seen a whale-boat adrift?"

Throttling his joy, Ahab negatively answered this unexpected question; and would then have fain boarded the stranger, when the stranger captain himself, having stopped his vessel's way, was seen descending her side. A few keen pulls, and his boathook soon clinched the *Pequod's* main-chains, and he sprang to the deck. Immediately he was recognized by Ahab for a Nantucketer he knew. But no formal salutation was exchanged.

"Where was he?—not killed! not killed!" cried Ahab, closely advancing. "How was it?"

It seemed that somewhat late on the afternoon of the day previous, while three of the stranger's boats were engaged with a shoal of whales, which had led them some four or five miles from the ship; and while they were yet in swift chase to windward, the white hump and head of Moby Dick had suddenly loomed up out of the water, not very far to leeward; whereupon, the fourth rigged boat—a reserved one—had been instantly lowered in chase. After a keen sail before the wind, this fourth boat—the swiftest keeled of all—seemed to have succeeded in fastening—at least, as well as the man at the mast-head could tell anything about it. In the distance he saw the diminished dotted boat; and then a swift gleam of bubbling white water; and after that nothing more; whence it was concluded that the stricken whale must have indefinitely run away with his pursuers, as often happens. There was some apprehension, but no positive alarm, as yet. The recall signals were placed in the rigging; darkness came on; and forced to pick up her three far to windward boats—ere going in quest of the fourth one in the precisely opposite direction—the ship had not only been necessi-

tated to leave that boat to its fate till near midnight, but, for the time,
to increase her distance from it. But the rest of her crew being at
last safe aboard, she crowded all sail—stunsail on stunsail—after the
missing boat; kindling a fire in her try-pots for a beacon; and every
other man aloft on the look-out. But though when she had thus sailed
a sufficient distance to gain the presumed place of the absent ones when
last seen; though she then paused to lower her spare boats to pull all
around her; and not finding anything, had again dashed on; again
paused, and lowered her boats; and though she had thus continued
doing till daylight; yet not the least glimpse of the missing keel had
been seen.

The story told, the stranger captain immediately went on to reveal
his object in boarding the *Pequod*. He desired that ship to unite with
his own in the search; by sailing over the sea some four or five miles
apart, on parallel lines, and so sweeping a double horizon, as it were.

"I will wager something now," whispered Stubb to Flask, "that
someone in that missing boat wore off that captain's best coat; mayhap, his watch—he's so cursed anxious to get it back. Who ever heard
of two pious whale-ships cruising after one missing whale-boat in the
height of the whaling season? See, Flask, only see how pale he looks—
pale in the very buttons of his eyes—look—it wasn't the coat—it must
have been the——"

"My boy, my own boy is among them. For God's sake—I beg, I
conjure"—here exclaimed the stranger captain to Ahab, who thus far
had but icily received his petition. "For eight-and-forty hours let me
charter your ship—I will gladly pay for it, and roundly pay for it—
if there be no other way—for eight-and-forty hours only—only that—
you must, oh, you must, and you *shall* do this thing."

"His son!" cried Stubb, "oh, it's his son he's lost! I take back the
coat and watch—what says Ahab? We must save that boy."

"He's drowned with the rest on 'em, last night," said the old Manx
sailor standing behind them; "I heard; all of ye heard their spirits."

Now, as it shortly turned out, what made this incident of the *Rachel's*
the more melancholy, was the circumstance, that not only was one of
the captain's sons among the number of the missing boat's crew; but
among the number of the other boats' crews, at the same time, but
on the other hand, separated from the ship during the dark vicissitudes
of the chase, there had been still another son; so that for a time, the
wretched father was plunged to the bottom of the cruellest perplexity;
which was only solved for him by his chief mate's instinctively adopt-
ing the ordinary procedure of a whale-ship in such emergencies, that
is, when placed between jeopardized but divided boats, always to pick

up the majority first. But the captain, for some unknown constitutional reason, had refrained from mentioning all this, and not till forced to it by Ahab's iciness did he allude to his one yet missing boy; a little lad, but twelve years old, whose father with the earnest but unmisgiving hardihood of a Nantucketer's paternal love, had thus early sought to initiate him in the perils and wonders of a vocation almost immemorially the destiny of all his race. Nor does it unfrequently occur, that Nantucket captains will send a son of such tender age away from them, for a protracted three or four years' voyage in some other ship than their own; so that their first knowledge of a whale-man's career shall be unenervated by any chance display of a father's natural but untimely partiality, or undue apprehensiveness and concern.

Meantime, now the stranger was still beseeching his poor boon of Ahab; and Ahab still stood like an anvil, receiving every shock, but without the least quivering of his own.

"I will not go," said the stranger, "till you say *aye* to me. Do to me as you would have me do to you in the like case. For *you* too have a boy, Captain Ahab—though but a child, and nestling safely at home now—a child of your old age too—Yes, yes, you relent; I see it—run, run, men, now, and stand by to square in the yards."

"Avast," cried Ahab—"touch not a rope-yarn"; then in a voice that prolongingly moulded every word—"Captain Gardiner, I will not do it. Even now I lose time. Good-bye, good-bye. God bless ye, man, and may I forgive myself, but ˙ must go. Mr. Starbuck, look at the binnacle watch, and in three minutes from this present instant warn off all strangers: then brace forward again, and let the ship sail as before."

Hurriedly turning, with averted face, he descended into his cabin, leaving the strange captain transfixed at this unconditional and utter rejection of his so earnest suit. But starting from his enchantment, Gardiner silently hurried to the side; more fell than stepped into his boat, and returned to his ship.

Soon the two ships diverged their wakes; and long as the strange vessel was in view, she was seen to yaw hither and thither at every dark spot, however small, on the sea. This way and that her yards were swung around; starboard and larboard, she continued to tack; now she beat against a head sea; and again it pushed her before it; while all the while, her masts and yards were thickly clustered with men, as three tall cherry trees, when the boys are cherrying among the boughs.

But by her still halting course and winding, woeful way, you plainly saw that his ship that so wept with spray, still remained without comfort. She was Rachel, weeping for her children, because they were not.

CHAPTER 89

THE HAT

A<small>ND NOW</small> that at the proper time and place, after so long and wide a preliminary cruise, Ahab,—all other whaling waters swept—seemed to have chased his foe into an ocean-fold, to slay him the more securely there; that he found himself hard by the very latitude and longitude where his tormenting wound had been inflicted; now that a vessel had been spoken which on the very day preceding had actually encountered Moby Dick;—and now that all his successive meetings with various ships contrastingly concurred to show the demoniac indifference with which the white whale tore his hunters, whether sinning or sinned against; now it was that there lurked a something in the old man's eyes, which it was hardly sufferable for feeble souls to see. As the unsetting polar star, which through the livelong, arctic, six months' night sustains its piercing, steady central gaze; so Ahab's purpose now fixedly gleamed down upon the constant midnight of the gloomy crew. It domineered above them so, that all their bodings, doubts, misgivings, fears, were fain to hide beneath their souls, and not sprout forth a single spear or leaf.

In this foreshadowing interval too, all humour, forced or natural, vanished. Stubb no more strove to raise a smile; Starbuck no more strove to check one. Alike, joy and sorrow, hope and fear, seemed ground to finest dust, and powdered, for the time, in the clamped mortar of Ahab's iron soul. Like machines, they dumbly moved about the deck, ever conscious that the old man's despot eye was on them.

Nor, at any time, by night or day could the mariners now step upon the deck, unless Ahab was before them; either standing on his pivot-hole, or exactly pacing the planks between two undeviating limits,—the main-mast and the mizzen; or else they saw him standing in the cabin-scuttle,—his living foot advanced upon the deck, as if to step; his hat slouched heavily over his eyes; so that however motionless he stood, however the days and nights were added on, that he had not swung in his hammock; yet hidden beneath that slouching hat, they could never tell unerringly whether, for all this, his eyes were really closed at times; or whether he was still intently scanning them; no matter, though he stood so in the scuttle for a whole hour on the stretch, and the unheeded night-damp gathered in beads of dew upon that stone-carved coat and hat. The clothes that the night had wet, the next day's sunshine dried upon him; and so, day after day, and night after night; he went no more beneath the planks; whatever he wanted from the cabin that thing he sent for.

At the first faintest glimmering of the dawn, his iron voice was heard from aft——"Man the mast-heads!"—and all through the day, till after sunset and after twilight, the same voice every hour, at the striking of the helmsman's bell, was heard—"What d'ye see?—sharp! sharp!"

But when three or four days had slided by, after meeting the children-seeking *Rachel*; and no spout had yet been seen; the monomaniac old man seemed distrustful of his crew's fidelity; at least, of nearly all except the Pagan harpooneers; he seemed to doubt, even, whether Stubb and Flask might not willingly overlook the sight he sought. But if these suspicions were really his, he sagaciously refrained from verbally expressing them, however his actions might seem to hint them.

"I will have the first sight of the whale myself,"—he said. "Aye! Ahab must have the doubloon!" and with his own hands he rigged a nest of basketed bowlines; and sending a hand aloft, with a single sheaved block, to secure to the main-mast head, he received the two ends of the downward-reeved rope; and attaching one to his basket prepared a pin for the other end, in order to fasten it at the rail. This done, with that end yet in his hand and standing beside the pin, he looked round upon his crew, sweeping from one to the other; pausing his glance long upon Daggoo, Queequeg, Tashtego; but shunning Fedallah; and then settling his firm relying eye upon the chief mate said,—"Take the rope, sir—I give it into thy hands, Starbuck." Then arranging his person in the basket, he gave the word for them to hoist him to his perch, Starbuck being the one who secured the rope at last and afterwards stood near it. And thus, with one hand clinging round the royal mast, Ahab gazed abroad upon the sea for miles and miles,—ahead, astern, this side and that,—within the wide expanded circle commanded at so great a height.

Now, the first time Ahab was perched aloft; ere he had been there ten minutes; one of those red-billed savage sea-hawks which so often fly incommodiously close round the manned mast-heads of whalemen in these latitudes; one of these birds came wheeling and screaming round his head in a maze of untrackably swift circlings. Then it darted a thousand feet straight up into the air; then spiralized downwards, and went eddying again round his head.

But with his gaze fixed upon the dim and distant horizon, Ahab seemed not to mark this wild bird; nor, indeed, would anyone else have marked it much, it being no uncommon circumstance; only now almost the least heedful eye seemed to see some sort of cunning meaning in almost every sight.

"Your hat, your hat, sir!" suddenly cried the Sicilian seaman, who being posted at the mizzen-mast-head, stood directly behind Ahab, though somewhat lower than his level, and with a deep gulf of air dividing them.

But already the sable wing was before the old man's eyes; the long hooked bill at his head: with a scream, the black hawk darted away with his prize.

An eagle flew thrice round Tarquin's head, removing his cap to replace it, and thereupon Tanaquil, his wife, declared that Tarquin would be king of Rome. But only by the replacing of the cap was that omen accounted good. Ahab's hat was never restored; the wild hawk flew on and on with it; far in advance of the prow: and at last disappeared; while from the point of that disappearance, a minute black spot was dimly discerned, falling from that vast height into the sea.

CHAPTER 90

THE "PEQUOD" MEETS THE "DELIGHT"

THE INTENSE *Pequod* sailed on; the rolling waves and days went by; the life-buoy-coffin still lightly swung; and another ship, most miserably misnamed the *Delight*, was descried. As she drew nigh, all eyes were fixed upon her broad beams, called shears, which, in some whaling-ships, cross the quarter-deck at the height of eight or nine feet; serving to carry the spare, unrigged, or disabled boats.

Upon the stranger's shears were beheld the shattered, white ribs, and some few splintered planks, of what had once been a whale-boat; but you now saw through this wreck, as plainly as you see through the peeled, half-unhinged, and bleaching skeleton of a horse.

"Hast seen the white whale?"

"Look!" replied the hollow-cheeked captain from his taffrail; and with his trumpet he pointed to the wreck.

"Hast killed him?"

"The harpoon is not yet forged that ever will do that," answered the other, sadly glancing upon a rounded hammock on the deck, whose gathered sides some noiseless sailors were busy in sewing together.

"Not forged!" and snatching Perth's levelled iron from the crotch, Ahab held it out, exclaiming, "Look ye, Nantucketer; here in this hand

I hold his death! Tempered in blood, and tempered by lightning are these barbs; and I swear to temper them triply in that hot place behind the fin, where the white whale most feels his accursed life!"

"Then God keep thee, old man—see'st thou that"—pointing to the hammock—"I bury but one of five stout men, who were alive only yesterday; but were dead ere night. Only *that* one I bury; the rest were buried before they died; you sail upon their tomb." Then turning to his crew, "Are ye ready there? place the plank then on the rail, and lift the body; so, then—Oh! God"—advancing towards the hammock with uplifted hands—"may the resurrection and the life——"

"Brace forward! Up helm!" cried Ahab like lightning to his men. But the suddenly started *Pequod* was not quick enough to escape the sound of the splash that the corpse soon made as it struck the sea; not so quick, indeed, but that some of the flying bubbles might have sprinkled her hull with their ghostly baptism.

As Ahab now glided from the dejected *Delight*, the strange life-buoy hanging at the *Pequod's* stern came into conspicuous relief.

"Ha! yonder! look yonder, men!" cried a foreboding voice in her wake. "In vain, oh, ye strangers, ye fly our sad burial; ye but turn us your taffrail to show us your coffin!"

CHAPTER 91

THE CHASE—FIRST DAY

THAT NIGHT, in the mid-watch, when the old man—as his wont at intervals—stepped forth from the scuttle in which he leaned, and went to his pivot-hole, he suddenly thrust out his face, fiercely snuffing up the sea air as a sagacious ship's dog will, in drawing nigh to some barbarous isle. He declared that a whale must be near. Soon that peculiar odour, sometimes to a great distance given forth by the living sperm-whale, was palpable to all the watch; nor was any mariner surprised when, after inspecting the compass, and then the dog-vane, and then ascertaining the precise bearing of the odour as nearly as possible, Ahab rapidly ordered the ship's course to be slightly altered, and the sail to be shortened.

The acute policy dictating these movements was sufficiently vindicated at daybreak, by the sight of a long sleek on the sea directly and lengthwise ahead, smooth as oil, and resembling in the pleated watery wrinkles bordering it, the polished metallic-like marks of some swift tide-rip, at the mouth of a deep, rapid stream.

"Man the mast-heads! Call all hands!"

Thundering with the butts of three clubbed handspikes on the forecastle deck, Daggoo roused the sleepers with such judgment claps that they seemed to exhale from the scuttle, so instantaneously did they appear with their clothes in their hands.

"What d'ye see?" cried Ahab, flattening his face to the sky.

"Nothing, nothing, sir!" was the sound hailing down in reply.

"T' gallant sails!—stunsails! alow and aloft, and on both sides!"

All sail being set, he now cast loose the life-line, reserved for swaying him to the main royal mast-head; and in a few moments they were hoisting him thither, when, while but two thirds of the way aloft, and while peering ahead through the horizontal vacancy between the main-top-sail and top-gallant-sail, he raised a gull-like cry in the air, "There she blows!—there she blows! A hump like a snow-hill! It is Moby Dick!"

Fired by the cry which seemed simultaneously taken up by the three look-outs, the men on deck rushed to the rigging to behold the famous whale they had so long been pursuing. Ahab had now gained his final perch, some feet above the other look-outs, Tashtego standing just beneath him on the cap of the top-gallant-mast, so that the Indian's head was almost on a level with Ahab's heel. From this height the whale was now seen some mile or so ahead, at every roll of the sea revealing his high sparkling hump, and regularly jetting his silent spout into the air. To the credulous mariners it seemed the same silent spout they had so long ago beheld in the moonlit Atlantic and Indian Oceans.

"And did none of ye see it before?" cried Ahab, hailing the perched men all around him.

"I saw him almost that same instant, sir, that Captain Ahab did, and I cried out," said Tashtego.

"Not the same instant; not the same—no, the doubloon is mine, Fate reserved the doubloon for me. _I_ only; none of ye could have raised the white whale first. There she blows! there she blows!—there she blows! There again!—there again!" he cried, in long-drawn, lingering, methodic tones, attuned to the gradual prolongings of the whale's visible jets. "He's going to sound! In stunsails! Down top-gallant-sails! Stand by three boats. Mr. Starbuck, remember, stay on board, and keep the ship. Helm there! Luff, luff a point! So; steady, man, steady! There go flukes! No, no; only black water! All ready the boats there? Stand by, stand by! Lower me, Mr. Starbuck; lower, lower,—quick, quicker!" and he slid through the air to the deck.

"He is heading straight to leeward, sir," cried Stubb, "right away from us; cannot have seen the ship yet."

"Be dumb, man! Stand by the braces! Hard down the helm!—
brace up! Shiver her!—shiver her!—So; well that! Boats, boats!"

Soon all the boats but Starbuck's were dropped; all the boatsails se
—all the paddles plying; with rippling swiftness, shooting to leeward
and Ahab heading the onset. A pale, death-glimmer lit up Fedallah'
sunken eyes; a hideous motion gnawed his mouth.

Like noiseless nautilus shells, their light prows sped through the sea
but only slowly they neared the foe. As they neared him, the ocea
grew still more smooth; seemed drawing a carpet over its waves
seemed a noon-meadow, so serenely it spread. At length the breathles
hunter came so nigh his seemingly unsuspecting prey, that his entir
dazzling hump was distinctly visible, sliding along the sea as if a
isolated thing, and continually set in a revolving ring of finest, fleecy
greenish foam. He saw the vast, involved wrinkles of the slightly pro
jecting head beyond. Before it, far out on the soft Turkish-rugge
waters, went the glistening white shadow from his broad, milky fore
head, a musical rippling playfully accompanying the shade; and behind
the blue waters interchangeably flowed over into the moving valle
of his steady wake; and on either hand bright bubbles arose and dance
by his side. But these were broken again by the light toes of hundred
of gay fowls softly feathering the sea, alternate with their fitful flight
and like to some flag-staff rising from the painted hull of an argosy
the tall but shattered pole of a recent lance projected from the whit
whale's back; and at intervals one of the cloud of soft-toed fowl
hovering, and to and fro skimming like a canopy over the fish, silentl
perched and rocked on this pole, the long tail feathers streaming lik
pennons.

On each soft side—coincident with the parted swell, that but onc
heaving him, then flowed so wide away—on each bright side, the whal
shed off enticings. No wonder there had been some among the hunter
who namelessly transported and allured by all this serenity, had ven
tured to assail it; but had fatally found that quietude but the vestur
of tornadoes. Yet calm, enticing calm, oh, whale! thou glidest on, t
all who for the first time eye thee, no matter how many in that sam
way thou mayst have bejuggled and destroyed before.

And thus, through the serene tranquillities of the tropical sea, among
waves whose hand-clappings were suspended by exceeding rapture
Moby Dick moved on, still withholding from sight the full terrors o
his submerged trunk, entirely hiding the wrenched hideousness of hi
jaw. But soon the fore part of him slowly rose from the water; for a
instant his whole marbleized body formed a high arch, like Virginia'
Natural Bridge, and warningly waving his bannered flukes in the air

he grand god revealed himself, sounded, and went out of sight. Hoveringly halting, and dipping on the wing, the white sea-fowls ongingly lingered over the agitated pool that he left.

With oars apeak, and paddles down, the sheets of their sails adrift, he three boats now stilly floated, awaiting Moby Dick's reappearance.

"An hour," said Ahab, standing rooted in his boat's stern; and he gazed beyond the whale's place, towards the dim blue spaces and wide wooing vacancies to leeward. It was only an instant; for again his eyes seemed whirling round in his head as he swept the watery circle. The breeze now freshened; the sea began to swell.

"The birds!—the birds!" cried Tashtego.

In long Indian file, as when herons take wing, the white birds were now all flying towards Ahab's boat; and when within a few yards began fluttering over the water there, wheeling round and round, with joyous, expectant cries. Their vision was keener than man's; Ahab could discover no sign in the sea. But suddenly as he peered down and down into its depths, he profoundly saw a white living spot no bigger than a white weasel, with wonderful celerity uprising, and magnifying as it rose, till it turned, and then there were plainly revealed two long crooked rows of white, glistening teeth, floating up from the undiscoverable bottom. It was Moby Dick's open mouth and scrolled jaw; his vast, shadowed bulk still half blending with the blue of the sea. The glittering mouth yawned beneath the boat like an open-doored marble tomb; and giving one sidelong sweep with his steering oar, Ahab whirled the craft aside from this tremendous apparition. Then, calling upon Fedallah to change places with him, went forward to the bows, and seizing his harpoon, commanded his crew to grasp their oars and stand by to stern.

Now, by reason of this timely spinning round the boat upon its axis, its bow, by anticipation, was made to face the whale's head while yet under water. But as if perceiving this stratagem, Moby Dick, with that malicious intelligence ascribed to him, sidelingly transplanted himself, as it were, in an instant, shooting his pleated head lengthwise beneath the boat.

Through and through; through every plank and each rib, it thrilled for an instant, the whale obliquely lying on his back, in the manner of a biting shark, slowly and feelingly taking its bows full within his mouth, so that the long, narow, scrolled lower jaw curled high up into the open air, and one of the teeth caught in a row-lock. The bluish pearl-white of the inside of the jaw was within six inches of Ahab's head, and reached higher than that. In this attitude the white whale now shook the slight cedar as a mildly cruel cat her mouse.

With unastonished eyes Fedallah gazed, and crossed his arms; but th
tiger-yellow crew were tumbling over each other's heads to gain th
uttermost stern.

And now, while both elastic gunwales were springing in and ou
as the whale dallied with the doomed craft in this devilish way; an
from his body being submerged beneath the boat, he could not b
darted at from the bows, for the bows were almost inside of him, a
it were; and while the other boats involuntarily paused, as before
quick crisis impossible to withstand, then it was that monomania
Ahab, furious with this tantalizing vicinity of his foe, which place
him all alive and helpless in the very jaws he hated; frenzied with a
this, he seized the long bone with his naked hands, and wildly strov
to wrench it from its gripe. As now he thus vainly strove, the jav
slipped from him; the frail gunwales bent in, collapsed, and snapped
as both jaws, like an enormous shears, sliding further aft, bit the craf
completely in twain, and locked themselves fast again in the sea, mid
way between the two floating wrecks. These floated aside, the broke
ends drooping, the crew at the stern-wreck clinging to the gunwales
and striving to hold fast to the oars to lash them across.

At that preluding moment, ere the boat was yet snapped, Ahab th
first to perceive the whale's intent, by the crafty upraising of his head
a movement that loosed his hold for the time; at that moment his hand
had made one final effort to push the boat out of the bite. But onl
slipping further into the whale's mouth, and tilting over sideways a
it slipped, the boat had shaken off his hold on the jaw; spilled him ou
of it, as he leaned to the push; and so he fell flat-faced upon the sea.

Ripplingly withdrawing from his prey, Moby Dick now lay at a
little distance, vertically thrusting his oblong white head up and down
in the billows; and at the same time slowly revolving his whol
spindled body; so that when his vast wrinkled forehead rose—som
twenty or more feet out of the water—the now rising swells, with al
their confluent waves, dazzlingly broke against it; vindictively tossing
their shivered spray still higher into the air. So, in a gale, the but hal
baffled Channel billows only recoil from the base of the Eddystone
triumphantly to overleap its summit with their scud.

But soon resuming his horizontal attitude, Moby Dick swam swiftly
round and round the wrecked crew; sideways churning the water in
his vengeful wake, as if lashing himself up to still another and more
deadly assault. The sight of the splintered boat seemed to madder
him, as the blood of grapes and mulberries cast before Antiochus's
elephants in the book of Maccabees. Meanwhile Ahab half smothered
in the foam of the whale's insolent tail, and too much of a cripple to

swim,—though he could still keep afloat, even in the heart of such a
whirlpool as that; helpless Ahab's head was seen, like a tossed bubble
which the least chance shock might burst. From the boat's fragmentary
stern, Fedallah incuriously and mildly eyed him; the clinging crew,
at the other drifting end, could not succour him; more than enough
was it for them to look to themselves. For so revolvingly appalling
was the white whale's aspect, and so planetarily swift the ever-contracting circles he made, that he seemed horizontally swooping upon them.
And though the other boats, unharmed, still hovered hard by; still they
dared not pull into the eddy to strike, lest that should be the signal for
the instant destruction of the jeopardized castaways, Ahab and all; nor
in that case could they themselves hope to escape. With straining eyes,
then, they remained on the outer edge of the direful zone, whose
centre had now become the old man's head.

Meantime, from the beginning all this had been descried from the
ship's mast-heads; and squaring her yards, she had borne down upon
the scene; and was now so nigh, that Ahab in the water hailed her;—
"Sail on the"—but that moment a breaking sea dashed on him from
Moby Dick, and whelmed him for the time. But struggling out of it
again, and changing to rise on a towering crest, he shouted, "Sail on
the whale!—Drive him off!"

The *Pequod's* prows were pointed; and breaking up the charmed
circle, she effectually parted the white whale from his victim. As he
sullenly swam off, the boats flew to the rescue.

Dragged into Stubb's boat with blood-shot, blinded eyes, the white
brine caking in his wrinkles; the long tension of Ahab's bodily strength
did crack, and helplessly he yielded to his body's doom for a time,
lying all crushed in the bottom of Stubb's boat, like one trodden under
foot of herds of elephants. Far inland, nameless wails came from him,
as desolate sounds from out ravines.

But this intensity of his physical prostration did but so much the
more abbreviate it. In an instant's compass, great hearts sometimes
condense to one deep pang, the sum total of those shallow pains kindly
diffused through feebler men's whole lives. And so, such hearts,
though summary in each one suffering; still, if the gods decree it, in
their life-time aggregate a whole age of woe, wholly made up of instantaneous intensities; for even in their pointless centres, those noble
natures contain the entire circumferences of inferior souls.

"The harpoon," said Ahab, half way rising, and draggingly leaning
on one bended arm—"is it safe?"

"Aye, sir, for it was not darted; this is it," said Stubb, showing it.

"Lay it before me;—any missing men?"

"One, two, three, four, five;—there were five oars, sir, and here are five men."

"That's good.—Help me, man; I wish to stand. So, so, I see him! there! there! going to leeward still; what a leaping spout!—Hands off from me! The eternal sap runs up in Ahab's bones again! Set the sail; out oars; the helm!"

It is often the case that when a boat is stove, its crew, being picked up by another boat, help to work that second boat; and the chase is thus continued with what is called double-banked oars. It was thus now. But the added power of the boat did not equal the added power of the whale, for he seemed to have treble-banked his every fin; swimming with a velocity which plainly showed, that if now, under these circumstances, pushed on, the chase would prove an indefinitely prolonged, if not a hopeless one; nor could any crew endure for so long a period, such an unintermitted, intense straining at the oar; a thing barely tolerable only in some one brief vicissitude. The ship itself, then, as it sometimes happens, offered the most promising intermediate means of overtaking the chase. Accordingly, the boats now made for her, and were soon swayed up to their cranes—the two parts of the wrecked boats having been previously secured by her—and then hoisting everything to her side, and stacking her canvas high up, and sideways outstretching it with stunsails, like the double-jointed wings of an albatross; the *Pequod* bore down in the leeward wake of Moby Dick. At the well-known, methodic intervals, the whale's glittering spout was regularly anounced from the manned mast-heads; and when he would be reported as just gone down, Ahab would take the time, and then pacing the deck, binnacle-watch in hand, so soon as the last second of the allotted hour expired, his voice was heard.—"Whose is the doubloon now? D'ye see him?" and if the reply was No, sir! straightway he commanded them to lift him to his perch. In this way the day wore on; Ahab, now aloft and motionless; anon, unrestingly pacing the planks.

As he was thus walking, uttering no sound, except to hail the men aloft, or to bid them hoist a sail still higher, or to spread one to a still greater breadth—thus to and fro pacing, beneath his slouched hat, at every turn he passed his own wrecked boat, which had been dropped upon the quarter-deck, and lay there reversed; broken bow to shattered stern. At last he paused before it; and as in an already over-clouded sky fresh troops of clouds will sometimes sail across, so over the old man's face there now stole some such added gloom as this.

Stubb saw him pause; and perhaps intending, not vainly, though, to evince his own unabated fortitude, and thus keep up a valiant place

In his captain's mind, he advanced, and eyeing the wreck exclaimed—
"The thistle the ass refused; it pricked his mouth too keenly, sir,
ha! ha!"

"What soulless thing is this that laughs before a wreck? Man, man!
did I not know thee brave as fearless fire (and as mechanical) I could
swear thou wert a poltroon. Groan nor laugh should be heard before
a wreck."

"Aye, sir," said Starbuck drawing near, "'tis a solemn sight; an
omen, and an ill one."

"Omen? omen?—the dictionary! If the gods think to speak outright
to man, they will honourably speak outright; not shake their heads,
and give an old wives' darkling hint.—Begone! Ye two are the opposite poles of one thing; Starbuck is Stubb reversed, and Stubb is Starbuck; and ye two are all mankind; and Ahab stands alone among
the millions of the peopled earth, nor gods or men his neighbours!
Cold, cold—I shiver!—How now? Aloft there! D'ye see him? Sing
out for every spout, though he spout ten times a second!"

The day was nearly done; only the hem of his golden robe was
rustling. Soon it was almost dark, but the look-out men still remained
unset.

"Can't see the spout now, sir;—too dark"—cried a voice from the
air.

"How heading when last seen?"

"As before, sir,—straight to leeward."

"Good! he will travel slower now 'tis night. Down royals and top-
gallant stunsails, Mr. Starbuck. We must not run over him before
morning; he's making a passage now, and may heave-to a while. Helm
there! keep her full before the wind!—Aloft! come down!—Mr.
Stubb, send a fresh hand to the fore-masthead, and see it manned till
morning."—Then advancing towards the doubloon in the main-mast—
"Men, this gold is mine, for I earned it; but I shall let it abide here till
the white whale is dead; and then, whosoever of ye first raises him,
upon the day he shall be killed, this gold is that man's; and if on that
day I shall again raise him, then, ten times its sum shall be divided
among all of ye! Away now! the deck is thine, sir."

And so saying, he placed himself half way within the scuttle, and
slouching his hat, stood there till dawn, except when at intervals
rousing himself to see how the night wore on.

CHAPTER 92

THE CHASE—SECOND DAY

At day-break, the three mast-heads were punctually manned afresh.
"D'ye see him?" cried Ahab, after allowing a little space for the
light to spread.

"See nothing, sir."

"Turn up all hands and make sail! he travels faster than I thought
for;—the top-gallant sails!—aye, they should have been kept on her
all night. But no matter—'tis but resting for the rush."

The ship tore on; leaving such a furrow in the sea as when a
cannon-ball, missent, becomes a plough-share and turns up the level
field.

"By salt and hemp!" cried Stubb, "but this swift motion of the deck
creeps up one's legs and tingles at the heart. This ship and I are two
brave fellows!—Ha! ha! Some one take me up, and launch me,
spine-wise, on the sea,—for by live-oaks! my spine's a keel. Ha, ha!
we go the gait that leaves no dust behind!"

"There she blows—she blows!—she blows!—right ahead!" was now
the mast-head cry.

"Aye, aye!" cried Stubb, "I knew it—ye can't escape—blow on and
split your spout, O whale! the mad fiend himself is after ye! blow
your trump—blister your lungs!—Ahab will dam off your blood, as
a miller shuts his water-gate upon the stream!"

And Stubb did but speak out for well nigh all that crew. The frenzies
of the chase had by this time worked them bubblingly up, like old
wine worked anew. Whatever pale fears and forebodings some of
them might have felt before; these were not only now kept out of
sight through the growing awe of Ahab, but they were broken up, and
on all sides routed, as timid prairie hares that scatter before the bound-
ing bison. The hand of Fate had snatched all their souls; and by the
stirring perils of the previous day; the rack of the past night's suspense;
the fixed, unfearing, blind, reckless way in which their wild craft went
plunging towards its flying mark; by all these things, their hearts were
bowled along. The wind that made great bellies of their sails, and
rushed the vessel on by arms invisible as irresistible; this seemed the
symbol of that unseen agency which so enslaved them to the race.

They were one man, not thirty. For as the one ship that held them
all; though it was put together of all contrasting things—oak, and
maple, and pine wood; iron, and pitch, and hemp—yet all these ran

into each other in the one concrete hull, which shot on its way, both balanced and directed by the long central keel; even so, all the individualities of the crew, this man's valour, that man's fear; guilt and guiltiness, all varieties were welded into oneness, and were all directed to that fatal goal which Ahab their one lord and keel did point to.

The rigging lived. The mast-heads, like the tops of tall palms, were outspreadingly tufted with arms and legs. Clinging to a spar with one hand, some reached forth the other with impatient wavings; others, shading their eyes from the vivid sunlight, sat far out on the rocking yards; all the spars in full bearing of mortals, ready and ripe for their fate. Ah! how they still strove through that infinite blueness to seek out the thing that might destroy them!

"Why sing ye not out for him, if ye see him?" cried Ahab, when, after the lapse of some minutes since the first cry, no more had been heard. "Sway me up, men: ye have been deceived; not Moby Dick casts one jet that way, and then disappears."

It was even so; in their headlong eagerness, the men had mistaken some other thing for the whale-spout, as the event itself soon proved; for hardly had Ahab reached his perch; hardly was the rope belayed to its pin on deck, when he struck the keynote to an orchestra, that made the air vibrate as with the combined discharges of rifles. The triumphant halloo of thirty buckskin lungs was heard, as—much nearer to the ship than the place of the imaginary jet, less than a mile ahead— Moby Dick bodily burst into view! For not by any calm and indolent spoutings; not by the peaceable gush of that mystic fountain in his head, did the white whale now reveal his vicinity; but by the far more wondrous phenomenon of breaching. Rising with his utmost velocity from the furthest depths, the sperm-whale thus booms his entire bulk into the pure element of air, and piling up a mountain of dazzling foam, shows his place to the distance of seven miles and more. In those moments, the torn, enraged waves he shakes off, seem his mane; in some cases, this breaching is his act of defiance.

"There she breaches! there she breaches!" was the cry, as in his immeasurable bravadoes the white whale tossed himself salmon-like to Heaven. So suddenly seen in the blue plain of the sea, and relieved against the still bluer margin of the sky, the spray that he raised, for the moment, intolerably glittered and glared like a glacier; and stood there gradually fading away from its first sparkling intensity, to the dim mistiness of an advancing shower in a vale.

"Aye, breach your last to the sun, Moby Dick!" cried Ahab, "thy hour and thy harpoon are at hand!—Down! down all of ye, but one man at the fore. The boats!—stand by!"

Unmindful of the tedious rope-ladders of the shrouds, the men, like shooting stars, slid to the deck, by the isolated backstays and halyards; while Ahab, less dartingly, but still rapidly was dropped from his perch.

"Lower away," he cried, so soon as he had reached his boat—a spare one, rigged the afternoon previous. "Mr. Starbuck, the ship is thine—keep away from the boats, but keep near them. Lower, all!"

As if to strike a quick terror into them, by this time being the first assailant himself, Moby Dick had turned, and was now coming for the three crews. Ahab's boat was central; and cheering his men, he told them he would take the whale head-and-head,—that is, pull straight up to his forehead,—a not uncommon thing; for when within a certain limit, such a course excludes the coming onset from the whale's sidelong vision. But ere that close limit was gained, and while yet all three boats were plain as the ships three masts to his eye; the white whale churning himself into furious speed, almost in an instant as it were, rushing among the boats with open jaws, and a lashing tail, offered appalling battle on every side; and heedless of the irons darted at him from every boat, seemed only intent on annihilating each separate plank of which those boats were made. But skilfully manœuvred, incessantly wheeling like trained chargers in the field; the boats for a while eluded him; though, at times, but by a plank's breadth; while all the time, Ahab's unearthly slogan tore every other cry but his to shreds.

But at last in his untraceable evolutions, the white whale so crossed and recrossed, and in a thousand ways entangled the slack to the three lines now fast to him, that they foreshortened, and, of themselves, warped the devoted boats towards the planted irons in him; though now for a moment the whale drew aside a little, as if to rally for a more tremendous charge. Seizing that opportunity, Ahab first paid out more line: and then was rapidly hauling and jerking in upon it again—hoping that way to disencumber it of some snarls—when lo!—a sight more savage than the embattled teeth of sharks!

Caught and twisted—corkscrewed in the mazes of the line, loose harpoons and lances, with all their bristling barbs and points, came flashing and dripping up to the chocks in the bows of Ahab's boat. Only one thing could be done. Seizing the boat-knife, he critically reached within—through—and then, without—the rays of steel; dragged in the line beyond, passed it, inboard, to the bowsman, and then, twice sundering the rope near the chocks—dropped the intercepted fagot of steel into the sea; and was all fast again. That instant, the white whale made a sudden rush among the remaining tangles of the other lines; by so doing, irresistibly dragged the more involved boats of Stubb and Flask towards his flukes; dashed them together like two rolling husks on a surf-beaten beach, and then, diving down into the sea, disappeared in a boiling maelstrom, in which, for a space, the odorous cedar chips of the wrecks danced round and round, like the grated nutmeg in a swiftly stirred bowl of punch.

While the two crews were yet circling in the waters, reaching out after the revolving line-tubs, oars, and other floating furniture, while aslope little Flask bobbed up and down like an empty vial, twitching his legs upwards to escape the dreaded jaws of sharks; and Stubb was lustily singing out for some one to ladle him up; and while the old man's line—now parting—admitted of his pulling into the creamy pool to rescue whom he could;—in that wild simultaneousness of a thousand concreted perils,—Ahab's yet unstricken boat seemed drawn up towards Heaven by invisible wires,—as, arrow-like, shooting perpendicularly from the sea, the white whale dashed his broad forehead against its bottom, and sent it, turning over and over, into the air; till it fell again—gunwale downwards—and Ahab and his men struggled out from under it, like seals from a sea-side cave.

The first uprising momentum of the whale—modifying its direction as he struck the surface—involuntarily launched him along it, to a little distance from the centre of the destruction he had made; and with his back to it, he now lay for a moment slowly feeling with his flukes from side to side; and whenever a stray oar, bit of plank, the least chip or crumb of the boats touched his skin, his tail swiftly drew back, and came sideways smiting the sea. But soon, as if satisfied that his work for that time was done, he pushed his pleated forehead through the ocean, and trailing after him the intertangled lines, continued his leeward way at a traveller's methodic pace.

As before, the attentive ship having descried the whole fight, again came bearing down to the rescue, and dropping a boat, picked up the floating mariners, tubs, oars, and whatever else could be caught at, and safely landed them on her decks. Some sprained shoulders, wrists, and ankles; livid contusions; wrenched harpoons and lances; inextricable intricacies of rope; shattered oars and planks; all these were there; but no fatal or even serious ill seemed to have befallen anyone. As with Fedallah the day before, so Ahab was now found grimly clinging to his boat's broken half, which afforded a comparatively easy float; nor did it so exhaust him as the previous day's mishap.

But when he was helped to the deck, all eyes were fastened upon him; as instead of standing by himself he still half-hung upon the shoulder of Starbuck, who had thus far been the foremost to assist him. His ivory leg had been snapped off, leaving but one short sharp splinter.

"Aye aye, Starbuck, 'tis sweet to lean sometimes, be the leaner who he will; and would old Ahab had leaned oftener than he has."

"The ferrule has not stood, sir," said the carpenter, now coming up; "I put good work into that leg."

"But no bones broken, sir, I hope," said Stubb with true concern.

"Aye! and all splintered to pieces, Stubb!—d'ye see it.—But even with a broken bone, old Ahab is untouched; and I account no living bone of mine one jot more me, than this dead one that's lost. Nor white whale, nor man, nor fiend, can so much as graze old Ahab in his own proper and inaccessible being. Can any lead touch yonder floor, any mast scrape yonder roof?—Aloft there! which way?"

"Dead to leeward, sir."

"Up helm, then; pile on the sail again, ship keepers! down the rest of the spare boats and rig them—Mr. Starbuck away, and muster the boat's crews."

"Let me first help thee towards the bulwarks, sir."

"Oh, oh, oh! how this splinter gores me now! Accursed fate! that the unconquerable captain in the soul should have such a craven mate!"

"Sir?"

"My body, man, not thee. Give me something for a cane—there, that shivered lance will do. Muster the men. Surely I have not seen him yet. By heaven it cannot be?—missing?—quick! call them all."

The old man's hinted thought was true. Upon mustering the company, the Parsee was not there.

"The Parsee!" cried Stubb—"he must have been caught in——"

"The black vomit wrench thee!—run all of ye above, alow, cabin, forecastle—find him—not gone—not gone!"

But quickly they returned to him with the tidings that the Parsee was nowhere to be found.

"Aye, sir," said Stubb—"caught among the tangles of your line—I thought I saw him dragging under."

"*My* line! *my* line? Gone?—gone? What means that little word? What death-knell rings in it, that old Ahab shakes as if he were the belfry. The harpoon, too!—toss over the litter there,—d'ye see it?—the forged iron, men, the white whale's—no, no, no,—blistered fool! this hand did dart it!—'tis in the fish!—Aloft there! Keep him nailed—Quick!—all hands to the rigging of the boats—collect the oars—harpooneers! the irons, the irons!—hoist the royals higher—a pull on all the sheets!—helm there! steady, steady for your life! I'll ten times girdle the unmeasured globe; yea and dive straight through it, but I'll slay him yet!"

"Great God! but for one single instant show thyself," cried Starbuck; "never, never wilt thou capture him, old man. In Jesus' name no more of this, that's worse than devil's madness. Two days chased; twice stove to splinters; thy very leg once more snatched from under thee; thy evil shadow gone—all good angels mobbing thee with warnings:—what more wouldst thou have?—Shall we keep chasing this murderous fish till he swamps the last man? Shall we be dragged by him to the bottom of the sea? Shall we be towed by him to the infernal world? Oh, oh,—Impiety and blasphemy to hunt him more!"

"Starbuck, of late I've felt strangely moved to thee; ever since that hour we both saw—thou knowst what, in one another's eyes. But in this matter of the whale, be the front of thy face to me as the palm of this hand—a lipless, unfeatured blank. Ahab is for ever Ahab, man. This whole act's immutably decreed. 'Twas rehearsed by thee and me a billion years before this ocean rolled. Fool! I am the Fates' lieutenant; I act under orders. Look thou, underling! that thou obeyest mine. —Stand round me, men. Ye see an old man cut down to the stump; leaning on a shivered lance; propped up on a lonely foot. 'Tis Ahab— his body's part; but Ahab's soul's a centipede, that moves upon a hundred legs. I feel strained, half-stranded, as ropes that tow dismasted frigates in a gale; and I may look so. But ere I break, ye'll hear me crack; and till ye hear *that,* know that Ahab's hawser tows his purpose yet. Believe ye, men in the things called omens? Then laugh aloud, and cry encore! for ere they drown, drowning things will twice rise to the surface; then rise again, to sink for evermore. So with Moby Dick—two days he's floated—to-morrow will be the third. Aye, men, he'll rise once more,—but only to spout his last! D'ye feel brave, men brave?"

"As fearless fire," said Stubb.

"And as mechanical," muttered Ahab. Then as the men went forward, he muttered on: "The things called omens! And yesterday I talked the same to Starbuck there, concerning my broken boat. Oh! how valiantly I seek to drive out of other's hearts what's clinched so fast in mine!—Fedallah—the Parsee!—gone, gone!"

When dusk descended, the whale was still in sight to leeward.

So once more the sail was shortened, and everything passed nearly as on the previous night; only, the sound of hammers, and the hum of the grindstone was heard till nearly daylight, as the men toiled by lanterns in the complete and careful rigging of the spare boats and sharpening their fresh weapons for the morrow. Meantime, of the broken keel of Ahab's wrecked craft the carpenter made him another leg; while still as on the night before, slouched Ahab stood fixed within his scuttle; his hid, heliotrope glance anticipatingly gone backward on its dial; sat due eastward for the earliest sun.

CHAPTER 93

THE CHASE—THIRD DAY

THE MORNING of the third day dawned fair and fresh, and once more the solitary night-man at the fore-mast-head was relieved by crowds of the daylight look-outs, who dotted every mast and almost every spar.

"D'ye see him?" cried Ahab; but the whale was not yet in sight.

"In his infallible wake, though; but follow that wake, that's all. Helm there; steady, as thou goest, and has been going. What a lovely day again! were it a new-made world, and made for a summer-house to the angels, and this morning the first of its throwing open to them, a fairer day could not dawn upon that world. Here's food for thought, had Ahab time to think; but Ahab never thinks; he only feels, feels, feels; that's tingling enough for mortal man! to think's audacity. God only has that right and privilege. Thinking is, or ought to be, a coolness and a calmness; and our poor hearts throb, and our poor brains beat too much for that. And yet, I've sometimes thought my brain was very calm—frozen calm, this old skull cracks so, like a glass in which the contents turned to ice, and shiver it. And still this hair is growing now; this moment growing, and heat must breed it; but no, it's like that sort of common grass that will grow anywhere, between the earthy clefts of Greenland ice or in Vesuvius lava. How the wild winds blow it; they whip it about me as the torn shreds of split sails lash the tossed ship they cling to. A vile wind that has no doubt blown ere this through prison corridors and cells, and wards of hospitals, and ventilated them, and now comes blowing hither as innocent as fleeces. Out upon it!—it's tainted. Were I the wind, I'd blow no more on such a wicked, miserable world. I'd crawl somewhere to a cave, and slink there. And yet, 'tis a noble and heroic thing, the wind! who ever conquered it? In every fight it has the last and bitterest blow. Run tilting at it, and you but run through it. Ha! a coward wind that strikes stark naked men, but will not stand to receive a single blow. Even Ahab is a braver thing—a nobler thing than that. Would now the wind but had a body; but all the things that most exasperate and outrage mortal man, all these things are bodiless, but only bodiless as objects, not as agents. There's a most special, a most cunning, oh, a most malicious difference! And yet, I say again, and swear it now, that there's something all glorious and gracious in the wind. These warm Trade Winds, at least, that in the clear heavens blow straight on, in strong and steadfast, vigorous mildness; and veer not from their mark, however the baser currents of the sea may turn and tack, and mightiest Mississippis of the land swift and swerve about, uncertain where to go at last. And by the eternal Poles! these same Trades that so directly blow my good ship on; these Trades, or something like them—something! so unchangeable, and full as strong, blow my keeled soul along! To it! Aloft there! What d'ye see?"

"Nothing, sir."

"Nothing! and noon at hand! The doubloon goes a-begging! See the sun! Aye, aye, it must be so. I've oversailed him. How, got the start? Aye, he's chasing *me* now; not I, *him*—that's bad; I might have known it, too. Fool! the lines—the harpoons he's towing. Aye, aye, I have run him by last night. About! about! Come down, all of ye, but the regular look-outs! Man the braces!"

Steering as she had done, the wind had been somewhat on the *Pequod's* quarter, so that now being pointed in the reverse direction, the braced ship sailed hard upon the breeze as she rechurned the cream in her own white wake.

"Against the wind he now steers for the open jaw," murmured Starbuck to himself, as he coiled the new-hauled main-brace upon the rail. "God keep us, but already my bones feel damp within me, and from the inside wet my flesh. I misdoubt me that I disobey my God in obeying him!"

"Stand by to sway me up!" cried Ahab, advancing to the hempen basket. "We should meet him soon."

"Aye, aye, sir," and straightway Starbuck did Ahab's bidding, and once more Ahab swung on high.

A whole hour now passed; gold-beaten out to ages. Time itself now held long breaths with keen suspense. But at last, some three points off the weather bow, Ahab descried the spout again, and instantly from the three mast-heads three shrieks went up as if the tongues of fire had voiced it.

"Forehead to forehead I meet thee, this third time, Moby Dick! On deck there!—brace sharper up; crowd her into the wind's eye. He's too far off to lower yet, Mr. Starbuck. The sails shake! Stand over that helmsman with a top-maul! So, so; he travels fast, and I must down. But let me have one more good round look aloft here at the sea; there's time for that. An old, old sight, and yet somehow so young; aye, and not changed a wink since I first saw it, a boy, from the sand-hills of Nantucket! The same!—the same!—the same to Noah as to me. There's a soft shower to leeward. Such lovely leewardings! They must lead somewhere—to something else than common land, more palmy than the palms. Leeward! the white whale goes that way; look to windward, then; the better if the bitterer quarter. But good-bye, good-bye, old mast-head! What's this?—green? aye, tiny mosses in these warped cracks. No such green weather stains on Ahab's head! There's the difference now between man's old age and matter's. But aye, old mast, we both grow old together; sound in our hulls, though, are we not, my ship? Aye, minus a leg, that's all. By heaven this dead wood has the better of my live flesh every way. I can't compare with it; and I've known some ships made of dead trees outlast the lives of men made of the most vital stuff of vital fathers. What's that he said? he should still go before me, my pilot; and yet to be seen again? But where? Will I have eyes at the bottom of the sea, supposing I descend those endless stairs? and all night I've been sailing from him, wherever he did sink to. Aye, aye, like many more thou toldst direful truth as touching thyself, O Parsee; but, Ahab, there thy shot fell short. Good-bye, mast-head—keep a good eye upon the whale, the while I'm gone. We'll talk tomorrow, nay, to-night, when the white whale lies down there, tied by head and tail."

He gave the word; and still gazing round him, was steadily lowered through the cloven blue air to the deck.

In due time the boats were lowered; but as standing in his shallop's stern, Ahab just hovered upon the point of the descent, he waved to the mate,—who held one of the tackle-ropes on deck—and bade him pause.

"Starbuck!"

"Sir?"

"For the third time my soul's ship starts upon this voyage, Starbuck."

"Aye, sir, thou wilt have it so."

"Some ships sail from their ports, and ever afterwards are missing, Starbuck!"

"Truth, sir; saddest truth."

"Some men die at ebb tide; some at low water; some at the full of the flood;—and I feel now like a billow that's all one crested comb, Starbuck. I am old;—shake hands with me, man."

Their hands met; their eyes fastened; Starbuck's tears the glue.

"Oh, my captain, my captain!—noble heart—go not—go not! see, it's a brave man that weeps; how great the agony of the persuasion then!"

"Lower away!"—cried Ahab, tossing the mate's arm from him. "Stand by the crew!"

In an instant the boat was pulling round close under the stern.

"The sharks! the sharks!" cried a voice from the low cabin-window there; "O master, my master, come back!"

But Ahab heard nothing; for his own voice was high-lifted then; and the boat leaped on.

Yet the voice spake true; for scarce had he pushed from the ship, when numbers of sharks, seemingly rising from out the dark waters beneath the hull, maliciously snapped at the blades of the oars, every time they dipped in the water; and in this way accompanied the boat with their bites. It is a thing not uncommonly happening to the whale-boats in those swarming seas; the sharks at times apparently following them in the same prescient way that vultures hover over the banners of marching regiments in the east. But these were the first sharks that had been observed by the *Pequod* since the white whale had been first descried; and whether it was that Ahab's crew were all such tiger-yellow barbarians, and therefore their flesh more musky to the sense of the sharks—a matter sometimes well known to affect them,— however it was, they seemed to follow that one boat without molesting the others.

"Heart of wrought steel!" murmured Starbuck gazing over the side, and following with his eyes the receding boat—"canst thou yet ring boldly to that sight?—lowering thy keel among ravening sharks, and followed by them, open-mouthed to the chase; and this the critical third day?—For when three days flow together in one continuous intense pursuit; be sure the first is the morning, the second the noon, and the third the evening and the end of that thing—be that end what it may. Oh! my God! what is this that shoots through me, and leaves me so deadly calm, yet expectant,—fixed at the top of a shudder! Future things swim before me, as in empty outlines and skeletons; all the past is somehow grown dim. Mary, girl! thou fadest in pale glories behind me; boy! I seem to see but thy eyes grown wondrous blue. Strangest problems of life seem clearing; but clouds sweep between— Is my journey's end coming? My legs feel faint; like his who has footed it all day. Feel thy heart,—beats it yet? Stir thyself, Starbuck! —stave it off—move, move! speak aloud!—Mast-head there! See ye my boy's hand on the hill?—Crazed;—aloft there!—keep thy keenest eye upon the boats:—mark well the whale!—Ho! again!—drive off that hawk! see! he pecks—he tears the vane"—pointing to the red flag flying at the main truck—"Ha! he soars away with it!—Where's the old man now? seest thou that sight, oh Ahab!—shudder, shudder!"

The boats had not gone very far, when by a signal from the mast-head—a downward pointed arm, Ahab knew that the whale had sounded; but intending to be near him at the next rising, he held on his way a little sideways from the vessel; the becharmed crew maintaining the profoundest silence, as the head-beat waves hammered and hammered against the opposing bow.

"Drive, drive in your nails, oh ye waves! to their uttermost heads drive them in! ye but strike a thing without a lid; and no coffin and no hearse can be mine:—and hemp only can kill me! Ha! ha!"

Suddenly the waters around them slowly swelled in broad circles; then quickly upheaved, as if sideways sliding from a submerged berg of ice, swiftly rising to the surface. A low rumbling sound was heard; a subterraneous hum; and then all held their breaths; as bedraggled with trailing ropes, and harpoons, and lances, a vast form shot lengthwise, but obliquely from the sea. Shrouded in a thin drooping veil of mist, it hovered for a moment in the rainbowed air; and then fell swamping back into the deep. Crushed thirty feet upwards, the waters flashed for an instant like heaps of fountains, then brokenly sank in a shower of flakes, leaving the circling surface creamed like new milk round the marble trunk of the whale.

"Give way!" cried Ahab to the oarsmen, and the boats darted forward to the attack; but maddened by yesterday's fresh irons that corroded in him, Moby Dick seemed combinedly possessed by all the angels that fell from heaven. The wide tiers of welded tendons overspreading his broad white forehead, beneath the transparent skin, looked knitted together; as head on, he came churning his tail among the boats; and once more flailed them apart; spilling out the irons and lances from the two mates' boats, and dashing in one side of the upper part of their bows, but leaving Ahab's almost without a scar.

While Daggoo and Queequeg were stopping the strained planks; and as the whale swimming out from them, turned, and showed one entire flank as he shot by them again; at that moment a quick cry went up. Lashed round and round to the fish's back: pinioned in the turns upon turns in which, during the past night, the whale had reeled the involutions of the lines around him, the half-torn body of Fedallah was seen; his sable raiment frayed to shreds; his distended eyes turned full upon old Ahab.

The harpoon dropped from his hand.

"Befooled, befooled!"—drawing in a long lean breath—"Aye, Parsee! I see thee again. Away, mates, to the ship! those boats are useless now; repair them if ye can in time, and return to me; if not, Ahab is enough to die—Down, men! the first thing that but offers to jump from this boat I stand in, that thing I harpoon. Ye are not other men, but my arms and my legs; and so obey me.—Where's the whale? gone down again?"

But he looked too nigh the boat; for as if bent upon escaping with the corpse he bore, and as if the particular place of the last encounter had been but a stage in his leeward voyage, Moby Dick was now again steadily swimming forward; and had almost passed the ship,—which thus far had been sailing in the contrary direction to him, though for the present her headway had been stopped. He seemed swimming with his utmost velocity, and now only intent upon pursuing his own straight path in the sea.

"Oh! Ahab," cried Starbuck, "not too late is it, even now, the third day, to desist. See! Moby Dick seeks thee not. It is thou, thou, that madly seekest him!"

Setting sail to the rising wind, the lonely boat was swiftly impelled to leeward by both oars and canvas. And at last when Ahab was sliding by the vessel, so near as plainly to distinguish Starbuck's face as he leaned over the rail he hailed him to turn the vessel about, and follow him, not too swiftly, at a judicious interval. Glancing upwards he saw Tashtego, Queequeg, and Daggoo, eagerly mounting to the three mast-heads; while the oarsmen were rocking in the two staved boats which had just been hoisted to the side, and were busily at work in repairing them. One after the other, through the port-holes, as he sped, he also caught flying glimpses of Stubb and Flask, busying themselves on deck among bundles of new irons and lances. As he saw all this; as he heard the hammers in the broken boats; far other hammers seemed driving a nail into his heart. But he rallied. And now marking that the vane or flag was gone from the main-mast-head, he shouted to Tashtego, who had just gained that perch, to descend again for another flag, and a hammer and nails, and so nail it to the mast.

Whether fagged by the three days' running chase, and the resistance to his swimming in the knotted hamper he bore; or whether it was some latent deceitfulness and malice in him: whichever was true, the white whale's way now began to abate, as i) seemed, from the boat so rapidly nearing him once more; though indeed the whale's last start had not been so long a one as before. And still as Ahab glided over the waves the unpitying sharks accompanied him; and so pertinaciously stuck to the boat; and so continually bit at the plying oars, that the blades became jagged and crushed, and left small splinters in the sea, at almost every dip.

"Heed them not! those teeth but give new rowlocks to your oars. Pull on! 'tis the better rest, the shark's jaw than the yelding water."

"But, at every bite, sir, the thin blades grow smaller and smaller!"

"They will last long enough! pull on!—But who can tell"—he muttered—"whether these sharks swim to feast on the whale or on Ahab?—But pull on! Aye, all alive now—we near him. The helm! take the helm! let me pass,"—and so saying, two of the oarsmen helped him forward to the bows of the still flying boat.

At length as the craft was cast to one side, and ran ranging along with the white whale's flank, he seemed strangely oblivious of its advance—as the whale sometimes will—and Ahab was fairly within the smoky mountain mist, which, thrown off from the whale's spout, curled round his great Monadnock hump; he was even thus close to him; when, with body arched back, and both arms lengthwise high-lifted to the poise, he darted his fierce iron, and his far fiercer curse into the hated whale. As both steel and curse sank to the socket, as if sucked into a morass, Moby Dick sideways writhed; spasmodically rolled his nigh flank against the bow, and, without staving a hole in it, so suddenly canted the boat over, that had it not been for the elevated part of the gunwale to which he then clung, Ahab would once more have been tossed into the sea. As it was, three of the oarsmen—who foreknew not the precise instant of the dart, and were therefore un-prepared for its effects—these were flung out; but so fell, that, in an instant two of them clutched the gunwale again, and rising to its level on a combing wave, hurled themselves bodily inboard again; the third man helplessly dropping astern, but still afloat and swimming.

Almost simultaneously, with a mighty volition of ungraduated, instantaneous swiftness, the white whale darted through the weltering sea. But when Ahab cried to the steersman to take new turns with the line, and hold it so; and commanded the crew to turn round on their seats, and tow the boat up to the mark; the moment the treacherous line felt that double strain and tug, it snapped in the empty air!

"What breaks in me? Some sinew cracks!—'tis whole again; oars! oars! Burst in upon him!"

Hearing the tremendous rush of the sea-crashing boat, the whale wheeled round to present his blank forehead at bay; but in that evolu-tion, catching sight of the nearing black hull of the ship; seemingly seeing in it the source of all his persecutions; bethinking it—it may be—a larger and nobler foe; of a sudden, he bore down upon its advancing prow, smiting his jaws amid fiery showers of foam.

Ahab staggered; his hand smote his forehead. "I grow blind; hands! stretch out before me that I may yet grope my way. Is't night?"

"The whale! The ship!" cried the cringing oarsmen.

"Oars! oars! Slope downwards to thy depths, O sea, that ere it be

for ever too late, Ahab may slide this last, last time upon his mark!
I see: the ship! the ship! Dash on, my men! will ye not save my
ship?"

But as the oarsmen violently forced their boat through the sledge-
hammering seas, the before whale-smitten bow-ends of two planks burst
through, and in an instant almost, the temporarily disabled boat lay
nearly level with the waves; its half-wading, splashing crew, trying
hard to stop the gap and bale out the pouring water.

Meantime, for that one beholding instant, Tashtego's mast-head
hammer remained suspended in his hand; and the red flag, half-
wrapping him as with a plaid, then streamed itself straight out from
him, as his own forward-flowing heart; while Starbuck and Stubb,
standing upon the bowsprit beneath, caught sight of the down-coming
monster just as soon as he.

"The whale, the whale! Up helm, up helm! Oh, all ye sweet powers
of air, now hug me close! Let not Starbuck die, if die he must, in a
woman's fainting fit. Up helm, I say—ye fools, the jaw! the jaw! Is
this the end of all my bursting prayers? all my life-long fidelities? Oh,
Ahab, Ahab, lo, thy work. Steady! helmsman, steady. Nay, nay! Up
helm again! He turns to meet us! Oh, his unappeasable brow drives
on towards one, whose duty tells him he cannot depart. My God, stand
by me now!"

"Stand not by me, but stand under me, whoever you are that will
now help Stubb; for Stubb, too, sticks here, I grin at thee, thou grinning whale! Who ever helped Stubb, or kept Stubb awake, but
Stubb's own unwinking eye? And now poor Stubb goes to bed upon
a mattress that is all too soft; would it were stuffed with brushwood!
I grin at thee, thou grinning whale! Look ye, sun, moon, and stars!
I call ye assassins of as good a fellow as ever spouted up his ghost. For
all that, I would yet ring glasses with thee, would ye but hand the
cup! Oh, oh! oh, oh! thou grinning whale, but there'll be plenty
of gulping soon! Why fly ye not, O Ahab! For me, off shoes and
jacket to it; let Stubb die in his drawers! A most mouldy and over
salted death, though;—cherries! cherries! cherries! Oh, Flask, for one
red cherry ere we die!"

"Cherries? I only wish that we were where they grow. Oh, Stubb,
I hope my poor mother's drawn my part-pay ere this; if not, few
coppers will now come to her, for the voyage is up."

From the ship's bows, nearly all the seamen now hung inactive;
hammers, bits of plank, lances, and harpoons, mechanically retained
in their hands, just as they had darted from their various employments;
all their enchanted eyes intent upon the whale, which from side to

side strangely vibrating his predestinating head, sent a broad band of overspreading semicircular foam before him as he rushed. Retribution, swift vengeance, eternal malice were in his whole aspect, and spite of all that mortal man could do, the solid white buttress of his forehead smote the ship's starboard bow, till men and timbers reeled. Some fell flat upon their faces. Like dislodged trucks, the heads of the harpooneers aloft shook on their bull-like necks. Through the breach, they heard the waters pour, as mountain torrents down a flume.

Diving beneath the settling ship, the whale ran quivering along its keel; but turning under water, swiftly shot to the surface again, far off the other bow, but within a few yards of Ahab's boat, where, for a time, he lay quiescent.

"I turn my body from the sun. What ho, Tashtego! let me hear thy hammer. Oh! ye three unsurrendered spires of mine; thou uncracked keel; and only god-bullied hull; thou firm deck, and haughty helm, and Pole-pointed prow,—death-glorious ship! must ye then perish, and without me? Am I cut off from the last fond pride of meanest ship-wrecked captains? Oh, lonely death on lonely life! Oh, now I feel my topmost grief. Ho, ho! from all your further bounds, pour ye now in, ye bold billows of my whole foregone life, and top this one piled comber of my death! Towards thee I roll, thou all-destroying but un-conquering whale; to the last I grapple with thee; from hell's heart I stab at thee; for hate's sake I spit my last breath at thee. Sink all coffins and all hearses to one common pool! and since neither can be mine, let me then tow to pieces, while still chasing thee, though tied to thee, thou damned whale! *Thus*, I give up the spear!"

The harpoon was darted; the stricken whale flew forward; with igniting velocity the line ran through the groove;—ran foul. Ahab stooped to clear it; he did clear it; but the flying turn caught him round the neck, and voicelessly as Turkish mutes bowstring their victim, he was shot out of the boat, ere the crew knew he was gone. Next instant, the heavy eye-splice in the rope's final end flew out of the stark-empty tub, knocked down an oarsman, and smiting the sea, disappeared in its depths.

For an instant, the tranced boat's crew stood still; then turned. "The Ship? Great God, where is the ship?" Soon they through dim, be-wildering mediums saw her sidelong fading phantom, as in the gaseous Fata Morgana; only the uppermost masts out of water; while fixed by infatuation, or fidelity, or fate, to their once lofty perches, the pagan harpooneers still maintained their sinking look-outs on the sea. And now, concentric circles seized the lone boat itself, and all its crew, and each floating oar, and every lance-pole, and spinning, animate and inanimate, all round and round in one vortex, carried the smallest chip of the *Pequod* out of sight.

But as the last whelmings intermixingly poured themselves over the sunken head of the Indian at the main-mast, leaving a few inches of the erect spar yet visible, together with long streaming yards of the flag, which calmly undulated, with ironical coincidings, over the destroying billows they almost touched;—at that instant, a red arm and a hammer hovered backwardly uplifted in the open air, in the act of nailing the flag faster and yet faster to the subsiding spar. A sky-hawk that tauntingly had followed the main-truck downwards from its natural home among the stars, pecking at the flag, and incommoding Tashtego there; this bird now chanced to intercept its broad fluttering wing between the hammer and the wood; and simultaneously feeling that ethereal thrill, the submerged savage beneath, in his death-gasp, kept his hammer frozen there; and so the bird of heaven, with archangelic shrieks, and his imperial beak thrust upwards, and his whole captive form folded in the flag of Ahab, went down with his ship, which, like Satan, would not sink to hell till she had dragged a living part of heaven along with her, and helmeted herself with it.

Now small fowl flew screaming over the yet yawning gulf; a sullen white surf beat against its steep sides; then all collapsed, and the great shroud of the sea rolled on as it rolled five thousand years ago.

EPILOGUE

*and I only am escaped alone to
tell thee*

Job

The drama's done. Why then here does any one step forth?—Because one did survive the wreck.

It so chanced that after the Parsee's disappearance, I was he whom the Fates ordained to take the place of Ahab's bowsman, when that bowsman assumed the vacant post; the same who, when on the last day the three men were tossed from out of the rocking boat, was dropped astern. So, floating on the margin of the ensuing scene, and in full sight of it, when the half-spent suction of the sunk ship reached me, I was then, but slowly, drawn towards the closing vortex. When I reached it, it had subsided to a creamy pool. Round and round, then, and ever contracting towards the button-like black bubble at the axis of that slowly wheeling circle, like another Ixion I did revolve. Till gaining that vital centre, the black bubble upward burst; and now liberated by reason of its cunning spring, and, owing to its great buoyancy, rising with great force, the coffin lifebuoy shot lengthwise from the sea, fell over, and floated by my side. Buoyed up by that coffin, for almost one whole day and night, I floated on a soft and dirge-like main. The unharming sharks, they glided by as if with padlocks on their mouths; the savage sea-hawks sailed with sheathed beaks. On the second day, a sail drew near, and picked me up at last. It was the devious-cruising Rachel, that in her retracing search after her missing children, only found another orphan.